HOPEFUL COWBOY

HOPE ETERNAL RANCH ROMANCE, BOOK 1

ELANA JOHNSON

Copyright © 2020 by Elana Johnson

All rights reserved.

No part of this book may be reproduced in any form or by any electronic or mechanical means, including information storage and retrieval systems, without written permission from the author, except for the use of brief quotations in a book review.

ISBN-13: 979-8635700051

CHAPTER ONE

Nathaniel Mulbury could smell something in the air. Something that indicated a change was coming.

A big change.

He stepped up to the window of the door of his dormitory and looked both ways down the hall. He'd been stationed in the wing on the far end of the hall, with only a few feet between his door and the one that led to the yard. And beyond that, the baseball fields. The track. The fresh Texas air.

He liked this dorm, because he didn't hear any of the scuffles from the indoor area, which sat to his left and down the hall about a hundred yards.

No one roamed the halls right now, as it wasn't the appropriate time. A count had just been called, and it wasn't even one of the normal times. The men at River Bay endured five daily counts, three of them between midnight and five a.m.

A count meant all prisoners had to be in their dormitory, and when one was called at an off-time, it was a standing count. So Nate stepped back and held very still at attention. He'd never been disciplined in the fifty-two months he'd been at the River Bay FCI. He was within six months of his release date, and that remained fluid due to his exemplary behavior in prison.

"You hear anything?" Ted asked.

Nate didn't even flick his eyes toward his friend. "Not a word."

"Because you're in that office a whole lot," he drawled.

Nate's teeth ground together, and he knew Ted would see the way his jaw jutted out. But he said nothing.

True, he worked in the office with the Unit leaders. Didn't make him privy to what they knew, and it certainly didn't give him insight as to why they'd called a stand up count at two-fifteen in the afternoon.

He'd been up most of the night, as usual. He assisted with the suicide watch, and one of their newboots had struggled mightily last night.

Nate could remember the day he'd come to River Bay as clearly as if it had happened yesterday. His brother, Ward, had dropped him off at the facility, after he'd gotten permission to self-surrender at the low security prison camp only two hundred and forty miles from White Lake, where his parents and both of his siblings lived.

Ward was the oldest of the three Mulbury children, and Nate had appreciated him more than anything the day he'd driven him to the FCI. He hadn't had to box up his clothes and mail them back to his mother. Ward had taken them.

I'll keep them for you, okay? he'd said.

Nate had just nodded, because he didn't want to do anything to upset Ward. Anything more than what he'd already done, that was. Nate was the only Mulbury to be convicted of a federal crime, and his heartbeat skipped when he thought about getting out of River Bay. What would be waiting for him out there?

The hair on the back of his neck stood at attention too, and Nate looked to his left. A pair of Unit Officers came down the hall, and Nate hoped this standing count would end in a moment. His unit was usually one of the last to be counted, and he focused back on his brother's words from the day he'd dropped Nate off.

We'll see if these clothes fit when you get out. Ward had smiled then, but all Nate could think about was the many things he'd missed while he'd been in prison. Ward's wife had been pregnant when they'd come to River Bay.

He'd missed the birth of his first nephew. He'd missed Ward and Jane's divorce. He'd missed his sister's wedding, and the birth of her two children. He'd missed birthday parties and Christmases and picnics and days out on the boat in the Gulf of Mexico.

The PA crackled. "Count complete. We're clear."

Nate sighed as his muscles relaxed. He climbed back

onto his bunk, exhaustion pulling though him. He stared at the bottom of the bunk above his, the towheaded boy Connor had grown into forming in his mind's eyes.

Ward's son.

Ward came to visit Nate every week, even after all these months. These years. Every week. Most holidays, he brought several people with him. Friends of his who knew Nate, and at least once a month, Nate's parents.

His parents had gotten old while Nate had been in prison, and he'd missed that too.

"You're up to shower," someone said, tapping his foot against the frame of Nate's bed. He heaved himself off the mattress that wasn't comfortable anyway and headed out the now-open door.

He'd learned to be vigilant when simply walking down the hall. He was housed in a low security prison camp, which meant he could come and go almost anywhere anytime he wanted. There were rules and limitations, which he'd learned quickly, and he didn't want to be caught going one direction while the other twelve hundred men at the camp were going the other.

He'd gotten a seven-year sentence for his role in investment fraud, but there were guys in here who'd used weapons during robbery, broken into homes, committed crimes against children, and more. Anything could happen if he didn't watch what was going on around him, all the time.

The only time he didn't need to do that was during the

ten-minute shower he got each day. Which was why he'd heaved himself off the bed and down the hall to the bathroom he shared with the other forty-seven men in his wing of Unit NF.

He soaped and shaved, then dressed in his standard prison clothes and reported to the unit office. He had a special pass to work there, and he'd been helping with files and doing simple data entry for a couple of months now. The work wasn't stimulating, but it was work.

Everyone in prison had to work, and most of the men needed the money. Nate hadn't told a single soul that he did not. Ward deposited money in his prison bank account every month, though he couldn't spend more than three hundred and ten dollars a month.

Nate, in all the months he'd been in River Bay, had not spent that much. He saw no need to call attention to himself. In fact, everything Nate had done over the last fifty-two months was to keep the spotlight off of him.

Head down. Mouth closed. That was how he'd avoided the fights, the disagreements, and the overload of tickets that seemed to fly from the Unit Officer's fingertips.

No one spoke to him, which suited Nate just fine. He knew all the men and women in the unit office, and he felt very lucky to have been assigned to this unit.

"How's Charles?" he finally asked when he and the unit secretary seemed to be the only ones still working.

She looked up from her computer, her eyes slightly glazed over. Nate wondered what that would be like, to feel so comfortable that he wasn't constantly scanning the windows just beyond the office for any sign of a threat.

"Oh, uh, he's okay," she said, her mind clearly somewhere else. Ellen had thin, wispy hair the shade of rich soil. She tucked it away, but it just spilled out again, because it was so fine.

"Think I'll get a full night's sleep tonight?" Nate asked, looking back to his own computer. His was at least five years older than the one Ellen pecked on, and it didn't connect to the Internet. Nate got thirty minutes each day to download and upload his emails, and just by communicating with his mother and then Ward, it wasn't enough time to stay caught up on everything.

"Probably," Ellen said. "We've got two more on call. You took your turn last night."

Nate thought of the three a.m. count, and though he didn't have to stand at attention for that one, he woke up every night when the Unit Officers came through the rooms, their flashlights as bright as spotlights.

He nodded anyway, thinking he'd made it through another day. Another day toward his release. Toward freedom.

<hr/>

NATE DID GET AWAKENED IN THE MIDDLE OF THE night, but it wasn't because of heavy boots on the floor and those sweeping lights crisscrossing the dormitory.

No, someone was talking.

The men in his wing didn't cause trouble, for the most part. Sometimes Ted could get a bee in his bonnet, but he had a louder bark than a bite. Though, Nate supposed he probably could have a mighty loud bite too. He'd been incarcerated for aggravated assault. He'd gotten into a scuffle at his law office, used his fists to get the other guy away from him, and found out the hard way that undercover cops could literally be anywhere.

To make matters worse, Ted had been holding a knife in one hand because he'd been cutting a cake for an office party.

Thus, he'd gotten aggravated assault on a police officer. The law office had been under investigation for some questionable activity with the drug cartel along the Southern border, and Ted had become the fall guy.

He hadn't used the knife, but he was in possession of it. He hadn't handled the wrong accounts, but he suddenly had a target on his back. He'd fought for the rights of his clients, and in the end, he'd lost his.ho

Nate thought sometimes the law could be downright comical.

"Nate," a man whispered, bending down to shine his light right into Ntae's eyes.

He knew the voice, even if he was blinded to Percy's face. "What?" he asked, trying not to sound irritated. Some Unit Officers handed out tickets for much more innocent questions than the one Nate had just asked. He held up one hand to shield his retinas from all that blasted light.

"Come with me." Percy straightened and walked away, leaving Nate confused as he tried to sit up and reason through why he'd need to go with Percy.

Rule number one in prison: Don't go off with a guard alone.

Nate flicked a glance at Ted, who slept on the bottom bunk only five feet from Nate. They shared the desk sitting between the two sets of bunk beds, but Nate got his own locker for his personal belongings.

"Come on," Percy said from the doorway, and Nate stood up.

"I need shoes," he said.

"Not for this."

"For what?" Nate asked, his pulse starting to beat a little too fast through his body. The weight of every eye in his wing was on him, but Nate had literally never caused a scene before.

Percy turned back to him, and anguish rolled across the man's face. "You better get dressed and put on your boots."

Nate nodded and got changed, not caring that everyone watched him. He had to get strip searched to go into the suicide unit, so switching out his sweat pants and T-shirt for the official prison uniform was no big deal.

Ready, he walked toward Percy, who still looked like he was one breath away from crying. Ellen appeared in the hallway, a panicked look on her face. Nate frowned at her and followed Percy out of the room.

The other guard said, "Go back to sleep."

"What's going on?" Ted asked. "You can't just take him. He's done nothing."

The door closed, sealing all the other inmates in while Nate was out. He looked through the unbreakable glass, his eyes meeting Ted's. He'd been in for longer than Nate, and he'd just reached nickel status.

Five years.

"The Commander and the Warden want to see you," Percy said.

"Why?" Nate asked, feeling courageous that evening.

"I'll let them explain."

Ellen marched at the head of their group as they left the building and started down the sidewalk under the watchful eye of the moon. Nate normally loved being outside, and he had all the paths of this place memorized.

He'd only met the Warden a handful of times, and the experiences had all been good. A tension rode on the air as the four of them walked, Ellen's heels making the most noise against the concrete.

She led the way into the Warden's office too, where five men stood around the man's massive desk. They all turned toward Ellen and the others as they entered.

Nate stopped in the doorway, everything in his body telling him not to enter this room. He scanned the men quickly, making a dozen observations. Prison could teach a man to notice the slightest of things, that was for sure.

The Warden looked as he normally did. Properly put together, with a tie knotted around his neck. Today's was blue with black stripes.

Two other police officers stood in the office, and they looked like they'd just stepped out of a coffee shop on their nightly beat.

Nate's fingers clenched into a fist when he met his lawyer's eye, and he raised his chin. "What's going on?" he asked. Lawyers didn't make house calls at one-thirty in the morning, that was for dang sure. Especially not Lawrence Matthews.

No one spoke. The people in the room all looked around at one another, their gazes ultimately coming back to his.

The last man in the room was Nate's Unit Manager, Gregory Fellows. He wore a grim look and nodded to Ellen.

"Nate, come sit down," she said.

Nate couldn't get his legs to work. "Ellen," he said as evenly as he could, but his nerves made everything inside him vibrate. "Just say it."

She sat down on a black leather couch just inside the door. Clearing her throat, she adjusted her legs and set a folder on her lap before she looked up at him with tears in her eyes.

Actual tears.

Nate wanted to run as far and as fast as he could. Whatever she was about to say wasn't good.

"Nate," she said again. "I'm so sorry to have to tell you this, but your brother has passed away."

A pit opened in his stomach, but he still managed to ask, "What?"

"Ward passed away," she said.

His brother's name echoed in Nate's mind. A shriek started in his soul. "But he's coming on Friday," he said stupidly. "He's bringing Connor." Ward didn't bring his son every time, but usually a couple of times a month. He'd emailed to say Connor had made something for Nate at preschool, so they'd both be coming that weekend.

"No, honey," Ellen said, standing. She put her hand on his arm, and Nate just stared at it. "There was an accident on the ranch, and they did everything they could." She swiped at her face with her free hand.

"But he just audits ranches," Nate said, not comprehending. "What kind of accident?" How did someone die when they carried around a clipboard and a ballpoint pen?

Lawrence stepped forward. "Nate, I got here as quickly as I could. Once the will was read, we moved swiftly to—"

"When did he die?" Nate asked, the words belonging to someone else. He looked from Lawrence to Ellen.

"Monday morning," Ellen whispered.

"But it's Wednesday," Nate said, confusion riddling his thoughts. They were so knotted, and Nate didn't know how to unravel them.

"You didn't miss the funeral," Ellen said. Her dark eyes

reminded Nate of his father's. Why he was thinking of that, he didn't know.

"Were you aware your brother named you the legal guardian of his son?" Lawrence asked, reaching into his fancy-pants briefcase. He removed a sheaf of papers and handed them to Nate.

He'd spent plenty of time on his bed, reading complicated legal documents. But not in the middle of the night, and not minutes after he'd been told his brother and oldest friend had died. Ward took care of everything—he took care of Nate—and Nate didn't know how to keep breathing.

"No," he said, staring at the black letters on white paper.

"Well, he did," Gregory said kindly. He guided Nate to a chair in front of the Warden's desk. "And Nate, your lawyer has petitioned for your release date to be Saturday, the day of the funeral. Then you can be there with your family and with Connor, and the two of you will be able to... start a life."

Nate gripped the edges of the paper, his eyes unseeing. Start a life. What a joke. He couldn't start life again.

"Since you're still six months out from your parole hearing, we've made arrangements for you and Connor." Greg placed another folder in Nate's hands. "It's not precedent, but this is an extenuating circumstance."

"The judge signed the order, Mister Fellows," Lawrence said.

"I'm aware," Greg bit out. He sat in the chair next to Nate's, and their eyes met. "You'll be released on Saturday,

Nate. But not to just wander in the world. You're being assigned to Hope Eternal Ranch, one of our Residential Reentry Centers. You'll finish your sentence there for the next six months."

"I haven't finished my release programming," Nate said.

"Hope Eternal will finish it with you," Greg said, his eyes actually softening as he spoke. "You'll live there, with Connor, and work on the ranch. They're a trusted partner, and they've taken several of our men over the years. You'll be in very good hands there."

Nate felt as if someone had encased his body in tight cloth, mummifying him. He didn't know what to say or do.

No one had asked him if he wanted to be released and live at this Hope Eternal Ranch. No one had asked him—not even Ward—if he wanted to, or was even capable of, taking care of a four-year-old boy.

"Okay," Lawrence said from behind him. "She's here."

The people in the room moved, and Nate twisted toward the door as they welcomed someone new. He couldn't see them through the press of bodies, which only made his heart rate accelerate.

Finally, the crowd parted, and the most beautiful woman Nate had ever set eyes on stood there. She wore a pair of jeans that seemed to go on and on—and on—as she easily stood close to his height and had legs that went for miles. She sported shiny, almost-copper-colored hair that fell to just below her shoulders. Her eyes could've been any color, because Nate couldn't quite see them in the shadows of her cowgirl hat.

She frowned at him, and then looked back at Lawrence. "Well? Does he speak? It's been a long drive, and I'm already tired."

"Nate," Greg said, helping Nate stand up. "This is Ginger Talbot. She runs Hope Eternal Ranch, and we're releasing you to her care on Saturday."

Nate wasn't sure if he'd hit the lottery or been condemned to death. By the growl in Ginger's eyes and the way she folded her arms instead of extending her hand to shake his, Nate had enough mental capacity to think, *I guess I did get the death penalty.*

He also had no idea how to be a father.

And the pain over Ward's death continued to radiate from deep within him, spiraling up and out until he was left bent over and gasping for air.

CHAPTER TWO

Ginger Talbot knew her stance and her cold question made her seem like the Ice Queen. Perhaps she was. When it came to men like Nathaniel Mulbury, she had to be. She'd worked with several of them over the years.

Because Hope Eternal Ranch was a completely female-run operation, she would only take prisoners in the RRC program that hadn't been convicted of sex offenses.

The man currently bent over in front of her, gasping for air, was a white collar criminal. She read every case and every conviction before agreeing to house the prisoner on her ranch. Nathaniel had been caught up in investment fraud in the firm where he'd worked for three years before the ceiling had fallen on everyone, from the CEO on the top floor to the secretary just inside the door, at Isotope Investments.

Her heart pounded in her chest at the sight of him still

struggling to breathe. She'd been told not to touch him, but her kind, compassionate side urged Ginger to take the few steps toward him. She let her hands drop to her side, then she lifted one and placed it on Nathaniel's shoulder at the same time the only other woman in the room said, "Nate, we've got a drink for you."

She took the plastic bottle of water from the man who'd gone to retrieve it, and she too joined Ginger at Nate's side. She put her hand on his other bicep, the two women flanking him.

"Come on now," she said quietly. "You're okay. You've been in here for fifteen hundred and eighty-one days."

Nate started to straighten, turning toward the other woman and not Ginger. She could see him in a cowboy hat, a pair of dark jeans, with cowboy boots on his feet. And he'd be even more handsome than he was now.

Ginger strengthened the walls around her heart and mind. She let her hand drop from his shoulder, the absence of heat from his body instant and causing some sort of regret to pull through her. She frowned at herself and fell back a couple of steps.

"Thank you, Ellen," Nate said, his voice soft and quiet, yet possessing a power Ginger couldn't name. "But it's eighty-*two* days," Nate said, taking the bottle. "Fifteen-eighty-*two*."

A ghost of a smile crossed the other woman's face, and she too moved back.

"Ginger," Lawrence said, and she retreated all the way

to his side. She knew him, because she'd been working with him for the past two days following the death of Ward Mulbury. She knew the Warden too, but he hadn't moved from behind his desk yet.

James Dickerson wasn't a small man, nor one to keep silent. But he still hadn't spoken. Ginger watched him, and it was clear the man was struggling with his own emotions. She looked at Nate again as he drank, and the picture before her cleared. These men and women here at the River Bay Federal Correctional Institution *liked* Nathaniel Mulbury.

Nate's gaze moved to hers, and the air in her lungs froze instantly. Several long seconds passed before the man who'd helped Nate stand stepped between them. "We'll make sure he's ready on Saturday, Miss Talbot." He gestured for her to leave the room, because she still had plenty to talk about with his Unit Manager.

Ginger held Nate's gaze for another moment, a flash of a heartbeat, and then she stepped out the door Lawrence held for her. Down the hall in another room, she paced to the window and turned to face the two of them as they came inside behind her.

"Ginger, this is Gregory Fellows. He's Nate's Unit Manager." Lawrence indicated the other man, who wore a uniform suggesting his status inside the correctional facility.

"Greg," the man said, reaching to shake her hand. She gave one pump and looked back at Lawrence.

"So?" the lawyer asked. "He's acceptable for your program?"

"Yes." Ginger lifted her chin, wondering if anyone else that partnered with the BOP had such strict rules for who they'd take in. She told herself not to back down. She had to protect her friends and colleagues, as well as all the visitors that came to Hope Eternal.

And yourself, she thought, hating that door that opened in her memory bank so easily. Ginger wasn't the type of woman to make the same mistake twice, and just because Nate was good-looking and grateful for a bottle of water didn't mean she'd allow herself to be anything but his parole officer for the next six months.

She wouldn't even have to do that. The Bureau of Prisons would send someone out every couple of weeks, and she could call at any time and have them come and get Nate if things simply didn't work out.

The image of the blond-haired boy paraded through her mind. Nate's situation certainly was complex, and he'd been hit with three very large items in the space of five minutes. All at once, Ginger was glad she'd let her compassionate side step over to him and offer him a brief touch of comfort.

She couldn't even imagine how she'd react to one of her siblings passing away, and her heart leapt into the back of her throat.

"I believe you wanted some insight to Nate," Greg said, adjusting one of the chairs by the door. He sank into the hardbacked seat, a long sigh coming from his mouth. "He's the best one in the wing—in the whole Unit. Probably out of any Unit here."

"Why isn't he in the satellite camp then?" Lawrence asked. "That has even looser security than here."

Greg glanced at Lawrence and then Ginger. He swiped one hand through his nearly black hair, and all the exhaustion he felt showed plainly on his face. "He was in the satellite camp for a while. Nine months, maybe? Ten. But it's crowded there, just like it is here, and we needed him to teach our business and finance classes." He issued a long sigh. "So we asked him if he'd come back over to River Bay Low, and he agreed. He's done two jobs here—he's my office assistant, and he works part-time with our suicide watch team as well."

Surprise moved through Ginger. This Nathaniel Mulbury really was the best of the best. She'd never heard of an inmate working in the Unit office with the team.

"With his good behavior," Lawrence said, tapping on his phone. "We have him getting released in five months and twenty-two days."

"Probably earlier even," Greg said. "He gets more days for every month of good behavior. He's never been in trouble in all the time he's been here. He has the least number of tickets out of any inmate currently in River Bay, through all security levels, and the ones he does have are for little things like not being in line on time, or dropping his shower shoes on the floor too loudly." He looked back and forth between Lawrence and Ginger.

"If he's so great," Ginger started. "Why couldn't you get

him out, Lawrence? Why does he have to finish the five months and twenty-two days at all?"

His brother had died. Nate now had a child to raise.

"The judge said other family members could take the boy," Lawrence said. "She wouldn't uphold the will to the point where Nate could just be released to his own care, the way he would've been in a few months. So our next best step was the Residential Reentry Center. This way, he's out, but under supervision. He can take the child with him. And he can have a decent transitional period to work through...everything."

Ginger nodded, a strangely fierce determination moving through her that Nate would get exactly that. She'd *help him* get exactly that.

"And the family is okay with that?" she asked.

"His parents are getting up there in years," Lawrence said. "The father has just been diagnosed with colon cancer, and no, Nate doesn't know yet." He sighed, and Ginger supposed even lawyers had a human side from time to time. "His sister is married with two kids under age four, neither of whom Nate has met." He read from his phone, though surely he had these familial facts about his client memorized.

"Her husband got in a motorcycle accident only six months after they got married, and he's disabled and in a wheelchair. She cried and cried when she told me she couldn't take Connor on too." He looked up and shrugged. "It's Nate or the foster care system."

HOPEFUL COWBOY   21

"Nate will never let that happen," Greg said. "Ward and Connor came to visit him all the time. He loves that boy."

Lawrence nodded. "Yes, I've heard. Which is why I petitioned the judge for RRC, and specifically at your ranch, Miss Talbot. It's only a ten-minute drive from his parents and sister. Bethany—the sister—said she could make that drive to see her brother and her nephew. All agreeable with you, of course."

"Of course," Ginger murmured. So many things ran through her head that she couldn't grab onto any one thought and examine it. She drew in a deep breath. "Okay, so I'll get the clothes on the request sheet, and I'll be back here on Saturday morning to get him." She looked between Greg and Lawrence. "Right?"

"Yes," Greg said, standing. "He'll be in the Special Housing Unit, Administrative Detention."

"Why?" Ginger asked.

"Because he's in crisis right now," Greg said. "And to lessen the questions and noise from the other prisoners. We put all inmates in Admin Detention during transfers or before hearings. That kind of thing. It's not like detention at the principal's office. He's not in trouble. It's to *spare* him trouble." He reached for her hand again, and they shook. "I'll be there to say good-bye to him as well. He's been a good inmate here." With that, he nodded and turned to leave the office.

Ginger waited until the door closed and then she took

his seat, combing her fingers through her own hair. "Is that all then?" she asked Lawrence.

"That should do it," he said. "Everything will be ready for you between now and then. You get the clothes. I'll meet you here with the boy. And...that's that."

That's that.

The words didn't seem like enough for a man who'd lost his brother and was about to become a father, all within a few minutes. So much was changing, and not for her. She'd have another cowboy on the ranch, which she desperately needed.

She seized onto the gratitude as it slipped through her veins and said, "Okay, then. I'll be ready, and I'll be here." She stood and followed Greg out the door, her focus only on making it back to her truck safely.

Once there, she allowed her mind to wander. Yes, she needed Nate's help on the ranch. She'd just had a cowboy quit last week, and his appointment through the Residential Reentry Program was a huge blessing for her.

"He's sure handsome," she muttered, her mood darkening. "And you're not going to let him use that against you."

No, she was not.

She *could* not.

The last time she had, she'd nearly lost everything, and it was only by God's grace that she'd managed to hold onto the ranch and her last shred of dignity.

That's that.

Decision made that Ginger would only speak to Nate if

she absolutely had to, she made the drive back to Hope Eternal Ranch, the pure blackness that existed to her left threatening to claw at her very soul.

The absence of light over the water of the Gulf sometimes brought her peace. Tonight, though, it only served to remind her of how far she'd come since she'd fallen in love with Hyrum Charles—an inmate from River Bay, just like Nate—and how far she could fall if she allowed something like that to happen again.

SATURDAY MORNING, GINGER ARRIVED BACK AT RIVER Bay with a small backpack. She'd gotten the requested clothes for Nate, as well as a couple of soft drinks, snacks, and a chocolate bar for both him and Connor.

She'd taken prisoners back to Hope Eternal before, and she knew how much they liked chocolate. Apparently, it was very expensive inside prison, and while she knew Nate had worked in investment banking before his time at River Bay, she suspected he didn't have a whole lot of money to be buying chocolate every week.

Someone met her in the lobby and took her outside to a nearby building, this one much closer than the one she'd trekked to on Wednesday night. It was early still, with the sun barely lighting the sky. She'd left the ranch last night and made the three-hour drive to the town of River Bay, where she'd slept in a lumpy bed and gotten up before dawn.

She smoothed down her hair, wishing it wasn't quite so bright. Over the years, she'd tried to tame the coppery color with hair dye, but she'd given up and embraced the auburn locks she had. Thankfully, she wasn't walking down the center aisle of a prison, with rows of inmates on both sides, leering at her through the bars.

In fact, this building felt like an office building and nothing more. The guard who'd met her took her into a nondescript room, where Lawrence waited with Connor.

Joy filled Ginger as the little boy spun in one of the chairs around the long, oval table. He had hair the color of cornsilk, and she wondered where that had come from. Nate had medium-to-dark brown hair, with blue eyes. So maybe there was some blond-haired, blue-eyed genes in his ancestral line.

"You must be Connor," she said, putting a wide smile on her face easily. Ginger had always loved children, even if she didn't have any of her own.

Connor looked at Lawrence, who nodded. He got down out of the chair and came toward her as he approached him. She crouched down several feet away and set the backpack on the ground. "Guess what I brought for you?"

The little boy peered at the backpack, but he didn't guess. She unzipped the top of it and reached inside slowly. "Did your daddy ever let you have...chocolate?" Ginger pulled the candy out of the bag and showed it to Connor.

His face split into a smile, and he said, "Yes, ma'am. Daddy bought me chocolate." His tiny, high-pitched voice tugged against her heartstrings, and he came all the way over to her and the pack.

"I brought two now," she said. "One for you." She handed him one of the chocolate bars. "And one for your uncle Nate."

"Uncle Nate loves chocolate," Connor said.

Ginger grinned at him. "I'll bet he does." She handed the child the second bar. "So you hold it for him, and when he comes out, you can give it to him. Okay?"

Connor took the candy but handed his back. He didn't have to ask for Ginger to know what he wanted. She got to work on ripping open the top of the package, and she gave it back to him. "It's got squares, so you can just break off what you want."

"It's the cookie kind." The child looked at her with wonder in his clear, bright blue eyes. "I love these." He broke off the top square and stuck it in his mouth.

Ginger wondered where his mother was, but she hadn't asked Lawrence. She straightened to do just that when the door in the back of the room opened.

Nate walked inside, wearing his prison uniform and carrying a medium-sized bag. It was clear, and Ginger could see everything he owned right there in his hand. Her heart beat out a song of remorse for him too, because she had no idea what it was like to have her entire existence reduced to what she could carry in a single, see-through bag.

"Uncle Nate!" Connor ran toward him, and Nate bent down to scoop the boy into his arms. He pressed his eyes closed as he hugged the little boy, and Ginger actually found herself getting emotional.

Ridiculous, she told herself, bending to pick up the backpack and zip it closed. She shouldered it and then squared her body toward Nate so she'd look tall and imposing. She was tall for a woman, she knew that. But she'd have to gain at least fifty pounds to even start to appear on the cusp of imposing.

Nate didn't look her way anyway. He set Connor on his feet and stayed down at the boy's level while they talked. Only when Connor gave him the chocolate and then turned to point at Ginger did Nate lift his eyes to hers.

That same magnetic power that had clenched their gazes together a few days ago roared to life. Nate straightened and opened his chocolate, biting off the first square while he simply stared at her.

"You have his clothes?" Lawrence asked, approaching her.

She blinked and ducked her head, glad for the distraction. "Yes." She handed him the backpack, and he took it over to Nate.

"Five minutes," Lawrence said after Nate had taken the pack and Connor back through the door. "And then he's all yours." He turned back to the table and picked up a folder. "Here's all the paperwork you need for him, as well as the first month's check. The address for the funeral is in there, as well as all of his family contacts." He looked at the other man who'd come in, and he too wore the uniform of a high-ranking officer at the facility. "Anything else?"

"I don't think so," the man said. "We'll say our good-byes out here. When he comes back in, he'll be ready to go."

"Great." Lawrence collected his bag and walked toward the door Ginger had come through at the same time the officer left through the one where Nate had disappeared.

She turned in a full circle, one door closing right after the other and sealing her inside the room alone. Alone, to wait for Nate and Connor to come back.

Then, they'd all leave together.

Every time she did this, Ginger felt so surreal. After all, who in their right mind would let *her* take a prisoner back to the ranch? Didn't they know she had no idea what to do for him, what to say, or how to help him?

Her legs urged her to flee. She could drop off the folder at the front desk and say she'd made a mistake.

Before she could move, the door opened and Nate walked through it, now wearing the dark suit, the black shiny shoes, and the blue and cranberry tie he'd requested for the funeral.

And Ginger couldn't move at all.

CHAPTER THREE

Nate held onto Connor's hand as if the small child could protect him from what was about to happen. He'd managed to carry his bag, the backpack Ginger had brought, and his nephew out of the facility.

Ginger drove a nice truck, and they'd made good time from River Bay to White Lake, Connor on the bench seat between them. She kept the radio on low, and the tension between them had bled out after only a few minutes.

Nate couldn't get enough of the scenery, and he kept trying to see everything as it passed. The flat fields, full of crops and waving in the morning light. The water towers fascinated him. And when Ginger had pulled onto the coastal highway, he simply couldn't get enough of the glinting water, the long stretch of tan the sand of the beach.

The beach.

The water.

The sky.

It was all different outside of the River Bay FCI, and Nate breathed in deeply through his nose, no fear of what he might smell.

"Uncle Nate," Connor said from on the seat beside him.

"Yeah?" Nate looked down at the child, his eyes so much like Ward's. Like, Nate's too. Those deep, bright blue eyes came from their father, and Nate couldn't find hardly any of Jane in her son.

"I have to go to the bathroom."

"Oh, yeah, sure." Nate looked at Ginger, who'd already started to decelerate.

"There's a place right up here," she said, easing one of her booted feet onto the brake. She made the turn and a couple of blocks down, she pulled into a fast food restaurant.

Nate sat there, because he didn't know if he could take Connor into the restroom alone. His heartbeat pulsed through his whole body, a pit of nervousness way down deep in his gut. He couldn't just walk into this place, though the scent of breakfast hung in the air and tempted him to get a sausage and egg biscuit.

"Come on," Ginger said, finally opening her door. "Get out my side, buddy. We'll meet your uncle inside." She tossed him a look as she slid from the truck and turned back to help Connor out.

The door slammed closed, and Nate flinched. He pressed his eyes closed and breathed through his nose again. He wasn't wearing the prison blues and oranges. No one here would even know who he was, or that he'd been a free man—kind of—for less than two hours.

He opened the door and got out of the truck, closing the door much softer than Ginger had. She'd taken Connor into the restaurant, and Nate followed, finding them standing in the short hallway that led to the bathrooms.

He took Connor's hand and went into the men's room, wondering what Ginger was going to do. Probably just stand watch to make sure he didn't try to run away with his nephew. He was pretty sure he could overpower her without even trying, but he had no desire to run.

He had nowhere to go.

He'd asked all kinds of questions on Wednesday night, but no one had known any of the answers. Finally, Warden Dickerson had said he'd find out everything he could—what Ward had done with the house, the bills, his money. Where his ex-wife was. Why his sister couldn't take Connor, all of it —and Nate had been led to a comfortable enough room in Administrative Detention.

He'd only gone back to Unit NF once to get his belongings. The officers had made everyone leave the dormitory, so Nate could have as much time as he needed to clean out his locker without having to answer a bunch of questions.

Questions he didn't have the answers to.

The Warden had learned that Ward had left everything to Nate. Absolutely everything, and he'd left him a long letter too, explaining everything. The Warden didn't have it and couldn't get it until that morning, when Lawrence the lawyer showed up again.

Nate had the letter now, but he needed complete privacy to study it again. He'd only had time to read it once, and he'd been sniffling when his Unit Manager had knocked and come inside.

Greg's last words to Nate still tickled in his ears. *Don't be the same man leaving as you were coming in.*

Nate didn't feel like he was, and he'd taken the card Greg had given him. It was a professional business card, but Greg had put his personal number on the back. "Call anytime, Nate. Day or night."

They'd hugged, and Nate had walked out with Connor. Easy as that. Too bad no one told him every step would be like torture. No one had told him the guilt would threaten to drown him as he left River Bay—and all the friends he'd made inside.

He'd left letters for Ted, Dallas, and Slate. The three men he was closest to. Ted had brought another man into their fold too, not long ago. Luke—not Lucas. That last bit was really important to the guy, and the reason he found himself in a low security facility with men who'd committed much worse crimes than assault with intent.

His crew. His friends. The Mulbury Boys Greg had called them. His throat closed again, and Nate didn't know how to deal with all the issues streaming through him. He'd thought he'd had problems before, but he now knew how simple prison had made his life.

HOPEFUL COWBOY   33

Nate blinked as Connor said, "Uncle Nate, my zipper's stuck."

He stepped over to the boy and helped him with his fly before they approached the sink to wash up. He had no idea what to say to Connor. He knew how to get a zipper up, though, and he knew he had enough money to buy the boy breakfast. Everything else, he'd have to learn one thing at a time.

Ward had told him to do exactly that.

I know you'll feel inadequate. Heaven knows I do on a daily and sometimes hourly basis. But Nate, just take it one thing at a time. Just like you did in River Bay. One day at a time.

One hour. One minute.

Nate dried his hands and stepped into the hall to find Ginger hadn't moved. "All good?" she asked, her eyes skating down to Connor.

"Yep."

"You hungry, Connor?" he asked.

The boy looked at him with wide, innocent eyes. "A little."

"Can we get a sandwich?" he asked Ginger, because he honestly didn't know the rules at all.

"Sure," she said. "We won't want to take long, though. The funeral."

He nodded and went around the corner to the line to order. No one looked at him. No one waved a book of tickets in his face and told him to keep his eyes forward or he'd get a citation. No one swore or jostled for a place or breathed threats if he didn't give up his spot in line.

These people had no idea how good their lives were.

He ordered for all of them and got a bag of biscuits and muffins and hashbrowns a few minutes later. Back in the truck with everyone, he started handing things out.

"Thank you," Ginger said, and Connor echoed her.

Nate took a moment before he bit into his bacon and egg biscuit to think back to the last time someone had thanked him. His friends did. Maybe Greg and Ellen had, in time.

It felt nice.

"CONNOR!" ANOTHER LITTLE BOY CAME RUNNING down the hall toward Nate and Connor, who let go of Nate's hand and ran toward him too.

Nate's step slowed, and not only from the unfamiliar child. Right around that corner sat his family. All of Ward's friends and associates. He really didn't want to be there, but there was no way Nate could skip his brother's funeral.

A woman came around the corner, her expression bordering on panic. "Milo," she said. "Oh." She came to a complete stop, and Nate did too.

He drank in the sight of his sister. Bethany was seven years younger than him, but they'd been good enough friends growing up. She'd been engaged when he'd gone into River Bay, and she hadn't come to visit him more than a handful of times. Usually on Christmas or his birthday, and that was all.

He knew why. Her husband had suffered the loss of both of his legs in a motorcycle accident, and she had her hands full. She rushed toward him then, tears spilling down her face. "Nate," she said, grabbing onto him and sobbing into his chest.

Nate clenched everything he had in order to keep his own emotions inside, but it sure did feel good to have a hug from someone he loved. Someone who loved him. For so long there, Nate had wondered if his family would even want to speak to him again. Everyone, seemingly, had abandoned him.

Except Ward.

"He must belong to you," Nate finally said as she stepped back. He wiped quickly at his own eyes before he looked to the two little boys. Her son showed Connor a toy car, and it was clear Connor wanted it.

"Yes," Bethany said. "My son Milo."

"And you have a daughter too," Nate said, not sure if he should introduce himself to his nephew or not.

"Yes," his sister said again. "Ella just turned two." She linked her arm through his. "Come on. Momma's been asking about you for at least an hour." She glanced at Ginger, who'd come into the church with them. She'd been wearing jeans and a blouse when she'd picked him up at the facility, and he'd been waiting for her outside the women's restroom when Milo had come sprinting around the corner.

She wore a denim skirt now, and she stepped forward to greet Bethany. "I'm Ginger Talbot."

"Of course," Bethany said. "The—at Hope Eternal Ranch, right?"

"That's right." Ginger smiled as if she and Nate were going to Disneyland instead of a ranch he knew nothing about. He'd never worked on a ranch, despite being a Texan, and a flutter of nerves stole through him.

He told himself that before his incarceration, he'd never assisted in an office either. He'd never worked in a library. He'd never taught business or finance classes, and he'd never done suicide watch. And he'd managed to figure out how to do all of those things too.

He could do whatever Ginger threw his way.

But when she turned to him, that perfectly pretty smile still on those full lips, Nate's whole world blacked out. She couldn't smile at him like that, because he was suddenly thinking about things he shouldn't be.

He hadn't kissed a woman in a very long time, though he didn't have the exact number of days counted the way he did for how long he'd been behind bars. *You won't be kissing Ginger either*, he thought, and he turned away from her stunning beauty.

Nate was very good at following rules. Very, very good at it. He could handle his time at Hope Eternal Ranch. It was less than six months, and Nate knew he could do anything for less than six months.

He let Bethany lead him around the corner and into the

chapel. The funeral hadn't started yet, and people sat in the rows, talking softly to one another. As he went by, though, all chatter ceased.

"Momma," Bethany whispered once they'd reached nearly the front row. "Nate's here."

His mother moved as if in slow motion, her eyes lit from within. "Nathaniel." She rose, using the bench in front of her to steady her.

Nate stepped toward her and engulfed her in a hug, this one ten times better than the one he'd gotten from Bethany. "Momma." He breathed in the soft, floral-powdery scent of her. At least that hadn't changed.

A murmur moved through the crowd, but Nate ignored it. He didn't want to talk to anyone. He just wanted to hug his father and sit down. Momma wept when she stepped back and traded places with Daddy.

"Hey, Dad." Nate hugged him too, hoping his father wasn't too disappointed in him. Ward had said he wasn't; that they'd all come to terms with the situation. His father held him tight. So tight, Nate started to believe what his older brother had told him, and he couldn't quite contain his emotions.

His eyes burned, and he closed them just as tightly as he held onto his father. They'd only come to visit him a few times. The drive was hard for them, and he'd kept his relationship going with them through emails and fifteen-minute phone calls and pictures Ward showed him.

Ward.

He sat down and looked up at the stained glass window. He couldn't believe his brother was gone. What in the world was Nate going to do without him? He'd been the only solid thing in Nate's life for the past fifteen hundred and eighty-two days, and he had no idea how to keep living without Ward only a message away.

He hadn't even realized he'd started to cry until a soft, chilly hand slipped into his. Ginger had calluses on her thumbs, and Nate sure did like that about her. It meant she worked hard around that ranch of hers, and Nate suddenly couldn't wait to get there.

He'd like to work outside if he could. Even though he hadn't had a lot of restrictions on his outdoor time in prison, he had fences surrounding him all the time. He couldn't wait to see the ranch and maybe, just maybe, scale the fence and stand on the other side. Just for a few minutes.

"Uncle Nate," Connor said, climbing into his lap. Nate had to let go of Ginger's hand to hold the boy, but that was okay. He and Connor were all the other had now, and Nate pressed his lips to the child's temple as if it was the most natural thing in the world.

"You okay?" he asked.

"I miss my daddy," he said, snuggling deeper into Nate's chest.

"I know," Nate whispered. "So do I, Connor. So do I." Beside him, Ginger stood up, and Nate looked at her. She motioned for him to follow her, but he wasn't sure why.

Then his mother said, "Go on, Nate. We're going into

the other room for a family prayer, and then we'll follow the casket in here."

Nate hadn't gotten all the memos, clearly, so he hurried to stand with Connor in his arms. He went into the room behind the chapel, catching plenty of side-glances from cousins and aunts and uncles. He ignored them all and stayed right beside his mother and father, Connor glued to him as if the child was afraid Nate would leave him too.

Please help me, he thought. He'd attended church services at River Bay, though he'd never been overly religious. Ward definitely was much more into worshipping, and Nate closed his eyes as the pastor started a beautiful prayer that was filled with warmth and comfort.

But when he had to walk in the processional behind his brother's casket, the panic that had been hovering just beyond Nate reared and roared and reverberated through his whole soul.

He tried to breathe and couldn't.

He tried to hold back his tears and failed.

He tried to find a solution—any solution—to his current situation, and saw...Ginger.

CHAPTER FOUR

Ginger had always been quite observant, but it didn't take much to see Nate begin to spiral. His face became the color of wet cement, and he'd stopped walking. With the crowd of family members still behind them, Ginger couldn't just let him stand there.

So she whispered, "Come here, sweetheart," and took Connor from him. Their eyes met, and she tried to give him the fiercest look she possessed. *Just a few more steps*, she wanted to say.

Nate somehow got the message, but Ginger still nudged him with her elbow as she passed, hoping he'd walk with her. He did, and she preceded him down the same row they'd briefly sat on earlier. She took the spot between him and his mother and settled Connor on her lap. Everyone around her was crying, and Ginger watched as the funeral director placed an enormous splay of red roses, bright pink carnations, and huge yellow sunflowers on the top of the closed casket.

She didn't know Ward Mulbury, but it was obvious the man was well-loved. To get distance from the sadness around her, she wondered who'd come to her funeral. Her friends and co-workers at the ranch, of course. Her parents. Her two sisters and one brother, none of whom were married. Aunts, uncles, cousins, friends.

The same type of people who had come to Ward's funeral.

She turned to look at Nate and found tears streaming down his face. Her heart broke in that moment, but it was a new and different kind of crack she'd never experienced before. Sure, she'd had her heart broken by a man before, but not because he wasn't afraid to show the world how he felt.

In her lap, Connor started to cry too, and Nate reached for him. She passed the child to him, and Nate put their heads together and whispered to Connor things Ginger couldn't hear. Connor twisted and pressed his back into Nate's chest, and Nate wrapped him up in a big hug. Someone got up and started talking, and all Ginger could think about was providing Nate and Connor with the safest, happiest place on earth.

She pulled out her phone during one of the hymns and texted Emma, the assistant on the ranch—and Ginger's best friend. They'd been working at Hope Eternal together for a decade, and there was no one better than Emma at making someone feel loved and special.

How's Nate's room coming? she asked.

All ready for him, Michelle responded. *I gave him the two bedrooms on the main floor, with the bathroom between them. Dylan moved to the basement with Josh. They were both glad to do it. Jill, Jess, and your sisters are working on a babysitting schedule for Connor now. We should have it ready by the time you arrive.*

Ginger's stomach growled despite the greasy breakfast sandwich Nate had bought for her. *And dinner?* she texted.

All set. Steak and baked potatoes. I even got Michelle to make her layered salad by telling her she had to bring a peace offering if she wanted to go over all the legalities with Nate tonight.

Ginger smiled at her phone. Michelle Trent was the ranch's lawyer, and she didn't really like it when Ginger participated in the BOP's program to help convicts get back on their feet and make a good transition from incarceration to real life.

The poor man. How's he holding up?

Ginger didn't need to look to her left to know. *He's dealing with a lot,* she said. The song ended, and Ginger quickly added, *Gotta go. Thanks, Em. You're the best,* before tucking her phone back into her pocket.

By the time the services ended, they'd gone to the cemetery, and they'd eaten a lunch that was cold but supposed to be hot, Ginger was ready to get out of her skirt and on the road. Hope Eternal Ranch sat down the highway about fifteen minutes—maybe ten if there was no traffic and no cattle—and she'd been gone for almost twenty-four hours.

She stood near the truck while Nate hugged everyone for what felt like the millionth time, coaching herself to be patient. She might be observant and quick to learn, but her impatience could really bring out the worst in her.

She employed every ounce of kindness she had, and then distracted herself with her phone until Nate finally came over. "Sorry," he murmured. "Thank you for waiting for me." He opened the passenger door and helped Connor onto the bench seat.

Ginger could hardly believe this man had broken the law and then gone to jail for any amount of time. She'd never met an inmate like him before, and she'd housed a couple dozen at Hope Eternal.

The drive happened in silence, but because summer was almost upon them, it wasn't dark when they arrived at the ranch. "Okay," she said, taking a deep breath a moment later. "Here we are." She pulled onto the dirt lane that led back off the highway. Around another bend, and the ranch spread before her. "Everything you see now is Hope Eternal land."

"Wow," Nate said, and he genuinely sounded awed. "It's beautiful."

"Well, we are here when the sun is hanging in the west," she said, easing the truck to a stop. "But it's a great view right now." The golden sunlight spread across the land like honey, bathing everything in a yellow shine.

"Do you raise cattle?"

"No," she said. "We have a few cows, of course, but mostly for milk. Dairy cows. We grow crops here that we sell to neighboring farms and ranches, and we have horses, chickens, goats, and pigs. And birds." Boy, did they have a lot of birds at the ranch.

Being so close to the water did that, and there were plenty of ponds and rivulets on the ranch too. "We do a variety of programs for people," she said. "Horseback riding lessons and excursions. Bird-watching. Nature experiences. Hummingbird demonstrations. Monarch butterfly classes."

"Oh, so you're more commercial."

"You could say that," she said. "I run the ranch with five or six other women, and there's definitely an aspect of ranching here. We have people to take care of the animals behind-the-scenes and all of that. I have cowboys who run my riding programs too, and we do a hog hunt four times a year in March and April. Last one was last weekend."

Nate nodded, his eyes scanning the landscape in front of him. She wondered what he was thinking, what he could see here that he hadn't seen for so long. She didn't ask.

"I'd like to respectfully request not to be involved in the hunting," he said quietly. "And to have something to do outside."

Ginger looked at him, another round of surprise moving through her. "You don't like hunting?"

"Not particularly." He met her eyes, and Ginger

couldn't help leaning toward him, as if he possessed a powerful magnet and she had no other choice but to get closer to him. Her heart started screaming a warning, but it took her brain several long seconds to get the message.

She cleared her throat. "Well, seeing as how our last hunt was last week, and you're only obligated to be here for five months, I don't think being involved in the hunt will even come up." She released her foot on the brake and let the truck inch forward again. "And something outside...I'm sure we can do that." She glanced down at Connor, who'd fallen asleep at some point during the drive.

A smile touched her mouth, drying up when Nate said, "He's cute, but I have no idea how to take care of him."

Ginger heard the apprehension in Nate's voice, and she once again didn't know what to do with it. "You did great today," she said. "You held him when he needed you, and you helped him with his lunch, and you kept him right beside you." In fact, watching Nate do all of those things had warmed Ginger toward him considerably.

"Will you help me with him?" Nate asked.

Ginger glanced at him, her eyebrows shooting up. "What?"

"I saw you with him," he said. "You're great. You know exactly what to do."

She started shaking her head, but Nate continued anyway. "You showed up with chocolate, and you handed him a napkin before I even knew he needed one. You knew when to take him from me, and when to give him back, and you picked up his tie when I didn't even see that he'd dropped it."

"Nate," she said, but she stopped. Of course she was going to help him. Hadn't she already decided to make this transition for him as easy as possible here?

She had, and she knew it. Instead of answering, she eased around the corner and said, "There's the homestead."

Nate finally took his eyes off her face, and Ginger felt the weight of them go. "Oh...wow," he said again. "Look at that place."

Ginger looked at it, trying to see what Nate did. The homestead was really two houses connected together with a three-car garage in the middle. The garages had doors on both sides, so she could get to the road she was driving down now, or out onto the ranch in the opposite direction. When they were open and the sky shone through the gaps, it really was spectacular.

But they were closed today, which only made the house seem much bigger than it was.

"I live on the left side," she said. "The West Wing, we call it. Like the White House."

"Alone?" he asked.

"No," she said. "I have three women that live there with me. We all work on the ranch. Emma, my assistant, is there. Jessica is my stable master. She lives there. And Jill is a ranch hand. She works in the behind-the-scenes stuff the most. She lives there as part of her room and board."

She passed through the front gate, where the fields

ended and an unruly patch of grass barely passed for a front yard. "On the right is where the cowboys live. The Annex. You'll live there with Connor. Emma put you on the main floor, where there's only three bedrooms. A great guy named Spencer Rust lives in the other one. Downstairs, we have three more bedrooms and three more bathrooms, and the boys double up down there."

Nate said nothing, and Ginger really wanted to know what he was thinking. So she asked, "What are you thinking about?"

"I get the whole bedroom to myself?"

"Yes," she said. "And Connor can have the other one. If you'd rather sleep in the same room, that's fine. We weren't sure—"

"It's fine," he said. "Anything is fine, honestly."

She reached up to press the button to get the far left garage door to lift.

"I lived in a dormitory with sixteen other men," he said. "I can't even remember what it feels like to have an entire bedroom to myself."

Ginger had been told that before, and she hated that she hadn't remembered. "Emma and the other girls have been working on a babysitting schedule for Connor. You'll come over to our kitchen tonight, where she also has a feast waiting for us. Then I'll take you to the men's wing—what we call the East Annex. Or just the Annex."

She pulled into the garage, her heart thumping in a

strange way. "And that's it. You can't come to the West Wing whenever you want. It's off-limits to cowboys."

"I don't know if you know much about me," he said. "But I'm not a cowboy."

Ginger grinned at him, feeling a little out of control. Definitely tired, which probably spurred her to say, "You will be, Mister Mulbury. Trust me on that," in a flirty tone. She didn't add a giggle to the statement, thankfully, and quickly got out of the truck.

As she busied herself with her luggage from last night and all the paperwork she'd been given at the FCI, she kicked herself for saying anything about Nate becoming a cowboy. She also couldn't allow herself to flirt with him again. She needed him on the ranch; that was all. He didn't get to know about her private life, and she'd had plenty of experience with keeping things professional between her and the cowboys. She could do it with him too.

Nate had a waking-up Connor in his arms while he waited near the tailgate, and Ginger hurried to go up the steps in the garage that led into the utility room. An entire wall of cabinets greeted her, as did a washer and dryer and four boot racks.

She passed everything, keeping her boots on, and went around the corner and into the kitchen. The scent of sizzling meat met her nose, and her taste buds perked right up.

"There you are," Emma said, turning from the oven where she'd just pulled out a tray of foil-wrapped potatoes.

She stepped over to Ginger and hugged her. "Long day, right?"

"Really long," Ginger said, setting her folder on the counter and her bag next to the island. She indicated Nate behind her. "This is Nathaniel Mulbury, and his nephew Connor. He goes by Nate." She smiled at Connor. "And you go by Connor, right bud?"

The boy nodded as if she were asking a serious question, and she reached out and lovingly swiped the hair off his forehead. "He just woke up, so he's a bit shy right now." She stepped further into the kitchen. "This is Emma Clemson," she said. "She's my right hand and my left hand. If it looks like I know what I'm doing around here, it's because of her."

Emma just smiled and shook her head, sending her dark curls cascading around her shoulders. "Not true."

"Come in, come in. Let's get over to the table." Ginger stepped that way, unsurprised to see Emma pick up her folder of important documents and move them to the file holder on the opposite counter, out of the way.

"I'll go grab the others," Emma said. She picked up Ginger's suitcase and took it with her, calling, "Jess, Michelle. They're here."

Nate still hadn't said anything, and he sat in a chair at the corner of the table. Connor stayed in his lap, and Ginger didn't know what to do to break the tension. She reminded herself that the first night was always like this, that he just needed some time to adjust to a new way of living. One where he didn't have to share a bathroom with dozens of other men.

Ginger sat beside him and folded her hands in her lap. "Do you like steak?"

He turned his head toward her as if in slow motion. "I haven't had steak in years. But yeah." He spoke slowly and nodded his head. "I think I used to like steak."

"Emma's a really good cook."

"Do you cook, Ginger?"

She really liked how he said her name, with all the tenderness of a really good man. She sighed and shook her head. "I mean, I can if I have to, but Emma's here, so I don't have to." She gave him a smile, and for the first time, he returned it. He obviously had no idea what a smile transformed his face into, though he probably had at one point in the past.

"All right," Michelle said, her voice too brusque for their current conversation. She breezed into the room like a hurricane and took the chair on the other side of Nate. "Do you want to do the business first, or eat, and then talk afterward?"

"I'm exhausted," he said. "So let's get this over with, and then I can go to bed after dinner."

Michelle's gaze barely flicked toward Ginger, but she still caught the anxiety there. "Good plan. So this outlines the rules of Hope Eternal Ranch. You can go over it whenever. Ginger will talk to you about your assignment, probably in the morning."

"Or a day or two," she said. "It's Sunday tomorrow."

"Oh, right." Michelle barely missed a beat. "We need you to sign this one for the Bureau of Prisons. The BOP really likes all their paperwork in line as soon as possible." She held up a page and set it on the table in front of Nate.

"What is it?" he asked, though he was already reaching for the pen.

"It states that you understand that you work here. That you'll get paid. That we'll provide adequate housing for you and Connor." She paused as she looked at the boy. "But you'll have to pay for your own groceries, gas, vehicle should you choose to purchase one." She let another beat or two of silence pass, because most inmates usually had questions about their pay, their budget, or how they were supposed to pay for things.

Nate said nothing.

Michelle looked at Ginger and took another breath. "It says that you'll have a parole officer visit at least once a month, unannounced, and that you'll do daily check-in's with Ginger for the first week, whereupon they'll move to weekly, and then peter out as time goes by." She craned her neck to look at the paper. "Oh, and that you can't leave the property for any reason."

"Ever?" He looked from the paper to Michelle and then Ginger. "How do I buy groceries if I can't leave the ranch?"

"There's a delivery service," Ginger said. "And you can go with someone else. If you want to leave the ranch by yourself, there is a for for your parole officer, and it's up to him whether you can go or notI." She glanced at Michelle. "Right?" It had been several months since they'd had anyone from the prison system come to Hope Eternal.

"Right." Michelle picked up the pen. "Sound good?"

"What choice to I have?" Nate asked, the first sign of attitude from him that Ginger had seen. He took the pen and signed with a few hills and valleys in ink that looked nothing like his name at all.

"Great." Michelle whisked the paper away and stood up. "Let's eat."

"Yes," Ginger said, her stomach quite upset with her dietary choices from that day. "I'm starving."

Nate once again said nothing, and Ginger wondered if staying silent was a lesson he'd learned behind bars that had allowed him to survive. She wanted to ask him, but she thought he'd probably had enough questions for one day.

She reached over and patted his hand where it lay over Connor's and said, "I'm glad you're here, Nate." She wasn't sure if her tone revealed too much or not, so she quickly added, "You too, Connor," and got up to go help Emma in the kitchen so she wouldn't further embarrass herself.

CHAPTER FIVE

Nate wanted nothing more than to get his shoes off. He hadn't worn such flat or stiff shoes in months. Probably years. And he'd been in these monstrosities all day long. He couldn't believe he used to wear shoes like this to work every day, twelve hours a day, sometimes six days a week.

He did not miss his old life, that was for sure. He realized now how stressed he'd been all the time, and it was no wonder that all of his relationships were in ruins.

"This is your room," Ginger said, bringing Nate out of the pain of his feet. He gazed at the bedroom, with the huge queen-sized bed all made up with a puffy blue comforter and more than one pillow. He marveled at that fact alone, not to mention how big it was. Cavernous almost.

"The closet is around the corner," Ginger said, still speaking in that soft voice she'd adopted sometime after dinner. Nate had stayed in the kitchen in the West Wing, sipping coffee for as long as he could. When he'd caught Ginger's eye, she seemed to get his telepathic message that he was done.

Beyond done.

"Can I take off these shoes?" he asked.

"Of course."

But before he could move, Ginger darted in front of him. "Nate, you don't have to ask my permission to do anything."

He simply looked at her, the concept of making his own decisions somewhat foreign to him. Of course, he did remember that he'd once lived this way. It had just been so long. He nodded and stepped around the corner to enter the closet. It too was massive—at least two men could sleep in here—and he found a neat stack of jeans and another of T-shirts. A single sweatshirt hung from a hanger, as well as a heavier coat and three long-sleeved shirts.

He took off his shoes and left them on the floor, turning and almost colliding with Ginger. "I got a few things," she said. "According to the size chart. I kept the receipts, so if something doesn't fit, let me know, and I'll get the money back."

"Thanks," Nate said, though the money wasn't important to him. Ginger, however, got paid to have someone like him at her ranch, and she'd definitely want it back.

"Maybe you can't wear regular shirts," she said, her eyes holding a question.

Nate blinked, trying to figure out what she meant.

"I just—I mean, your shoulders are so broad." Instantly, a pink hue crept into her face, and she spun away from him. "Just let me know." She strode away from him and into the bathroom. "The bathroom is here. It has a door straight into Connor's room."

Nate wasn't sure if he had shock running through him or warmth. Maybe both. He knew this day had felt like a year, and he couldn't wait to lie down in that bed that looked made of clouds. He cast it a look before following Ginger, who'd taken Connor by the hand and was showing him the bed he could sleep in.

"Look, Uncle Nate." Connor jumped on the bed a couple of times, far too smiley and energetic for the day they'd had.

"I see," he said to the boy. "Now don't jump on the bed, Connor. It's not ours." He picked up his nephew and smiled at him. "Let's find you some pajamas." His eyes crossed Ginger as he located the dresser in the room—which was twice as big as the locker he'd used for almost five years.

He'd seen the kitchen—huge, with lots of glinting silver appliances—and the living room with two comfortable couches. She hadn't taken him downstairs, and Nate suspected he'd have plenty of time to get a feel for his new home.

He found a pair of dinosaur pajamas in the top drawer, and he started helping Connor get changed. He had no idea how to put a shirt on a child, but Connor helped by lifting up his arms, and the shirt just went right on. Ginger hung back in the doorway, watching, and Nate really wanted to get away from all the eyes.

Especially hers for some reason. Maybe because her observant gaze made him too hot, and he definitely couldn't handle the heat.

"All right," he said to Connor. "Into bed you go."

Connor climbed up onto the bed, and Nate pulled the blanket down to tuck him in. He leaned over and kissed Connor's forehead. "I'm right next door, okay? Right through the bathroom. Come get me if you need me."

"Uncle Nate?"

"Yeah?"

Connor just looked at him, though, and Nate had gotten good at seeing things inside the facility, but he couldn't read minds.

"Love you," he said through a tight throat, and he turned to face Ginger. She wore a look on her face that suggested she'd have done something differently.

Sure enough, when he approached, she whispered, "You're not going to have him brush his teeth or use the bathroom before bed?"

Foolishness filled Nate, and he stopped in his tracks. "Uh, yeah." He turned back to Connor. "Come brush your teeth, Connor. And you should use the bathroom before bed." He reached for the boy, still unable to think of him as his son, and Connor slid out from beneath the blanket.

Nate supervised while Connor got the tasks done, but he didn't go back into his bedroom. Nate finally crouched down in front of the wisp of a child and put his hands on Connor's slight shoulders. "What is it, bud?"

"I'm not going to see Daddy tomorrow, am I?"

Nate's lungs froze, cracking as they tried to exhale. "No, Connor," he said. "I'm going to take care of you now."

Connor reached out and put his hand on the side of Nate's face, the touch so innocent and so pure it made Nate's chest ache. "Can I sleep with you, Uncle Nate?"

Relief like Nate hadn't known in a while ran through him. "Of course." He picked up Connor and took him into the other bedroom, pulling down the comforter on the side closest to the bathroom. He got Connor tucked into bed, and he told Ginger he was going to change and come check with her.

Once he'd dressed in a more comfortable pair of gym shorts and one of the T-shirts—which did pull weirdly along his shoulders—he went out into the living area to find Ginger chatting with two other men, both of whom wore cowboy hats.

Once again, Nate froze. These men shouldn't scare him, and scared wasn't the right word. Everything in Nate's life had been blended up, poured out, and reblended, and he just wanted to disappear into the bedroom.

"Oh, here he is," Ginger said with a warm smile. "Nate, come meet Spencer and Nick. They share the master suite."

Nate managed to get his feet moving, and he shook hands with a dark-haired man Ginger introduced as

Spencer Rust, and then a blond man that couldn't be older than twenty.

"This is Nick Talbot," she said. "He's my cousin."

"And he works here?" Nate asked.

"Yep," Nick said, keeping the wide smile on his face. "Aunt Ginger is an awesome boss." He beamed at her and walked around the island in the kitchen to get a chocolate chip cookie from the plate of them Ginger had brought from their dinner next door.

Nate just looked at Ginger. "So tomorrow..."

"Tomorrow is Sunday," she said. "We run a skeleton operation on Sundays. You should take the day to enjoy the ranch and spend time with Connor. Explore."

Nate nodded, thinking about the fences and gates he still had in his life. But Hope Eternal Ranch was at least a thousand times better than where he'd slept just last night, so he wasn't about to complain.

"I serve breakfast at six-thirty," Spencer said. "But you can eat whenever you get up. Nick here snores until at least nine on Sundays." He jabbed the younger man in the ribs, the two of them laughing together.

"And don't let him fool you with 'I serve breakfast at six-thirty,'" Nick said, dropping his voice to imitate Spencer on the last few words. "He puts out boxes of cereal with a few bowls and spoons."

"So if you have any requests, let me know," Spencer said, grinning like he'd really said something funny.

Nate liked both of them, as they seemed full of joy. He

wondered what it would be like to be carefree, and he tried to turn over the feelings and examine them. Now that he was out, he could work on getting to where they were.

He had money, so he didn't have to worry about that. He had a job. He had somewhere to live that was so nice he almost didn't dare touch anything. If he could figure out how to take care of Connor, and work through the grief eating at the bottom of his stomach, Nate thought he actually had a chance to start the life Greg had mentioned that he could.

"Thank you," he said to Spencer and Nick. "Well, I'm exhausted, so I'm going to turn in. I'm sure I'll see you in the morning."

They both tipped their hats at him, and Nate found himself wanting to do the same. He caught Ginger's eye, and she nodded once and smiled at him before he left the kitchen and went back down the hall that led alongside the stairs. Through an arched doorway sat the two bedrooms joined by the bathroom, and he cast a look at the front door only a few feet away before making the turn.

Anyone could come through that and with just a few steps, be in his bedroom. He detoured to make sure it was locked—it wasn't—and then he joined Connor in the bedroom. He locked that door too, a faint slip of relief accompanying the click of the lock.

He closed the bathroom door, but it didn't lock from this side. So he went through it again and locked the bedroom door into Connor's room. Then the bathroom door that led into the same bedroom.

Finally, he lay down on his side of the bed, barely able to comprehend the soft pillows and blankets and mattress beneath him. A sigh leaked out of his mouth, and he closed his eyes, sure sleep would claim him instantly.

Unfortunately, it didn't, and Nate lay awake, his mind moving a hundred miles an hour. He hadn't spoken to Ted today, and that didn't feel right. Phone calls in River Bay were coveted and expensive, but maybe Nate could put some money in Ted's account now that he was out.

He needed to get to the bank first thing on Monday morning and figure out his money situation. He had no debit or credit card, and no cash. He needed to get more clothes and boots to wear around the ranch. Connor needed clothes and shoes too. Probably some toys or a bike or something. Nate needed groceries too. Spencer and Nick seemed like nice guys, but he didn't think they'd take kindly to him if he kept eating everything they bought.

He needed more toiletries than the travel-sized ones Ginger had given him. He needed to get out on the ranch and see how far he could go. He needed to take a deep breath of the outdoor air as a free man.

He needed to figure out how to get along in the world without Ward. He needed to untangle his complicated feelings for Ginger. Strange she'd already introduced herself into his life, and he'd spent only a day with her.

He rolled over, frustrated he was still awake when everything from his brain to the bottom of his feet was so tired.

It all started with making sure he could get to his money, so his first order of business on Monday morning would be to get to a bank. His thoughts morphed then, twisting and turning around the money in his account and whether or not he deserved it.

An image of a face flashed through his mind, and Nate shivered as he brought the blanket all the way to his chin. He'd been safe from Oscar Dominguez while in River Bay. Now that he was out, how long before Oscar came looking for him—and his money?

THE NEXT MORNING, NATE EMERGED FROM THE bedroom with Connor a few minutes before seven. True to his word, Spencer had set a few boxes of cereal on the cupboard, with a stack of bowls and a pile of spoons.

"Lucky Charms?" He picked up the box and showed it to Connor. Once Nate had finally fallen asleep, he'd slept great. It was amazing the rest a man could get when he wasn't being counted at midnight, and at three a.m, and again at five.

The smile grew on Connor's face as his eyes widened. Nate chuckled as he lifted the flaps on the box. "Your daddy doesn't let you eat these, does he?"

"No, sir," Connor said, sobering. "Do you think he'll be mad?"

"Nope," Nate said, pouring the sugary cereal into a bowl for Connor. "I think your dad probably wishes he'd eaten a few more bowls of Lucky Charms." Nate was going to have the unhealthy cereal too, despite the label on the box claiming it was made with whole grain.

Yeah, and a whole lot of sugar, Nate thought. Ward had been a bit of a health nut, and he could only imagine the types of cold cereal he'd allow Connor to consume. A bitterness entered Nate's mind, because for all of Ward's running and consumption of brown rice and quinoa, he'd still died very young.

Forty-one was barely starting life, and everything inside Nate tightened again. He didn't relax until his first bite of the sugar-filled puffs, and even then, his mood had worsened. His head hurt a little, which made no sense given the amount of sleep he'd gotten last night.

The house sat in silence, and he wondered if the other cowboys were really asleep or if they had chores to attend to on the ranch. His money—if he were still a betting man—was on the latter, as animals needed to be cared for around the clock, a man's sleep schedule notwithstanding.

He finished eating and put his bowl in the sink before he started hunting through the many drawers and cupboards in the giant kitchen. Even the chow hall at River Bay hadn't been this big, and sixty men ate in there at the same time. He found neatly labeled shelves with everything from granola and protein bars to Pop Tarts to boxes of gelatin on them.

He counted seven other names, and his heart constricted and then tried to burst out of the tiny box it had folded itself into. He'd just opened a cabinet and spied the little white bottle that surely had painkiller in it when the back door opened.

Nate glanced at Ginger as he picked up the bottle, and then he focused on pressing and turning the lid to get it off. "Morning," he said.

"What are you doing?" Ginger asked, taking three long strides and snatching the bottle from him.

He blinked, trying to catch up to the situation. "I have a headache."

"These are sleeping pills." She shook the bottle like he should know that, but he hadn't even looked at it.

"Okay," he said, frowning. "I didn't even have a chance to look at it."

Her eyebrows drew down, and her dark hazel eyes flashed with fire. "Did you sleep okay last night?"

"Once I fell asleep," he said. "Before then...it was so *quiet*." And that had left his mind to churn over too many thoughts.

"You should've been in the West Wing," she said dryly, putting the bottle back on the shelf. She rummaged around for a few seconds and pulled out a much larger container. "These are your painkillers."

"Was it noisy over there?" he asked, taking the bottle from her.

"Oh, Ursula must've been able to smell something. Foxes or coyotes or something. She barked all night."

Nate tapped a few pills into his palm. "So Ursula is a dog."

"She's my German shepherd," Ginger said as if he should've known.

"I didn't see a dog last night."

"She was out with Spencer," she said. "She likes him *almost* as much as me, and he takes her for me when I have to leave the ranch overnight."

As if on cue, a dog barked somewhere beyond the back door, and Ginger turned just as the huge black and orangey-gold shepherd came into the house. Ursula's tongue hung out of her mouth, and she had big, brown, keen eyes.

"Oh, there she is," Ginger said, pure joy in her tone. She bent down and scrubbed Ursula's head and neck. "You're a good girl, aren't you? Noisy last night, but such a good girl."

Nate didn't know how to make the demanding version of Ginger who'd walked through the door a few minutes ago line up with the one talking like a baby to a dog who could easily knock her down and bite off her face. Not to mention the soft, kind woman who'd held his hand yesterday and bent to his every whim.

A wicked thought ran through his mind—*what else could he get her to do for him?*—and he banished it quickly. Number one, all of his mental energy went to Ursula as she came over, her nails clicking against the hard floor, to sniff him.

He wasn't afraid of dogs, but he didn't want one all up in his business either. He bent down and patted the German shepherd, because she was a magnificent creature. She seemed to like him well enough, and then she went over to Connor, who still sat on the barstool. The boy squealed and then laughed as he slipped off the stool to pet the dog. Ursula licked his face, and Connor giggled and giggled.

When Nate looked at Ginger, she wore such a blissful expression on her face that made Nate want to be able to put that look there again and again. He had no idea what that meant, and he filed the thought to think about later.

"I need to go to the bank tomorrow," he said. "Do you drive me? Or should I ask someone else? Or...?" He let his question hang there, because he honestly didn't know how to finish it.

"I'll take you," she said. "You can't go anywhere alone, Nate, except around to do your work on the ranch."

He nodded, suddenly needing a very strong cup of coffee. The brew behind bars was always too hot and too bitter, but Nate had grown accustomed to it. He glanced down the counter and didn't even see a coffee machine. That would definitely have to change.

"I'm thinking I'll put you with the horses," she said as Spencer entered the house.

"Oh, Ursula made it back," he said, grinning at the dog. "She barked at everything that moved today."

"And last night," Ginger said with a sigh. "I need to get her into that agility program."

Nate's interest piqued, because they'd had a couple of prison dogs, and he'd enjoyed working with them.

"He's doing horses?" Spencer asked, stepping over to the sink to wash his hands.

"And I'm going to give him the beginning riding lessons." Ginger looked at him, the questions right in her eyes. "And then the outlying work of fixing fences and bird blinds."

"Sounds good to me," Spencer said.

"What do you think?" Ginger asked Nate, who honestly had no idea how to do anything she'd just listed.

He told himself he could learn, so he just said, "Sounds great," and hoped he'd be left alone to figure things out without too much embarrassment.

"Great," Ginger echoed. "We'll go to the bank and do any shopping you want to do tomorrow, and then I'll get you started."

The idea of him getting to mess up and fix it before she found out disappeared, but at least he'd get to have Ginger at his side.

He wasn't sure if the thought was traitorous or exciting, but he knew for certain it was very confusing.

"Oh, and my girls are coming this way in a few minutes," she said. "To go over a babysitting schedule with you." She glanced around the kitchen. "Now, why isn't there any coffee over here?"

Amen, Nate thought, a smile coiling through him that he didn't let touch his mouth.

CHAPTER SIX

Ginger left Nate alone for the afternoon on Sunday, telling herself she couldn't glue herself to his side just because she found him handsome. She'd seen a glint in his eye a couple of times, but she had no idea what it meant. In her experience, ex-cons could lie like it was breathing, and she had all the proof she needed of that in her past.

So she'd made herself scarce while Emma and Jess went over the babysitting with him, while Spencer ordered pizza for the cowboys in the East Annex, and while Nate took Connor down the dirt path behind the huge homestead and out onto the ranch. She'd watched them for a few minutes, ducking down behind the counter when Nate turned and looked back toward the house, as if he could sense her eyes on his broad shoulders.

Monday morning, she arrived at the East Annex at nine o'clock, already having put in three hours out on the ranch.

Nate wore a pair of the jeans she'd bought with the money from the BOP, as well as one of the T-shirts, this one in a dark gray that made him seem stormy and sexy at the same time. She'd been right, and the shirt didn't fit well around his shoulders. But she wasn't going to embarrass herself again, and she said nothing.

Jill arrived to take Connor for the morning, and the boy skipped happily with her across the back deck and down the steps to the yard, Ursula going with them. "I think she likes Connor more than Spencer," Ginger said, still watching them.

"That's because Connor lets that beast lick his face," Nate said, and Ginger burst out laughing.

Nate chuckled with her, and their eyes met in that same magnetic power they had before. She wondered if he'd laughed a lot in prison, but she felt like she already knew the answer to that question, so she didn't ask it.

"Ready?" she asked instead, clearing her throat afterward.

"Yes," he said. "I found my personal ID, so I think I'm good." He reached into his back pocket and pulled out his old driver's license. He had nothing else, and Ginger had known he wouldn't. She'd just forgotten she needed to schedule a few days of errands so her ex-cons could get their lives settled before they started on the ranch. She was simply desperate for the manpower, and she'd been hoping Nate could start that day.

"Is that still good?" Ginger asked. She hadn't looked at any of his personal effects.

"Yes," he said. "I have a couple of months until my birthday."

Ginger's extreme curiosity got the best of her. "And then you'll be…?"

"Thirty-six," he said, his expression turning cold for a moment. Just as quickly, he thawed again. "And I know better than to ask a lady her age." He gave her what she would classify as a flirty smile. Maybe sly. Whatever it was, it held some heat behind it.

Ginger felt that heat rise through her whole body, and she turned away from him. "I don't mind." She wanted to share a few things with him. She told herself she didn't have to date him or kiss him if he knew how old she was. "I'm already thirty-six."

"How long have you been running this place?" he asked from behind her as they walked toward the front door.

"Oh, about six years now," she said. "I'm the oldest child in my family, and my father had sustained an injury, so." She shrugged. "I've always wanted the ranch, and now I have it." She flashed him a smile as she opened the door. He held it for her, and she went through first. She couldn't help thinking about the time she'd almost lost the ranch, but she wasn't going to detail that for Nate. Not right now.

Not ever, she told herself firmly. If she was talking about Hyrum Charles—her last boyfriend, as well as the last man she'd taken from the BOP into the RRC program—that meant she was talking about her past relationships. And she only did that with a potential boyfriend—or a man who'd already become her boyfriend.

Nate wasn't going to be either. *Nope, nope,* she told herself. *Not happening.*

She had about five hundred things to get done that day, so she drove a little fast on the way into town. Nate directed her to the bank he wanted, and Ginger stared at the steel and glass building. "You bank here?"

"Ward does," Nate said without any inflection in his voice. Ginger tossed a look in his direction to see if speaking his brother's name bothered him. It didn't seem to. "Do you come in, or wait here...?"

"I'll come in," she said. "Don't worry, I'll sit clear across the room." That way, she could observe him better, and he wouldn't know. Ginger couldn't believe her hormones were betraying her so badly. No wonder she'd never agreed to another inmate.

She recited to herself all the work around the ranch that needed to be done, and how with Nate, she could get caught up faster. *New fields to plow for next year.*

Six more bird blinds to be built.

A waiting list for horseback riding lessons. With Nate, she could register everyone on the list and make a lot more money.

The fact was, she needed him. Just not in a romantic way. But as he reached the door and opened it, stepping back to let her go in first, Ginger had the thought that he was the most polite ex-con she'd ever met.

Everything about Nate wasn't what she'd expected based on her past experience with Hyrum, and her mind betrayed her by thinking, *Maybe we can get to know him. Maybe we can hold his hand. Maybe we can kiss him...*

She cut off the thoughts there, because they were already too dangerous. "I'll be right here," he said, plunking herself down in a plush chair just inside the lobby, near the door they'd come in. She didn't think Nate would make a run for it, though there was another door on the far side of the bank.

He proceeded over to a desk and started speaking with a man, who took him up the steps and into a fancy office where Ginger could see through the walls of glass. The two of them sat down at an oversize desk and started talking.

She just watched, but grew bored of that very quickly. Nate took an enormous amount of time at the bank, and by the time he came downstairs, he was tucking a couple of cards into a brand-new wallet. Ginger gaped at him. Since when did banks give out genuine leather wallets?

She rose, her back protesting at her long lapse in movement. "All good?"

"Yes," he said. "Sorry that took so long."

She waved off the apology and asked, "Where to next?"

"Connor and I need some clothes," he said. "And toiletries. And groceries." He cut a look at her out of the corner of his eye. "Can you take me somewhere to do all of that at once?"

"Let's try the department store over on Wall," she said. "It has a grocer right next door."

"Great."

She drove, and Nate rode along. He wasn't a particularly chatty man, and the silence was driving Ginger insane. But all the questions she wanted to ask seemed inappropriate, so she kept her mouth shut too.

By the time he finished shopping for everything, lunchtime had come and gone. Her stomach growled as he loaded bags of cereal and granola bars and eggs into the back of her truck.

"I heard that," he said, grinning at her. "Do you have time for lunch?"

No, Ginger really didn't have time for lunch. She supposed no one had called or texted her with an emergency yet, and she might as well enjoy her time off the ranch. "Okay," she said, looking around. They were right downtown in Sweet Water Falls, and they had their pick of at least a dozen places. "What do you like?"

"Ginger," he said, his voice made of magic and warm honey. "I've been eating prison food for almost five years. Everything here has to be better than that."

She turned toward him and met his eye. He smiled, and his whole countenance transformed with that simple gesture. Ginger felt like someone had poured cement in her veins, because she couldn't move.

Her mind raced, though, and all she could think about was being this man's girlfriend.

"I would like some amazing pizza," he said, glancing around, his gaze coming back to hers a moment later. "Do you think that's possible?"

"Yes," she said dumbly. She gave herself a mental shake and blinked her way out of the heated trance she'd fallen into. "There's a great place just around the corner called Papa Bear's."

"Oh, wow." He chuckled and gestured for him to lead the way. "Close enough for us to walk?"

"Yes," she said, already moving. Maybe a walk would clear her head, though Papa Bear's was literally five minutes away.

"So tell me," Nate said after he'd matched her stride with his. "Are there other rules around the ranch I need to know about?"

"Other rules?"

"Yeah, you know, like where I can put my groceries in the house. Those shelves were all labeled."

"Oh, well, that's because Jack's crazy." She giggled, actually mortified at the sound. She tried to suck it back in and ended up choking. As she coughed, Nate just grinned, almost like he knew the effect he held over women.

He hadn't lost everything in prison, that was for dang sure.

"Who's Jack?"

"He lives downstairs," she said. "He's an amazing

cowboy, but he has a little bit of an issue with OCD. Likes things a certain way. He'll have some shelves labeled for you by the time we get back, or I'll treat you to lunch again."

"I don't need you to treat me this time," he said.

"No?" She looked at him. "I suppose Ward did leave you everything."

"That's still being worked out with the lawyers," he said. "I have money from...before."

"Oh." Surprise darted through Ginger, and she nearly fell down when Nate put his hand softly on the small of her back and said, "I think it's down there."

She'd been preparing to cross the street, but he was right. Papa Bear's was to their left, just beyond the grocery store where he'd seemingly bought everything he wanted. Ginger's skin sparked, sending electricity up her back, across her shoulders, and down her arms.

"Anything else I need to know?" he asked. "You know, cowboys to avoid. How to make sure I'm safe when I go out on the ranch. That kind of thing."

"Nate," she said, coming back to the present, though she still felt like shivering from his touch. "You're not in prison anymore. You're safe at Hope Eternal Ranch."

"You don't have farm equipment that could cause some damage?"

"Sure," she said. "But you won't be using it."

"I have no idea how to work with horses," he said. "And believe it or not, there were no riding lessons in River Bay."

He gave her a smile that seemed too tight around the edges. "Lots of other classes, but not that one."

"You're smart," she said, deciding that was a compliment and not a flirtation device. "I think you'll pick it all up quickly." She turned to go inside the pizza parlor, adding, "Now, there's this white pizza that is simply amazing that I think you'll like. Have you had white pizza?"

"Yes," he said. "But not for a long, long time."

GINGER ATE WAY TOO MUCH AT PAPA BEAR'S, WHERE the furniture was as big as the pizza. She carried half of their meal in a box while they walked back to the truck. They'd had an enjoyable lunch, making small talk about her family, and his, and the people who worked around the ranch.

He hadn't met all of them yet, but he claimed to be looking forward to it. She turned up the radio on the truck, and started thinking about an afternoon nap instead of going out to the stables to check on the riding program.

A new batch of riders was starting that day, and Ginger really needed to be out there at three-thirty to make sure everyone got checked in and had a good experience. So she'd go, even if she did just want to lie down for a little while.

She knew she felt like that because she'd eaten too much, and a brisk walk around the ranch to help prep for the class would settle her stomach.

She pulled into the garage closest to the West Wing and

killed the engine, ready to get going. Nate, however, didn't move.

"You okay?" she asked, and he turned his attention to her.

"I wanted to ask you one more thing," he said.

Ginger draped one arm over the steering wheel. "Shoot."

"It's about the rules here at the ranch."

She grinned at him, at the way he stayed so serious. "Didn't I say there weren't really rules?"

"That's not true, though," he said. "For example, I can't just come over to the West Wing whenever I want."

"Well, that's true." She reached for the pizza box on the seat between them. "So what's your question?"

"It's about dating," he said.

Ginger froze, her fingers curled around the cardboard. "Dating?"

"Yeah." Nate cleared his throat. "Is that allowed? You know, for me?"

"Well, I mean." She blew out her breath. "You can't leave the ranch, so I suppose if your date is okay coming here or whatever, then yeah, you can date."

"What if I wanted to date someone who works at the ranch?"

Her eyebrows shot toward the sky. "Here? At the ranch?" She narrowed her eyes at him.

"Yeah," he said, finally tearing his gaze from hers.

"Someone here at the ranch. Can cowboys date the women in the West Wing?"

Ginger needed to get out of this truck immediately. Her skin itched now, and she wondered who had caught his eye. Probably Michelle. All men liked Michelle. She had the curves they wanted, with the long legs and the flat stomach. Ginger didn't have curves, which made buying jeans really hard, for the record.

"I mean...I don't know."

"You don't know?" Nate watched the door that led into the West Wing, as if the woman he desired would walk through it at any moment. "So there's no rule against it?"

"No," Ginger said dumbly, though her heart beat with the reverberations and sound of a gong through her whole body. She should've told him there was a rule against cowboys dating the women out here. Then she wouldn't have to watch him go out with one of her friends.

In that moment, Ginger recognized and acknowledged that she had a crush on this man. Horror filled her, laced with excitement. She hadn't been out with a man in years. Years and years, if she were being honest.

No one since Hyrum, in fact.

And she couldn't get involved with another prisoner. Could she?

"Great," Nate said. "Do you want to have dinner with me sometime?" He looked at her again, and Ginger's eyes widened.

Her fingers scrabbled for the door handle, finding it after

only a moment. She yanked, and the door opened. She practically jumped from the truck with the words, "I'll be right back," and strode out of the garage as quickly as her long legs could take her.

She didn't remember breathing, so by the time she made it across the dirt lane to the small shed there, her lungs felt like they'd been set on fire. She hurried through the door and closed it, leaning against it and sucking at the air.

Had Nate just asked her out?

And worse, had she run away from him afterward? A moan started somewhere in the bottom of Ginger's boots and worked its way up, tearing through her insides before it came out of her mouth.

And the worst part? She wanted to say yes, she'd love to have dinner with him. She slid down the door until she met the ground, and she stared straight ahead, trying to decide what to do.

Last time she'd allowed herself to fall for an ex-con, he'd stolen from her, broken her heart, and almost managed to get the ranch in his name.

Would the consequences of a relationship with Nate be worse?

Ginger didn't want to find out. At the same time, she really did. Since she was now at war with herself, she simply continued to stare, hoping an answer to this new dilemma would present itself inside the shed.

CHAPTER SEVEN

Nate kept his eyes on the rear-view mirrors, and he saw Ginger high-tail it down the driveway and across the lane to the shed. She ran the last few steps, and he made an angry sound.

"Idiot," he chastised himself. But surely the feelings he felt for her couldn't be one-sided. She had to feel *some*thing. Didn't she?

Nate had been out of the dating game for a while. A very long while. So long that he'd probably go out with anyone at this point.

"Not true," he muttered. He knew what he liked in a woman, and he liked Ginger. At least he knew what the old Nate had liked in a woman, but he knew the financial sector Nate would've never looked Ginger's way for longer than a few seconds.

He was looking now.

He was different now.

He got out of the truck and decided to face Ginger before retreating to the massive bedroom inside the huge house where he now lived. He went down the driveway and across the lane too, knocking a couple of times on the door.

"Ginger," he said. "I'm going back to the Annex. Forget I said anything, okay?"

She didn't answer, but Nate wasn't going to stick around and add insult to injury. He turned and returned to the truck to get his groceries, and then he walked through the Texas sunshine to the Annex, where he found Jill coloring with Connor.

"I'm back," he said, setting a few bags on the kitchen counter. He hated this uncertainty streaming through him. He just wanted someone to tell him where to put his coffee and creamer, but the house felt very quiet. "I can take him now, Jill."

"Great," she said. "I have to go get the horses ready for riding lessons this afternoon."

"Oh, I think I'm helping with those," he said. "What time do they start?"

"Three-thirty," she said. "You can come watch if you want. I'm sure Ginger didn't intend for you to start today." Jill flashed him a smile that didn't make his heart boom through his chest the way Ginger's did.

So he definitely liked her. He wasn't just lusting after her because she was a woman and he was a man who'd been in prison for nearly five years.

Jill left, and Nate abandoned the groceries on the counter. He sat at the table with Connor. "What are you drawing?"

"It's a leopard," Connor said. "See his spots?" He pointed with a brown crayon.

"Oh, yeah, I see that," Nate said, though he couldn't see spots anywhere on the page. He got up again and started unpacking the bags. "Listen, Connor, I have some things here I want you to take in your room."

He made a stack of clothes, socks, and underwear, and called the boy over to get them. "Take them to the dresser, okay?"

"Okay."

"Then I'll show you the toys I got for you." He smiled at the little blond boy, his heart squeezing painfully at the parts of Ward he could see.

Connor grinned and hurried down the hall to put his things away. All Nate could think was that at last he'd done one right things that day by buying Connor some toys.

As he went through the cupboards and drawers and found slots for his things, as he showed Connor how to play Go Fish, as they got settled in their lives, Nate's thoughts revolved around Ginger.

"All right," he said just after three. "Let's go see if we can find the horses." He reached for Connor's hand, glad when the boy put his chubby fingers in Nate's. The simple touch reminded Nate of how much good there was in the world, and he hoped he could experience a lot more of it right here at Hope Eternal Ranch.

The walk along the path, with the bright May sunshine overhead, soothed Nate's soul. He'd been unsure about coming here, but now, he couldn't imagine being anywhere else. He'd gotten a new phone and a new computer, and he needed some time to get them set up. He'd wished he could've bought them privately, but he was used to doing everything in the view of someone else.

He just wished it wasn't Ginger. She'd asked about his money, and he'd managed to put her off in a way that he hoped she wouldn't come back to it. Nate needed to do a lot more at the bank than he had, but he'd made Ginger sit there for almost an hour, and the vice-president had said Nate could call his personal line to finish the business they'd started.

"Look, Uncle Nate," Connor said. "Look at all those horses."

Nate looked up from the dust puffing up from his boots to the sight of dozens of horses. The majesty of them took his breath away, and his steps slowed. Several people, both men and women, seemed to be scurrying around, getting the horses in line and putting equipment nearby.

Nate had no idea how to saddle a horse, and his pulse started picking up speed. And when Ginger stepped around a particularly beautiful brown and white horse, Nate thought someone had turned up the intensity of the sun.

Jill stepped in front of him, and Nate blinked until he

focused on her. She had light features, with minty eyes and blonde hair. She spent so much time in the sun that her tan skin didn't quite go with her fairer features.

"Hey," she said. "The kids are gathering on the other side of the stables. You could take Connor over there and keep an eye on them, if you want."

"Okay." Nate wasn't sure where the other side of the stables was, and he had no idea what to do with kids. He led Connor away from Ginger, though he desperately wanted to talk to her, and they moved around the horses.

The stables spread before them, a sprawling, single-story red wood building that looked like something from a classic Texas farm. Several aisles led through the building, and he took Connor down the closest one to get out of the heat.

The sound of chattering and children laughing told Nate that he was headed in the right direction. Thankfully, a couple of other adults stood above the heads of the children. And even better, they were Spencer and Nick, the two cowboys Nate had already met.

"Hey." Spencer grinned at him and turned back to the boy he'd been talking to. The kids that had swarmed into the corral all seemed to be about ten or twelve years old, not that Nate could really judge the age of children. They were a lot taller than Connor, though, and they had really big front teeth.

Connor let go of Nate's hand, and panic reared through him. "Stay here," Nate told him. The noise reminded him of the inmates jeering when someone would get in a fight. It happened rarely in the low-security facility, but it happened. Sometimes just an argument would break out about someone talking too loud while others wanted to sleep, and the Unit Officers would have to come tell everyone to be quiet and go to sleep.

Nate backed up a step and looked at Spencer. "This is a lot of kids."

"Right?" He grinned out at all the little people. "The eleven-year-old introductory lesson is our most popular one."

So all these boys and girls were eleven. They'd all gotten a memo about what to wear, and they had on long pants, boots, and hats.

"Ready?" Spencer asked, looking at Nick.

"Let's go."

"All right," Spencer said, holding up both hands. The children began to quiet. "I need y'all to settle down." He paused for a moment as more children stopped talking. "Quiet on down now."

They did, and Spencer stepped up onto the bottom rung of the fence, so he was even taller than the children. "I've just gotten word that the horses are almost ready." A twitter of excitement ran through the crowd. "We're going to go over a few rules before we go back, and there's a lot of us, so we expect everyone to follow the rules. If you don't, you'll be right back here, waitin' for your mom to pick you up."

He sounded like he meant it too, and Nate watched the children's faces. They believed him too.

"First, horses don't like the noise. So we need to use a quiet voice when we leave here. You'll stand where we tell you to stand. You'll hold the reins how we show you. There will be someone for every four of you, and you'll need to remember that person's name and ask any questions you have. Each cowboy or cowgirl will give you specific things to do once you get back there."

He grinned out at them. "So who's ready to ride a horse?"

The children cheered, and Nate caught some of their excitement as it filled the air. He didn't think the instructions were adequate for eleven-year-olds to know how to ride a horse, but he wasn't in charge of this group. He didn't even know how to be in charge of a group like this.

"All right," Spencer called out. "Three lines, boys and girls. Three lines. Make three lines. One will follow me. One will follow Nick here." Nick stepped forward and raised his cowboy hat. "And one will follow Nate."

Nate swung his attention from a cute red-headed girl to Spencer, who looked at him expectantly. He quickly swept the hat off his head too and lifted it into the air. The children began to make the lines Spencer requested of them, and Nate took Connor's hand again and stepped to the front of a line.

Thankfully, Spencer took his line of boys and girls first, and surprisingly, Nate didn't have to wait that long to follow him. Spencer split them up and assigned them out to the dozen cowboys and cowgirls waiting with the horses, and

Nate became quickly overwhelmed with how many animals stood ready for a ride.

He hung back, because he had no idea where he fit in. He kept Connor at his side so the boy wouldn't get hurt, and he simply gaped at the sheer number of people and horses.

"It's a bit overwhelming, isn't it?"

He turned toward the female voice to find a brunette standing there. The same one who'd fed him last night. She nodded toward all the people now talking to groups of four. They demonstrated and instructed, and then the saddles started going on the backs of horses. "It's completely overwhelming," Emma said. "And I've been around for the first day of eleven-year-old lessons many times."

"There's a lot of them," he admitted. He watched Ginger weave around one horse and then a group of people. She caught Emma's eye and then looked at Nate—and stumbled.

He wanted to leave, but he'd told Jill he'd come observe today. "Is this what I'll do?" he asked. "Ginger said I'd do the riding lessons, as well as some fence fixing and something with bird blinds?"

"She'll want you to watch this class for a week, and then she'll want you to be Spencer there." Emma nodded to the other cowboy. "He entertains them while they wait for the lesson to start. He gives them a little speech, lines them up, and brings them back. He organizes everything. Then, the riders take them out, and he's done for a bit. When the horses and kids come back, he takes care of the horses while the parents pick up their kids."

"How long are lessons?" Nate asked.

"An hour," she said. "We do them four days a week. So you'll get to hear Spencer's speech four times this week, and you'll be ready by Monday." She gave him a warm smile and refocused on the chaos in front of them.

"I'm going to need a riding lesson," Nate said. "And some instructions on how to take care of a horse after it's been ridden."

"Spencer and Nick will get you ready," she said easily. "You'll go out with them in the morning and stick to them like a shadow for the next several days."

"Yes, ma'am," he said. The first child swung up onto a nearby horse, and very soon after that, the rest of them did too. They wore the biggest, brightest smiles Nate had ever seen, and he let their joy lift his spirits.

Ginger caught his eye, and some of that happiness leaked out. She nodded toward the stable, and Nate understood her non-verbal communication. He bent down and looked at Connor. "Can you stay with Emma for a minute?" He passed the boy's hand to Emma and straightened to meet her eye. "I'll be back in a second."

As he went toward the stable, he could only pray that he could handle whatever Ginger said to him.

CHAPTER EIGHT

Ginger paced in the stables, sure Nate had seen her indicate he should meet her there. She turned and stalled when she saw him framed in the doorway. "Hey," she said.

"Hey." He shoved his hands in his pockets, and the way he radiated contriteness from his very being made Ginger's perfectly prepared speech dry right up.

"Look," she said. "I've kind of had...a rough time in the whole going-to-dinner thing, and I just got a little flustered."

"Perfectly understandable." He made no attempt to come closer to her. With the sun haloing him from behind, and with that sexy cowboy hat perched on his head, it was difficult to see his face.

Ginger nodded. "So, do you think you can do the riding lessons?"

"Oh, there's no way I can do this," he said, and while he spoke with a tease in his voice, she suspected he believed his words.

"You'll learn it," she said.

"You sound so confident," he said. "I wish I had some of that."

"Did you grow up in White Lake?"

"Yes."

"Never rode a horse?"

"I mean, I did," he said. "But that doesn't mean I can teach others how to do it. Especially kids."

"The kids are the easiest group, trust me," Ginger said.

"Did you grow up in Sweet Water Falls?"

"Right down the road," she said. "My grandparents lived in the house where I live now, and my father added the East Annex when he moved there. I was fifteen, and he taught me how to shingle a roof and texture a wall before painting it." She put a smile on her face, because she'd enjoyed learning things from her father.

"And I suppose you've been riding since you could walk."

"Of course not," she said. "We don't start riding until we're three or four, and that's *years* after we first learn to walk."

Nate let a beat of silence go by, and then he laughed. It was a wonderful, deep sound that set Ginger's heartbeat racing. She joined in, glad for this single moment in time and hoping they'd have more.

She took a few steps toward him, wanting to reach out and take his hand in hers. She wasn't quite brave enough for that. "So, you know, I eat dinner every night, and if you really wanted to eat with me, I think that could be arranged."

"I don't want to break the rules," he said.

"There are no rules about who can eat dinner with who."

"I don't want to make your life harder."

"Nate, I brought you here to make my life easier."

"Then I will do my best to do that," he said, and he was just so wonderful. In that moment, Ginger realized just how different he was than Hyrum too, and she allowed herself to believe that perhaps they could have something that went beyond friendship.

THE DAYS PASSED, AND GINGER SAW PLENTY OF NATE. She had to, because she had to complete a daily check-in with him. She also kept in constant contact with Spencer and Nick, who were helping him learn the ropes, literally. They both said he was agreeable, and a quick study, and very, very good with horses.

Ginger finally went out to the stables on Sunday morning to see for herself. Sure enough, Nate worked with the horses as if he'd been born to do it. Even one of their newer, wilder horses settled right down the moment Nate took the reins from another cowboy. He talked to the equine in a quiet voice, and everything about Nate was a very strong version of quiet.

He put the horse in its stable and turned, catching her standing there, watching him. "Hey," he said. "What are you doing out here?" He took off his gloves and clapped them together as he came toward her.

"I've been getting good reports about you," she said. "So I came to see for myself." She smiled at him as he neared. "How are you feeling? Ready to start the riding lessons tomorrow?"

"You know what?" he asked. "I think I am."

Ginger nodded, glad he'd settled in so quickly. "Good." She'd run out of things to say already, and she couldn't imagine eating dinner with him. He'd not asked again, and Ginger couldn't get herself to bring it up either. "All right, well, I have work in the fields to do. I'll see you later?"

"Maybe for dinner," he said, touching a couple of fingers to the brim of his hat, turning, and walking away.

Ginger simply stared at him as he retreated, her pulse pounding through her whole body. He'd gotten a new cell phone when they'd gone to town on Monday, and she had the number. In fact, she could take him to town. They could make up any excuse—not that anyone would truly ask.

Ginger couldn't believe these crazy thoughts as they wound through her head. The guy had gone to prison for almost five years. Could he really be a different man than the one who'd gone along with a scheme to defraud people out of their money?

She'd never truly believed a person could change that much, but everything she'd seen from Nate was making her question that belief. He *had* worked in the Unit Manager's office, and he'd been nothing but hard-working and just... good since she'd picked him up a week ago. She could hardly believe it had only been a week since his arrival at Hope Eternal Ranch, as it seemed simultaneously much longer than that but also the days had passed by in the blink of an eye.

She got herself out of the stable and into the fields to test the soil and make sure the sprinkling system was working after the maintenance that had been done last week. Now that May was a couple of weeks old, the sun had really intensified, but Ginger didn't mind the sweat running down her face. It testified of a good day's work, and she needed to feel like she'd done something worthwhile every day.

By the time she returned to the West Wing, her stomach roared for food. Emma had put something in the slow cooker that morning, because the house smelled like something slow-roasted and full of garlic.

"French dip sandwiches," Emma said as Ginger walked through the kitchen.

"Gonna shower first," she said.

"Okay, but don't take forever," Emma said. "Spencer, Nick, and Nate will be here in fifteen minutes."

Ginger stumbled, throwing out her hand to balance herself against the doorjamb. "Really?"

"Yeah," Emma said, not even looking over to Ginger. "I caught Nate as he finished with our weekend riders, and I invited them." She glanced over her shoulder. "Is that okay?"

"*You* invited them? Or you invited *him*?"

Emma put down the tongs and turned toward Ginger. "I invited them all," she said. "He was alone, but I told him to pass on the invite, and he said the three of them would come. He's a nice guy, Ginger."

"No, I know." Ginger's voice pitched up too much, and Emma would hear it. Her eyes narrowed as she took a couple of steps closer to Ginger.

"What does that mean?" she asked.

"Nothing," Ginger said. "It means nothing."

But Emma could clearly see it meant something. They'd been friends since the moment Emma had first brought her students to the ranch, and she'd been living and working at Hope Eternal for ten years now. "Ginger."

"It's nothing," she said. "I need to shower." She left quickly then, because Emma's questions could be relentless. Ginger had no answers for them either. She'd been so sure about how things would go with the new inmate she'd agreed to.

But Nate wasn't anything like what she'd expected. He wasn't anything like Hyrum, and Ginger didn't know how to make the two of them line up.

By the time she finished showering and left her bedroom, she could hear deeper voices in the kitchen. *It's not a date*, she told herself. Emma would be there, as would Spencer and her cousin. And if there was anyone who could see through her easier than Emma, it was Nick.

She squared her shoulders and shook her hair out. It was still damp from the shower, and a tremor of nervousness moved through her. She should've dried it and put on makeup. But if she did that, everyone would know why. And Ginger didn't even know why.

"Go on," she muttered to herself as the people in the kitchen laughed. She went down the hall and entered the kitchen, where Jill and Jess had joined them.

Her eyes went straight to Nate, and he wore a smile but he wasn't laughing with the others. His gaze flicked to hers too, and the chemistry between them bubbled and boiled.

"Ginger," Connor said, and she looked down at the boy.

"Oh, hey." She grinned as she dropped into a crouch. "Have you had a good week on the ranch?"

"Yeah," he said, extending an envelope toward her. "Uncle Nate and I made you a card."

"You did, huh?" She smiled at him, his blue-blue eyes too much for her to handle. "That's so sweet of you."

"He made it himself," Nate said, appearing at the child's side. "I just found an envelope."

"It was too big," Connor said.

Ginger flipped over the envelope and slid her finger under the sealed flap. "It's just perfect." She grinned at him again and took out the card. Clearly, Connor had done this, and she couldn't quite tell what the brown and black lines were meant to be. "Show me," she said.

"That's Ursula," he said. "See her purple collar?" He pointed to it, and pure happiness flowed through Ginger.

"Oh, she's beautiful," she said. The dog came over and licked Ginger's arm, and she showed her the card. "Look, Ursula. It's you."

The dog didn't much care about the card, but she did take a step toward Connor. He threw both arms around the dog's head and hugged her.

"Not too tight, bud," Nate said, but Ursula didn't seem to care. Ginger straightened, because her knees couldn't take the crouching for much longer, and opened the card. She could make out a couple of the letters—a T, an A or two, and some O's. A lot of O's.

"What does this say?" she whispered to Nate, tilting the card toward him.

"He wanted to tell you thank you for letting us come live with Ursula." He smiled, and Ginger's heart grew and grew and grew. Emotion gathered in her throat, and she couldn't believe it, but tears burned behind her eyes.

She'd had no idea that having Nate and Connor at the ranch would affect her so much. She felt like someone had tied her to the end of a yo-yo, and she was being thrown down and then lifted back up, over and over again.

Reaching down, she lifted Connor into her arms and said, "Thank you for coming to the ranch so Ursula would have a new friend." He hugged her back, and Ginger had never known pure love as strongly as she did in that moment.

"All right," Emma said. "We're ready to eat. Everyone gather over here."

Ginger took Connor with her, moving the child to her hip, and joined the others gathered around the kitchen island. Nate followed her, easing into the perfect place just behind and to the side of her. His hand slid along her back, and her blood popped as if someone had poured fizzing candy into her veins.

She wanted this to be her reality every day. She wanted him solidly in her life, and while she still couldn't quite believe that she did, she also couldn't keep denying it.

THE DAYS AND WEEKS PASSED. MAY BLURRED INTO June, and Ginger had started meeting with Nate on a weekly basis instead of a daily one. They'd gone to town several times for groceries and errands, and Nate was always proper and polite.

He'd eaten dinner at the West Wing a few times now, but they had not gone anywhere alone. With so many people at Hope Eternal, catching a moment alone wasn't that easy. They'd gone to lunch when they came to town, and Ginger didn't mind the slow pace of the relationship.

If anything, it actually helped her undo another sticky

point with each day that passed. Nate never got angry. He never lashed out. He barely spoke in a voice louder than normal. He worked amazingly well with children, and he seemed to have a great rapport with Connor.

He was almost a little *too* perfect, if Ginger were being honest.

His one real flaw was how little he spoke. She didn't get a whole lot of time to ask him about his personal life, and the once or twice she had, his answers had been short and clipped. She liked him. She liked his work ethic. But she felt like she didn't *know* him.

The second Monday of June found her waiting in the house for his parole officer to show up. Martin Landy had called last week, and Ginger had been on the phone with him for an hour. They'd arranged this visit, of course, but Nate didn't know it was happening. He'd never been hard to find on the ranch, as he seemed to stay fairly close to the epicenter.

The appointed time for Martin to arrive came and went, and frustration built in Ginger's chest. She had work to do, and she hated it when people showed up late. Of course, everyone ran late sometimes, but Martin had her phone number. He could've called her.

Finally, almost thirty minutes later, the doorbell rang. Ginger looked up from her phone, where she'd been playing a card game, as Ursula filled the house with a few barks.

"Hush," Ginger said. She answered the door to find a tall, silver-haired man standing on the stoop.

"Ginger Talbot?" he asked, already smiling.

"That's me." She extended her hand for him to shake, which he did. "You must be Martin."

"That I am."

"Come in." She stepped back, keeping one leg in front of Ursula. "Are you dog-adverse?"

"Absolutely not," he said, stepping inside. "I have four dogs."

"Oh, wow," Ginger said. "Ursula will love you." The dog moved around her to make her initial sniff of Martin. He smiled and patted her, and they took their business into the kitchen.

"How's he doing?"

"He's been the best inmate I've ever gotten from River Bay," Ginger said.

"That's what I like to hear." Martin put his briefcase on the kitchen table and opened it. "Says here he's got his brother's son?"

"Yes," Ginger said. "He's doing great with him. At least he seems to be. They both seem to be eating and sleeping. Connor isn't in school yet, so we have a rotation of cowboys and cowgirls that watch him out here."

"Good, good." Martin pulled out a paper. "We talked a lot last week, so if you're comfortable with that, and you don't have any other questions, I just need you to sign this."

"I'm good," Ginger said. She knew the drill. This wasn't the first time she'd had a parole officer out to the ranch. She signed her name and added, "Should I call Nate and get him here?"

"If you would, please," Martin said, taking a seat at the table. "If he's as good as you say he is, this shouldn't take long."

Ginger nodded and stepped back to pull out her phone. She dialed Nate, and the line started ringing. And ringing. And ringing. He didn't answer, and she got sent to voicemail. She frowned. "Strange," she said, already dialing again. She'd only had to call him once in the past few weeks. Texting was much easier, and much less immediate, and anything she needed to talk with him about certainly wasn't urgent.

He didn't answer for a second time, and Ginger's nerves heaved. "He's not answering."

Martin looked up from a stack of paperwork he'd pulled from his briefcase. "Should we go find him?"

"Sure," she said, pocketing her phone. "He works in the stables. It's not far." She led him out of the house, trying to find something they could talk about on the ten-minute walk from the house to the stables. But her mind raced in so many different directions, she couldn't land on any one topic.

They finally reached the stable that took her entire crew a week to paint and Ginger went down row F, where Nate usually worked. He wasn't there. Everything was still and calm, and all the evidence pointed to the fact that he had been there. The horses had been fed; Domino's leg had been re-bandaged. The tack was neat and polished and ready for use.

"Strange," she said again. "This is where he should be." She turned in a full circle, her embarrassment increasing with every moment that Nate didn't appear.

CHAPTER NINE

Nate really disliked the sound of the voice on the other end of the line. He'd known the unknown number calling him would be Oscar, and he'd quickly left the chickens to peck at their feed. He probably had twenty minutes before someone would notice he wasn't with the horses, and even then, he could simply say he'd taken a walk.

He was allowed to walk.

"...so I'll just need to know where you want my guy to come," Oscar finished. Of course, he wouldn't come to deal with Nate. He had underlings to help with that. Nate frowned at the far fence line, though the morning sunshine should've lifted his spirits.

"I can't get you what you want in one delivery," Nate said. "I'm sure you know I'm on parole, and in a re-entry program."

"That is what I was told," Oscar said, his voice never

hitching. Nate never could tell how he was feeling, not even when they'd met in person. No matter what, though, Oscar wanted his money. And if he couldn't get his money, he wasn't happy. That was all Nate really needed to know.

"So I have to get a ride to town," he said. "I'm never left alone." He looked over his shoulder. He was alone right now, but Oscar surely wouldn't know that.

"Yeah, the pretty redhead waits downstairs for you," Oscar said, and Nate's blood turned cold.

"That's right," he said, playing some of that coolness into his voice. "And she'd notice if I left the bank with a huge bag of cash." He looked back out at the waving fields beyond the chicken pens. A semblance of peace existed here, and Nate didn't want to crack it. He wouldn't put Connor in jeopardy, nor anyone else on this ranch.

Things were different when it was just his neck on the line. Just his bet going to the bookie. Just a few thousand dollars.

But Oscar had accelerated things from simple horse betting and sports to investments, and Nate owed him a lot more than a few thousand dollars. He'd been ready to pay too, but then the indictments had come, and if Oscar wanted his money, he'd have to wait.

Which he'd been doing for almost five years.

"So I'll send a guy to talk to the banker."

"You will not," Nate said. "I have my brother's son now, and I have to live here. The money is there, Oscar. I know you've seen the account." He probably hadn't let a day go by of Nate's sentence where he didn't check that bank account.

When Nate got time on the computer, he used a few minutes of it to check the account himself. Still there, week after week. Still accumulating interest. Still bigger than Nate thought possible.

Now, with Ward's money too, Nate wouldn't need to work once he completed his six months at Hope Eternal Ranch. He would, though, because he'd had plenty of idle time in prison, and he didn't like it. Not one little bit.

Oscar exhaled in a rare showing of his irritation. "Fine. When can I get the first installment?"

"I have it here at the ranch," Nate said. "But you absolutely cannot come here." His brain whirred through the week's upcoming activities. "I can probably get to town on Friday or Saturday."

He'd asked Ginger to eat dinner with him, and they had several times. Always with her friends and Spencer and Nick. Never alone. Maybe this weekend, he could achieve two things at once—dinner with Ginger alone, and a drop for Oscar.

"They have lockers at the mall," Nate said. "I can put the bag in one of them, pay for it, and get your guy the code to open it."

"Okay," Oscar said. "Friday or Saturday."

"I'll have to see how it goes," he said. "I don't exactly make my own schedule like I used to."

Oscar chuckled, which grated against Nate's nerves. "Don't call," he said, still laughing. "Text, and delete."

Nate was familiar with the T&D method Oscar preferred, and he couldn't help feeling a little slimy as the call ended. A sigh passed through his whole body then, because he just wanted to be done with everything from his previous life.

"As soon as you pay him back, you will be," he muttered to himself.

His phone rang again, and Nate recognized a number he was well-versed with. He'd sat at the phone where this call originated from, and he quickly swiped on the call from River Bay. "Ted?"

"How'd you know it'd be me?" Ted asked, a smile in his voice.

"Maybe because you're the only person I gave this number to," Nate said, smiling on back. No one had told him he'd miss his friends inside the prison. He'd thought he'd want to walk away from those fifteen hundred days without any baggage too. He'd been wrong, and he missed his boys that were still inside.

"How's the ranch?" Ted asked.

"You know what? It's pretty great." Nate glanced around at the barn to his left, the vast stables about a hundred yards behind him to the right, the gently waving grasses and further out, stalks of corn.

"Not too many mosquitoes?"

"A few," he said. "It is by the water." He'd taken Connor

out to a pond in the middle of the ranch, where Spencer had told them to go to catch a few small fish. They hadn't caught anything though, and Nick said they had to take bacon to get the crawdads to come up. Nate was planning on doing that with Connor in the near future. "So you get fifteen minutes," he added. "And I know you didn't call to chat about the ranch."

To an inmate, their outbound calls were precious. With only three each week, and only fifteen minutes long, every call had to be really important. The prison monitored every call, except those to lawyers, but Nate wasn't worried about something Ted would say. They'd banded together inside River Bay for a reason, and that was so they'd be able to watch each other's backs.

"Right," Ted said, another chuckle coming from his mouth. "Down to twelve minutes. I wanted to ask about the RRC program."

Surprise darted through Nate. "Oh." He'd never given it much thought, because he hadn't dreamed Ward would die or that he'd altered his will. Nate had asked his lawyer to find out where Ward's ex-wife was, but he hadn't heard anything yet. "What about it?"

"Do you like it?"

"It has some advantages," Nate said. "For sure. For one, I have a place to live. A job. A way to earn money. Someone to help me with all the things it takes to live."

"Bank account, utilities, stuff like that," Ted said.

"Yeah, all of that," Nate said. "But I can't leave the

ranch. I can't go to town myself. I'm driven everywhere." He didn't want to dwell on the negative. "It's nice having my daily interview with Ginger, though. We're to weeklies now, and I haven't heard from my parole officer yet. So that's nice too. She's nice, and she's actually pretty easy to work with." He'd never truly met with a parole officer, so he couldn't say if he'd like it or not, but he knew it wouldn't be as casual or as enjoyable as chatting with Ginger about what help he needed and what he was doing fine with.

"I'm wondering if she'd take me," Ted said, his voice made of ice. He wouldn't give away if he wanted the RRC at Hope Eternal or not, that was for sure. But him just asking about it meant he wanted it.

"Oh." More surprise danced through Nate. "I mean, I don't know. Is she allowed to have more than one inmate here at a time?"

"No idea."

"I suppose your six months is coming up in what? Three months?"

"Eighty-eight days," Ted said. They'd talked many times about their release dates, and what they'd do once they got out. The meals they'd eat. The things they'd see and do.

Nate hadn't done any of them. *Yet*, he told himself. He wasn't really out yet anyway.

"Let me find out," he said. "You sure you want to come here? It's a lot of work, and Ginger expects you to know it all already. There's very little training, and a *lot* of horses, and I don't think I've worked less than twelve hours a day since I got here."

"I'm not afraid of hard work," Ted said at the same time someone behind Nate said, "Of course I expect a lot of you, *especially* that you're where you said you were going to be."

He spun around at the angry—no, furious—tone in Ginger's voice. He wasn't sure how many minutes Ted had left on the call, but he knew they wouldn't go into a bank his friend could use later. He took in Ginger's blotchy, red face and her folded arms, and decided his friend would have to eat the leftover minutes.

"I have to go," he said to Ted, who started to protest. "Sorry. Call me next week." He hung up the phone and glanced at the man who'd come up behind Ginger, huffing and puffing and clearly not wearing the right kind of footwear for a ranch. Nate knew, because he hadn't been for the first week either.

"I'm sorry?" he asked, his nerves fraying a bit. He knew who that guy was, and he'd rather go shovel manure out of a stall than deal with an angry Ginger and then sit through an interview with his parole officer.

"You're supposed to be in the stable," Ginger said, practically shooting fire from her eyes. "And you didn't answer when I called."

"I was on the phone." He lifted his phone as if she hadn't overheard him talking on it. He'd actually considered asking her about bringing Ted here too, but there was no way that could happen. At least not right now.

"Yes, I heard." Ginger's glare could take an entire herd down, but only a flicker of annoyance started in Nate's gut. It fanned into a flame that burned up and up, and he found himself glaring back.

"I'm sorry," he said. "But I am entitled to a fifteen-minute break in the morning." He looked at the other man. "I don't think we've met. I'm Nathaniel Mulbury."

"Oh, of course," the man said. "I'm Martin Landy." The two shook hands, and he nodded back toward the more civilized parts of the ranch. "Should we go talk at the house?"

"Sure," Nate said, casting one more glance at Ginger. She hadn't softened at all, and Nate's ire went right back up. He couldn't believe he'd told Ted she was nice or easy to work with. Right now, she seemed like a simmering pot about to boil over, and he'd be the one to clean it all up.

Martin walked away, but Nate held back for a few moments. He turned to Ginger, who still wore that growl right on her face. "It sure is nice to know for certain that you don't trust me," he said, his voice on the growly side too.

"I didn't say that."

"I'm at least a mile from the fence," he said, taking a menacing step closer to her. "And I don't have to drop everything in my life and answer your calls, Ginger. That's not part of the program." He glared down at her, actually satisfied when she started to wilt. "And you *do* expect a lot, and you're demanding, and you know what? I haven't cared, because I'm just so dang glad to be here. But that doesn't mean it's been easy for me."

"Who were you talking to?"

"None of your business," he said. "Who I talk to is another thing I don't have to clear with you." With his heart pounding in his chest, he fell back a step. "If you'd have told me my parole officer was coming this morning, I'd have met you at the house."

"I thought—" She cut off when Nate held up his hand, and he supposed he probably wore a storm on his face too. They looked at one another, and Nate had a lot more to say. Instead of letting it out and regretting it later, he simply shook his head and turned around to follow Martin.

THE INTERVIEW WITH MARTIN PASSED IN A BLUR where Nate only tuned in half the time. He must've done a good enough job to pass, because Martin took his phone number and said he'd call next month.

Once he was gone, Nate focused on his chores, but he found himself slamming buckets down when he should just set them. A hurricane blew through him, and he didn't know how to get it to move on.

The sound of crying met his ears, and it was far too early for the kids to be on the ranch for their riding lessons.

"Connor," he said under his breath, his mood morphing from anger to concern in less time than it took to breathe. He abandoned the buckets of oats he'd been distributing to the horses and jogged out of the stables, already searching for his nephew.

Hannah Otto, the accountant for the ranch, carried the little boy, who clung to her as if his life depended on it. "I'm sorry," she said. "He fell while riding his bike, and nothing I did could calm him." She passed him to Nate, who took the dribbling, sniffling boy and drew him right into his chest.

"It's fine," he said to Hannah. "Thank you for bringing him. I'd have come if you'd called."

She stepped back and put her hands in her back pockets, her short blonde hair sticking out at odd angles. "I have to get back. I have an appointment in ten minutes."

"Go," Nate said. "I'm fine."

The woman walked away, and once again, Nate felt nothing with her, though she was slim and pretty and educated. She spent the most time with Connor during the day, as she had an office in the house with a TV in it. Connor said he liked her, and that she had boxes of cookies in her bottom drawer that he could have whenever he wanted them.

"Are you hurt, bud?" he asked Connor, trying to get him to let go of his neck. Connor finally did, and Nate looked at his face. "I don't see any blood."

"My knees hurt," Connor said with a whimper.

Nate glanced down, though the boy still had his legs around Nate's waist. "All right," he said as calmly as he could. "Let's have a look." He took Connor into the stables and set him on the top of one of the doors that led to an empty stable. "Oh, yeah, look at that." He looked at Connor and smiled. Anything to put on a brave face. "Skinned knees."

Connor's bottom lip trembled, and Nate wanted to fold him into a hug and never let go. "I can fix these."

"Can you, Uncle Nate?" One big alligator tear fell down Connor's cheek, and Nate's heart turned to mush. This kid needed him, and Nate was as committed as ever to make sure he was there for his nephew. As much as possible, he was going to be there.

Don't go to the mall, ran through his mind, and Nate's smile slipped. "Sure I can," he said, wishing he had an older brother to call. Ward would know what to do with skinned knees on four-year-old boys—and what to do about the money drop this weekend.

He stepped over to a first aid box attached to the wall and pulled it down. "It'll be quick, and then you can help me with the horses for the riding lessons."

"Can I?" Connor's voice held so much hope, and Nate didn't want to tell him no.

So he said, "Yep. You'll have to stay right by my side."

"I can, Uncle Nate."

He smiled at Connor as he quickly cleaned his knees and then put two Band-aids over the bloodiest parts. "All done."

Connor looked at him like Nate held the world in the palm of his hand, and the whole sky got brighter for just that one moment.

"Hey, little man," Nick said as he entered the stable. "You helpin' with the horses today?"

"Sure am," Connor said, made of smiles now. Nate helped him down, and he ran over to Nick, who picked him up and swung him around, both of them laughing.

Nate smiled too, because Connor was happy again. As he watched Nick set Connor down and take his hand, all the while talking about a horse named Willowwood, Nate wondered if maybe he could have the other cowboy make his drop for him this weekend...

He's Ginger's cousin, Nate told himself. And then Ginger lodged herself in his mind, and Nate started working on the words he needed to apologize to her. A whole new kind of sigh moved through his body, but he needed Ginger on his side. So he'd swallow his pride and make sure he got back on the same page with the woman he wanted to spend more time with. Go to dinner with.

Maybe even kiss...

CHAPTER TEN

Ginger hovered out of sight while Nate got the kids in line and took them around the stables. He really was great with them, and it seemed like every person he came in contact with fell under his charm.

Herself included.

She frowned and ducked deeper into the shadows, the scent of hay and hooves filling her nose. She loved the smell of the horses and the saddles, and she reached out and ran her fingertips down the stable doors.

They used every available horse and saddle for their riding lessons, which left the stable empty enough to hold her thoughts.

She didn't think Nate was being disingenuous. He didn't seem to know how to be anybody or anything but himself, and that only made him more endearing.

Sighing, Ginger sank onto a chair outside a stall, her

mind flowing back over the situation from that morning. She hadn't meant to snap at him, though she definitely had. Martin Landy had been late, and that alone had annoyed Ginger. Then she hadn't been able to get in touch with Nate, and he wasn't in the stables, or the barn, or with the chickens.

Martin's eyebrows had gotten higher and higher and higher, and Ginger's embarrassment had too. By the time she'd seen Nate standing out in the fields beyond the coops, she was ready to go nuclear.

He hadn't taken it well, but he had taken it.

It's a lot of work, and Ginger expects you to know it all already.

Nate's words filled her ears, and she wished she could shake them out. She'd been trying for hours, and yet, they still lingered, vibrating against her drums and consuming her mind. He'd said something after that, but it was all a blur. All she could hear was that he thought she was demanding.

He'd said so right to her face.

"Well, maybe you are," she muttered, and she knew there was no *maybe* about it. She wasn't sure how long she sat there, outside an empty horse stall, but it was long enough for all the kids to mount their horses and leave the area.

Long enough for Nate to come walking toward her, leading a horse with a simple rope around its neck. "Hey," he said, his eyes glued to hers. "What're you doing in here?"

HOPEFUL COWBOY   119

"Nothing." Ginger sounded miserable about it too. She was miserable at the moment. She studied her hands while he opened a stall a couple down from her and across the aisle. "Look, I need to apologize for this morning."

"I do too," Nate said, leading the horse inside her stall. He came back out and closed the bottom half of the door. "I shouldn't have said you were demanding."

"No," Ginger said. "I am demanding."

Nate kicked a grin in her direction. "Yeah, you kind of are." He came toward her, but there was no other chair for him to sit down in. He crouched in front of her, his head down so she could only see the top of his cowboy hat. "But I get why you are. Really, I do, and I was just being cruel." He looked up, and he was easily the best-looking man in the state with those striking blue eyes. "And I don't like being cruel. So I'm sorry."

Ginger's chest vibrated, and she felt one breath away from crying. She told herself not to do it, because then she'd be embarrassed—again. She nodded instead, drawing in a slow, deep breath. "I'm sorry too. Of course I trust you. I just couldn't find you, and by the time I did, I was embarrassed and frustrated, and well, you took the brunt of that." She looked back at her hands, because his gaze was simply too much for her to hold.

She played with her fingers, letting them go round and round each other. Then, Nate put his hand over both of hers, stilling her fingers. Stilling her heart. Stilling everything.

Someone had pressed pause on her life, because it all just came to a halt. She looked at him, and he looked at her, and things were...okay.

He twisted and sat down on the ground beside her chair, a groan coming out of his mouth. His hand returned, taking hers this time and lining his fingers up so they fit right in between hers.

A sigh moved through her whole soul, and while Ginger couldn't believe she was currently sitting in the stable, holding hands with an ex-con, it felt like exactly the right thing to be doing.

She slipped off the chair to the ground too, glad she *demanded* her cowboys keep the cement swept clean, and sat shoulder-to-shoulder with Nate. He said nothing, and Ginger simply leaned her head against his bicep, the moment sweet and tender between them.

Ginger never slowed down like this during the day. Once she got back to the West Wing, sure. But not out in the stables. Not when there was so much work to be done. Somewhere on the ranch, a dog barked, but it wasn't Ursula. Spencer had taken the German shepherd and Connor back to the house once Nate had started the lessons.

"Is Connor okay?" she asked. She'd seen Band-aids on his knees.

"Yeah, he just fell on his bike." Nate's deep voice tickled in her ears as he hardly spoke loud enough for her to hear. "He'll be okay."

"Will we be okay?" Ginger asked, surprised at her own boldness.

"Yeah," Nate said, lifting her knuckles to his lips. "I think we'll be okay too."

A smile slipped across Ginger's face, and she closed her eyes for a moment. Or maybe a few minutes. It wasn't until Nate said, "Ginger, I have to tell you something," that she even realized she'd drifted off.

"All right." She yawned, suddenly knowing why she didn't allow herself to slow down like this during the day. She'd fall asleep, and then it would be terribly difficult to get back to work.

Several beats of silence passed before he said, "We're almost out of cocoa crispies, so I need to go to town again this weekend."

"Didn't you buy three boxes just last week?"

"We like them," he said. "What can I say?" He added a chuckle to his question, and it sounded a tad bit forced to Ginger.

She shook her head and stood up. "All right. I'll look at my schedule. We're moving into harvest season." She extended her hand toward him to help him up.

"Already?" He put his hand in hers, and for one breathtaking moment, she thought he'd pull her onto his lap and kiss her. How much she wanted him to do just that surprised her and made her legs tremble.

He stood too, still looking at her.

"Yeah," she said, though she barely remembered the

question. "We've got peas and carrots already in the gardens. We'll be setting up the beaver traps and we've got bird blinds to build. Our tour groups start this weekend, and summer is a very busy time on the ranch."

"You need a lot of help then," he said.

"Always," she said. "Though you taking the riding program has helped Spencer be able to get more done with the agriculture." She smiled at him, because she was glad he was there. He had to know that. "I can try to be less demanding."

He shook his head as they walked down the aisle toward the rectangle of sunlight. "It's not necessary, Ginger." He paused on the threshold between being in the stable and out of it. "You do a great job here."

"Thanks." She watched him, sure there was more he wanted to say. But he didn't say it

He tipped his hat and said, "Well, I have work to do. I'll catch up with you later," before he walked away.

Ginger watched him go, though she had plenty of work to do too. Spencer came out from another aisle of the stable, and he and Nate started talking. They laughed and went inside together, and Ginger did like that the two of them got along so well. She was never quite sure what kind of man she was bringing back to the ranch when she got someone in the RRC program, but Nate seemed to be the cream of the crop.

She liked him, even though she'd tried not to. Still, she coached herself to go slow, because she wanted to get to know him before anything serious happened. Really know him, not just *think* she knew him, the way she had with Hyrum.

The alarm on her phone went off as she walked back toward the homestead, and she looked at it. *Lumber* flashed at her, and she glanced up, her pulse prancing through her now.

"Shoot." She broke into a jog, because if she didn't meet the Anderton brothers and give them specific instructions for where to deliver the lumber she'd bought for the bird blinds, it would end up on the front lawn.

She arrived at the same time the delivery truck pulled around the corner, and she waved her hand at them to get them to stop. Michael Anderton rolled down his window and stuck his elbow out. "Heya, Ginger."

"Hey, Mike. We're taking this down the same road you did last time. All the way to the last bird blind."

"Jump in and show me."

Ginger wanted to roll her eyes, but she didn't. "All right." She circled the truck and climbed in the other side, which caused George Anderton to slide into the middle of the bench seat. She didn't care, as long as it wasn't her.

She'd been out with Michael a couple of times, and sometimes he forgot their relationship had never really gotten off the ground.

"How's your momma?" she asked George, proud of her Texas manners.

"She's convinced we're all about to die," he said with a

chuckle. "She's been hoarding toilet paper, and she won't drink anything anyone gives her."

"Oh, wow," Ginger said, something in her chest releasing.

"Are you going out to the bay festival in a couple of weeks?" Michael asked.

"Uh, maybe," Ginger said. "Depends on how much we get done here." She did enjoy the beachside music festival held every year in Sweet Water Falls, which was located near the water. Not the Gulf itself, but an inlet, where islands dotted the waters and created bays.

Falling Oak Bay was the closest one to the ranch, and the site of the festival every year. Ginger hadn't missed it in at least a decade, maybe longer. She always said she'd maybe make it to something when Michael asked, but this year, she could see herself dancing barefoot on the sand with one very serious cowboy who used to be in prison.

Did Nate dance?

For some reason, she couldn't imagine him doing something like that, and a smile touched her lips at the very idea of him holding her while they swayed to a ballad.

"Here?" Michael asked, pulling her from the beautiful daydream with his somewhat reedy voice.

"No, keep going," she said. He always tried to drop off the lumber in the most convenient location for him. He kept going though, and Ginger directed him all the way down the road to the last bird blind. "Here."

"We're really far out here," he said, peering through the

windshield. "You sure this is still your land?" He grinned at her and got out of the truck before she could respond. It wasn't a question that needed a response anyway.

She got out too, her phone chiming as she did. It was Nick, and he'd said, *Can I take Nate to town tonight for steak and seafood? He says he's never been to Maddox. Can you imagine?*

Ginger shook her head at her cousin. He really was innocent about a lot of things. *Just you and him?*

And Spencer and Connor. Maybe Bronco if he'll stop texting Katie.

"Oh, Katie," Ginger said, making a face. Her brother really could pick out some of the worst women to date. And she'd thought his last girlfriend would definitely be the worst. Then he'd brought Katie Holbrook to the ranch, and the woman had obviously thought he was taking her to get a salad and that the ranch would be the dressing.

Ginger had never seen such a look of disgust. She'd never been back to the ranch, and Bronco bent to her whims.

So can we go? Nick asked. *Nate said we had to ask you.*

Yes, she sent back. *Go. Have fun.*

She wanted to go and have fun too, but she knew better than to invite herself. Number one, she'd never gone on their steak and seafood excursions before. Number two, maybe Nick could stop at the grocery store and get the cereal Nate wanted.

See if you can get his cocoa crispies while you're in town, she sent next, the deafening crash of wood on wood alerting her to the unloading process happening on the other side of the truck.

Okay, Nick said. *Thanks, Ginger.*

She stuck her phone in her pocket and rounded the truck to find a pile of lumber that would take her hours to sort through.

"Just need your signature right here," Michael said, sliding up to her with a clipboard and a pen—and that smile that told her she wasn't going to like what he said next. As she signed, he asked, "What are you doin' tonight? Wanna grab a drink or a bite to eat?"

"Oh, I can't," she said, making her voice sugar-sweet. "I just made plans with my brother."

"Oh? What's Bronco got himself into this time?"

"Well, he's dating this woman who's just all wrong for him. So I need to talk to him about her." Not entirely a lie, and she had just made plans to talk to him about Katie. Just now. Just the moment Michael had asked about going out with him.

"Good luck with that," Michael said with a smile, but Ginger didn't know what he meant.

"Yeah," she said anyway, handing the clipboard back. "And I have a meeting with my activities staff I need to be to in ten minutes. I can hitch a ride with you on the way back, right?"

"Sure thing." He looked over his shoulder to George. "George, you drive us back, all right?" He grinned at Ginger

HOPEFUL COWBOY   127

like he'd just won the lottery, but she groaned way down deep in her gut.

She'd have to sit on her hands to make sure he didn't hold one of them, and walking back to the ranch sounded like a better idea than getting a ride.

But she'd already asked, and Anderton Lumber was the best in town. So she hitched her smile in place, turned to go back around the truck, and hunched her shoulders as she sent the emergency word to Emma.

As she climbed into the truck and sat beside Michael, her phone rang. "Oh, I have to take this," she said, swiping on the call. "Hey, Emma, what's up?"

"How long are we talking?"

"Oh, I'll be back in ten minutes or so." Ginger used her left hand to hold the phone to her ear, creating a semi-barrier between her and Michael. She put her elbow on the armrest of the door on the right side and leaned even further from him. "The Anderton brothers delivered our lumber, and they're giving me a ride back."

"Oh, that sneaky Michael Anderton. Did he ask you out again?"

"Yes," Ginger said. "It's in the drawer in the bottom of my desk."

"I swear, I don't know how he doesn't know you're not interested. Maybe I should just pull him aside and tell him."

"Don't you dare," Ginger said, perhaps a little too forcefully. She cut a glance at Michael, who was watching her. "I put that chocolate in that drawer for a rainy day, and it's *not* raining."

"There's chocolate in your bottom desk drawer?" Emma asked.

"Emma," Ginger warned, but she knew her friend was already checking. A squeal came through the line a few moments later, and Ginger's heart dropped to her boots.

"I can't believe this was in here and you didn't tell me. I was *dying* for a treat last night."

"Clearly, you didn't die," Ginger said in a deadpan, wondering if she should've just let Michael Anderton hold her hand. At this point, she wasn't sure which was worse: That, or losing her coveted dark chocolate to her best friend and assistant.

Definitely Michael, she thought. She didn't want rumors of a relationship with him getting back to Nate.

Oh, no. That couldn't happen, because she was sure the hopeful cowboy wouldn't like that. He'd probably back right off and never trust her again. So she listened while Michelle detailed how the coconut and chocolate had hit the spot and then started in on how the bird photography classes had already started to fill into July.

Ginger was bored to tears, but anything was better than trying to ward off Michael's advances. Plus, while Emma talked and the delivery truck bounced over the dirt road back to the homestead, Ginger could continue her daydreams about kissing the handsome and hardworking Nate Mulbury.

CHAPTER ELEVEN

Nate felt the eyes of every single person in the bank on him while he waited for the withdrawal to go through. Of course, there wasn't a problem, and the woman who brought in the envelope smiled at him like he was one of their VIPs.

In her eyes, he was. He absolutely was, with how much money he had here at the bank and how close his father had been to the man behind the desk in front of him.

"It's all there?" Sam Wiseman asked.

"I'm sure it is," Nate said, slipping the envelope into his briefcase. He was planning to leave the whole thing in the locker in the mall, and he'd started praying last night that Ginger wouldn't ask him about the absence of his briefcase after the drop.

He didn't see how she wasn't going to ask. The woman

saw everything. So much, that Nate wondered if she had eyes in the back of her head.

She knew everything that happened around the ranch, because she had people everywhere. They all reported to her, and she seemed genuinely interested in their lives as well as making sure they did their jobs to her satisfaction.

His stomach squirmed as he stood and shook hands with Sam. "Good to see you again," he said, though he didn't really feel that way. He and Sam had an interesting relationship, because neither of them wanted to see the other ever again.

But they had a partnership that had to be seen through to the end, and Nate had started praying that end would come sooner rather than later.

Sam said nothing, and Nate left his office on the second floor. His briefcase handle felt too hard, but it was probably the way he was strangling it. He felt ridiculous carrying the briefcase at all, but he couldn't carry around an envelope big enough for a clipboard filled with cash. It had to be concealed somehow.

He also had to get Ginger to the mall somehow. He'd been stewing about it all week while he studied the blueprints for the bird blind and then started to build it. He worked on it alone, so thankfully, when he did something wrong, there was no one there to witness it. He'd put things together, realized they weren't right, and taken them apart at least ten times over the last few days.

In truth, Nate was tired. So mentally tired. He'd been

thinking about this drop for far too long, and he realized another thing prison had afforded him. Peace from so much thinking. Out here in the real world, he had to deal with things he'd left behind previously.

"Hey," he said when he met Ginger on the first floor. "Can we run to the mall real quick? I need to get my sister a birthday present." Not entirely a lie. Bethany's birthday was coming up, and the mall was a perfectly logical place for him to find a gift for her.

"Sure," she said. "I got a call while you were upstairs though. Can you just run in while I deal with something?"

"Absolutely," he said, his face filling with a grin. "Something I can help with?"

"No." She sighed as they left the bank. "Just some paperwork with...something." She looked at him, clearly flustered by this paperwork.

"That's so vague," he said, teasing her.

"Yeah," she said, sighing again. "It's *your* paperwork, Nate. The BOP is saying they didn't get it, but I mailed it weeks ago."

"That's not good."

"No, it's not." She went around the hood to the driver's side. They got in the truck, and she added, "I didn't make copies."

"So we'll just do it again," he said, knowing how important paperwork was to the Bureau of Prisons.

"We might have to," she said. "I'm going to call them again. We got cut off when...we got cut off."

"Fight?" he asked.

"How did you know?"

"Everything stops when there's a fight," Nate said, looking out his window, his mind automatically moving far away from his present situation. "Even phone calls about important paperwork."

She drove the few blocks to the mall, and Nate jumped from the truck. Every step felt like he was committing himself to something deceitful and wrong. He felt like everyone was looking at him strangely, like they knew what he concealed in his briefcase and that he'd served hard time in prison.

He entered the mall and hurried now. There was a virtual reality experience in the mall, and they didn't allow purses or bags inside. Thus, a couple of rows of lockers had been installed just around the corner from the experience.

He quickly found an available one and put in the quarters required to unlock it. He placed the briefcase inside, checking over both shoulders. His stomach hurt from how clenched it was, and his pulse raced through his veins. No one seemed to care what he was doing.

After closing the locker, a ticket got spit out from the machine, and Nate quickly snapped a picture of it. He wadded up the ticket and threw it in the trash can, then ducked around the next row of lockers and texted the picture to Oscar, along with the word *Done*.

Then he got the heck out of there and down to the bath

store, where he could find something citrus-smelling and soothing for his sister.

He hated sneaking around, and all he could think about was what Ginger would say if she found out. They'd been getting along well since the mishap with the parole officer, and Nate really didn't want to mess things up between them.

Good luck, he told himself as he checked out with a tube of six bath bombs. It seemed like everything Nate touched blew up at some point, and he anticipated the same would be true with Ginger. He just didn't know if it would be sooner or later, and if he'd have his heart intact when all the pieces came crashing down.

NATE HAD HIS HAND IN GINGER'S, THEIR MID-MORNING stroll down a remote road lined with trees about halfway over, when his phone rang. His heartbeat tripled for a second, and he released Ginger's hand to pull his phone from his back pocket.

"I don't think it'll be..." He cut off when he saw Lawrence's name on the screen. "It's my lawyer." He came to a full stop, because he was used to having conversations with his lawyer in private. Even the prison didn't listen in on legal calls.

He was just glad he hadn't said Ted's name. He still hadn't brought up the idea of having Ginger request another inmate from River Bay to come to the ranch, though his friend behind bars had called twice more.

Three weeks had passed since that initial phone call and his first meeting with his parole officer. Two and a half since he'd left the envelope of money in the locker at the mall. A few days later, he'd found the empty briefcase leaning against the old post that held up the mailbox at the end of the lane that led to the ranch.

It was as far as Nate could go on the ranch, and he'd been volunteering to get the mail each morning ever since Oscar had texted to say he'd returned the bag. Nate hadn't breathed properly until the next day, when he'd found the bag. At least Oscar—or more likely, someone low on his totem pole—hadn't come down to the house.

Nate had called him standing next to that mailbox and told him to never, ever come to the ranch again. Ever.

Oscar had laughed, but Nate wouldn't back down until he agreed he wouldn't come again. Next time, he agreed to leave the briefcase in the locker, where Nate would have to retrieve it before he went to the bank.

How he was going to do that, he had no idea. He couldn't even think of another reason he needed to go to the mall, though his mind ran around the problem morning and night.

"Lawrence," he said while Ginger turned around and kept walking. He faced away from her, back the way they'd come, the sun already hot today. It was almost June, and

Nate had lived in Texas his whole life. It would be hot from now until at least October. Probably November.

"I found Jane," Lawrence said, never one to mince words. "She's in Jamaica, and she's not interested in returning to the United States."

Nate frowned, because he couldn't imagine what kind of mother wouldn't want her child. "She knows Ward is gone, right?"

"She didn't know, and I had to tell her," Lawrence said, and he didn't sound happy about it. Nate wasn't sure why. The man seemed to thrive on delivering bad news. "She asked where Connor was—but she called him Conway—and I said Ward had named you the legal guardian. She said great."

"Great?" Nate shook his head, pure disbelief flowing through him. "That can't be true. She *hated* me. And secondly, she knows I went to prison."

"I don't know what to tell you," Lawrence said. "I asked her if she planned to try to get custody of Connor, and she said no. She had no interest in coming back to the US, and she hoped you'd take good care of Connor, because Ward would want that."

Nate struggled to make sense of everything his lawyer had said. In the end, he said, "All right. Thanks, Lawrence."

"Sure thing. Hey, how are things on the ranch?"

Nate turned around again and found Ginger down the road about a hundred yards, perched on a tree stump and looking his way. "Great," he said. He still hadn't kissed her, and he wondered what he was waiting for. They seemed to find plenty of time to be alone, without the chance of interruption. She sure seemed to like him, and he definitely liked her. In his mind, though, a barrier existed, and he needed to find a way past it before he could lean toward her and hope he didn't crash and burn.

Nate had lived so much of the past six years on hope alone, and he knew it could sustain a man as easily as it could consume him whole.

"Really great?" Lawrence asked. "Or is this one of those times where you tell me everything is great, but you've just gotten beat up by the punk kid who still has a chip on his shoulder?"

Nate chuckled, the laughter just right there beneath his tongue. It had never come that fast before, and Nate sure did like the appearance of it. "No, this isn't like that," he said. "It's really great here. I'm figuring things out slowly, and I actually like the reentry program."

"Good," Lawrence said with plenty of surprise in his voice too. "You were skeptical."

"That I was." He started walking toward Ginger. "But I actually like the cowboy hat, and working with the horses, and I don't know. There's something soothing about this place."

"I'm glad," Lawrence said. "Your paperwork was sorted. Will you let Ginger know?"

"Sure," Nate said. "I should see her later." Hey, a minute or two was later, wasn't it? He grinned as he kept walking toward her, the cowboy boots he'd thought he'd never get used to now the most comfortable shoes he'd ever worn.

"Thanks. Well, I hope we don't have to talk a ton in the future."

"You'll take care of all the actual release stuff, though, right?" Nate asked, a moment of trepidation overcoming him.

"Absolutely," Lawrence said. "But that's four months from now. We'll talk then."

"Sounds good." The call ended, and Nate re-pocketed his phone. Ginger stood from the stump as he neared, wearing a mask of apprehension on her face.

"What did he want?"

"Don't you know calls with lawyers are privileged?" he teased.

Ginger's smile broke through her anxiety, and she swatted at his chest. Nate dodged her futile attempt and instead took her into his arms. He'd never held her like this before, and he had absolutely no idea what he was doing, though he'd had girlfriends before.

Girlfriend.

Was that was Ginger was?

Nate's hope shot toward the sky, and he gazed down at her, glad she wore a flirty smile on her face still. "I asked him to find Jane," he said soberly. "He did, and she doesn't want Connor. So he's really mine. I'm going to adopt him." Then maybe Connor could call him Dad instead of Uncle Nate.

"Well, I'm going to talk to him about adopting him," Nate said. "See what he says."

"He's only four."

"Doesn't mean he can't think." Nate looked up and out over the ranch, a sigh of contentment moving through him. "I sure do like it here, Ginger. Thanks for taking me into the residential program."

She leaned her head against his chest, inching closer to him. He thought he could stand there in the shade and hold her for a good long while, the scent of her flowery perfume filling his nose. "Of course," she said. "I'm glad I took the gamble again."

"Would you consider having more of us here?" he asked, his throat almost closing around the question.

"Depends."

"On what?"

"On if I can get another guy like you."

Nate shifted back and looked at her as warmth and excitement dove through him. "Is that right? I guess I'm pretty awesome."

She giggled to go along with his chuckle, but neither of them continued on for very long.

"I know a guy," Nate said, his throat so dry. He glanced down at her mouth, and he couldn't look away. "He'd be great here."

"I don't want a guy just like you," she whispered.

"I don't want that either," he said.

"Why?"

"Because then maybe you'd like him more than you like me."

Ginger shook her head, a soft smile tracing its way across her mouth. Nate slid both hands up her arms to her face, cradling it in his palms. She stilled, and her eyes widened.

"I...can I kiss you?" he asked, his voice little more than a croak.

Ginger seemed to be moving in slow motion as she reached up and took off his cowboy hat. "You can, but not with this on. It's one of the hazards of being a cowboy."

"Noted," he whispered as he lowered his head toward hers. The moment his lips touched hers caused an explosion of sparks to move through his bloodstream, and Nate knew then that there was nothing half so great as kissing Ginger Talbot.

CHAPTER TWELVE

Ginger had never been kissed the way Nate kissed her. The level of care he took with her was exquisite, and she wanted to hold onto the moment for as long as possible. He eventually broke the kiss, and only then did Ginger realize how her heart sprinted in her chest.

She pulled in a breath, because her body had been shocked by such an amazing kiss that her involuntary functions had stalled.

"All right," Nate said quietly, securing his hand in hers again. He started down the road again, walking slowly the way they always did. She went with him, though she still felt a bit numb. She wasn't sure why, because her skin felt like someone had injected electricity into her cells.

She crackled with every step, a smile curving her mouth and refusing to straighten even when she looked at Nate. He grinned back at her, and Ginger ducked her head again.

"Oh, my hat." He released her hand and strode back to where she'd dropped it on the ground. She'd meant to hold it for him, but that kiss had literally melted her muscles into marshmallows.

"Sorry," she said as he came back toward her. "I don't normally just throw a man's hat on the ground."

"It's fine," he said. "Thanks for the tip." He took her hand again, and they continued their walk. When the barn came into sight, he dropped her hand and tucked his in his pocket, the way he'd always done. No one knew they stole away for thirty minutes after she completed her morning chores and before he went out to the bird blinds and fences.

Even if they did, Ginger could simply say she needed privacy to interview Nate for something the BOP wanted. No one had to know anything else.

You won't be able to keep this secret for long, she thought as Nate tipped his hat at her and went into the equipment shed to get his tools. He'd expressed some frustration with the building aspect of the bird blinds, but when she'd gone out to look at the one he'd completed, it was perfect.

"I rebuilt it four times," he'd admitted, and Ginger may have started to fall for him then.

Or maybe the slope had become a little slippery when she'd watched him lift Connor above his head and buzz like an airplane as the boy giggled and shrieked with delight. Or when he charmed the children in the riding lessons. Or stood at the window and watched him, Nick, and Spencer load into a pickup truck and go to town for chicken wings and cheese fries.

No matter when it had started, Ginger had definitely started to fall for Nate Mulbury. She'd told herself to go slow, and she'd been pulling on the reins of their relationship for a couple of weeks.

Now that he'd kissed her, Ginger wanted to climb onto the nearest roof and shout the news to the world. Emma would be able to tell something had changed in her, and Ginger decided not to go back to the homestead for lunch like she usually did.

Or maybe she should. If she didn't show up, Emma would for sure know something was wrong.

Not wrong. Different. Changed.

Ginger just needed something to happen on the ranch. A sick horse. A tourist that had gone off the path. Heck, she'd even take a swarm of locusts.

Okay, maybe not a swarm of locusts. Life at Hope Eternal Ranch was usually fairly quiet, though there were days when she'd texted her friends and told them she wouldn't be in for lunch. Otherwise, the women in the West Wing gathered for their midday meal.

Before she could turn fully away from the shed where Nate had disappeared, her phone rang. Only a moment later, the siren they used on the ranch filled the air. Cowboys and cowgirls started to spill out of sheds, barns, and stables, and Ginger couldn't hear her phone ringing anymore.

Spencer's name sat on the screen, and another call came in over his. Emma.

Ginger's mind raced, and her heart sprinted, but she swiped away Emma's call and answered Spencer's. "Talk to me," she said, plugging her left ear as she held the phone at her right.

"Accident in field four," he said, breathless. "I need you here."

"Did you activate the siren?"

"Yes," he said. "Someone's down out here, and I don't know who. We need a count, and Emma's calling the paramedics."

Confusion needled her mind. "She called me." She took several steps toward the equipment shed. Field four was too far away to run there in a reasonable amount of time. "Doesn't matter. I'll be there in five." She hung up and stopped next to the nearest person, who happened to be Jessica Morales, her chief stable master and one of the women who lived in the West Wing.

"Send out the call for a count at the homestead," Ginger said, her voice demanding and crisp. "Group text. And find out if Emma did call the paramedics. Text me who's missing and what's going on with medical assist."

Jess didn't ask any questions; she nodded and got busy on her phone.

Nate met Ginger at the door. "How can I help?"

"Go to the homestead and keep everyone calm," she

said, wishing she was one of those he could comfort. "I'll be back as soon as I can."

He let his fingers trail down her arm as she went past, and Ginger appreciated the touch. She threw her leg over the nearest ATV and zoomed out the back of the shed, turning sharply to get going in the right direction toward field four.

Spencer's truck idled near the fence line when Ginger arrived, and she parked beside him. She also didn't bother to turn off the ATV as she hurried to climb the fence and get out to where he stood, waving both hands above his head.

She jogged toward him, hoping she didn't land on a divot or hole in the field and twist her ankle. Her phone pealed, and she answered it.

"It's Nick," Emma said, her voice panicked. "Besides you and Spence, he's the only one not here."

Ginger's blood ran cold, and she forced her feet to move faster. "Thanks," she panted into the phone before she lowered it from her ear. It couldn't be Nick.

He can't be hurt, she thought over and over again.

Spencer started yelling, but Ginger was still too far away to hear the words. Just noise entered her ears, and she felt something wet on her face. Crying. She was crying.

What would she tell her aunt? She'd promised to take care of Nick, who wasn't even twenty years old yet.

As she neared, she could make out Spencer's words. "He's okay, Ginger! He's okay!"

She didn't slow down, her eyes focused solely on her

cousin, who was on the ground and not moving. How was that okay?

She finally arrived, Spencer talking a mile a minute. "I saw the tractor out here going this morning, but I didn't think anything of it. Then, the next time I drove past, Ursula was running in a circle out here, and there was no one in the tractor. So I pulled over and jumped on-board to get it stopped. I tried to get Ursula to come, but she wouldn't. She barked and barked and barked.." He scrubbed down Ursula, who paced in front of Nick.

She barked on cue, and Ginger focused on the dog.

"She'd come toward me for a few feet, bark, and then go back to him," Spencer continued. "Remember how you asked where she'd gone this morning and I didn't know? I think she's been out here with him."

Ginger reached for the German shepherd, needing the extra support. Ursula didn't stop pacing though, and she whined before she licked Nick's face. He wasn't bleeding, and Ginger didn't know where to put her hands.

The dog barked again, and Ginger knelt down on the ground next to her cousin. "Nick?" she asked. "It's Ginger. Can you hear me?"

"He said a couple of things a few minute ago," Spencer said. "I think he's okay."

"He's clearly not okay," Ginger snapped, her anxiety reaching a boiling point. "Sorry," she said immediately afterward. "He's hypoglycemic. He needs orange juice." She stood up, frantically searching for the tractor. "He'll have had something with him. Did you check his pockets?"

"No," Spencer said. "I didn't know he was hypoglycemic." He just stood there, and Ginger wanted to shake him.

She started toward the green tractor in the distance. "Check his pockets," she called over her shoulder. "If he has something to suck on—a piece of candy, a mint, anything—put it in his mouth."

"Ginger," Spencer called after her, but she faced forward and focused on breathing as she ran. The tractor was closer than the ATV, and she hurried to climb up into the cab. A handful of butterscotch candies sat in the tray right below the key, and she grabbed however many would fit in her palm.

A jolt went up her legs when she jumped back to the ground, but she pressed on. Nick could be slipping into a coma by now if he'd been out here for hours. What time was it? What time had she noticed Ursula was missing?

Ginger didn't have any of the answers to her questions, and a couple of the candies fell from her fingers as she ran. "Hold on," she said, but she wasn't sure if she was talking to herself or to Nick.

She made it back to his side, and Spencer said, "He didn't have anything."

"Help me hold his head up so he doesn't choke," she said, frantically unwrapping one of the butterscotches. "He had these in the tractor."

"I thought he just liked those," Spencer said, kneeling on the other side of Nick. He moaned as Spencer lifted him so he was lying in Spencer's lap.

"Have you ever seen him eat one?" Ginger asked, taking a moment to look at Spencer.

He just shook his head, and Ginger reached out to put the candy in her cousin's mouth. "All right, Nick," she said. "Here's one of your candies. Come on now. Eat it all, okay?"

"The ambulance is coming," Spencer said, nodding over her shoulder. Ginger turned to look, quickly refocusing on Nick. A bit of dribble came from the corner of his mouth, and she wiped it away.

Panic built in her chest—until Nick groaned, his mouth moving around the candy.

"That's right," she said. "Chew it, Nick."

He didn't wake completely before the paramedics arrived, but some of the color had returned to his face, and he was moving a lot more. So much that Ginger worried he'd spit out the candy.

She stood to let the two paramedics get closer to him. "He's a diabetic," she said. "Hypoglycemic." She held out the few remaining candies she had. "He always carries these with him, and we gave him one."

"All right," one of the paramedics said. "What's his name?"

"Nick," Spencer said. He came to stand beside Ginger, and he put his arm around her. She leaned into him, because he was taller and stronger than her, and Ginger felt one moment away from falling apart completely.

"Nick," the man said. "My name is Carlos. We're going to take real good care of you." He looked at the other man. "Byron, check his pulse."

Carlos continued to give Byron instructions, finally turning back to Spencer and Ginger. "He's new on the job."

"New on the job?" Ginger almost shrieked. This was her cousin's life. She wanted the most seasoned paramedic in the force. "How is he?"

"His pulse is strong," Byron said. "He's not feverish, but he is sweating, which is a common sign of hypoglycemia. Shaking, also a sign."

"Should we give him another candy?" She held one out to Carlos, who looked at it like it was a poisonous snake.

"Let's get him to the bus and put in an IV," he said to Byron. "Careful now." They got him on the stretcher easily, as Nick was made of more bones than muscles.

As they took him past Ginger, Nick turned his head and said, "Ginger."

"I'm right here," she said, hurrying to his side and taking his hand. Walking with the paramedics like that wasn't easy, but Ginger didn't care. "You're okay. You're going to be fine."

"Candy," he said, his eyes fluttering open. "Ursula."

"She's right here too," Ginger said. "She got Spencer's attention. She saved you." A sob gathered in the back of her throat, but Ginger swallowed against it. No one needed her tears and panic right now. She could sob into the shower later.

She left the ATV with Spencer, and told him to let everyone at the ranch know what was happening. She climbed in the back of the ambulance with her cousin, and they'd barely reached the highway when Nick opened his eyes.

"What's going on?" he asked, trying to sit up.

"Whoa, there, Nick," Carlos said. "You're strapped down for safety, but it's nothing to be worried about." He looked up at Byron. "Looks like the drip worked." He grinned at his partner, then Ginger, then Nick. "We're taking you to the hospital so you can be fully checked. Can you tell us what happened?"

"I was out in the fields," Nick said, settling back to a prone position. His eyebrows drew down. "I got really thirsty, but I didn't have any water. So I was going to go in and get some, but my heart started beating too fast. My vision blurred. I...don't know after that."

"Did you know you were going to pass out?" Carlos asked, putting on a pair of glasses as he started filling out a sheet on a clipboard.

"Yes," Nick said. "I got out of the tractor, because I could tell. I couldn't think though. I usually have candy with me, and I just pop one of those in. I couldn't fine them." He looked at Ginger, tears gathering in his eyes. "I didn't eat breakfast."

"It's okay, Nick," she said, though a measure of frustra-

HOPEFUL COWBOY 151

tion filled her. He was never supposed to go out onto the ranch without eating. Without water. And without his candy. Ever.

"I was in a hurry," he said, closing his eyes. "I have a date with Miss Samantha tonight."

Ginger worked hard not to roll her eyes, though her cousin wouldn't see her with his eyes closed. Carlos chuckled. "Well, Nick, she might have to come see you in the hospital."

"No way," he said, his eyes jerking open. He looked from Carlos to Ginger. "Ginger, you can't let her come to the hospital."

She leaned closer, trying to be compassionate but really wanting to crack her knuckles against his forehead. "I'll keep her away this time," she promised. "But if you rush out to work without eating again, I'll put you in the hospital myself."

Nick just blinked at her, but Carlos and Byron both chuckled. She straightened and looked at them. "I won't," she said. "Not really. But come on, Nick. You scared all of us. Spencer sent off the siren."

"I'm sorry," Nick said, sounding absolutely miserable. "I'm sorry, Ginger. It won't happen again."

Seeing her cousin unconscious on the ground wasn't what she'd wanted to keep her from the homestead, but it had worked. She got busy sending texts then, and she accompanied Nick into the hospital, where his mother soon arrived.

Only then did Ginger step out and lean against the wall, a sigh pulling through her whole body.

Her phone rang, and Nate's name on the screen reminded her of the bone-bending kiss they'd shared that morning.

That morning.

It felt like a year ago.

"Hey," she said after she'd connected the call.

"Hey," he said. "Connor and I want to come to the hospital and eat lunch with you. Would you let me bring your truck in?"

"Alone?"

"Yes," he said. "I'd be alone with Connor from the ranch to the hospital." He waited for her to answer, and Ginger's mind went around and around. He wasn't supposed to leave the ranch without someone with him, but he did have a driver's license. And she would like to see him and Connor.

"Okay," she finally said. "Tell me when you're leaving, so I know when you should be here."

"I can stay on the line with you if you'd like," he said.

"That's not necessary," she said. "My keys are in the top drawer in the West Wing. Emma can probably find them for you."

"I've already got them, sweetheart," he said. "We'll be there in fifteen minutes."

CHAPTER THIRTEEN

Nate pulled the rope tight to keep the barrels in place. He needed to get them out to the new bird blind he'd finished last week. Sweat ran down the side of his face, but he ignored it. He'd been at Hope Eternal for eight weeks now, and he finally felt like he knew how things worked.

"You got that?" Spencer called, and Nate finished tying the knot around the metal pole.

"Yep," Nate said. "Done." He turned to the other cowboy, who drank from a bottle of water.

He finished the whole thing and said, "You can't go out unless you drink. Ginger will kill us both."

Spencer was right, so Nate stepped over to the cooler just inside the shed and got a bottle of water. He managed to swallow a few mouthfuls to appease Spencer, and the two of them loaded up in the ranch truck.

Nate hardly ever drove, and today was no different.

Spencer took them over the bumpy roads to the far north side of the ranch, which surprisingly was pretty swampy. And water and tall reeds meant a lot of birds. People paid quite a bit to come to Hope Eternal and see the birds that lived here, as Nate had learned over the weeks.

They came to see beehives and wear bee suits to harvest the honeycomb too. Children and adults alike came to ride horses. Summer campers came to learn about butterflies and farming. The number of people who came to the ranch had alarmed Nate at first, but now he was used to seeing the dirt parking lot to the west of the homestead full of cars and trucks.

"All right." Spencer let out a sigh that spoke of his exhaustion. "Let's get these unloaded."

"You stayed up too late, didn't you?" Nate asked as they got out of the truck.

"Only a little." Spencer wore a guilty grin as he came to the back and started on the rope on his side. "I just couldn't quit in the middle of the level."

"Yeah, and that's why Nick didn't shower before he left." Nate chuckled and untied the rope on his side. "You know Ginger is going to be cranky about that."

"Yeah, well, Nick can deal with that. I managed to get up when my alarm went off." Spencer hauled the first barrel off the truck. "And anyway, if you just take a walk with Ginger, she won't be so cranky anymore." He shot a knowing look at Nate, who froze.

"What?"

"Oh, come on, man," Spencer said with a laugh. "You two disappear every morning, and she comes back like she met Santa Claus out there and got a year's supply of gifts."

"I—" Nate cut himself off, because he didn't know what to say. He had no defense. He honestly hadn't known anyone knew about his and Ginger's morning walks.

"You're seeing her," Spencer supplied for him, reaching for another barrel. "Right?" He cut a glance at Nate, who still couldn't get himself to move.

"I mean, I guess?" Nate guessed.

"Oh, boy," Spencer said, grunting as the barrel came off the truck and he had to bear the full weight of it. "Okay, I'm just going to tell you this, and then you can do what you want with it."

"I really don't want to hear it," Nate said, pulling his gloves on and reaching for the nearest barrel.

"Too bad," Spencer said. "I didn't want you to tell me I couldn't aim to save my life, but you said it anyway."

"That was a video game," Nate said. Spencer and Nick loved their video games, and Nate didn't mind watching after Connor went to bed. He still slept with Nate at night, and Nate didn't mind at all.

He'd asked Connor about adoption, and then Bethany when she'd come to the ranch for a few hours one weekend. Her kids played well with Connor, and she'd told him he should definitely adopt Connor.

Nate had talked to his parents, and he'd learned that his

mother was starting to forget things and that his father had been diagnosed with stage one colon cancer.

He called them a few times a week, because he was the oldest now and Ward wasn't around to do it. Sometimes the fact that Ward wasn't around hit Nate pretty hard, and thinking about adopting Connor usually sent him into a depression.

In the end, Nate had decided to go forward with the adoption. He'd filed all the paperwork with his lawyer, and now they were just waiting.

"This is real life," Spencer said. "And you should know Ginger's dated a guy like you before."

Nate's blood pressure rose. "A guy like me?"

"A guy in the RRC program," Spencer said. "He seemed like a nice guy. I actually liked him. Then, one day, he disappeared, and the next thing I know, Ginger is telling us she might lose the ranch and that this guy had stolen thousands of dollars from us all." He'd stopped unloading to tell his tale.

Nate didn't know what to make of it. "I'm not going to do that," he said.

"Yeah, because Hyrum's back in prison," Spencer said.

"I'm not going back there," Nate said, fierce determination in his voice. He wasn't. He had Connor to think about now, and he couldn't be irresponsible to the point where he could lose the boy he was going to adopt.

He thought of the next drop he needed to make, and fear slid through his whole body. He kept his head down and kept working, his thoughts tangling about this weekend's activities. Ginger had actually suggested they go to the mall, because she needed a day away from the ranch, and she wanted some Chinese noodles from a restaurant next to the mall.

He'd asked if she'd wait for him at the bank again, and she'd said she would. He could see the questions in her eyes, but to her credit, she hadn't asked them. Nate figured he'd have to tell her something soon enough, but she hadn't revealed her dating history to him, and as he pulled the last barrel off the truck, he realized his relationship with Ginger wasn't as deep as it could be.

He told himself it was still new, and it was. But he wanted it to be deeper, so he'd have to dig down and find something to share with her.

Spencer's phone rang, and he answered it with, "Hey, boss," the way he always did when Ginger called. "Yeah, I can be there. I'm just out at the north bird blinds with Nate." He looked over at Nate, who waited for Spencer to tell him what to do.

They weren't anywhere near done here. The barrels needed to be moved to the six blinds out here, and they'd have to walk through some watery areas the truck couldn't go to get the job done.

"He'll have to be here alone," Spencer said, half-turning away from Nate. A couple of seconds passed before he said, "All right, boss. See you in a minute." He hung up and faced Nate. "Ginger needs me back at the ranch."

"And I'm not going." Nate wasn't asking.

"She said it's fine if you work out here on your own." Spencer went around to the driver's seat. "I'll come back and get you, okay?" He paused before he got in the truck. "And Nate, for the record, I think you're nothing like that other guy that was here."

Nate nodded, though his chest squeezed too tight. "Thanks, Spencer."

"She trusts you, and so do I."

"I appreciate that."

Spencer nodded and got in the truck. Nate got straight to work, even before Spencer had gone. He wanted to show everyone that they could trust him. He could work hard. He could accomplish what they wanted him to accomplish.

And in four months, he'd be on his own, achieving his own dreams. If only he knew what those were.

He used to know what he wanted from his life, but that had all changed when he'd gotten caught up in the fraud scheme. Now, he needed a new purpose, one that would take him and Connor somewhere amazing.

He didn't really want to leave Texas, as Connor only had one set of grandparents, and Nate didn't think it fair to go too far from them. He'd spoken to his mom and dad several times over the weeks, and Bethany picked up the phone when Nate called too. Those relationships had been damaged, and he'd been rebuilding them for years.

He felt like they were almost there, and he hoped to move to White Lake with Connor to continue the work he'd been doing to reconstruct the trust he'd ruined with just a few bad decisions.

By the time he'd moved all the barrels, his breath huffed and puffed from his mouth, and his back, shoulders, and arms burned with the exertion he'd had to use to get them where Ginger wanted them.

Spencer still hadn't returned, and Nate's stomach growled for lunch. He looked down the road, trying to estimate how far it was back to the homestead. Probably an hour by foot, and Nate looked up into the bright, blazing sun.

He wasn't making that trek without water, and he'd left his bottle in the truck. He retreated to the shade of the bird blind, though it wasn't any cooler there.

His phone rang, and Nate quickly swiped on the call from the Bureau of Prisons, expecting to hear Ted's voice. Nate didn't want to tell him he hadn't followed up with Ginger about bringing him to the ranch, but he wouldn't lie to a friend.

Instead, he heard Dallas Dreyer said, "Nathaniel Mulbury," followed by a big belly laugh.

Nate chuckled too, because only a few people called him by his full name, and one of them was Dallas. At least the first time they talked. "What's up, Dallas?" he asked after they'd quieted down.

"Nothing much. Wondering how ranch life is."

"You know what? It's not bad." Nate could honestly say that now. "I think maybe I missed my calling in life the first time I chose a career."

"Oh yeah? Are you a cowboy now?"

"I think I am," Nate said. He hoped he could be a good cowboy. "It's good work." He rolled his aching shoulder, thinking maybe he shouldn't have fought the mud so much.

"I'm glad," Dallas said.

"What's new there?" Nate asked, surprised he wanted to know. But he missed his boys behind bars, and Dallas had needed a strong core group to watch out for him. Nate worried about what would happen to him once Ted left, as then Dallas would be the one with the most days behind him. Slate Sanders would probably rise to the top, because he had a stronger personality than Dallas, and Luke was happy to let someone else lead.

And as far as Nate knew, they'd added more men to their ranks. The five of them, Nate included, had formed a camaraderie that Nate missed powerfully every time he thought of his friends.

He did have Spencer now, and Nick, and a few other cowboys that lived in the house with him. He had Connor, and Ginger, and Emma. And his family, though he didn't get to see them much.

He let Dallas talk about River Bay, and how nothing much had changed. "Oh, except guess who just took over your job in the office?" he asked.

"Who?" Nate asked.

"Josiah Manuel."

All sound ceased as Nate absorbed that information. "You're kidding."

"I wish. And he's strutting around now like he's wearing the Manager's uniform or something. He's headed for a big fall."

"I didn't realize he had so much sway." Nate hadn't really either, but Josiah held a ton of tickets, and he'd almost been moved up a level of security because he loved to start fights.

"He doesn't," Dallas said. "Greg just wants him where he can keep an eye on him, because one of our wings is going through a remodel."

"Ah, I see." Nate wondered if he'd been in the office for a reason like that, but he dismissed the idea quickly. A beep sounded on the line, which meant that Dallas had one minute left on his call. So they said their goodbyes, and Nate hung up.

He moved to the edge of the bird blind and looked down the road, still finding it empty. He looked up into the clear sky, the hot sun burning straight through him. Frustration built inside him at his situation, so Nate decided to make one more phone call before he went back to the more populated areas of the ranch.

Sam Wiseman picked up his personal line after only one ring with the words, "Hello, Nathaniel. What can I do for you?"

"I need another withdrawal," Nate said. "In the same amount as last time. Same envelope too, if possible."

"It's possible," Sam said crisply. "I can have that ready for you for this afternoon."

Nate started thinking about possibilities, and he asked, "Can you deliver it to someone for me?" He couldn't imagine detailing how to put the money in a locker at the mall, not to Sam.

"No, sir," Sam said. "We can't do that."

"Can I pick it up tomorrow?"

"Absolutely. The counter is open from ten until two. I'm not in on weekends."

"How would I get it?" Nate asked.

"I'll put it in your safety deposit box, if that works for you?"

"That works," Nate said. He wasn't sure how he'd carry the briefcase around the mall, disappear, and come back without it. He needed a new bag, one that would conceal the envelope and that he could carry with him reasonably. Did men carry backpacks around the mall?

He shook his head at this situation. He hated it. He just wanted to give Oscar his money and be done with it. But Oscar refused to take more than nine thousand dollars at a time, and for the twenty-six thousand dollars Nate owed Oscar, that required three drops.

Tomorrow would only be the second, which meant Nate had to go through this again.

His phone rang, and when he looked at the screen, he found Ginger's name on the screen. "Hey, sweetheart," he said.

"Hey," she said. "You still out at the bird blinds?"

"It's good to hear your voice."

Ginger gave him a light laugh, and that made him smile. He wanted to confide in her, but he didn't know how. She probably felt the same way about telling him about her ex-boyfriend.

A guy like him.

"And yes," he added. "I'm out at the bird blinds. Done, but I can't bear the thought of walking back in this heat."

"I have good news for you then," she said. "I'm about five minutes away, and the air conditioner in this truck works really well."

"Bless you," he said, actually sighing in relief.

She laughed again and said she'd be there soon. Nate decided he could brave the sun for a few minutes, and he stepped out of the bird blind and headed down the road. Sure enough, Ginger rounded the bend and came toward him. She pulled to a stop beside him and said, "You lost, Mister?"

He grinned at her and sighed as he got in the passenger seat. "It's *hot.*"

"That it is," she said. "I brought you a water." She indicated it sitting in the console between them. Nate also spied something there that made his mouth water. "And yes, I got you a hamburger."

"You're the best," he said, reaching for the food and then the water. "Seriously, Ginger, thank you."

She gripped the steering wheel tightly. Her voice was a

bit too high when she said, "Thanks for being someone I can trust."

Guilt cut through Nate, but he said nothing. Once all the drops were done, once Oscar had his money and no reason to contact Nate ever again, then he'd tell Ginger. He'd tell her everything, share his whole life with her.

But for now, he had to keep this one secret. After all, how much damage could one little secret do?

CHAPTER FOURTEEN

Ginger had looked for ways Nate could potentially mess up. After the one time he hadn't been in the stables where she'd expected him to be, her stomach clenched whenever she went to find him. But he was always right where he said he'd be. He learned quickly, and he was one of the hardest working men she'd ever met.

She'd been toying with the idea of offering him a permanent position on the ranch once his reentry term expired. But he didn't seem to be hurting for money, and he'd mentioned moving into Ward's house in White Lake more than once.

So Ginger had kept her mouth closed. White Lake was only about twenty minutes down the road, and she could easily make the drive to see him. Heck, after his residential program ended, he'd be a free man, and *he* could drive to see *her*.

She set the curling iron down, deciding she couldn't make every lock of hair into a wave. Nate would know she'd spent an hour in front of the mirror, and she didn't want him to think she was trying so hard. Even if she was.

They were going to the mall today to get her favorite Chinese food. She hadn't told him it was to celebrate her birthday, but it was. She should probably text him just to let him know. As soon as she thought so, she recalled the idea. *No*, she told herself. *It's fine.* She didn't need him to buy her anything.

She knew he liked her, because he poured everything into his kisses, and Ginger had felt it time and time again over the past few weeks.

"There you are," Emma said, leaning into the doorway. "I just put the cheesecake in. Jill, Jess, Michelle, and Hannah have all confirmed for tonight. So did both of your sisters."

"Both of them?" Ginger turned away from her reflection. She was as beautiful as she was going to get, and another layer of lip gloss wouldn't help. "Sierra isn't going out with Max?"

Emma rolled her eyes. "She actually asked if she could bring him, and I told her irrevocably that she could *not*."

"I'm surprised she's coming then." Her sister couldn't do anything without her fiancé, and no one had the heart to tell Sierra that she and Max had been engaged for four years. Ginger wanted a man who couldn't wait to get her to the altar, not one that put the wedding off and off and off...

No one in the family—or anyone who'd been around for the past four years—believed Sierra and Max would actually get married. In fact, the plans for the non-existent wedding had stopped years ago.

But Sierra worked the weekend tours, and she helped with Connor, so Ginger respected her. She loved her because they were related, but sometimes Sierra could pull a diva card out of nowhere.

"We'll see if she actually does," Emma said, scanning Ginger. "How are things with Nate?"

"Fine," Ginger said with an air of coolness. She didn't make direct eye contact with Emma as she approached the door, and her best friend fell back into the hallway.

"Must be," Emma said. "You've gone to The Green Dragon by yourself for five years. Wouldn't even let me come so you didn't have to be alone on your birthday."

"I'm never alone on my birthday," Ginger said, pausing in front of Emma. She had gorgeous dark hair that had a natural wave, not like the too-tight one Ginger had put in her hair with a curling iron. Emma's big, brown eyes looked at Ginger, practically begging her for all the details.

It seemed that everyone around the ranch knew Ginger and Nate were something. They just didn't know how serious it was. Ginger herself didn't know that either, though she'd felt herself slipping more and more the past couple of weeks.

Everything Nate did and said made her foothold on reality a little less sure. She wanted a fantasy life with the strong, handsome cowboy, and the towheaded little boy. She could admit she loved Connor, but going all the way there with Nate...Ginger still had a tight grip on those reins.

"You always make me an amazing cake and a delicious dinner." Ginger smiled at Emma and leaned into her for a hug. She did love this other woman, who had been by her side for the past ten years here on the ranch. Emma had started as a teacher's aide, bringing first and second graders to the ranch to do the Monarch butterfly classes.

She loved horses, and soon enough, Ginger had pulled her from the school system and onto the ranch, where she'd been ever since. Ginger didn't trust anyone more than she did Emma, and they worked incredibly well together to make sure Hope Eternal Ranch thrived under any circumstances.

Emma held her tight and breathed in deep. "Okay, but I know you and Nate are something serious, even if you won't admit it."

"I never said I wouldn't admit it," Ginger said.

"You've never even admitted that you've kissed him," Emma said with a laugh, pulling away from Ginger. "And I don't get why. We all know you have."

"Maybe I just don't want to talk about it over dinner," Ginger said.

A new light entered Emma's eyes, "Great. I'm going to get a ton of butter pecan ice cream, and you'll come to my room tonight. Ten o'clock. Wait. Nine. And then we'll chat."

She turned and started down the hall before Ginger could protest.

When she finally did, Emma just waved over her shoulder. "Nine o'clock," she said, disappearing around the corner. That was that. Ginger would go, because she'd always talked to Emma about her boyfriends.

Boyfriend.

Was that what Nate was? Would he classify her as his girlfriend?

She hoped so.

Several minutes later, she sat in the truck as Nate helped Connor onto the seat. "Slide over, bud. All the way."

Connor did, and Ginger helped him with his seatbelt. "How's the little cowboy?" she asked. Nate slammed the door, so she didn't hear the beginning of what Connor said, but it didn't matter. The boy had been dipped in magic, and then gold, and she couldn't imagine a better child than Connor.

"You guys hungry?" she asked as she pulled through the garage and circled the house instead of backing out into the driveway.

"I am," Connor said, bouncing a little on the seat. "Uncle Nate wouldn't let me eat breakfast."

"Is that so?"

"No," Nate said, somewhat crossly. He wore a displeased look on his face as he gazed at Connor. "That is not true. You ate French toast, Connor. And bacon. I wouldn't let you eat a Twinkie fifteen minutes ago, because we're going to lunch with Ginger." He looked at her from across the cab. "For her birthday."

She sucked in a breath and dang near drove them into the fence post. She corrected sharply, throwing them all to the right. Nate started laughing, and Connor said, "Whoa there," like a real cowboy.

"Who told you?" Ginger asked.

"Nick," Nate said.

"I'm going to kill him."

"Why?" Nate's gaze on the side of her face was too heavy. "What's the big deal if I know it's your birthday?"

"Yeah, don't you want any presents?" Connor asked in his innocent little boy voice.

"Yeah," Nate echoed. "We could've gotten her so many presents. Now we'll just have to settle for what we can find at the mall."

"No," Ginger said. "I don't want presents."

"Who doesn't want presents?" Nate asked.

"I don't," she said. "My friends throw me a big birthday dinner with cake every year. I just want Chinese food and good company."

"You don't like your friends?"

"I love my friends. They're just...loud."

"The mall is loud," Nate said.

"But it's not the ranch," Ginger said, finally letting herself look at him. "So, to the bank first? Chinese second? Mall third?"

Nate nodded, a curious look on his face still. Thankfully, Ginger had to look away to check the traffic before she pulled onto the highway.

"You gotta be good," Nate said in a mock whisper to Connor. "She said she wanted good company."

"What's company?" Connor asked back, and Ginger's face broke into a smile.

"It's who you spend your time with," Nate said. "So she wants to spend lunch with us, but only if she likes us."

"She likes me," Connor said. "Does she like you, Uncle Nate?"

Ginger looked at Nate then, and he looked at her. "Yeah," he said with a wide grin. "I think she does."

"Then we'll be good," Connor said, satisfied now.

"And I'm buying lunch," Nate said.

Ginger shook her head, but she wasn't going to argue with him. If he wanted to buy her lunch, that was fine. Perhaps she could use the topic of who paid to find out if they were dating, casually walking in the mornings and kissing each other, or what kind of labels he might use if he introduced her to say, his mother.

Or how she might introduce him to her sisters, both of whom were coming that night. Her heartbeat picked itself up and threw itself down, causing a slight echo in her pulse.

She and Connor waited in the car while Nate ran inside the bank for a few minutes. This was definitely his shortest trip to the institution, and he came out a few minutes later with an envelope he tucked into his backpack.

At the Chinese restaurant, he insisted on sitting beside

her instead of across from her, and as Connor colored all over the animals that comprised the Chinese New Year, Nate slipped his hand into Ginger's and leaned real close to her. "Happy birthday," he said. "What would you wish for?"

She liked the intimacy between them, and how dim the inside of the restaurant was even in the middle of the summer. "That's a hard question."

"Is it?"

"What would you wish for?"

"Oh, let's see. Cooler summers, for one." He grinned at her, and Ginger couldn't contradict his wish. "The ability to sleep in every day. And world peace."

Ginger giggled and nudged him with her shoulder. "That's a good list."

Nate chuckled and lifted his water glass to his mouth with his free hand. "Oh, that's not good. That tastes like flowers." He made a face and looked at her. "You like this place?"

"The lo mein is incredible," she said. "And the shrimp fried rice. That's what I'm getting."

He looked down at the menu. "What do you want, bud?" he asked Connor.

"Sweet and sour chicken," the little boy said as if he'd frequented many Chinese restaurants.

Surprise crossed Nate's face, but he said, "All right," and ordered the child what he wanted when the waiter came. Ginger loaded up on carbs, because it was her birthday and she could. Nate got teriyaki beef and pork fried rice, and she watched as he took his first bite.

"Good, right?" she said as his face lit up.

"Really good."

"Now you know why I come here on my birthday every year." She happily dug into her shrimp fried rice, more joy coursing through her than she'd felt in many long years.

"Do you always come with 'good company'?" he asked.

"I usually come alone," she said. "At least since...." She trailed off, not sure how to bring up Hyrum. But she felt like it was time. Nate had been at the ranch for over two months now. Ten weeks, maybe. They'd been kissing for a while.

He didn't press her to finish her sentence, and she twirled her chopsticks through her noodles, focusing on the bean sprouts and green onions as she said, "I used to be with a guy named Hyrum. We came together once."

"Was he the last guy you've been out with?" Nate asked.

Ginger nodded and scooped up her noodles. "What about you? Pen pal girlfriend from prison?"

Nate chuckled and shook his head. "Nope. Not much of a love life before prison either. I was pretty focused on my career."

"Oh, come on," she said. "You expect me to believe that? A handsome guy like you didn't have a girlfriend?"

"It's true," he said. "Though, I mean...yeah, I can tell you." He put his fork down and glanced at Connor. "The last woman I dated—her name was Brittany. She's the one who introduced me to the guys who got us all entwined in the fraud. So...yeah, I'm not really that lucky in the girl-friend department."

Ginger nodded, trying to sort through which question to ask. The fraud? The girlfriend? "So...what are we?" she asked, going with girlfriend. "If you saw someone you knew, for example, right outside those doors." She pointed with her chopsticks. "How would you introduce me?"

Nate reached for his fork again, his head bent. "Well, I guess I'd say you were my boss."

"Oh, that's the wrong answer," Ginger said as his words dove deep into her heart and gouged out a hole. But by making her tone flirty and adding a plastic smile to her face, maybe she wouldn't spiral into self-loathing.

"In that case," he said. "I'd say you were my girlfriend."

"Yeah, because it's kind of icky to be kissing your boss, right?" she asked.

"Is it icky to kiss your boss?" he asked, throwing her a flirty smile too. "Oops. Done that."

A beat of silence passed, and Ginger burst out laughing. "See?" she asked when she'd sobered up enough to talk. "You have had other girlfriends."

"No." He shook his head, still chuckling. "No, I haven't. The boss was Brittany. Same woman. She's still in prison too. Got ten years."

"Oh, wow." Ginger quieted all the way, and Nate seemed to disappear inside himself for a minute.

He drew in a breath, and she imagined him to be throwing off the cobwebs in his mind, because when he looked at her again, those bright, striking blue eyes danced. "I'm going to run next door for a minute. Will you be okay here with Connor?" He tossed his napkin on the table, already starting to stand.

She shouldn't let him go off on his own, but how could she say no? "I don't need any gifts," she said. "Really, I don't. Lunch is what I wanted, and you're buying that."

"Give me fifteen minutes to find something," he said, reaching into his back pocket and pulling out his wallet. He tossed a card on the table that actually made a thud like it was made of metal. "Use that to pay. If I can't find anything in fifteen minutes, you'll get lunch and that's it." He grinned and acted like he was getting ready to run a race. "Okay?"

"Okay," Ginger said with a laugh.

Nate took off for the exit, taking his backpack with him. He didn't look back, and Ginger couldn't help giggling as he left. She looked at Connor, who had bright orange sauce around his mouth. She tapped his napkin. "Wipe your lips, bud."

He did, and then he said, "Nate is gonna be my dad."

"Yeah," Ginger said. "I heard that. Are you excited about that?"

"Yeah," Connor said, and that was all. She wondered what it was like inside a four-year-old's head, but she couldn't remember when she was four.

So she asked him why he liked sweet and sour chicken, and he said, "My dad used to get it all the time," he said, launching into other foods his dad used to make or feed him.

Ginger handed the credit card to the waiter when he came by, and it was indeed made of metal. She'd never seen such a fancy, metal card before, and she was once again reminded that Nate Mulbury was not like other inmates.

Fifteen minutes came and went. So did twenty. When she and Connor had been sitting there alone for thirty minutes, Ginger reached for him. "Come on, bud," she said. "Let's go find Nate."

Worry ate at her insides, and she couldn't believe she'd let him go to the mall by himself. He could be anywhere by now. Literally anywhere.

Ginger stepped out of the dark restaurant and into the bright sunshine, blinking as if she'd never stepped foot into downtown Sweet Water Falls. The truck still sat in the parking lot only a few yards away, so he hadn't stolen that.

Just the fact that she'd assumed he might've stolen from her made her frown. But why hadn't he come back?

"Hey," he said a moment later, rushing toward them. "Sorry. I'm sorry. Did you get my texts?"

Ginger could only blink. There he was. He hadn't left. He hadn't hitched a ride to the bus station and gotten on the first Greyhound to come by. He'd never given her a reason not to trust him, and guilt gutted her.

"No," she said. "Sorry, I didn't look." She pulled her phone out of her purse, and sure enough, Nate had texted several times. "Long lines, huh?"

"They were having a big sale," he said, still trying to

catch his breath. He thrust a fancy, gold-foil lined bag toward her. "I think you'll like this."

A brand name was embossed on the bag, and Ginger wondered how in the world he knew she loved Arbortia lotions. A smile filled her from top to bottom as she pulled the tissue paper out of the bag and found not only the hand cream she adored, but a fancy, sparkling bottle of perfume.

"Nate," she breathed, lifting it out. She'd seen this perfume before, and she knew it was very, very expensive. "Thank you."

Their eyes met, and Ginger suddenly didn't care who was watching. Not the general public. Not Connor. She stepped into his arms, still clutching the gorgeous bottle of perfume, and kissed her boyfriend.

CHAPTER FIFTEEN

Nate emerged from his bedroom, leaving Connor to sleep. He got up before the sun now, because the chores on the ranch still needed to be done, but the heart of the summer brought such extreme temperatures that Ginger had ordered everyone to be back inside by noon.

She'd made a rotation for who had to go out and do the evening chores, and no one ever went alone so someone didn't get overheated and not have help nearby.

Spencer stood in the kitchen with Jack, another cowboy that lived in the basement of the Annex. Two dozen blueberry muffins steamed on the counter, and Spencer put a plate of butter next to them while Jack chopped pineapple.

The amount of food that went through the Annex still impressed Nate. The food in prison wasn't bad, but it wasn't delicious either. There was never enough, Nate knew that. Here, though, he always had enough to eat—and more.

Jack put the bowl of pineapple on the counter too, and then turned to get the pan of breakfast sausage that had scented the air with salty maple goodness.

"Morning," Nate said. "What's with the spread?"

"Samantha broke up with Nick," Jack said, and Nate sure did like how these men took care of each other.

"That's rough," Nate said. "They seemed to get along great." He'd met the woman several weeks back when Nick had brought her back to the Annex after one of their dates. He'd seemed absolutely smitten with the blonde, and Nate supposed she was beautiful.

Not Ginger-level gorgeous, but Nate knew everyone had their own chemistry and attraction. In his opinion, Ginger should've been snapped up a long time ago, and he wondered if somehow, she'd just been reserved for him.

No matter what, he liked being her boyfriend, and with half of his reentry period over, Nate thought he had a very good chance of leaving this ranch with so much more than he'd arrived with.

Of course, the knowledge and skills he'd acquired over the past three months would be invaluable too. As would the friendships. He opened the fridge and got out the flavored creams Jack, Spencer, and Nick liked. He enjoyed them too, especially the caramel one.

"Bill's on the evening shift with me?" Nate asked.

"That's right. So he's sleeping in, and he'll make sure Connor's looked after," Spencer said.

"Great." Nate tried to vocalize his appreciation every

chance he got, because everyone at this ranch had helped with Connor. There were no other kids here, besides the ones that came out to the ranch for riding lessons, and everybody seemed to love Connor.

Nate sure did, and he couldn't wait to be the boy's legal father. He hadn't heard anything about it in a while, and he wondered if he should make a call to his lawyer.

His phone buzzed in his back pocket, but he ignored it. Whoever was texting him at four-ten in the morning could wait, at least until after breakfast.

"Here he comes," Spencer hissed. "Places, guys."

Nate got out of the way, joining Jack and Spencer on the other side of the island, though he hadn't gotten the memo about where his place was. He heard Nick's boots against the tile, and then he entered the kitchen. He stopped and took in the counter full of food, his eyes then moving to the three of them waiting for him.

"You guys," he said.

"Sorry about Samantha," Spencer said.

Misery streamed across Nick's face, and Nate's heart went out to him. "Yeah, well."

That was all. Nate had been in similar situations. Maybe not with women, but plenty of things that the only response could be, "Yeah, well." There simply wasn't anything else to say.

Nick picked up a plate and started putting muffins on it. The others joined in, and between the four of them, they barely managed to save enough for Bill and Connor for when they got up later.

Nate left the house stuffed full, with Nick right behind him. "At least we get to go to the beach this weekend," Nick said.

"Yeah," Nate said, remembering his phone. "I'm looking forward to that." He pulled his device out of his pocket and looked at it, his stomach clenching around the huge meal he'd just eaten. Oscar.

Last drop. This weekend. Then we're done.

Anticipation and excitement combined with his raw anxiety, and he quickly shoved his phone back into his pocket. He didn't want Nick to see it, as he wouldn't be able to explain much about it. He'd need to delete this text as soon as possible, after confirming with Oscar.

Now that he could call the bank and have them get his money ready before he showed up, it shouldn't be too hard to do this last drop. He'd been lucky last time when it had been Ginger's birthday. That had allowed him to sneak away without having to come up with an excuse.

He worked through his animal chores, loaded his tools into a bin on the ATV he'd use later, and prepped the boxed lunches for the birdwatchers. They arrived, and Nate greeted them with smiles and the tablet, checking them in and assigning them a bird blind.

They waited off to the side until everyone was checked in, and then he swung his leg over the ATV to lead the group out to their assigned blinds. They'd spend three days and two nights here at Hope Eternal Ranch, and if Nate rode out to the wetlands on the ranch tonight, he'd find their domed tents behind the blinds he'd spent a month improving and even building.

Other cowboys drove big side-by-sides with the people who'd paid to come find the birds they'd never seen before, and they followed him in order of when they'd drop people off. Once there, Nate went over the rules with them and made sure each blind didn't need any last minute repairs or trash removal.

After the last drop-off, he drove back to the ranch with the last side-by-side behind him, and he and Ken parked in the equipment shed and marked all the paperwork so whoever looked at it would know who was where and for how long.

"Done," Ken said, sighing. "I'm over in the stables. Where you goin'?"

"I have to run back to the Annex," Nate said. Connor should be up by now, as it was almost nine o'clock, and Nate liked to check in with him early in the day to make sure he was okay and knew Nate would be back by lunchtime. "I'll walk with you over to the stables."

Once there, Nate bent to get a cold bottle of water out of the cooler at the end of the row, and when he straightened, he found Ginger coming toward him. "Hey," he said, grinning at her. They hadn't really had a conversation about taking their relationship out of the shadows, but after her birthday lunch and shopping afternoon, it had just happened.

"Hey." She kissed him quickly, and added, "Are you headed back to see Connor?"

"Yep."

"I'll walk with you."

He wasn't going to argue with a woman who wanted to be with him, so they set off for the homestead.

"Are you excited to go to the beach this weekend?" she asked.

"Definitely," he said. "I see what you mean about getting off the ranch sometimes."

"It's big, but it can feel really small at times," Ginger said. "But you're doing okay?"

"Just fine," he said.

"Your meetings with Martin are going good?"

"Just fine," Nate said, not wanting to talk about his parole officer. He didn't like being reminded that he was still technically in the Bureau of Prisons, and he couldn't wait to be a free man.

"Good," Ginger said, seeming to get the hint that Nate wasn't interested in expounding on these topics. "Are you excited for the beach?"

"Sure," Nate said. "I haven't been in years." Sometimes, he tried to see the Gulf of Mexico from the ranch, but even if he thought he could, he knew he couldn't. Any water he could see wasn't the whole, huge Gulf. A couple of islands existed between this part of the coastal bend of Texas, and he wanted to stand on the edge of the continent, dig his toes in the sand, and look out over the vast water.

"I'm not excited at the early wake-up call," she said. "But one day we'll be able to sleep in."

Nate's pulse slammed against his ribcage, because he didn't know the details of their weekend beach excursion. He didn't have to know. He just did whatever Ginger told him. "What time are we leaving?"

"Seven, probably," she said. "The beach is about a half-hour away, and it's the best until about ten or eleven."

"Mm," he said, his brain whirring around how he could spend the morning on the beach when he needed to make the last drop for Oscar. He had to get Oscar off his back and out of his life. He'd never negotiated the date or time of the cash drop-off, so maybe he could try to postpone it until next weekend.

"Then, my parents will bring lunch and all these tables so we don't have to eat on the sand. My sisters and brother will be there." She cast him a look, completely unaware of the panic building and building in his chest. "You ready to meet all of us?"

"Sure," Nate said, his voice only a little scratchy.

Ginger laughed and nudged him with her hip. "You'll be fine. They'll love you."

"They know I'm in the Residential Reentry Program, right?" he asked, trying to find something he could grab onto to get out of this beach day.

"Yes," she said. "They know I operate the ranch as a

center for the BOP." She glanced at him. "You're not seriously worried about that, are you?"

"Of course I am," he said. "You aren't?"

"I don't know," she said, her voice at half its usual volume.

Nate let the conversation stall there, because they were almost to the Annex, and he really needed some silence and privacy to figure out what he was going to do on Saturday. It didn't sound like they'd be leaving the beach before two, and the bank was only open from ten to two on Saturdays.

The panic stole through him, but he kept it dormant, a silent scream moving through him as the back door opened and Connor came running across the deck. "Dad!" he yelled, and Nate fully stopped then.

"Dad," Ginger whispered, and Nate bent to scoop Connor into his arms.

"Hey, bud," he said, his heart expanding at a rate he'd never felt before. "Did you get some muffins?"

"Yep," Connor said, leaning into Nate's shoulder. "Cowboy Bill let me take Ursula to get the mail."

"Is that right?" Nate asked. "Did we get anything?"

"Bill said we did. Something from the layer-yer."

Nate tried to figure out what he'd said, and he glanced toward the deck, where Bill had come out and now held up an envelope. "The lawyer," he said, and Nate's pulse rioted again.

He felt like a yo-yo—up one moment and down the next. Panicked one moment, and anxious the next.

"Let's see what it is," Nate said, setting Connor back on his feet. His legs felt like he was bending them backward, but he made it to the deck and up the steps. He took the envelope from Bill and opened it, not sure what he'd find inside. He didn't pretend to understand how the adoption of a family member worked, but Lawrence had said he'd take care of it.

This letter wasn't from Lawrence, though. It bore the letterhead of the same firm, and Nate realized he'd passed the case onto a family lawyer in the same building.

"Jill didn't contest the adoption," he said as he read. "And neither did anyone in her family." Relief streamed through him, and he beamed down at Connor. "That means we're good to go ahead, bud." He handed the paperwork to Ginger, because she liked to read it for herself, and Nate scooped the little boy back into his arms.

All cares and worries about that weekend's drop-off disappeared as he and Connor laughed together, and Nate bent to touch his forehead to Connor's. "I love you, Connor," he whispered. He'd always loved his nephew, but this was something different. Something more.

Something parental.

Nate hated himself as he glanced over his shoulder to the sleeping form of Connor. They were packed and ready to hit the beach at seven a.m. tomorrow morning, but Nate hadn't been able to move his drop-off.

Instead, he'd gotten Nick to do it. He could drive himself. He could leave the beach for forty minutes and get the job done.

Nate had had to explain a couple of things he wished he hadn't had to, but Nick hadn't judged him at all. He hadn't asked too many questions either.

Nate slipped out of the room and closed the door behind him silently. Spencer and Nick shared a room, and Spencer got vicious if someone interrupted his sleep. So Nick had agreed to meet Nate on the back deck.

The location made him nervous, because anyone could overhear the conversation, and he didn't want anyone else on the ranch to know about his deal with Oscar Dominguez. It was almost over, and then he could breathe.

And when he became a free man in just eighty-seven days, he wouldn't have anything or anyone in his way to start his life again, with a son.

He slipped out the back door, and thankfully, Nick already stood against the railing. He turned toward Nate and smiled.

Nate did not. He felt like he'd swallowed one of the beehives out on the ranch, and he pushed against the nausea. "Hey," he said, joining Nick. "Thank you for doing this."

"No problem," Nick said. "It's going to the bank. Picking

up the envelope. Putting it in the backpack, and taking that to a locker in the mall."

"That's right." Nate took a deep breath. "Then you text me the number and the code, and I'll take care of the rest. Come back to the beach. Done." The weight of the money in Nate's pocket seemed to weigh him down. "And I have something for you." He pulled the bills out and tried to slip them to Nick quickly.

But Nick wouldn't take it. "I don't need to get paid. Friends do favors for each other."

Nate shoved the money back in his pocket. "Okay."

"How much money do you have?" Nick asked.

"A lot," Nate said.

"How?"

"I inherited Ward's entire estate," Nate said. "And I invested wisely before prison."

"You were in investments, right?" Nick asked.

"Yes."

"This is legal money?"

"Mine is," Nate said. "This drop is too. It's just something I wasn't able to pay out before I got arrested." He looked at Nick. "Honestly."

"And Ginger doesn't know." He wasn't asking.

"It's not illegal," Nate said. "I just want it to be over, so I don't have this hanging over my head anymore."

"I get that."

But Nate wasn't sure how he could. Nick was nineteen years old.

"Thank you," Nate said. "I really will pay you for this."

"It's not necessary," Nick said, clapping Nate on the shoulder. "See you in the morning."

Nate hardly slept, and when he lifted his backpack over the tailgate of Ginger's truck the next morning, he felt like it weighed a hundred pounds.

Thankfully, Connor had enough energy for both of them, and he occupied Ginger's attention. Nate watched as they laughed together, and he had a flash of a future with the three of them as a family.

So much about him had changed, as he'd never really envisioned himself as a husband and father. But he sure did now.

That hope that had been growing inside him swelled, and he took a moment to revel in the fantasy of him and Ginger, married, with Connor as their son.

"Ready?" she asked, breaking through the image in his mind.

"Yep," he said, hoping he could make it through this morning.

Hours later, Nate couldn't focus, though Connor kept calling to him from the waves. Nick should've been back fifteen minutes ago. Then twenty. Then thirty.

He checked his phone over and over, but there were no calls and no messages. Ginger's family was set to arrive in only twenty minutes, and Nate couldn't remember any of their names, though he and Ginger had been talking about them all week.

Flipping over his phone again, Nate considered what to do. He couldn't just sit here and do nothing. "I've got to use the restroom," he said to Ginger. "Keep an eye on Connor?"

"Of course."

He bent down and kissed her, easily slipping his hand into her purse and taking her car keys. He walked away, his muscles vibrating with his pulse. Around the side of the small brick building that housed the bathroom, Nate dialed Nick.

"Come on," he muttered. Maybe the kid had met a girl at the mall. Maybe he'd spied his favorite hamburger joint. Nate prayed for either of those as the line rang.

"Nate," a man said, but it wasn't Nick.

It was Oscar.

Nate strode toward the parking lot. "Where is he?"

"Dad," Connor said, and Nate spun toward him while Oscar said he didn't appreciate someone else making the drop.

Nate pulled the phone away from his mouth. "Come on," he said to Connor. "We have to go for a ride." He picked up his son and hurried toward the truck.

"I had a thing," Nate said. "Nick is nothing. He doesn't even know how much or why I'm giving you money."

"He knows it's me," Oscar said.

"Also not true," Nate said, opening the door and sliding

Connor in the passenger seat. "I didn't tell him anything but how to get the money from my bank and where to drop it." He ran around the hood and opened the driver's door.

"Nate."

He turned toward Ginger, who wore confusion on her face.

"Where are you going?"

"I'll be right back," he said, getting behind the wheel. He slammed the door and said to Oscar, "Tell me where he is right now. You got your money, and we're done. You don't need Nick." He took off even as Ginger stepped toward him, a look of extreme anger on her face.

He couldn't go back though, and try to explain to her that he'd put her cousin in danger. He knew how much Nick meant to her, and Nate kicked himself for putting the kid in danger.

He was going to make this right.

He was going to end this. Today.

Then he would explain everything to Ginger and hope that she could forgive him.

CHAPTER SIXTEEN

Ginger couldn't believe what had just happened. Fury roared through her as the taillights of her truck disappeared around a bend in the road that led back to Sweet Water Falls.

Her parents were due to arrive in ten minutes. They were expecting to meet her boyfriend and his son. And they'd both just disappeared.

Her torso felt like someone had hollowed her out and filled her with bleach. And where the heck was Nick? He'd left over an hour ago to go get a new battery for his phone. He should've been back by now.

She turned in a full circle, trying to figure out what to do. She was supposed to report anything the inmate did that went against his terms of the reentry program. And leaving without telling her where he was going—and all by himself —was definitely against Nate's terms.

Unrest rolled through her gut. She didn't want him to get in trouble. She also didn't want to stand here on this beach, alone and wondering if Nate was making a run for the Southern border the way Hyrum had.

"He's *not* Hyrum," she told herself, not for the first time. She faced the water, wishing it would confirm what she'd just said. Only the whooshing of waves against sand met her ears. Spencer laughed from the towel where he lay, looking at something on his phone. Emma looked over at him, then back at her paperback.

Everything seemed normal and serene, but Ginger didn't fit in the scene. Not without Nate and Connor. She glanced at the parking lot, but he didn't return with her truck, and Ginger realized she could report him for stealing the vehicle. She really didn't want to do that. Why had he left and put her in this position?

He knew he couldn't go anywhere by himself. "This is why you shouldn't have let him run over to the mall alone," she muttered, as her feet took her toward her friends and co-workers enjoying themselves in the sun and surf.

That episode where Nate had gone to the mall to buy her a birthday present was weeks old, and he'd never indicated he was anything but happy at the ranch. He'd told her time and time again that he was grateful for the opportunity to be at Hope Eternal.

So what had changed?

She sighed as she sank into the beach chair next to Emma. She had to call the BOP. If she didn't and they found out that Nate had gone missing, even for an hour, and she hadn't reported it, she'd never get another inmate at the ranch.

She'd already contacted the Warden at River Bay and said she'd take someone else if he had them, and James Dickerson had said he'd look through his files. Ginger knew who she wanted, because Nate had talked to her about a friend of his. Ted Burrows.

She frowned, and she wasn't sure how long she flipped her phone over in her palm before Emma asked, "What's going on?"

"Nate left," Ginger said as quietly as she could. "With Connor."

Emma abandoned her book completely, her eyes widening. "What? When?"

"Just now. A few minutes ago." Ginger shook her head, the first threat of tears burning behind her eyelids. "I have to call the Bureau."

Emma stood up so fast, her beach chair flipped onto its back. "He took your truck?"

"Ginger," Spencer said, pushing himself up on his elbow. "Look at this." He wore a concerned look on his face and pressed on the side of his phone.

"...breaking news from the Sweet Water Mall." Spencer turned the phone toward Ginger, and Emma came back to peer at the device too. A female reporter stood in front of the camera, the panorama of the mall behind her. "The police have already shut down the mall to new shoppers, and they're apparently moving through the building in a grid pattern, searching for this man."

An image of Nick came up on the screen, and Ginger yelped, immediately pressing her hand over her mouth.

"No way," Emma said, her voice little more than air.

"Nickolas Talbot," the reporter continued speaking though Nick's picture remained on the screen. "The nineteen-year-old was last seen walking with an unidentified man, who reportedly had a handgun. We'll bring you more as this story develops."

"No," Ginger said. She needed more now. Right now. She scrambled for her phone, her heart beating out of control. She couldn't quite get enough air, and her fingers slipped on the phone.

"I'm calling him," Spencer said, but Ginger stabbed at her screen anyway.

The line rang on Spencer's phone, and he'd put it on speaker, so they could all hear. It rang and rang and rang. "This is Nick," his voicemail said.

Spencer tapped the red phone icon to hang up, and Ginger tried calling Nick too. Ringing. Same voicemail.

"We have to go to the mall," Ginger said, standing. She didn't have the mental capacity to fold up her chair or find her sandals, not right now.

"We can't go to the mall," Spencer said, jumping to his feet and darting in front of her.

"Why is he even at the mall?" Ginger didn't care if tears

made her weak, because she couldn't hold them back for another second.

Spencer engulfed her in an embrace, and Ginger wanted Nate to be the one standing in front of her, trying to get her to see reason.

A terrible, awful, horrifying thought crossed her mind.

Nate.

He'd rushed out of here like the devil himself was chasing him. Had he known Nick was in trouble? And if so, how?

He'd been talking on the phone. Perhaps he'd been talking to Nick.

"Come on," Jack said, and Ginger stepped away from Spencer. She wiped her eyes and kept her head down. She'd known her cowboys for years now, but she still didn't want to be seen as the weak girl-boss that cried over her cousin.

Ginger told herself it was okay to have feelings, and she bent to pick up the shopping bag she'd brought with all the crackers and chips.

"I've got it," Jack said. "Let's get back to the ranch and figure things out."

Ginger nodded and had taken three steps when she realized she didn't have a ride back to the ranch. "He took my truck."

"You can ride with me," Emma said, linking her arm through Ginger's and keeping her moving.

Numbness spread through her, and Ginger only made it to Emma's car because her friend had a hold on her arm.

"It's going to be fine," Emma said. "We'll get back to the ranch, and Nate will be there. I just can't see him taking your truck and fleeing."

Ginger's brain felt encased in quicksand, and she was sinking fast. She wanted to tell Emma that neither of them had believed that Hyrum had stolen a truck from the ranch either. They couldn't see him doing that, not when he'd told Ginger he loved her and hoped to be with her after he got fully released.

At least Nate hadn't done that.

"I have to call the Bureau," Ginger said, pure misery streaming through her. "If I don't...." She didn't even want to think about what might happen if she didn't. She could be arrested too, for helping an inmate escape.

She tapped to her favorites and chose number two. The only person higher than the Bureau of Prisons was Emma, and Ginger didn't recognize her life in that moment.

The line only rang once before someone answered with, "Bureau of Prisons, how may I direct your call?"

"I need to speak to Warden James Dickerson," Ginger said. "Immediately. My inmate at the Residential Reentry Center number two-four-seven-one-nine has fled."

"Hold please," the woman chirped, as if Ginger wanted to order a pepperoni pizza.

The Warden must've had a Bat-phone or something, because he came on the line only ten seconds later with, "Ginger? Nate's gone?" He sounded as stupefied as Ginger felt, and all she could do was nod.

Only when she realized that Warden Dickerson couldn't see her did she pull in a deep breath and get herself together. "Yes, sir," she said. "I need to report him as missing. He took my truck and his son." Her voice clamped around the last word, and she couldn't continue.

"How long ago?" the Warden asked.

She honestly didn't know. She could've been standing on the beach for an hour before she went to sit beside Emma. But then her parents would've arrived.

"Maybe fifteen minutes," she said. "Probably ten."

"License plate?"

Ginger rattled it off for him, and the call ended with him saying, "Stay at the ranch. I'm going to text you my personal number. If he comes back, I need you to call me instantly. Understand?"

"Yes, sir," she said miserably. She was never going to get another inmate from the BOP, and the ranch benefited from that money. She slouched into the passenger window thinking, *I never want another inmate from the BOP anyway. Never, never, never.*

Hours later, Ginger sat on the couch having given up trying to entertain the Unit Officers that had made the drive from River Bay. The local police had been at the ranch by the time Ginger and Emma had returned from the beach, but no one had seen Nate leave except Ginger.

She'd given them every detail she could remember, and they'd conveyed it all to their counterparts at the mall. Emma had tried to put on the news, but that only upset Ginger even more, and they'd sat in silence until the officers had arrived.

Emma had served coffee and leftover cookies from the night before. Ginger gave the same interview. They tried calling Nate and Nick, and neither one answered. The worry sitting in the bottom of Ginger's stomach felt like acid, and she couldn't get rid of it no matter how hard she tried.

A radio beeped, and a voice came from one of the officer's belts. "Be advised, we have the suspect's truck turning onto the road. Again, the suspect's truck with license plate four-seven-seven-alpha-charlie-beta-alpha has just turned onto the ranch road."

Ginger shot to her feet despite one officer saying, "Ma'am."

But a rush of adrenaline, combined with anger, had her marching toward the door and yanking it open. The radio beeped again and the same voice spoke, but Ginger couldn't hear it through the windstorm in her ears. She went out onto the front porch and right on down the steps as her truck came into view.

Her truck.

With Nate behind the wheel. Oh, boy, he was going to get it, and get it good. Her fingers clenched into fists as she stomped down the sidewalk.

Nate pulled past the gate and kept on coming, and every

regret Ginger had ever had in her life streamed through her. If she'd just have waited a few hours, he'd have come back. No one would've had to know he'd been gone.

Ginger realized then that he wasn't alone in the truck. Of course, she'd expect to see Connor. But she saw Nick too.

A sob wrenched itself from her throat, and she started running. Nate couldn't pull into the garage with all the police and prison vehicles in the driveway, and he simply parked behind one of them.

He got out of the truck with his hands up, calling, "I'm not armed. I came back. I'm not armed." He only took a few steps away from the truck before he dropped to his knees, his hand still straight up in the air,

Ginger wanted to rage at him, but Nick was getting out on the other side of the truck, and she raced toward him. "Nick."

"I'm okay," he said. "I'm fine." He caught her and held on, but the reunion was short lived as he turned to help Connor out of the vehicle. "Stay by me," he muttered to the little boy, his attention past Ginger and toward the house.

She turned and watched as no less than six armed men approached Nate with their weapons raised. She stepped in front of Connor and said, "Don't watch this, bud." She reached behind her and pressed his face into the back of her leg, because no one should have to see their father figure get pushed to the ground and handcuffed from behind while five other men pointed guns at him.

They hauled Nate to his feet, and when he came up, the

first thing he did was look at Ginger. "I'm sorry," he called. "I had to go, and I'm sorry. Nick will tell you everything." The officers wrenched him around, and Nate walked the way they wanted him to as they marched him over to a prison van and loaded him into the back of it.

Then the six of them stood there as if they didn't know what to do next.

Ginger sure didn't.

Slowly, she turned back to Nick, questions racing through her head. "Well?" was all she could get out.

"You should really have him tell you," Nick said. "It's so much better when he explains it."

"I don't think I have that option," Ginger growled.

"Yes, you do," Nick said, his dark eyes narrowing at her. "If you wanted to talk to him, they'd let you talk to him. All you have to do is ask." He bent and pick up Connor. "Come on, buddy. Let's go see if Emma has any cookies left or if those nasty prison guards ate them all."

Ginger watched him walk away, dumbfounded. Nasty prison guards? No explanation? He'd just flitted off to the mall to do who-knows-what and he was going to walk inside and ask for cookies as if nothing had happened?

She cast a look toward the prison van and the men guarding it. All it would take was one step to get her going in the right direction. The problem was, she didn't know if that one step should be toward Nate or toward the homestead.

So she didn't take it.

Couldn't take it.

CHAPTER SEVENTEEN

Nate went to the place inside his mind where only self-loathing lived. In this place, which was a small compartment in his mind that only existed of slate-gray walls, he didn't have to feel. He didn't have to think. He didn't have to listen to anyone, or wonder what would happen to him now.

He could just be.

When the back door of the van opened, Nate didn't even look toward it. Someone would come in and make a big sigh and tell him he'd screwed up. As if he didn't already know. And he hadn't just messed up with the Bureau. He'd seriously compromised Connor's safety, and he'd put Ginger in a no-win situation, and he honestly just wanted to go back to River Bay.

At River Bay, he knew who to be. He knew how to act. He knew what to eat, and what time that would happen. He knew how to stand at attention for count, and he knew how to count down the days until this entire nightmare would end.

Everything at the ranch had grown increasingly complicated. Maybe he simply wasn't cut out for a regular life.

The whiff of sunscreen and sand met his nose, and he got jolted out of the gray place. He looked up, and Ginger sat down across from him in the narrow space. Surprise filled him, and he actually looked to see if the guards were going to let them be in there alone.

The door drifted closed, but didn't latch, and Nate got his answer.

"Nick wouldn't tell you, would he?"

The whole way back from the storage facility where Nate had gone to pick up Nick, the young man insisted Nate should tell Ginger everything himself. Nate wanted to, but he also knew he'd be driving into the exact situation that had happened.

"I had to call the Bureau," Ginger said.

"I know." Nate nodded, wishing so many things could be different. But he'd spent plenty of time in his life wishing he'd have made a different decision. Done something just a little different. Taken a different way to work one day, or not answered the phone when Oscar had called the first time.

So many seemingly small things had brought his life to this point. Including a small thing like reaching out and holding Ginger's hand. He did that, surprised and amazed that she let him touch her.

She did pull away after only a few seconds, though, and Nate felt his world shift one more time that day.

"Okay," he said. "What'd they give you? Ten minutes?"

"Yes."

"And we've been sitting here for at least one." He drew in a deep breath. "So this is a nine-month story in nine minutes." He looked up and met her eyes, because he didn't want to be ashamed of himself anymore. And this particular thing wasn't illegal.

"I met Oscar Dominguez almost a year before I got indicted for investment fraud," he said. "We did a few minor deals together, mostly so he could test me. See how I handled his money, and if I paid him out on time. All of that."

Nate could easily see himself from seven years ago. Young. Thought he was hot stuff. Rich. Good-looking. He'd felt invincible.

"I did, and we worked together well. I made money on his investment; so did he. It was a win-win."

"This wasn't illegal?"

"Nope. All straight up investments. Lucrative. High-risk. But legal." He took another breath. "I'd put a larger amount of money into a pharmaceutical company for him, and it was going well. They got bought by one of the big giants, and we were all thrilled. I called to sell the stocks, which usually happened by the close of business. It did, and we were set to cash out. I had a dummy account for cash outs. That way, I could take my cut of the profits, and then transfer the rest to the client. It kept things neat." He sighed and leaned back, closing his eyes as he remembered the day. He could see it clearly in his head, as clearly as if it had just happened yesterday.

"It was raining that day in Austin," he said, his voice almost a ghost of itself. "I'd ducked under the eaves of a bakery when my phone dinged at me, because it was a notification of money. I saw we'd been cashed out, and all I needed to do was make the split and the deal would be done. Next thing I know, I'm shoved against the brick. My phone is gone. And I'm in handcuffs. I couldn't finish the cash out."

"So you've had the money all this time," she said.

"I do like how smart you are," Nate said with a smile. He opened his eyes and looked at Ginger, who did not smile back. "And yes. That money has sat in that dummy account all this time. I owed him just over twenty-six thousand dollars, and I've been paying him back in cash drops in a locker in the mall."

Ginger just stared at him, unblinking. He hated the look on her face, and he hated even more than he'd put it there. He could tell she felt stupid, tricked, betrayed.

"I'm sorry," he said. "My last drop was today, and we had this beach thing. I tried to move it, and Oscar wouldn't. So I asked Nick to make it for me."

"You put my cousin in danger."

"Oscar isn't—okay, yes." Nate didn't want to lie. Oscar Dominguez was absolutely dangerous if he didn't get his money. "It was a simple pick up and drop off."

"Obviously not."

"Oscar was watching the lockers," Nate said. "He didn't like that it was Nick and not me. They took him. I went to get him. We sorted it all out. We're done." He made it sound like he'd gone to pick Nick up from a birthday party or something simple. Going to the storage facility had been anything but simple, especially with Connor in the car.

"Listen," Nate said, leaning forward. "I'm sorry. I didn't mean for Nick to get hurt, which he didn't by the way. He was a little shook up, but he's fine. Not a bruise or a scrape on him. I didn't mean to take your truck. I didn't mean to keep this secret from you. I just...wanted to handle this myself, and it was fine."

"Until it wasn't."

"Until it wasn't," he conceded. "And listen, Ginger, they're going to take Connor from me. I'm going to have to go back to River Bay or somewhere like that." He leaned even closer to her. "Will you please take him? He knows you, and he loves you, and I'll come get him when I'm out, and you'll never see me again."

Ginger balked and leaned away from him, not quite the reaction he'd been hoping for. He chided himself for being so darn hopeful all the time. But he'd imagined a scene where Ginger leaned toward him too, and maybe cradled his face in her palm, and said, "I don't want you to go. When you get out, you'll come stay here with me and Connor."

Instead she asked, "Why can't your parents take him?"

"They just can't." Nate shook his head, his only concern for the child. "I'll ask Spencer."

"Really, Nate. Why can't your parents take him? Why did Ward name you as his guardian?"

"They're too elderly," he said. "My dad has a temper *and* colon cancer. My mom forgets things. A four-year-old paired with them would be a disaster."

The back of the van opened, and a Unit Officer stood there. Nate didn't know him, but he had a feeling they were going to be good friends. "Time's up, ma'am."

"Please," Nate whispered, reaching out and taking Ginger's hand again. He managed to get in one good squeeze before she pulled away.

"I can't believe I trusted you," she said.

"I'm sorry," Nate said again. The words weren't adequate, but they were all the Good Lord had given to humans. What else could Nate say? What else could he do?

He sat there and watched as Ginger climbed out of the van and walked away, his heart cracking right down the middle. In that moment, he knew he was in love with Ginger Talbot, but he was absolutely powerless to keep her in his life.

NATE GOT A FIFTEEN-MINUTE CALL EVERY OTHER DAY in Administrative Detention. He'd called Spencer the first day, as he'd received word that Connor had indeed stayed at

Hope Eternal Ranch. He'd gotten to speak to his nephew for thirteen minutes, where he tried to reassure the child that he'd be coming back for him soon.

Sooner than Nate even knew, as he'd been assigned a hearing to review his blunder with the Residential Reentry Center where he'd been assigned.

His second call went to Nick, who talked for most of the fifteen minutes about how he'd been calling everyone in the state of Texas about getting Nate out of prison and back on the ranch.

Apparently, the Talbots had some deep pockets if the right one got involved in something they were passionate about, and Nick had somehow bonded with Nate and wanted him and Connor to get their familial happily-ever-after.

He'd talked to Connor again a few times, and once he'd tried to call Ginger, but she wouldn't pick up his call. And that was all the answer he needed.

"You ready?"

Nate looked up at the deep voice of Warden Dickerson. "Yes, sir." He stood, the jangling of the handcuffs in the Warden's hands reminding Nate that he wasn't in Admin Detention because he was leaving the facility for a fun time on a ranch somewhere along the coastal bend of Texas.

He was going to the hearing, and he fully expected to get sentenced to finish out his original punishment of six years. He'd been shaving days off because of his good behavior for years, all to have it undone by one single act.

One single decision.

It was the right one, he told himself. He couldn't have lived with himself if Nick had been permanently injured—or worse. Ginger would've never forgiven him then.

She hasn't forgiven you now, he thought as the Warden opened the cell door.

"I don't need these, do I?" he asked, staring a hard look in Nate's direction.

"No, sir." He approached the warden, wishing so many things could be different.

"Nate," Dickerson said. "I've done everything I can for you. I don't know what will happen today."

"I know," Nate said. "I've drawn Billings." And he was the toughest judge in the county.

"He's got grandsons," Dickerson muttered. "All I'm saying is don't give up. You're a good man. You came in one person, and you're not him anymore. You did what we hope everyone will do when they come to prison."

"What's that?" Nate asked, surprised by this more human side of the warden. He'd never seen it before.

"You didn't leave the same way you came in."

Nate wanted to say he hadn't left yet, but he couldn't. He had left. He'd gone to Hope Eternal Ranch, and everything inside him wanted to go back there again. Brush down those horses. Pick up that hammer and fix the leaning wall of the bird blind. Hold Ginger's hand on that dusty road, and kiss her in the shade of those windfall trees.

A tiredness pulled through his whole body as he nodded. "Thanks, Warden. I'm sorry I made you look bad."

"Oh, you didn't," the warden said.

"Someone looked bad with what happened," Nate said.

"Yeah," Warden Dickerson said. "But not really. What we got to show the public was that our residential programs have failsafes in place, and the system works. Ginger called. We came. You got apprehended."

"I came back," Nate said dryly.

The Warden grinned and pocketed the handcuffs meant to go around Nate's wrists. "And it all worked out."

Sure, Nate thought. Everything seemed to work out for everyone but him. He knew that was his fault, though, and he was going to own the decisions he'd made that had gotten him to this point in his life.

They walked down the hall together, and the Warden handed Nate the cuffs at the exit. He couldn't go walking around the grounds without being restrained, but the Warden let Nate put the cuffs on himself, so they weren't terribly tight.

He rode to the courthouse, the sun reminding him that the world hadn't come to an end. He went inside through a side door, and he sat at the table with Lawrence, who looked at him with pinched lines around his eyes, almost a glare of annoyance though Nate kept his bills paid.

Nate didn't have to apologize to his lawyer, so he didn't. At the same time, he'd probably cost the man a lot of sleepless nights, so he leaned close to Lawrence and said, "I'm sorry, Lawrence. How are things going with the adoption?"

"They're on hold," Lawrence said. "Depending on what happens today, we'll see what I can do."

Nate nodded, and Judge Billings came through the corner door, and everyone rose. Nate had been in court many times, and he could stand and sit without specific direction from his brain. The judge read the issue at hand, and Lawrence stood up.

"I want to hear from Nathaniel," Judge Billings said. His eyes bored a hole into Nate's. "Step up to the mic, son."

It had been a very long time since anyone had called Nate "son," but he did what the judge asked. "You left the center with the child you've been entrusted with?"

"Yes, sir."

"Why?"

Nate held his head high as he related the same story he'd given to Ginger, and Nick, and the Warden. His Lawyer. His mother. Spencer. Ward, though his brother hadn't responded.

"So you went to rescue the person you'd drawn into your scheme?"

"It wasn't a scheme, Your Honor," Nate said. "This particular investment and payout was legal. It was Oscar who didn't want the full payment in one lump sum. I guess he can't move that much cash safely, and that is not my fault."

"We'll agree to disagree on that, Mister Mulbury," the

judge said, glancing down. "All right. Do you have anyone present in the courtroom today to speak for you?"

Nate didn't even have to check behind him. His parents wouldn't make such a long drive for a hearing like this. Bethany had her hands full. Nate was on his own, and he felt it more keenly in that moment than any other.

"No, sir," he said, his throat tightening.

"Yes, he does," someone said, and Nate spun around to see Warden Dickerson pushing his way into the courtroom.

"Warden, you can't be a character witness for an inmate," Judge Billings said.

"I'm not," the Warden said. He stepped to the side, and Ginger stood there.

Nate's heart swelled so big, it stuck in the back of his throat. That blasted hope that he hadn't managed to scrub from his soul ballooned, lighting up the room and making his spirits soar. Their eyes met, and time slowed to nothing. Everything fell away, and it was just Ginger and Nate. Nate and Ginger.

"What's your name, ma'am?" the judge asked.

Ginger cleared her throat and tugged on the hem of her pink blouse. She'd paired it with a black pencil skirt and a sensible pair of heels. She strode forward and said, "Ginger Talbot, sir. And I'm here as a character witness for Nathaniel Mulbury."

CHAPTER EIGHTEEN

Ginger worked to keep her hands at her sides instead of fidgeting with the folder she'd brought with her or adjusting her clothes. She'd already pulled down her already perfectly flat shirt.

She could feel the magnetism of Nate, and she also had to work not to turn and stare at him. Whispers ran through the courtroom, though there weren't very many people there.

"Ginger Talbot," the judge said. She couldn't remember his name, but he looked like a wise, no-nonsense man she wouldn't want to cross. "You own Hope Eternal Ranch, correct?"

"Yes, sir. Your Honor. Yes." She cleared her throat and wished she'd accepted the bottle of water the Warden had offered her. Her head spun, because she still couldn't believe she was here.

The judge peered over the top of his glasses at her. "Mister Mulbury worked at your ranch for almost four months, correct?"

"That's right," she said.

"Tell me about how it went." He settled back into his seat and crossed his arms.

Ginger took a deep breath and opened her folder. She and Emma had been up for the last two nights to prepare the contents in the folder. When Ginger had finally admitted that she couldn't go to work around the ranch as if she didn't know Nate had a hearing this afternoon, everyone had chipped in to help her.

"Nate is an excellent cowboy," Ginger said, her voice shaking the tiniest bit. She really didn't want the judge to know how she felt about Nate, but Spencer and Emma had told her that it was obvious she was in love with him.

"I only have to look at you for half a second to see how miserable you are," Emma said.

"Just go talk to him and get him back," Spencer had said.

"Everyone knows you're in love with him but you," Nick had told her.

The last month had been torture for Ginger, and she'd spent a lot of time walking the road she and Nate had used to stroll together, wondering where she'd gone wrong. Nick had finally texted her in all caps: *IT'S NOT WRONG TO FALL IN LOVE.*

She cleared her throat and continued with, "Not only that, but he stepped up to the challenge of becoming an instant father. He was always concerned about Connor, his four-year-old nephew, and I have several statements from the cowboys that he lived with about how Nate would sit with Connor in the bathroom while the boy bathed, reading to him from a paperback book, doing voices for the different characters."

She tried to breathe and focus on the letters that formed the words on the page in front of her. She did not want to cry in court, not in front of the judge. Certainly not in front of Nate. She'd never witnessed the reading during bath time, but it was just so Nate, and she wished she had.

"He always made sure Connor had what he needed, and most of what he wanted. We all helped take care of Connor on the ranch, and we've all grown to love him. But none as much as Nate, obviously." She shuffled her papers, because she had too much evidence, she was sure. "And Your Honor, Connor loves Nate with his whole heart."

She paused again, this time not caring that her voice had pitched up slightly. "Just this morning, when I went into his bedroom to tell him I was coming to speak for Nate, he said, 'Tell Daddy I love him.'"

Ginger settled her weight on one foot. "But that's just one side of Nate. He has a hard-working side too, which I'm sure if you asked his Unit Officers or Manager about, they'd tell you the same thing. He didn't get selected to work in the Unit Office because he was lazy. I assigned him to build new bird blinds on the ranch, something he'd never done before. When he showed me the finished product, it was perfect.

Only then did he admit that he'd rebuilt it four times to get it right."

She looked up, hoping the judge was actually listening. He looked one breath away from falling asleep. "Who does that? Who builds something four times just to make sure it's right?" She shook her head. "No one I've ever hired. They would've come to get me to ask a million questions, or they would've given up. Nate did neither. He figured it out."

She could sense she needed to wrap things up. "I put him in charge of our eleven-year-old riding program. He interacted with the children, worked with horses, and managed a ton of moving pieces." She closed the folder. "He's a great cowboy, Your Honor. I'd take him back at the ranch in a heartbeat. But he's more than a cowboy. He's a good father. He's a good friend. He's a good man."

Ginger nodded, because she didn't have anything else to say. "He was only trying to make things right with his past, so he could move forward into the future without the baggage. Don't we all have something we wish we could tie up so it can't weigh us down anymore? I know I do. The difference between Nate and I is that he's brave enough to do what it takes to cut ties with those things holding him back. I learned that from him, and I'm trying to do the same now so I can have a brighter, more hopeful future."

She backed up a step, wondering where she was supposed to go now.

"Are you finished?" the judge asked.

"Yes, sir." She turned when someone touched her arm,

and she let the Warden lead her to the first row of chairs behind the railing. Ginger's heel caught on the leg of one chair, and she almost fell. Instead, she just landed hard in the seat, but the embarrassment felt the same as a fall.

"Mister Brandt? Your argument?"

The lawyer at the table opposite of Nate's stood. "We have nothing, Your Honor. Nathaniel Mulbury was an exemplary inmate, and we believed him a perfect candidate for the RRC program." He glanced at Nate and his lawyer. "We still do."

"Your Honor," Nate's lawyer said, standing. "River Bay is over-crowded, and Mister Mulbury's been in Administrative Detention since his return to the facility. That's hardly ideal, and we request he be returned to Hope Eternal Ranch to finish out his sentence."

"Ah, the sentence," the judge said, and Ginger's stomach clenched. She'd emailed Greg several times, asking what could happen to Nate, and the bottom line was, he'd probably have to complete his whole sentence now. "Let's talk about that."

The judge started talking, and honestly, Ginger got lost in all the legal talk about sentences served and punishments given and accolades for good behavior and how that affected the sentence.

In the end, he said, "I'm ready to make my ruling."

Nate stood up, as did his lawyer. Everyone in the courtroom seemed to be holding their breath, Ginger included.

"Mister Mulbury, I don't see you as a flight risk, nor do I

believe you were fleeing when you took Miss Talbot's truck. I think if Miss Talbot will have you back, you should go." He looked down at his paperwork. "Let's see, you were doing a reentry program of six months there. You were there for nearly four...back for one...."

He sighed like this whole proceeding was just too taxing. "I can't just look the other way when you've broken the number one rule of the reentry program. So, Mister Mulbury, do you think you can handle six more months at Hope Eternal Ranch?"

"Yes, Your Honor," he said. "I can handle that."

"Miss Talbot?" the judge asked. "Can you handle having this man at your ranch?"

"I think so," she said, excitement parading through her. She tamped it down, because she didn't think it would be appropriate to squeal in court. It definitely wouldn't do to kiss him either.

So Ginger stood very still while Nate and his lawyer exited the courtroom, and then she went with the Warden.

"Thank you for coming," Warden Dickerson said as they left the courtroom. "I think you made all the difference."

"I doubt it," Ginger said, looking over her shoulder. "So now what?"

"Now we process him, and then he'll be ready to go back to the ranch."

"How long does that take? The processing."

"A couple of days."

Ginger thought of Connor and Spencer, waiting for her at the hotel where they'd all stayed last night. They could stay for a couple of days. She could probably use the time to get the words of her apology in order anyway.

"Watch, Ginger," Connor said, and Ginger was beginning to think the child didn't know any other words. She looked up from her phone and employed her patience. He watched her for an extra moment to make sure she was watching him, and then he jumped into the pool.

Again.

She'd taken him to the beach again yesterday, but today, he said he was fine with just going to the pool. Ginger had brought her tablet and her wireless keyboard so she could at least go through the end-of-month statements for the ranch. She also had to submit all the items for the payroll by the fifth, and that was tomorrow.

She grinned at the little boy when he came bobbing up out of the pool. "Nice one, bud," she called to him, wishing Spencer hadn't met a woman at the beach yesterday and asked her to breakfast. It wasn't like their relationship would last through the weekend, since he lived and worked hours from River Bay.

But neither he nor Cassandra seemed to care about that. He'd promised he'd be back by lunchtime, but Ginger had her doubts.

A sigh slipped through her lips as she tried to focus back on her screen. Her attention had been wandering after only a few seconds for days now, and she still hadn't heard anything from the River Bay facility, Nate's lawyer, or Nate himself.

She told herself it had only been a day and a half, and she could stay in the hotel as long as necessary. The ranch waited only a few hours southwest of here, and Ginger could easily take everyone home too. But she wanted to be here—and Connor had to be with her—the moment she got the call.

In her experience, the BOP didn't usually call until things were already in motion, and that didn't allow for a three-hour drive. She didn't want Nate to have to wait one more moment to be reunited with Connor, and selfishly, she wanted to see him as soon as possible too.

She glanced at her phone, but it didn't ring or flash. No messages. No calls. Nothing.

"Watch, Ginger," Connor called, and Ginger looked toward the little boy. He sat on the side of the pool now and started kicking his legs and churning up the water when he was sure she was looking at him.

"Wow," she said, infusing a lot of false enthusiasm into her voice. "Go faster, Connor."

His face scrunched in concentration as he tried to make his little legs move quicker. Ginger giggled at him and added, "Don't hurt yourself, Connor."

The splashing stopped, and Ginger practically lunged

toward her phone when it rang. But it wasn't Greg or Lawrence or Warden Dickerson. "Hey, Emma," she said, still using that fake tone. "What's up?"

"I don't want you to freak out," Emma said, and that caused Ginger to start freaking out. "But, Jack just called in to say that Scalloped Potato was lying down in her stall this morning."

"She's going into labor," Ginger said immediately. Her adrenaline kicked into gear at the same time her stomach dropped to the pool deck.

"We think so," Emma said. "Okay, that was a lie. Jack is sure of it. He's called the vet, and they'll be here in twenty minutes."

"It's fine," Ginger said, wondering if she was going to use a normal voice at all today. "Can you get out there when it's time and video chat me? I want to see the foal so I can name it." Ginger liked to be present for all equine births on the ranch, because she could tell a foal's personality before she named them. And she named all of them.

"Of course," Emma said. "I was just going to suggest that."

"How long do you think?"

"Jack didn't say. I'll call you back."

"Thanks, Em." Ginger hung up and let her phone fall to her lap while she watched Connor start to talk to another little boy that had arrived at the pool. The chair beside Ginger scraped, and another mom sat down.

"How old is your son?" she asked.

Ginger glanced at her and then Connor, trying to decide if this woman needed to know that Connor wasn't her son. She really didn't. "Four," Ginger said.

"Mine too," she said. "We're from Chicago."

"Oh, great," Ginger said, though she wasn't particularly great at small talk. She just wanted the BOP to call. The two little boys played well together, and Ginger went back to her books on the screen.

She worked steadily through the financial reports, and everything looked like it was in order. They'd sold an extraordinary amount of hay last month, and Ginger had more money in her ranch account than she'd had in a while.

Turning her attention to the payroll, she simply selected everything and kept the wage the same as last month. She had to go through the extra timecards and the overtime, but those typically weren't too time-consuming.

"Watch, Ginger," Connor called, and she looked up from her work. Both boys stood on the pool deck now, and they took a few steps toward the edge of the pool and jumped in, creating double splashes.

The mom next to her started clapping, and she whooped for her son as he came out of the water. Ginger realized she had no idea how to be a mom, though if what she wanted to happen with Nate actually happened, she'd be Connor's stepmother.

She opened her mouth to tell Connor how amazing his jump was when someone said, "That was amazing, bud."

She knew that voice.

Ginger turned toward Nate, shock moving through her so fast it rendered her immobile.

"Dad!" Connor ran toward Nate, though running wasn't allowed in the pool area.

Nate chuckled as the two embraced, and Ginger felt the vibrations of that laugh way down deep in her soul. She stood up, practically throwing her tablet to the cement. She managed to put it in the seat she'd just vacated, her heart pounding so hard it entered every organ.

Nate said something to Connor she didn't hear, and the little boy nodded. Only then did Nate turn his attention to Ginger.

He looked different somehow, but she couldn't pinpoint why. He wore jeans and a T-shirt—what anyone would wear. He looked clean, his brown hair swooping to the side while those intense eyes drank her right up.

"What are you doing here?" she asked, glancing toward the door. "Who brought you? Do you—?" She cut off, suddenly remembering they weren't alone at the pool. She couldn't look away from Nate, though, to see if the other mom was watching or listening. Of course she was.

"I'll tell you later." Nate set Connor down. "Go jump in and show me how you can swim," he said, and Connor ran off.

Ginger felt frozen though the sun was plenty hot already this morning. She met Nate's eyes as he focused back on her, and it seemed like both of them moved toward each other at the same time.

He took her easily into his arms, and whispered, "I missed you so much."

"I'm so sorry," she said as they started to sway together.

"Thank you for coming to the hearing." His lips caught on the bottom of her earlobe, and icy shivers ran through Ginger's body.

"I'm in love with you," she whispered.

Nate lifted his head and looked at her, a dozen things storming through his bright blue eyes. "I love you, too."

And finally, finally, he kissed her, and everything in Ginger's life suddenly made perfect sense.

CHAPTER NINETEEN

Nate had never told a woman he loved her, and he'd never kissed a woman he loved. He'd just done one and was currently doing the other, and he'd never known such joy. How an amazing woman like Ginger could love him, Nate didn't understand.

But he believed it, because he could feel it in her kiss.

He'd seen the other woman sitting beside Ginger at the pool, so he didn't kiss her as long as he wanted to. He couldn't believe the Warden had said he could walk through the hotel to the pool by himself, but he had. Apparently, the guy who owned this hotel used to work at River Bay as a Unit Manager, and when he'd retired from the prison system, he'd bought the hotel. He'd called to say Connor and Ginger were at the pool, and the Warden had simply let Nate get out of the car and walk inside.

No one had looked at him. No one could tell he'd been in prison just by looking at him.

"I have to be back at the ranch tonight," he said. "It's part of the release paperwork."

"Do you have that paperwork?" Ginger asked, turning in his arms and leaning into his body. She kept her arms wrapped around his waist as they watched Connor adjust his goggles and dive under the water again.

"Yes," Nate said. "I set it on the table back there."

"So six more months," Ginger said.

"I'm actually hoping for longer than that," he said.

"You have always been quite hopeful," she teased, and Nate liked that there was absolutely no tension between them. No need for more apologies. No wordy declarations. "My hopeful cowboy."

"Thank you for forgiving me."

"Thank you for forgiving *me*," she repeated. "We'll go as soon as Spencer gets back."

"Where is he?"

"You're never going to believe this," she said. "But he met a woman at the beach yesterday, and they went to breakfast."

Nate laughed, and the sound was glorious and wonderful, and Nate wanted to laugh this freely every day for the rest of his life. "Sounds like Spencer."

"Right?" Ginger nodded toward the chair she'd been sitting in. "I was just getting my payroll done."

"Go finish it," Nate said. "I'll go sit with Connor." He

pressed his lips to her temple, and Ginger stepped over to the chair and picked up her tablet. Nate stepped out into the sun and said, "Connor, show me how you float on your back."

LATER THAT NIGHT, AFTER THEY'D PACKED AND LOADED Ginger's truck, after they'd driven back to Hope Eternal Ranch, after Nate had been out to the stables to see the horses he'd left behind, he picked up his cowboy hat and said, "Come on, Connor. We're eatin' next door tonight."

Somehow, everyone else had left the Annex without him and Connor, so Nate took the little boy's hand and led him out the back door, across the deck, and down the stairs to the grass. "What did you and Ginger do while I was gone?"

"I got to sleep in Spencer's room," Connor said, though Nate already knew that. He'd spent some time this afternoon gathering all the little boy things from Spencer's bedroom and thanking the man profusely.

"Yep," Nate said. "And what else?"

"One time, Jack took me on the four-wheeler."

"Did you like it?"

"Yep."

"What did you eat?"

"Dad, Emma made grilled peanut butter sandwiches." Connor danced in front of Nate, his face animated with wide eyes. "Can you believe it? They were so good, and maybe she'll make them again."

"Maybe I can ask her how she did it, and then I can make them." He wasn't sure how to make the two pieces of bread stick together if the peanut butter melted, but Emma would tell him.

"But you have to use the right kind of bread," Connor said.

Nate smiled at his drama. "Yeah? What kind of bread is that?"

"It's the blue bag bread."

"Oh, the blue bag bread." They climbed the steps to the back porch of the West Wing, and Nate reached over the top of Connor's head to knock on the door before they went inside. With the door open, Nate couldn't hear anything, and that immediately alerted him that something wasn't right inside.

His heartbeat stuttered, but he kept moving. Connor skipped ahead of him, clearly not concerned by the silence inside. But Nate was. He'd never been to the West Wing where there weren't at least two women talking and laughing. Never.

He rounded the corner to enter the kitchen, and he took in the group of people all standing together across the room, facing him. "Welcome home!" they shouted as a single unit, and Nate stalled.

He couldn't stop smiling, especially as Emma went over

the pizza on the counter, the macaroni salad—"Your favorite," she said—and the giant chocolate-frosted cake.

"Thank you," he said. "Thank you all."

Everyone seemed genuinely happy to see him, and while that was somewhat difficult for Nate to believe, he'd never known any of the men or women here at Hope Eternal to be fake. He enjoyed dinner, with all of the chatter and laughter he'd come to expect from the West Wing.

"Let's go, Connor," Spencer said, and Nate lifted his head from the conversation he'd been having with Jack and Jessica. "I'm gonna take him back. Is that okay?"

"Sure," Nate said. "You sure?"

"We're both tired, huh, bud?" Spencer grinned down at Connor.

"Can Ursula come?"

"If you can get her to come, she can come." Spencer glanced down the table to where Ginger sat, Ursula at her feet. In the end, Connor couldn't convince the dog to come with him, and Ginger promised to bring her over later so she could sleep with Connor.

Spencer and Connor left, and the party broke up in little pieces after that. Nate felt like he could sleep for a year, but he didn't want to leave without kissing Ginger. Now that he knew he loved her, he wanted to be at her side all the time.

"Go," Emma finally said, and Ginger tossed down the wash rag she'd been using to wipe the counter. She met Nate's eyes, and he started for the back door. Behind him,

Ursula barked, and then she came out of the house with Ginger.

"Walk with me?" Nate asked, reaching for Ginger's hand. She slipped her fingers between his, and Nate sighed. "Thanks for that dinner."

"Oh, that was Emma."

"I know, but you let her."

"Did you hate it?" She looked at him with a bit of apprehension in her expression.

"No," he said. "You thought I'd hate it?"

"You don't really like crowds."

"No, I don't." He gazed up into the clear, night sky. He loved how dark it was out here, and how the stars seemed to be caught in this wide, black net. "But I like the people here, and I could eat that cake every day of my life."

"Emma is a genius with butter and flour," Ginger said.

Nate sighed, relaxing more and more the farther from the homestead they walked. He took her down the road where they'd shared their first kiss, the silence between him and Ginger so soothing.

"I'm so glad to be back," he said. "I really am sorry I left. I'm sorry I involved Nick. I'm—"

"Nate, you don't owe me any apologies," Ginger said.

Nate nodded. "Sometimes the apologies aren't for the person receiving them," he said. "So can I just finish them?"

"All right."

"I'm sorry I asked you to take care of Connor. You're amazing for doing it, but it wasn't fair." He pressed his teeth together, making his jaw jut out. "I'm sorry I put you through all of this, and I'm hopeful that once the six months are up, that you'll consider hiring me on full-time here."

"This is what you want? I thought you were going to go live in Ward's house in White Lake."

"I belong here," he said simply. "And if you'll have me, I'd love to stay."

"I'd love for you to stay," she said. "And Nate, we should probably talk about you know, what we said earlier."

"Which part?"

"Oh, come on." Ginger rolled her eyes by the light of the moon, and Nate's heart softened toward her again.

"You mean the part where I said I was in love with you?"

"Yeah," she said. "That part."

"You think I was lying?"

"No," she said. "I'm just wondering what you think the next step *for us* is."

Nate had been thinking about Ginger nonstop since he'd been pushed to the ground and re-arrested in front of her. For weeks now. Weeks.

"Well, I think most people get married," he said, watching her closely.

She nodded, and he didn't detect any apprehension in her. "And that's something you want to do?"

Nate let a smile spread across his face. "With you, Ginger, it's exactly what I want to do." He leaned down and kissed her, feeling her melt right into him, and for once, his reality was much better than what he'd imagined from the inside of his prison cell.

———

THE DAYS, WEEKS, AND THEN A FEW MONTHS PASSED. Nate enjoyed working around the ranch as much now as he had the very first time he'd entered the stables.

Connor turned five one week and started kindergarten the next. Nate, still in the reentry program, couldn't go pick him up alone, so he and Ginger made the drive together. They talked about everything, from Ginger's favorite horse on the ranch to whether she wanted children or not.

Both she and Nate did, but he hadn't asked her to marry him yet. He didn't want to get married as an inmate, and he still had two months left of his six-month sentence in the Residential Reentry Program. But he couldn't go ring shopping by himself, and he didn't want Ginger along for that ride.

Spencer had offered to go with him, and Nick had actually taken him to the mall and said, "Let's get her a ring today," one day near Thanksgiving. But Nate wasn't in the right mental state, and for some reason, he wanted to take Connor and have the two of them pick out the ring for Ginger together.

He still got the mail most days for the ranch, that walk out to the mailbox one of his favorites.

Just after Thanksgiving, he opened the mailbox and

pulled out a very large, white envelope. His heart fell to his boot tips and rebounded back to its rightful place in his chest. He flipped the envelope over and saw the seal from Lawrence's law firm.

All the other mail forgotten, Nate focused only on the envelope. It had his name on it, and he ripped it open, his mouth beyond dry. He pulled out the sheaf of paperwork and started reading the cover letter, which had been printed on ultra-soft paper that almost reminded Nate of cotton.

Congratulations Nate and Connor! the letter began.

Tears burned behind his eyes as he continued to read that his adoption of Connor had been approved by the state of Texas, and they had a hearing to attend in two and a half weeks, just before Christmas.

He hurried to put everything back in the envelope, his excitement multiplying exponentially as his fingers shook. He left the rest of the mail, and he didn't even know if he'd closed the mailbox as he jogged back to the homestead.

Ginger wasn't there, and Nate pulled out his phone and called her. "Hey," he said when she answered. "So I'm going to need Tuesday, December twentieth off."

"What?" Ginger asked.

"You'll need to clear your calendar too," he said.

"Nate, is that your release date?"

"No," he said, and he couldn't imagine what that kind of relief and joy would feel like. Right now, he felt like he was flying on clouds, and he chuckled as he said. "It's the hearing date Connor and I have to finalize the adoption."

"You're kidding," Ginger said, the words mostly air.

"I'm not," Nate said, letting his laughter out. "And I want you there. Connor will want you there."

"I'll be there," Ginger said. "Of course I'll be there."

"Thank you," Nate said. "Is Connor with Nick in the stables?"

"He's with Nick, but they're out in the fields," Ginger said. "I can call him."

"No, it's okay," Nate said. "I'll tell him when I see him this afternoon." Connor always came to help with the riding lessons in the afternoon, and he and Nate spent the afternoons and evenings together, sometimes working and sometimes just going back at the Annex.

"We should go celebrate tonight," Ginger said.

"Sweetheart, I can't eat more Chinese food." He made sure his voice carried a tease, but he was being dead serious.

Ginger pealed out a string of laughter that made Nate's heart happy, and then she asked, "What about a nice, juicy steak?"

"Oh, now you're talking my language."

"Pick me up at six?"

"Absolutely," he said. "I can ask Nick to babysit Connor so we can go alone." Nate had plenty of opportunities to see Ginger alone, and he exploited them as much as possible. The woman had lips he sure did like to kiss, and she didn't seem to mind when he took her hand and hurried her around to the back of the barn so he could do so.

"This is about the two of you," Ginger said. "He should come."

"Good point."

"All right," she said. "See you tonight."

"Love you," he said.

"Love you too, my hopeful cowboy."

Nate ended the call and tipped his head back to look up into the sky. "Thank you," he murmured, not sure if he was talking to God or to his brother. His hope grew and grew, and he hoped he could be the kind of father Connor deserved. He hoped he could be a good husband for Ginger. He hoped he would always be full of hope and dreams, and that he could work hard enough to make them come true.

"First, the adoption," he said. "Then my release. Then—get a ring on Ginger's finger."

CHAPTER TWENTY

The weeks until Connor's adoption hearing flew by, as December was a very busy time around ranches in Texas. It was birthing season, and most of Ginger's cowboys went to neighboring cattle ranches to help with all of that, and that left Hope Eternal shorthanded.

Ginger worked from sunup to sundown—and beyond, as the sun set a bit earlier than usual in the winter time.

Nate didn't go anywhere, and together, they kept the ranch going, and Ginger couldn't wait until February or March. Of course, then there was something new to be done around the ranch.

The morning she needed to be ready to accompany Nate and Connor to court, she fed the horses with Emma, who rarely came out onto the ranch. But dire circumstances required everyone with even one good leg and one good arm to help out.

Emma didn't hate working around the ranch, but she much preferred observing it from behind the safety of the windowpane. Not only that, but Emma really couldn't handle the heat. Thankfully, this close to Christmas, the sun's heat wasn't really an issue. At least not yet.

Ginger moved steadily down the right side of the stable while Emma fell rapidly behind on the left side. The ranch housed and cared for over seventy horses, and Ginger had never fed them all by herself.

That morning, she very nearly did, though Emma helped and Nate worked in the next aisle over. Ginger didn't often get a chance to just bend and empty yesterday's buckets, get new ones, check on every animal. She thought she needed to take a shift in these stables more often, but overseeing the ranch required almost all of her energy.

After a few hours of checking, feeding, and watering, an alarm went off on her phone.

"Time to go," Emma said, straightening and stretching her back. "I can finish."

"There's just three left," Ginger said, silencing the alarm.

"I can do it." Emma flashed her a smile and stepped over to give Ginger a hug. "I hope it goes well today. Call me as soon as it's done."

"I will." Ginger clung to her best friend, so glad she'd been able to convince Emma to come out to Hope Eternal all those years ago. She did like living off the beaten path too, so it hadn't really taken all that much convincing.

Emma nodded after she stepped back, and Ginger headed for the rectangle of bright light that signaled the doorway. Her nerves weren't cut out for court hearings, she knew that. She'd only been to the one, but it had taken a miracle to get herself dressed that morning. If Connor hadn't been there, looking at Ginger with those wide, hopeful eyes, she might not have gone.

She honestly didn't know.

But she was going to go today, and she looked left as soon as she exited the stable. Only a moment later, Nate came out, peeling his gloves from his hands. "Ready?" he asked.

"Ready to go get changed," she said. "Where's Connor?"

"He should be at the Annex," Nate said. "I told him to stay in bed when he woke up. We put Pop-tarts and his dinosaurs on the bedside table last night."

Ginger grinned as Nate reached her. He bent down and kissed her, smelling like horses and oats and leather. She loved the sight of him, the smell of him, the taste of him.

"Mm," he said, pulling away. "Come on. He's probably been awake for about fifteen minutes."

"I guess you'll know by how many crumbs he has in the bed."

Nate groaned. "This was a bad idea."

"But we got the horses fed," Ginger said as they started back toward the house. "Emma will finish, and she'll get the chickens taken care of too."

"We should stop and get her one of those bundt cakes she likes."

"She'd like that," Ginger said, impressed that Nate remembered Emma liked the miniature bundt cakes from a shop that didn't make anything else. "She really doesn't like working on the ranch."

"We'll get her two then," he said. "Because she had to help so we could go to court." He reached for her hand and squeezed it tight, a clear indication of his nerves.

"It's going to be okay," Ginger said. "It's all approved."

"I've never been to an adoption hearing," Nate said.

"Neither have I, and neither has Connor. It'll be okay." Ginger had to keep telling herself that as they separated to go to their respective parts of the house to get ready. Twenty minutes later, Ginger hurried down the steps and into the garage. Nate and Connor waited in her truck, both of them wearing dark suits, complete with a white shirt and matching striped tie in blue, maroon, and gold.

"Wow," Ginger said, sliding behind the wheel. "You two match."

"Daddy bought us the same suit," Connor said. "But mine is small."

"It sure is." Ginger grinned at the little boy, whose blond hair had been buzzed into a respectable cut only a few days ago. He'd sat in the kitchen in the West Wing while Jess used the clippers and then the scissors to get his hair just right. She'd then cut Nate's hair too, and they both looked clean-cut and respectable.

HOPEFUL COWBOY   243

Ginger drove them to the county courthouse, where they went through the metal detectors and then into the elevator to go to the fourth floor, where the courtrooms were for family court. There was nowhere to sit on the fourth floor, and Nate paced toward the window and back several times before Ginger took his hand in hers and forced him to stand still.

Some people already milled about, and more kept coming and coming. Ginger realized in that moment that this was not going to be a private hearing, and she wondered if the judge would know Nate wasn't quite out of prison yet. Her stomach jiggled and dropped, but she said nothing. He was already keyed up, and she didn't need to add to it.

"Where is he?" Nate asked, craning to look at the elevator bank. His lawyer was supposed to be there that morning, but they hadn't seen him yet.

"He'll be here," Ginger said. Lawrence might wear snakeskin sometimes, but he did a good job. He'd always done right by Nate, and surely he'd arrive any minute now.

Finally, the door opened to courtroom seven, their assigned courtroom, and a bailiff came out into the hall. "We've got our ten-thirty group entering," he said, stepping back. "Any requests to go first?"

"We'd like to go first," a man said, and Nate made a startled noise. "It's the Mulbury adoption."

"That's Lawrence," Nate said, but Ginger had spotted him on her own. "I didn't even see him." He released Ginger's hand, and said, "Come on, bud," to Connor, scooping him into his arms a moment later. He hurried toward the door and Lawrence, and by the time Ginger made it through the press of people to one of the rows inside the courtroom, Nate, Connor, and Lawrence sat at the front table.

"Guess we're going first," she muttered, taking a seat on the end of the row as the bailiff kept telling everyone to move down. Keep moving down.

People filled the room, and Ginger was suddenly glad Lawrence had stepped up and demanded to go first. At the same time, Ginger wished she had a moment to catch her breath, and she'd like to have seen how this procedure worked before it was Nate and Connor on the hot seat.

She reminded herself that she didn't need to know the procedure here. That was why Nate paid Lawrence.

Once everyone was settled, a silence descended on the room. At least until the door in the back opened, and out came two women. Everyone scrambled to their feet to show respect. One woman took her place in a booth on floor-level, and the other sat behind the bench.

"Ready, Randy?" she asked, a smile on her face.

The bailiff grinned back at her. "Everyone's here, ma'am."

"And we have our first case already seated," she said, gesturing to Lawrence, Nate, and Connor. "So I guess we're ready."

"The Mulbury's," Randy said, before turning to the

courtroom. "This is courtroom seven, with the honorable Judge Denise Jerry. You're up, sir."

Lawrence stood up and asked the judge how she was. "Fine," she drawled, still shuffling papers on her bench.

"All of our paperwork is in order," Lawrence said. "There was no contest from Jane Copeland, Connor Mulbury's birth mother. No contest from any of her family members, or any of Nathaniel's. Both Connor and Nate want to form this family unit and start new when the time comes."

The judge looked up, first at Lawrence and then to Nate and Connor. "Sir, please stand up."

Nate did, quickly buttoning his suit coat jacket. He nudged Connor, who also stood up. Nate smoothed his hair and they both faced the judge again. "Your Honor."

"This is your late brother's son?"

"Yes, Your Honor."

"His will named you the legal guardian, with specific instructions to adopt Connor as soon as you could."

"Yes, Your Honor."

She looked down at her papers again, a tiny crease appearing between her eyebrows. Ginger pulled in a breath and held it.

"You're still in state custody," the judge finally said.

"Yes, ma'am. Until February seventeenth."

"You're at Hope Eternal Ranch?"

Ginger glanced away from the bench when Nate didn't answer. He was bent over whispering something to Connor.

He straightened, and Connor said, "Yes, Your Honor. We live at Hope Eternal Ranch."

A collective "aw" rose into the air, and Ginger's heart swelled with so much love for him.

"Who's responsible for you there?" Judge Jerry asked.

"My dad," Connor said, looking up at Nate. "And Spencer. And Jack. And Nick. There's Emma, Jess, Jill, and Ginger too. And so many horses, and—" He stopped when Nate put his hand on the top of his head, and several people in the courtroom chuckled.

Including the judge. "So you have a lot of people looking after you."

"And Ursula," Connor said.

"And you, Mister Mulbury?"

"I report to Ginger Talbot, ma'am. She reports to the BOP."

"Did Miss Talbot come with you?"

"Yes, ma'am." Nate turned toward the audience, his eyes searching for her.

Ginger hadn't realized she'd need to be part of the proceedings. She stood up, lifting her right hand halfway as if everyone wasn't looking at her now.

The judge gestured for Ginger to join Nate and Connor at the small table on the other side of the short wall keeping the audience back from the podium. She made it to the table and reached down and pressed her palm flat against the wood, using it to steady herself.

"Your reports have been favorable," Judge Jerry said, clearly a prompt.

"Yes, Your Honor," she said, her voice scratchy. "Nate is such an excellent cowboy, I'm hoping to hire him on permanently once he's eligible."

She shuffled some more papers, which seemed to take a very long time. "And young man Connor. You want your Uncle Nate to be your father?"

He looked up at Nate, who nodded a couple of times. "Yes," Connor said.

"Anything to add, Mister Matthews?"

"Only that Nathaniel is capable and ready for this responsibility, Your Honor. He's already been doing it for months now."

"Yes," the judge mused. She finally closed the folder and looked up. "All right. I see no reason for the two of you not to be a family. I'm signing this now to make this a legal adoption, and to make things even easier, no one has to change any names." She beamed out at them, and Nate did something Ginger had never seen him do before.

He whooped and picked up Connor, who laughed as he looked down at his new father.

Ginger wanted to commit this moment to memory, because it was so full of joy and so precious.

"You can have two minutes for a picture," the bailiff said. "We're ready for the Jacobsen's." He stepped over to the separating wall and Ginger moved forward with

Lawrence. They stood back while Nate and Connor posed by the judge.

Ginger snapped pictures, the smiles now captured digitally forever.

Then they left the courtroom. Nate clapped Lawrence on the back of his shoulder, and said, "Thank you."

"Anytime," Lawrence said with a big smile. "I'll see you in a couple of months." He held up one palm. "Not a day before, okay, Nate? I don't want to see you until February."

"Deal," Nate said. They watched Lawrence leave, and Nate finally turned his attention to Ginger. He burst out laughing again, and he wrapped his arms around her and lifted her right off her feet. She giggled with him, and Nate bent to pick up Connor. "Come on," he said. "This calls for the biggest ice cream cone in Texas, and I know just where to get one."

"Yeah!" Connor cheered, and it was a good long while before Ginger could stop smiling.

CHAPTER TWENTY-ONE

Nate threw his cowboy hat into the air along with the other people wearing hats as the cheers went up and the clock clicked to midnight. "Happy New Year!" chorused through the West Wing, and Nate raised his voice along with the others.

He slipped his arm around Ginger's waist and pulled her into his body before he kissed her. They laughed together, and the kiss was pretty sloppy. But it didn't matter. Nate finally felt like his future held more than sleeping in a dormitory with a bunch of other men.

This year, he'd be free.

This year, he could start a new life.

This year, he would learn how to be a better father—and hopefully a husband.

He hugged Nick and wished him a Happy New Year. Everyone went around, laughing and talking and embracing.

Nate had never been part of such of tight-knit community, and he sure did like it. He didn't want to leave Hope Eternal, and he and Ginger had started talking about life after February seventeenth.

The date felt impossibly far away but also very, very close. He had no diamond ring to give to Ginger. He wasn't sure where they'd live, as they both currently had a room in a house filled with other people. He wanted to talk to Connor and find out how he felt about Ginger being his stepmother.

He wanted to go visit his parents and his sister in White Lake, and he wanted to be more involved in their lives. He wanted Connor to have them in his life.

He needed a vehicle of his own, and he wanted to go through Ward's house and see what had been left there. All of Nate's personal property from his life before should be at Ward's. He wasn't even sure he'd want any of it, but he wanted to see what there was.

Ward had once gone through Nate's apartment and boxed up what he deemed important. Now Nate would have to do the same for his older brother, his hero.

If he thought too hard about it, his chest started to collapse and Nate couldn't quite remember how to breathe.

His smile faltered, and he suddenly felt so tired. Cowboys didn't stay up until midnight, that was for dang sure. Not when their chores started by six the next morning.

So he kissed Ginger again, this time not as sloppily, and went down the hall to the front room, where the girls had a piano and a small loveseat. Connor slept there, his face smashed into the upholstery. Nate smiled down at him, slipped the little boy into his arms, and disappeared out the front door to the quiet night beyond.

In the Annex, he took Connor into their bedroom and laid him on his side of the bed. Nate went to brush his teeth and change into his pajamas, and as he looked at himself in the mirror, he hardly recognized the man looking back at him. His skin had tanned in the moths he'd been working on the ranch. His eyes almost seemed electric, because they possessed a quality he hadn't been sure he'd ever feel again.

Happiness.

No, joy.

He had gone into prison as one man, and he'd come out a different one. A better one. "A hopeful one," he said to his reflection. He reached up and ran his hand through his hair, which had just started to grow out from his cut from a couple of weeks ago.

He couldn't believe how much his life had changed in the last six months. Heck, in the last six years, Nate had grown more than he thought possible.

He was sure he was going to make stupid decisions again, but he hoped they wouldn't have such devastating consequences. "I'm going to do my best, Ward," he said. "I am. I'm going to do my best with Connor."

The sweetest feeling of peace moved through him, and Nate turned and went back into the bedroom. He lay down on the other side of the bed from Connor, a powerful sense of relief moving through him. He listened to Connor's steady, deep breathing, a smile dancing through his soul, before he fell asleep.

"ALL RIGHT," NATE SAID, STEPPING INTO THE JEWELRY store and stopping immediately. "We only have a few minutes. Have you got that list?" He loked down at Connor as a salesman came toward them. Thankfully.

"Yep." Connor held up the lined, yellow paper Nate had scrawled a few notes on. He and Connor had been slipping questions into normal conversation with Ginger for the past few weeks to find out what kind of ring she might like.

He'd learned she didn't like anything too big or gaudy. Connor had learned she liked gold more than silver. Nate had asked Emma about the cut on the diamond, and learned that Ginger liked the sparkliest things.

Nate could use the Internet, and he'd learned about a brilliant diamond with the most shiny facets—the Gassan diamond. He wanted that one, and he wanted it to be simple.

"Good morning," the salesman said. "My name is Chandler. What are you looking for today?"

Connor looked at Nate, and Nate looked at Connor. "An engagement ring," he said, a smile immediately following the words. "And we have a list." He nodded to the boy, and Connor handed it to Chandler.

HOPEFUL COWBOY   253

"Oh, okay." Chandler grinned at Connor, and then he focused on the list. "Something small, but expensive. Princess or brilliant cut. Gold band. Simple. Gassan diamond." He lifted his eyes to Nate's, his eyebrows going right up too. "A Gassan diamond is *very* expensive, sir."

"And I want it to be very white," Nate said with a smile. "Do you have something like that, or do I need to special order it?" He knew the Gassan diamonds came from the Netherlands, but he assumed he'd be able to talk to a good jeweler and get some answers.

Ginger had agreed to give him twenty minutes in the mall alone with Connor, though Nate wouldn't tell her what they wanted to shop for without her. She had to know, though.

"We have a catalog," the man said. "If you'll come over here, I'm sure we can find you something, and I'll make a call."

"Let's go look at the catalog," Nate said to Connor, though he knew the child wouldn't be any help. Nate wasn't one to beat around the bush, and he knew what he wanted. The salesman probably studied this catalog in his spare time, because he flipped straight to the section with the gold banded, brilliant-cut rings with all the facets that made them the shiniest diamonds in the world.

Ginger was going to love her ring.

He found the one he wanted—a chunkier band, with the stone set down in but also raised up because of its size—on the third page. He pointed to it. "That one. Can we get that one?"

"Let me find out." He took the catalog through a back door and into an office, and Nate glanced at his phone to judge the time. They had maybe ten minutes, and then Nate needed to get out of this store. Thankfully, Chandler came back within a couple of minutes and said, "I can get you this one. It's thirteen thousand dollars."

"How long?"

"They'll put it in the mail this evening, and it'll be here by Friday."

As it was Tuesday already, Nate thought Friday was fairly fast. Quite fast, in fact. "Perfect," he said, reaching for his wallet. "If I know the size, can I call and get it sized before I pick it up?"

"Of course."

"Okay, I'll work on that." He handed Chandler his credit card, and the transaction only took a few moments. Chandler took down all of Nate's information, and he herded Connor out into the busyness of the mall, glancing around to see if Ginger had come in yet.

He didn't see her, so he hurried Connor across the way to a smoothie shop. He'd ordered and had all three treats before turning around to look for the woman he loved again. This time, she raised her hand from over by the indoor fountain, and Nate said, "Over there, bud. Go on, now."

Connor skipped through the people to where Ginger sat on a bench, and she grinned at him and took him right onto her lap. Nate walked at a much slower pace, the noise and chaos around him fading to nothing as he looked at Ginger and Connor. No, they didn't look like they came from one another, but that didn't matter. Connor's shocking white hair reminded him of himself and Ward as children, and Ginger, with her auburn hair and those dark, hazely eyes, took his breath away every time he caught a glimpse of her.

"Hey, beautiful." Nate handed her the Styrofoam cup with her mango and orange smoothie and sat beside her.

"So, did you get your shopping done?" she asked, making a show of looking for a bag. "You don't have anything with you."

"Couldn't really find anything," Nate said casually. "We'll have to come back this weekend." He sipped his smoothie like he loved hanging out at the mall, and for how often he'd come here, an outsider would probably think he did.

"Mm hm," Ginger said, sipping her smoothie too.

"Ginger?" Connor asked. "You got any coins?"

"Sure thing, baby," she said, dipping down to get her wallet out of her purse. She handed him a quarter and a penny, and he went to toss them into the fountain.

"Thank you for loving him," Nate said quietly, and Ginger whipped her attention back to him.

Her wide eyes drank him in, and he just smiled at Connor before looking at Ginger. "He's a great kid," she said.

"Yeah," Nate said. "He is. And his dad was great too."

"Missing Ward today?" Ginger linked her arm through Nate's.

"Every day," he said. "Some days worse than others."

"Only a month until release."

Nate nodded, wondering how on Earth he was going to conceal a thirteen-thousand-dollar diamond ring from her for a month. "Listen," he said. "I wanted to ask you something." He hesitated, because he really didn't want to ask her to marry him while they sat on a bench in the mall.

"Yeah?"

"You hungry? I hear there's a great Chinese place around here somewhere."

Ginger giggled and laid her head against his bicep. Nate liked how she made him feel strong. He liked how she made him feel necessary. He simply liked being with her.

"Let's go," he said, standing up. "Come on, Connor. We're gonna go get noodles."

Connor skipped back over to them, and Nate took one of his hands while Ginger took the other. They went back to her truck, and she drove through the parking lot to the Chinese restaurant.

"Hey, Laura," Nate said as he walked in.

"Oh, my favorite family." She grinned at them and didn't bother with menus. Nate wasn't sure if that was a good thing or not. She led them to a table out of the way, and said, "I'll send over Kiki."

"Sounds good." Nate helped Connor sit, and then he

handed the boy his phone. "You can do the airplanes or the teddy bears."

"Do you have that snake game?"

"Snake game?" Nate shook his head. "No, I deleted that one."

"Why?"

"Because I couldn't download something else I needed."

Connor stabbed unhappily at the phone, and Nate had half a mind to take it from him and say he couldn't use it at all. Instead, he turned his attention to Ginger, who sat across from him.

His heart pounded in his chest, getting louder and more violent with every passing second. He could propose here, and then Ginger would love this restaurant even more than she already did. But he couldn't get the words out.

Kiki appeared at the end of the table and said, "Drinks?"

"Diet Coke," Ginger said.

"Same," Nate said. He didn't particularly enjoy soda, but it would be better than the rose water they served here. "And he wants Sprite."

"Sounds good. Do you know what you want?" She looked at the table. "You don't have menus."

"We don't need them," Ginger said. "I'll have the pork fried rice and the teriyaki noodles."

"Sweet and sour chicken," Connor said. "Please."

Nate grinned at him, glad he'd remembered his manners. "And I'll have the steak and shrimp stir fry."

"Be right back with the drinks."

Connor was already absorbed back into the phone, and Nate didn't have anything to distract him. He looked at Ginger and decided to just blurt out what was in his head.

"I love you, Ginger," he said. "And I want to spend the rest of my life with you. Today, Connor and I looked at engagement rings, and we bought one for you. It'll be here on Friday."

Her eyes widened and her mouth dropped open. "You're kidding."

"I am not," he said, ducking his head and smiling. "It's really pretty, and I just know you're going to love it." He looked at her again. "What I'm wondering is if you love *me* enough to marry me?"

Tears filled her eyes, but she was already nodding. "Yes," she said. "Yes, I love you, Nate."

He got up and rounded the table, meeting her as she stood too. He kissed her, not caring about anyone or anything else in the restaurant. He cradled her face in both of his hands. "I love you so much," he said. "Thank you for taking a chance on me."

"I love you too," she said, resting her cheek against his. "I love you and your big, beautiful, hopeful heart." She kissed him again, and Nate hoped he could be the kind of man she wanted, needed, and deserved.

"Diet Coke," the waitress said, and Ginger pulled away from him.

"Sorry," she said, giggling as she sat down. "But we just got engaged!"

Kiki gasped, looking between the two of them. "Really?"

"Really," Nate said. "The ring is coming from Amsterdam."

"It is?" both women asked together, and Nate felt like he'd done a very good thing with his engagement ring choice.

"It is," Nate said.

Kiki grinned at both of them and said, "I'll be right back with your food."

He reached across the table and took Ginger's hand in his. "I really think you're going to love it."

"I'm sure I will," Ginger said.

"I love you, Ginger," he said.

"I love you too, Nate," she said, which were the best words in the whole world.

Read on for a sneak peek of Chapter One in
OVERPROTECTIVE COWBOY.

THE END

SNEAK PEEK: OVERPROTECTIVE COWBOY CHAPTER ONE

Ted Burrows grinned when he saw the man sitting across the room, wearing a cowboy hat. His heart leapt at the familiar sight of Nathaniel Mulbury, though Ted hadn't seen Nate in months.

He started chuckling a couple of tables away, and Nate stood up, a giant grin on his face too. "Nathaniel," Ted said, engulfing Nate in a hug. The other man didn't particularly like his full name, but he laughed too. Ted clapped him on the back a couple of times. "What are you doing here?"

Nate stepped back, something new lighting his eyes. Ted recognized the shine of freedom in his friend's face, and he wondered what it would look like on him.

Ted was getting closer to his release date, but he'd been working very hard not to count down the days until he could walk out of the River Bay Federal Correctional Institution. He'd been counting up for so long, that counting down happened naturally. Somewhere in the back of his mind, he knew exactly how many days he had left inside these walls.

"I thought you were going to transfer to the camp," Nate said, sitting back down in the seat where he'd been waiting for Ted. "Drive tourists from the ships to the restaurants and stuff."

"Nah." Ted sat down too, the chairs in this tiny cafeteria-like room too small for him. "The opportunity came up, but if I moved to the camp, I'd forfeit the opportunity for a halfway house."

"Or the Residential Reentry Program," Nate said.

"That too," Ted said. "But I only have three and a half months. I think they put people in those programs who have six months."

"Well, I'm not getting strip searched again," Nate said with a smile. "So I guess this'll be the last time I see you before you show up at the ranch." He reached into his back pocket and pulled out a folded piece of paper. It was a compact square that he fumbled to unfold, and when he finally did, he smoothed it on the tabletop and slid it toward Ted.

Ted's heart beat strongly in his chest, and he didn't dare hope for the chance to go to the same ranch where Nate had been. His friend had sent plenty of communications about how much he loved it, and how much he thought Ted would love it. He wouldn't wear the cowboy hat though, and he glanced at the dark gray one perched on Nate's head. It felt

SNEAK PEEK: OVERPROTECTIVE COWBOY CHAPTER O... 265

as natural to Ted as it felt unnatural, and Nate caught him looking.

"You don't have to wear the hat."

"No?"

"You haven't even looked at the paper."

"Do I want to look at the paper?"

"Yes, Ted," Nate said, with some measure of exasperation in his voice. "You want to look at the paper."

Ted held his best friend's eyes for another moment, and then he looked at the form Nate had put on the table. They'd both spent plenty of time in prison reading over their sentences and appeals, so a simple release form that listed Hope Eternal Ranch as the location of his Reentry Program was easy to understand.

The date made him suck in a breath, and Nate didn't miss that. Another chuckle came from his mouth, and he said, "So we'll be here on Monday morning, and we'll see how long you last without a hat." He grinned like he knew something Ted didn't, which was entirely possible.

Ted's life had changed a lot over the past eight years, and one of the key moments was the day Nathaniel Mulbury had joined him in prison. They'd become fast friends and blood brothers, always looking out for each other and forming a band of boys that wasn't to be trifled with. They didn't cause problems. They didn't issue threats. Theirs was a mission to provide safety and security to everyone inside River Bay, and since it was a low-security facility, their strong presence ensured that the life was fairly easy for everyone.

In a lot of ways, life inside the low-security prison was like high school. There were a few cliques, but for the most part, everyone got along with everyone else. There wasn't much drama, and only a few fights, depending on who was in the facility with them, and for how long.

"Monday?" Ted looked up, trying to remember what day it was now. Had to be a Friday or Saturday, as those were visiting days. Wasn't a holiday.

"Four days, bud," Nate said, glancing up as a guard walked by their table. "Hey, Johnny."

The guard turned, surprised, but his face melted into a smile when he recognized Nate. "Nate," he said. "Wow." He glanced at Ted as he stuck out his hand to shake Nate's. "How's life out there?"

"So great," Nate said. "I'm engaged now, and Connor hasn't died yet."

Johnny laughed, and Ted did a little as well. "Wow, engaged."

Nate cut a look at Ted, who'd heard this news before. "Yeah, she owns the ranch where I did my reentry."

"And you're going there too, right Ted?" Johnny asked.

"I suppose so," Ted said, annoyed that he'd known before Ted had. But he knew that was just how things were done in the Bureau of Prisons. The prisoner was always the last to know his own fate, it seemed.

SNEAK PEEK: OVERPROTECTIVE COWBOY CHAPTER O... 267

The bell rang, and Nate got to his feet. "That's yours, Ted. See you Monday."

Ted stood up and hugged Nate again, realizing he only had to count down three more days. He watched Nate head for the exit along with all the other visitors, and a flash of gratitude and appreciation for the man filled him.

Ted didn't get a lot of visitors, as his family lived a few hundred miles away, and his parents couldn't make the drive alone anymore. They emailed still, and he talked to his mother on the phone every week, even if the conversation was only fifteen minutes long.

He waited in the room with all the tables and chairs where visiting took place until the guards released them, and he had to make a decision about that afternoon's automotive class. It would be his last one, and he hadn't anticipated that.

So he'd go, because Dallas ran the workshop, and the man who was part of the Mulbury Boys never went anywhere without the scent of grease accompanying him. He loved running the workshops, and he even had special permission to work in the shop when he wasn't doing classes. The beauty of the low-security facility.

There were plenty of rules too, and Ted had bucked against them at first. He'd been in the unit for eight months before Nate had shown up, wide-eyed and clenching his fingers into fists as he entered the unit for the first time.

Ted remembered exactly what it was like to walk into the facility for the first time, and he and Nate had tried to make the transition as easy as possible for newboots after that.

He wouldn't be tinkering with an engine for a couple of hours though, so he returned to the dormitory, choosing not to go outside quite yet. Spring had arrived in Texas, and Ted wondered what the air tasted like at Hope Eternal Ranch. Nate had told him about the bees the ranch cultivated, and Ted closed his eyes, almost able to hear the buzzing and taste the honey.

Almost

Ted had lived his whole life with the word *almost* riding on the back of his tongue. The fact that he'd *almost* used a knife in the brawl he'd gotten into had landed him in this facility.

"I saw Nate leaving," a man said, and Ted opened his eyes to look at Slate Sanders. He'd joined the Mulbury Boys the moment he'd come into the facility, because he was a little bit older, a little bit wiser, and extremely laid back.

"Yeah," Ted said. "He came to visit me. I'm going to Hope Eternal."

A smile formed on Slate's face, though Ted could see the longing in his eyes. He'd only received a sentence of thirty months, though, and he'd be out in ten. He could be in the camp too, but he'd stayed in the low because of the opportunities here. With more people, there was more access to health care, and infinitely more classes and opportunities to learn something.

Slate needed something else once he left this place, and

SNEAK PEEK: OVERPROTECTIVE COWBOY CHAPTER O... 269

he'd wanted the chance to take as many classes as possible so he could find something he could do after his sentence was up.

He came from the financial sector as well, the same as Nate, though Slate had been a stock broker out of Dallas, and Nate had been an investment banker in Houston.

Dallas had been a surgeon who liked to take apart engines on the weekends, and he'd really embraced his mechanic side behind locked doors and high fences.

"That's great," Slate said.

"Yeah," Ted agreed. He honestly had no idea if the ranch was great or not. Nate acted like it was, but Ted had spent so much time here, with his schedule decided for him, his meals chosen for him, and his wardrobe handed to him.

He could barely remember life beyond the bars, and a tremor of nervousness ran through him.

"See you later," Slate said, and just as quickly as he'd come, he left. Ted sighed and closed his eyes again, images running through his mind. He wasn't sure if they were memories of imaginations, because he'd had plenty of time to daydream in here. The fact was, Ted could barely distinguish between what was real and what wasn't, what his life before he'd come to River Bay had been like, and what he'd wished it had been.

Three more days, he told himself.

Then it was two days. Then one.

Monday dawned, and Ted had everything packed and ready to go before the sun rose. The door to the dormitory opened for the five a.m. count, but this time Gregory Fellows walked in. "Ready, Ted?"

He looked at the men he was leaving behind. He'd said all of his goodbyes already, and he met Dallas's eyes, then Slate's, then Luke's.

"Yeah," he said, shouldering his bag that held all of his worldly belongings. He'd have to surrender it when he left, and it would be searched. He didn't mind. He had nothing left to hide. All of his secrets, all of his dirty laundry, had been exposed, and Ted had survived.

Buoyed by the thought, he followed Greg out of the dormitory as the men he'd shared his sleeping and living quarters with cheered and clapped for him.

Outside in the hall, no one was cheering and applauding, but Ted rode the energy the other inmates had given him. Every step that took him farther from the dorm made his heart pound harder, and he went outside with the guards, getting a pair of handcuffs around his wrists before they went down the steps to make the move between buildings.

Ted hated the jangle of shackles, but he held still as a Unit Officer put them on his ankles. Once he had all his jewelry on, he shuffled down the steps and along the sidewalk, wondering what waited through the door. The Warden? Nate and Ginger, a woman he'd never met in real life? His lawyer?

Greg opened the door with a keycard, and he stood back as a couple of officers entered first, followed by Ted. His lawyer did stand there, and he took Ted's bag and handed it to a couple of officers who wore gloves and unzipped his duffle. Ted tried not to care, and really, he didn't.

Prison really had removed the anger from him. Then Jarrell Rose shook his hand, and Ted didn't hate seeing his lawyer, maybe for the first time. When he'd first been indicted, he'd thought his lawyer could help him, but Ted had learned painful lesson after painful lesson until all his faith in lawyers was gone.

The Warden came into the room, and all the paperwork got reviewed. Ted had learned to be patient over the years, and how to hold very still, a mask on his face, hiding his emotions. Inside, his muscles itched, and he wanted someone to say something, do something.

Finally, Warder Dickerson looked up and said, "All right, boys. He's ready." The Warden ran a tight ship here, and he didn't make personal connections with the inmates. Ted had never seen him wear anything but a suit and tie, just like he was now, despite the early hour on a Monday morning.

Ted stood still while all the restraints got taken off him, and one of the officers handed him his duffle bag. No one preceded him to the door, and Ted wasn't sure if he should just walk out.

Thankfully, Jarrell moved first, guiding Ted by the elbow, and they did walk out of the office, down the hall, and right on out of the building. A huge, black truck waited in the circle drive, the early morning sunlight glinting off all the chrome. Jarrell strode toward it, extending the thick folder of paperwork toward whoever was inside.

Nate got out of the passenger side and took the folder with the words, "Thanks, Jarrell." His gaze switched to Ted, a smile blooming on his face. "You ready?"

He was going to have to be, Ted supposed, and he swallowed and nodded. He relaxed as Nate embraced him again, as Jarrell promised to follow up with him in a couple of weeks, and as he got in the truck after Nate had slid into the middle.

"Ted," Nate said. "My fiancée, Ginger Talbot." He looked from Ted to Ginger. "Ginger, this is Ted Burrows, my best friend."

"Nice to meet you," Ginger said, and she gave him a real nice smile too, as if she actually meant it.

"And you," Ted said, because he'd been taught manners once upon a time in his life. He settled into the comfortable seats as Nate told him they had about a three and a half hour drive ahead of them.

Ted didn't care; he wasn't behind the walls of River Bay, and when Ginger turned down road after road and then onto a highway with the water on the left, all Ted could do was stare.

Nate didn't try to engage Ted in conversation, thankfully, as Ted felt like he was having an out-of-body experience. The sky was so blue. The water so beautiful. The sunshine so bright.

SNEAK PEEK: OVERPROTECTIVE COWBOY CHAPTER O... 273

Eventually, they reached the town of Sweet Water Falls, and Ted thought even the name was too good to be true.

Then Ginger turned onto the dirt lane that led to the ranch. The instructions started then, and he learned where he'd live, and where the women on the ranch lived, and when he'd meet with Ginger.

She pulled into a garage that had doors on both sides, so she could essentially drive straight through the house in one of the three stalls separating the West Wing—where the women lived—from the Annex—where the cowboys lived.

"Your room is right by mine," Nate said. "And Connor's. We'll share a bathroom."

Ted made a sound of affirmation, because he wasn't sure what to vocalize. He'd met Connor before, because Nate's brother used to bring him to the prison to visit.

"Emma will have lunch ready," Ginger said, opening her door. "You hungry, Ted?"

He looked over at her and nodded. "I didn't get breakfast."

"We should've stopped," Nate said. "Why didn't you say something?"

"I'm fine," Ted said, though he did get grumpy if he didn't eat enough. His stomach growled at the same time it told him not to eat, because it was nervous and wouldn't know what to do with the food he gave it.

"Let's go eat." Nate got out on the driver's side, and Ted finally got himself to move. Ginger had gone into the house ahead of them, and Nate met Ted's eye. "It'll be overwhelming for a little bit. But this is a great place, I swear, and you just do the same thing here that you did at River Bay."

"What's that?"

"Take it one day at a time." Nate gave him another smile and said, "Okay, so you're going to meet a bunch of people at once. Don't try to remember all of their names. You just need to know Ginger's."

"Ginger," Ted repeated. "Got it."

Nate climbed up the couple of steps and opened the door, and Ted followed him, a little weirded out that there wasn't any clinking of chains accompanying his footsteps. Just like he'd had to get used to life at River Bay, he'd have to figure out how to get used to life here at Hope Eternal Ranch.

"All right, guys," Ginger said over the gaggle of people inside, most of whom were talking. Ted saw several more men wearing cowboy hats. Women wearing cowgirl hats. One in an apron. All of them looked fresh, and happy, and almost like they *glowed*.

Ted felt completely out of place, and he'd wished he'd asked Ginger to pull over so he could change his clothes. He stood halfway behind Nate as Ginger continued with, "This is Ted Burrows, our new cowboy. I expect everyone to welcome him to Hope Eternal Ranch the way we do."

He wondered what way that was, and Nate glanced at him, questions in his eyes.

"I need to change," Ted hissed, and recognition lit Nate's face.

"Emma has your clothes." He nodded toward a brunette, who was walking toward them with the widest smile on her face. "Ted, this is Emma Clemson."

Ted blinked at her, because he knew that name. He *knew* this woman. His eyes narrowed at her, because she didn't quite look like the woman he'd thought he'd known. He'd compartmentalized things from his past, and he wasn't sure of anything anymore.

Emma smiled at him, and everything in Ted's world got brighter. She had a gorgeous smile, with straight, white teeth, and an inner light that shone out of her dark eyes. She wore a sleeveless, purple shirt with a pair of jeans, and she said, "I'll show you where you can change."

Her voice sounded familiar to him too, and he followed Emma while another woman started explaining the food covering the counter. Ted hadn't seen so much food in a long time.

He followed Emma away from the fray, ready to be away from the crowds. He'd lived the last five years with dozens of other people in close quarters, and he just wanted to be alone.

"Here you are," she said, handing him an obviously brand new backpack.

Ted took it but hesitated. "Have we met?"

Something like fear flickered across her face, but she kept her smile hitched in place. "I don't think so."

"Of course not," he said, feeling stupid for asking. But her voice was so familiar, and he'd definitely seen her face before. At least he thought he had. "Thanks."

He ducked into the bathroom and closed the door, locking it behind him. And finally, it was quiet.

Oh, I think they've met... Find out what happens between Ted and Emma in OVERPROTECTIVE COWBOY.

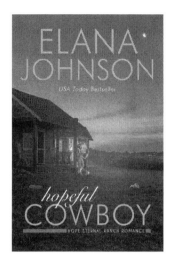

Hopeful Cowboy (Hope Eternal Ranch Romance, Book 1): Nathaniel Mulbury is released early from his six-year term in prison to care for his brother's four-year-old son. Dealing with grief over his brother's death and continued guilt for his role in the embezzlement scheme that landed him in jail, Nate has one more problem. He's never been a father and has no idea how to take care of Connor.

Make that two problems: He's released, but only to the care of Hope Eternal Ranch, a work-parole ranch run by the beautiful and smart Ginger Talbot. He's never been a cowboy, and he's got no room in his life for a woman.

Can Ginger and Nate find their happily-ever-after, keep up their duties on the ranch, and build a family? Or will the risk be too great for them both?

Overprotective Cowboy (Hope Eternal Ranch Romance, Book 2)

Rugged Cowboy (Hope Eternal Ranch Romance, Book 3)

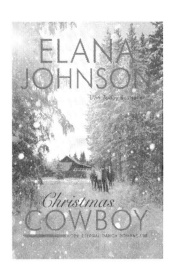

Christmas Cowboy (Hope Eternal Ranch Romance, Book 4)

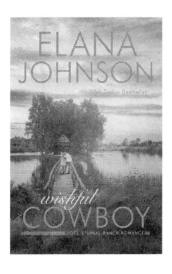 Wishful Cowboy (Hope Eternal Ranch Romance, Book 5)

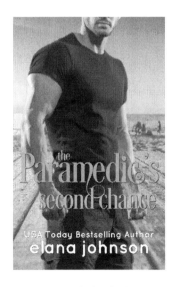

The Paramedic's Second Chance (Hawthorne Harbor Second Chance Romance, Book 1): Paramedic Andrew Herrin delivered Gretchen Samuels's daughter on the side of the road when she and her husband couldn't make it to the hospital in time. When their paths cross again in small-town Hawthorn Harbor, she's a widow and the baby is ten-year-old Dixie.

Dixie gets along great with Drew, and Gretchen finds herself falling in love with the man who's rescued her twice now. But when Drew's ex-girlfriend comes back to town, Gretchen's trust issues rear their ugly head. Can she and Drew find their way toward finding love in the lavender?

The Chief's Second Chance (Hawthorne Harbor Second Chance Romance, Book 2): Janey Germaine is tired of entertaining tourists in Olympic National Park all day and trying to keep her twelve-year-old son occupied at night. When longtime friend and the Chief of Police, Adam Herrin, offers to take the boy on a ride-along one fall evening, Janey starts to see him in a different light. Do they have the courage to take their relationship out of the friend zone?

The Firefighter's Second Chance (Hawthorne Harbor Second Chance Romance, Book 3): Bennett Patterson is content with his boring firefighting job and his big great dane...until he comes face-to-face with his high school girlfriend, Jennie Zimmerman, who swore she'd never return to Hawthorne Harbor. Can they rekindle their old flame? Or will their opposite personalities keep them apart?

The Officer's Second Chance (Hawthorne Harbor Second Chance Romance, Book 4): Trent Baker is ready for another relationship, and he's hopeful he can find someone who wants him and to be a mother to his son. Lauren Michaels runs her own general contract company, and she's never thought she has a maternal bone in her body. But when she gets a second chance with the handsome K9 cop who blew her off when she first came to town, she can't say no... Can Trent and Lauren make their differences into strengths and build a family?

The Soldier's Second Chance (Hawthorne Harbor Second Chance Romance, Book 5): A wounded Marine returns to Hawthorne Harbor years after the woman he was married to for exactly one week before she got an annulment...and then a baby nine months later. Can Hunter and Alice make a family out of past heartache?

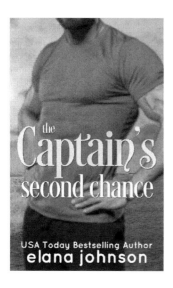

The Captain's Second Chance (Hawthorne Harbor Second Chance Romance, Book 6): A Coast Guard captain would rather spend his time on the sea...unless he's with the woman he's been crushing on for months. Can Brooklynn and Dave make their second chance stick?

BOOKS IN THE BRIDES & BEACHES ROMANCE SERIES

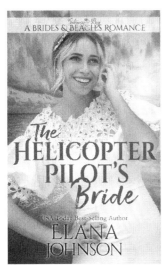

The Helicopter Pilot's Bride (Brides & Beaches Romance, Book 1): Charlotte Madsen's whole world came crashing down six months ago with the words, "I met someone else." Her marriage of eleven years dissolved, and she left one island on the east coast for the island of Getaway Bay. She was not expecting a tall, handsome man to be flat on his back under the kitchen sink when she arrives at the supposedly abandoned house.

But former Air Force pilot, Dawson Dane, has a charming devil-may-care personality, and Charlotte could use some happiness in her life. **Can Charlotte navigate the healing process to find love again?**

BOOKS IN THE BRIDES & BEACHES ROMANCE SERIES

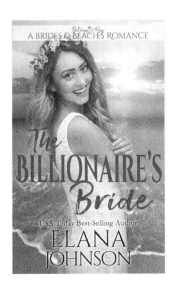

The Billionaire's Bride (Brides & Beaches Romance, Book 2): Two best friends, their hasty agreement, and the fake engagement that has the island of Getaway Bay in a tailspin...

BOOKS IN THE BRIDES & BEACHES
ROMANCE SERIES

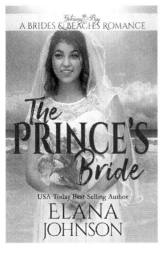

The Prince's Bride (Brides & Beaches Romance, Book 3): She's a synchronized swimmer looking to make some extra cash. He's a prince in hiding. When they meet in the "empty" mansion she's supposed to be housesitting, sparks fly. Can Noah and Zara stop arguing long enough to realize their feelings for each other might be romantic?

BOOKS IN THE BRIDES & BEACHES ROMANCE SERIES

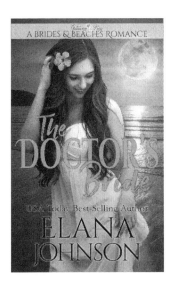

The Doctor's Bride (Brides & Beaches Romance, Book 4): A doctor, a wedding planner, and a flat tire... Can Shannon and Jeremiah make a love connection when they work next door to each other?

BOOKS IN THE BRIDES & BEACHES ROMANCE SERIES

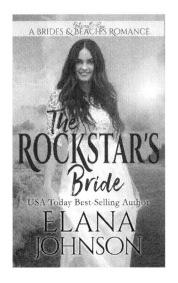

The Rockstar's Bride (Brides & Beaches Romance, Book 5): Riley finds a watch and contacts the owner, only to learn he's the lead singer and guitarist for a hugely popular band. Evan is only on the island of Getaway Bay for a friend's wedding, but he's intrigued by the gorgeous woman who returns his watch. Can they make a relationship work when they're from two different worlds?

BOOKS IN THE BRIDES & BEACHES
ROMANCE SERIES

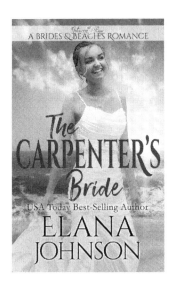

The Carpenter's Bride (Brides & Beaches Romance, Book 6): A wedding planner and the carpenter who's lost his wife... Can Lisa and Cal navigate the mishaps of a relationship in order to find themselves standing at the altar?

BOOKS IN THE BRIDES & BEACHES
ROMANCE SERIES

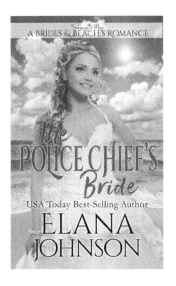

The Police Chief's Bride (Brides & Beaches Romance, Book 7): The Chief of Police and a woman with a restraining order against her... Can Wyatt and Deirdre try for their second chance at love? Or will their pasts keep them apart forever?

Love and Landslides (Stranded in Getaway Bay Romance, Book 1): A freak storm has her sliding down the mountain...right into the arms of her ex.

As Eden and Holden spend time out in the wilds of Hawaii trying to survive, their old flame is rekindled. But with secrets and old feelings in the way, will Holden be able to take all the broken pieces of his life and put them back together in a way that makes sense? Or will he lose his heart and the reputation of his company because of a single landslide?

Kisses and Killer Whales (Stranded in Getaway Bay Romance, Book 2): Friends who ditch her. A pod of killer whales. A limping cruise ship. All reasons Iris finds herself stranded on an deserted island with the handsome Navy SEAL...

Sentiments and Storms (Stranded in Getaway Bay Romance, Book 3): He can throw a precision pass, but he's dead in the water in matters of the heart...

Crushes and Cowboys (Stranded in Getaway Bay Romance, Book 4): Tired of the dating scene, a cowboy billionaire puts up an Internet ad to find a woman to come out to a deserted island with him to see if they can make a love connection...

BOOKS IN THE CLEAN BILLIONAIRE BEACH CLUB ROMANCE SERIES

The Billionaire's Enemy (Book 1): A local island B&B owner hates the swanky high-rise hotel down the beach...but not the billionaire who owns it. Can she deal with strange summer weather, tourists, *and* falling in love?

Driving the Billionaire Boss (Book 2): A car service owner who's been driving the billionaire pineapple plantation owner for years finally gives him a birthday gift that opens his eyes to *see* her, the woman who's literally been right in front of him all this time. Can he open his heart to the possibility of true love?

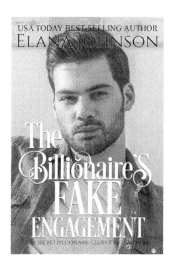

The Billionaire's Fake Engagement (Book 3): A former poker player turned beach bum billionaire needs a date to a hospital gala, so he asks the beach yoga instructor his dog can't seem to stay away from. At the event, they get "engaged" to deter her former boyfriend from pursuing her. Can he move his fake fiancée into a real relationship?

The Billionaire's Cinderella (Book 4): The owner of a beach-side drink stand has taken more bad advice from rich men than humanly possible, which requires her to take a second job cleaning the home of a billionaire and global diamond mine owner. Can she put aside her preconceptions about rich men and make a relationship with him work?

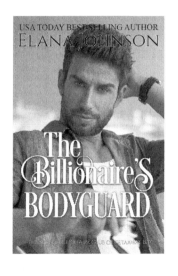

The Billionaire's Bodyguard (Book 5): Women can be rich too...and this female billionaire can usually take care of herself just fine, thank you very much. But she has no defense against her past...or the gorgeous man she hires to protect her from it. *He's her bodyguard, not her boyfriend.* Will she be able to keep those two B-words separate or will she take her second chance to get her tropical happily-ever-after?

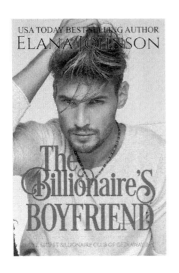

The Billionaire's Boyfriend (Book 6): Can a closet organizer fit herself into a single father's hectic life? Or will this female billionaire choose work over love…again?

Managing the Billionaire (Book 7): A billionaire who has a love affair with his job, his new bank manager, and how they bravely navigate the island of Getaway Bay...and their own ideas about each other.

Remarrying the Billionaire (Book 8): A silver fox, a dating app, and the mistaken identity that brings this billionaire face-to-face with his ex-wife...

Boyfriend By Mistake (Carter's Cove Sweet Romance, Book 1): She owns The Heartwood Inn. He needs the land the inn sits on to impress his boss. Neither one of them will give an inch. But will they give each other their hearts?

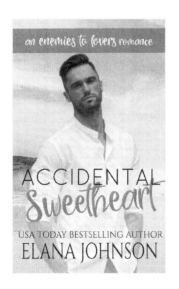

Accidental Sweetheart (Carter's Cove Sweet Romance, Book 2): She's excited to have a neighbor across the hall. He's got secrets he can never tell her. Will Olympia find a way to leave her past where it belongs so she can have a future with Chet?

Bodyguard, Not Boyfriend (Carter's Cove Sweet Romance, Book 3): She's got a stalker. He's got a loud bark. Can Sheryl tame her bodyguard into a boyfriend?

Not Her Real Fiancé (Carter's Cove Sweet Romance, Book 4): He needs a reason *not* to go out with a journalist. She'd like a guaranteed date for the summer. They don't get along, so keeping Brad in the not-her-real-fiancé category should be easy for Celeste. *Totally* easy.

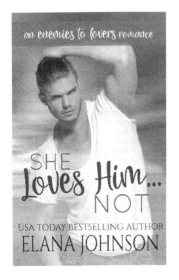

She Loves Him...Not (Carter's Cove Sweet Romance, Book 5): They've been out before, and now they work in the same kitchen at The Heartwood Inn. Gwen isn't interested in getting anything filleted but fish, because Teagan's broken her heart before... Can Teagan and Gwen manage their professional relationship without letting feelings get in the way?

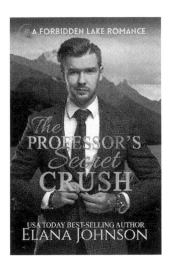

The Professor's Secret Crush (Forbidden Lake Romance, Book 1): She's about to break her university's rules and date a student...

The Lumberjack's Secret Guest (Forbidden Lake Romance, Book 2): He's about to let in his enemy and call her a guest...

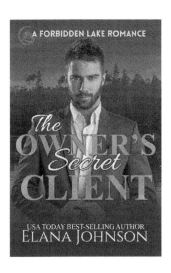

The Owner's Secret Client (Forbidden Lake Romance, Book 3): He knows it's against the rules to date his au pair...he just doesn't care.

The Billionaire's Secret Flame (Forbidden Lake Romance, Book 4): He's her boss and her biggest crush. He's also got secrets that could burn them both...

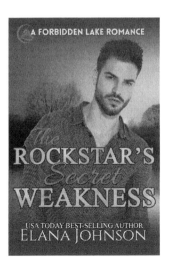

The Rockstar's Secret Weakness (Forbidden Lake Romance, Book 5): She's about to sign him as a client just to be able to see him...

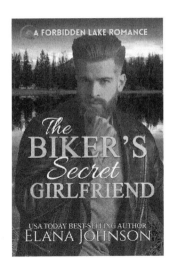

The Biker's Secret Girlfriend (Forbidden Lake Romance, Book 6): He wants the widow, but she belongs to the rival motorcycle club...

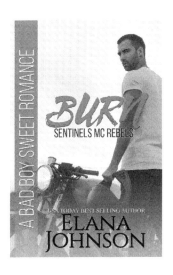

Burn (Sentinels Motorcycle Club Romance Series, Book 1): There's nothing more dangerous than a bad boy making decisions with his heart.

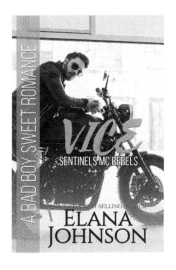

Vice (Sentinels Motorcycle Club Romance Series, Book 2): There's nothing more dangerous than a bad boy giving into his vices...

Crash (Sentinels Motorcycle Club Romance Series, Book 3): There's nothing more dangerous than a bad boy with secrets...

ABOUT ELANA

Elana Johnson is the USA Today bestselling author of dozens of novels, from YA contemporary romance to adult beach romances. She lives in Utah, where she teaches elementary school, taxis her daughter to dance several times a week, and eats a lot of Ferrero Rocher while writing. Find her on her website at elanajohnson.com.

Text
SAND
to 474747
and get sales, free
stuff, and contests
from Elana

CITIZENS AND
FOUNDERS

CITIZENS AND FOUNDERS

A history of the Worshipful Company
of Founders, London
1365–1975

by

GUY HADLEY

PHILLIMORE

1976
Published by
PHILLIMORE & CO. LTD.
London and Chichester

Head Office: Shopwyke Hall,
Chichester, Sussex, England.

© Guy Hadley, 1976

ISBN 0 85033 233 8

Set in Intertype Baskerville
and printed in Great Britain
by The Compton Press Ltd
The Old Brewery, Tisbury, Wilts

To the Family of the Founders,
past, present and yet to come,
this History of their Worshipful Company
is dedicated in friendship and affection

Contents

	List of illustrations	*p. viii*
	Foreword	*p. ix*
Chapter I	The Beginning	*p.* 1
Chapter II	The Spring of Years	*p.* 8
Chapter III	Winds of Change	*p.* 20
Chapter IV	London Pride	*p.* 30
Chapter V	The Sun Queen	*p.* 41
Chapter VI	Matters of Weight	*p.* 56
Chapter VII	Royal Charter	*p.* 67
Chapter VIII	Civil War	*p.* 83
Chapter IX	Ordeal by Fire	*p.* 101
Chapter X	False Colours	*p.* 115
Chapter XI	A Georgian Summer	*p.* 128
Chapter XII	Imperial Crown	*p.* 142
Chapter XIII	A Sea of Troubles	*p.* 159
	Postscript	*p.* 169
	Appendices	*p.* 177
	Principal Sources	*p.* 191
	Index	*p.* 193

Illustrations

Between pages 92 and 93

Plate 1   The Weoley Cup

Plate 2   St. Lawrence Church, Jewry. 1798

Plate 3   a. The Hall in 1848, when occupied by the Electric Telegraph Company
b. Bowen's Spoon, 1625
c. Poor's Box. Gift of Stephen Pilchard

Plate 4   Grant of Arms to the Founders' Company by Robert Cooke, Clarenceux, 1590

Plate 5   Founders' Company Window, West Crypt, Guildhall

Plate 6   Sketch plan of the old City, showing Founders' Hall

Plate 7   St. Margaret Church, Lothbury. Circa 1815

Foreword

WHEN MR. J. D. K. BEARDMORE, as Master in 1972, first suggested that I should write a History of the Founders' Company, I felt honoured by the invitation but also doubtful whether I should accept it. The amount of research likely to be required in covering a period of over 600 years was a daunting prospect for one no longer young and not a practising historian. Further enquiry showed, however, that a great deal of the basic research had already been done by Mr. William Meade Williams, Master in 1852 and 1853, in his *Annals* of the Company privately printed in 1867; and by Mr. Guy Parsloe in his masterly editing of the *Wardens' Accounts from 1497 to 1681*, published in 1964 by the Athlone Press of the University of London. I was further encouraged by the support of my colleagues on the Court of Assistants, and by the interest expressed by Dr. A. E. J. Hollaender, at that time Deputy Keeper of Records at the Guildhall.

No proper history of the Founders' Company has previously appeared. The *Annals* compiled by Mr. Williams were extracts taken from the Guildhall records which demanded years of patient search and sacrifice of leisure from a man already actively engaged in business. Mr. Williams had hoped to write a history from his own extracts, but was unable to do so, and it is therefore all the more fitting for the present writer to acknowledge his debt to such a distinguished and devoted example. In 1925, a History of the Company was compiled by Dr. W. Nembhard Hibbert, Master in 1923, and published by Unwin Brothers, but Dr. Hibbert himself pointed out that his book was based on Williams' *Annals*. He merely reproduced the extracts and comments made by Williams, while making some minor changes in presentation and adding a few references to developments between 1867 and 1925.

Much of the raw material for this present work is drawn from the earlier research done by Mr. Williams and Mr. Parsloe, to whom I gladly and gratefully pay tribute. In my references to Richard Weoley, donor of the Weoley Cup, I have been aided by the monograph on Weoley written by Dr. Hugh Stannus, Master in 1930, and privately printed. There still remained the formidable task of welding this material into a coherent and readable narrative extending over more than 600 years of history. It would have been relatively easy to confine the treatment to the internal administration and organisation of the Company in its various stages of evolution and compose a text mainly from dry lists of names, copies of ordinances, and other documentary extracts. This I rejected, because I felt that it would not do proper justice to the theme, nor be likely to interest more than a handful of academic specialists. I have chosen instead to set the development of the Company within the broader framework of English national history and the social conditions experienced by successive generations of Founders in their own times. While there are obvious risks in thus trespassing on the preserves of the professional historian, I have done my best to reduce them by extensive reading and an objective analysis of the principal sources.

I have also sought, wherever possible, to portray individual characters in the Company's long story, not as ciphers in dusty records, but as kindred creatures of flesh and blood. It is worth remembering, amid our present grave dangers, that our predecessors suffered civil war, pestilence, fire, threats of invasion, and internal inflation and left us an example of courage and endurance which should give us strength in our own troubles.

In addition, I felt that this History would not be complete without an account of the technical development of the foundry industry with which our Company was first associated, a connection which has been happily and strongly revived in recent years. Mr. Michael Hallett kindly agreed to fill this gap and he is admirably qualified to do so, both as a leader of the modern foundry industry and as a Liveryman of the Founders' Company, who has rendered it some outstanding services. To a layman like myself, his note is as lucid and interesting as it is to the technical expert.

In a historical work of this kind, certain questions of editing and presentation are bound to arise, and opinions often differ. In the matter of footnotes, for example, I personally regard them as an annoyance and distraction to the ordinary reader, and I agree with those authors who feel that, if a point is worth making or illustrating at all, it should be woven into the main text. In cases where documentary sources need to be quoted at some length, they have been reproduced as Appendices. In dealing with the old English spellings of many words and names, it has sometimes been difficult to decide between an exact verbal repetition which conveys the charm of the old language, or a modern version which makes more sense today than the old one. I have adopted a flexible attitude here and tried to judge each case on its merits.

I have already acknowledged my great debt to Mr. Williams for his work in mid-Victorian times, and to Mr. Parsloe for his mine of information in the Wardens' Accounts. I am also grateful for the support and encouragement given me by Mr. Beardmore as Master, and by his successors, Mr. Peter Blaxter, Mr. John Cully, and Mr. Frank Rowe; and for the help of the Clerk, Mr. Wilson Wiley, and the Beadle, Mr. John Fountain. My warm thanks are also due to Dr. Hollaender and the Guildhall Library, City of London, for their help, and for kindly allowing me to reproduce the prints of St. Lawrence and St. Margaret churches. Nor must I forget the patience shown by my wife in coping with a husband immured for a long period of solitary confinement, and a study so littered with paper that it made cleaning a nightmare.

I would only add, in conclusion, that my book has no claim to be regarded as a final verdict. There is still ample scope for further research on many aspects of the Company's evolution, and I can only hope that the present work will encourage

FOREWORD xi

others. Nobody can look back over the six centuries of existence which the Founders have achieved without feeling deeply conscious of the lasting links between the generations which bind us all together. Long may it so continue.

GUY HADLEY

Lealands House,
Groombridge, Sussex
1st March 1976

CHAPTER I

The Beginning

THE EARLIEST surviving record of the Founders' Company is a petition in Norman French translated into English and preserved at Guildhall, in which the 'Good Men of the Mistery of the Founders of the City of London' submitted their Ordinances to the Mayor and Aldermen and asked for them to be approved and enrolled. The petition was granted in 1365 and the newly-elected Master of the Founders, John de Lincoln, was presented on 29 July that year to the Mayor, Adam de Bury, and Aldermen. The fact that the petition was written in French, including the names of the Mayor and the Master, shows that this was still the custom in official documents 300 years after the Norman Conquest, although it was rapidly dying out in ordinary life. The Guildhall Letter Books also show that the ceremony of presenting a new Master to the Mayor was still performed in 1391, when two Masters were elected, Thomas Grace and Robert Newman. There are some indications that this practice was maintained for a much longer period, but it was later discontinued at some date unknown.

The wording of the Founders' petition makes it clear that a 'Mistery of the Founders' already existed in 1365 and consisted of craftsmen making candlesticks, large washing vessels called 'lavers', stirrups, spurs and buckles, and apparently working in brass or an alloy called 'latten'. We do not know when these early founders were joined together in a common body, but this seems to have originated, as with many other City gilds, in a parish brotherhood which helped its members in distress and gave them decent burial. The medieval craftsmen were often living and working as neighbours in the same street, and the transition from parish brotherhood to craft gild was thus a natural sequence. Religious belief was an integral part of medieval life, and from their earliest days as a gild, the Founders were attached to St. Lawrence church, Jewry, and had their own 'Brotherhood of St. Clement' named after their patron saint. It gave help in rent, food, and fuel for those members too old or ill to work. When they died, it met the cost of winding-sheet, burial pit, and tolling of bells, and escorted the body in procession to its grave. This aid was financed by a levy of 'Mass money' on all members and gifts of property or money from pious benefactors who endowed 'Chantries' for Mass to be sung and prayers recited in memory of the donor and his family.

Before the Founders were recognised in 1365 as an independent gild, they seem to have had some connection with the Brass Potters, whose own Ordinances of 1316 call for the appointment of 'four dealers and four founders' to take part in a 'joint assay'. Perhaps it was an increasing degree of specialisation which led the Founders to form their own gild, and it is even possible that they absorbed the Brass Potters. If so, this would have been contrary to the general trend in the 14th century, which was a period of rapid growth in the number of City gilds. Between 1328 and 1377, no less than 35 new ones were formed as separate and self-governing 'misteries'. The word 'Mistery' was probably derived from the Italian 'Mestiere', which was used in the great commercial city of Venice to describe a craft or trade.

The main purpose of a gild was to secure a monopoly of its particular craft and to protect it from outside competition by exercising control over all who worked in that craft. These aims had much in common with the 'closed shop' of a modern trade union, but the gilds also imposed on their members high standards of workmanship and conduct which the modern trade union leader would never himself accept or dare to propose to his own members. The Ordinances granted to the Founders in 1365 provide a good example of the principles on which a gild was based. The full text is given in Appendix A, but a summary of the chief clauses may be useful here.

First, it was ordered that every member of the Mistery should use only 'good, fine and pure metal', a rule also applied to 'closwork', meaning the repair of breaches or fractures. The use of white solder was prohibited, except in the pipes of laverpots and similar vessels. Second, nobody working as a founder in the City was allowed to keep a house or workshop unless he had first been examined and approved 'by the Masters of the said Mistery who are elected and sworn to govern such Mistery'. It was they who decided whether he was 'able, sufficient and knowing' and then presented him to the Mayor and Aldermen as a man 'good, sufficient and profitable to the common people and to the City'.

Thirdly, rules were laid down for maintaining discipline in the gild and high working standards. The Masters were authorised to carry out 'searches' for defective wares made of false or brittle metal, and could call on the aid of a City Sergeant. Moreover, these searches were not confined to the houses and workshops of the members, but could be extended to any premises where articles produced by the craft were being made or sold. False work could be seized on the spot and declared forfeit to the City Corporation.

Nobody outside the Company was permitted to employ any servant, apprentice, or hired man belonging to it in the founding craft. Nor could any member of the Company engage a hired assistant unless that person had been tried and approved by the Masters, who also decided what his daily wage should be. The master-craftsmen were required to pay wages fixed by contract and forbidden to keep any 'varlet' or servant against his will when his term of service had expired. Conversely, those found wanting in their duty were subject to punishment 'at the discretion of the Mayor and Aldermen, according to the degree of the trespass'. Other clauses forbade the 'poaching' of labour, either by taking over a servant who had quarrelled with his master, or an apprentice who had not completed his original term of service. Offences against the Ordinances incurred a fine of 40 shillings, no small penalty in those days.

THE BEGINNING

3

The Ordinances of 1365 also called for the selection of 'two or three of the best Men of the said Mistery' to watch over it, but did not say how they were to be chosen. A rule was added later, at some date before 1497, whereby the Master and Wardens in office, together with all who had previously served as a Warden, chose the new Wardens from two men who had already held that post and two of the Company who had not, and elected one from each pair. The candidates were named on the Saturday 'after the Feast of the Assumption of our Lady', 15 August, and the election was made on the Sunday following at a lunch or supper. The new Master was elected for the next two years by the retiring Master and Wardens and the two new Wardens.

Although John de Lincoln is given the title of 'Master' in 1365, this was for many years an exception and not the rule. It would seem that all three office-holders had the same status, with the Master ranking as first among equals. In 1497, the first year on record in the Wardens' Accounts, the officers are all described as 'Wardens', with no mention of Master, though it is fair to assume that the first-named was so regarded. The term 'Master and Wardens' first appears in 1501 and was used in most years up to 1565, when 'Master' was replaced by either 'Master Warden' or 'Upper Warden'. The title of 'Master' was re-established in the Charter of 1614. The first distinction between Wardens, as compared with Master, occurs in 1541, when the junior Warden is shown as 'Younger', and in 1547, when the senior Warden is called 'Second Warden'.

Whatever their descriptions, the men who held office in the Company in those times carried a heavy burden of work and responsibility. It was they who had the tasks of defending the interests of the craft against interference, contesting action by Crown or Parliament which might harm the Founders, searching out cases of bad workmanship, and maintaining good order within the Company itself. All this entailed frequent attendance at Westminster or Guildhall at the expense of time normally spent on private business. As will be seen in later pages, it also involved considerable risks of prosecution or even imprisonment.

The gilds certainly constituted vested interests as expressed in the economic conditions of their time, but people who today regard them as feudal survivals have not read their history. The gilds made a vital contribution to the development of English civil liberties and self-government, and this is well summed up by George Unwin in his book on the *Gilds and Companies of London* :

> The political liberty of Western Europe has been secured by the building up of a system of voluntary organisations, strong enough to control the State, and yet flexible enough to be constantly remoulded by the free forces of change. It is hardly too much to say that the foundations of this system were laid in the gild. It was in the gild that voluntary association first came into a permanent relation with political power.

The Founders can be justly proud of their modest part in this process, and still more so in our own time, when the political trend has been reversed and the State threatens to become omnipotent.

The birth of the Founders' Company coincided with the rise of a new English

4   CITIZENS AND FOUNDERS

nation on the foundations laid by the Norman Conquest. By 1365, the merging of
Norman and Saxon elements into a native English people, speaking its own tongue,
was virtually accomplished. The teaching of English was replacing French in the
grammar schools, and a statute passed in 1362 decreed that English was to be used
in future in the law courts. Above all, this was the England of Geoffrey Chaucer,
the first great English poet, whose *Canterbury Tales* breathed a new spirit of English national vigour and unity, expressed in robust and racy language which his
readers could understand and enjoy.

The tide of cross-Channel invasion had long been reversed and it was the English
kings who now ravaged France with fire and sword to uphold their feudal claims.
By 1365, the English Crown had lost Normandy, but still held large territories in
Poitou, Guyenne, and Gascony. Memories of the English victories at Crécy in 1346
and Poitiers in 1356 must have been strong in the first generation of the Founders,
and it was not until 1455 that the Hundred Years' War with France ended with
the loss of all the English possessions across the Channel except Calais.

The emergence of craft gilds goes back to much earlier times. An Exchequer list
of 1180, in the reign of Henry II, shows that tax was then being levied on 18
'adulterine' gilds, so called because they had not obtained a Royal licence, and
there were other gilds which had done so. Only four of the 'adulterine' gilds are
identified by their craft, namely the Goldsmiths, Pepperers, Clothworkers, and
Butchers. The others are only described by their patron Saint or ward Alderman, or
by the word 'Bridge', which may refer to their location near London Bridge, then
being built, or to their participation in this work.

The gilds were helped by the struggle for power between the Crown and the
barons, since both sides sought to win financial support from the City of London
and were willing to pay for it by making political concessions. In 1180, the government of London was still directly controlled by the Crown through its appointment
of the Mayor and his chief officials. The citizens were only entitled to elect their
Ward Alderman and hold meetings with him to discuss their affairs. But the signature of Magna Carta by King John at Runnymede in 1215 weakened the Royal
authority and was followed by a long struggle between the Crown and the feudal
lords, both competing for help from London. The gilds took full advantage of this
situation, and their position was further strengthened by the accession of a weak
King, Edward II, in 1307.

In 1312, the gilds sent a deputation to the Mayor and Aldermen which claimed
that the City 'ought always to be governed by the aid of men engaged in trades
and handicrafts'. They also demanded that no stranger, English or foreign, should
be admitted to the City freedom 'until the merchants and craftsmen, whose business he wished to enter, had previously certified the Mayor and Aldermen of his
condition and trustworthiness'. In 1319, Edward II granted the City a new Charter
which stipulated that no person, whether living in the City or elsewhere, should
receive the civic freedom of London unless he belonged to one of the London
trades or 'misteries' and was accepted by the whole body of citizens. The Charter
also declared that 'no man of English birth, and especially no English merchant,

THE BEGINNING   5

who follows any specific Mistery or craft is to be admitted to the City freedom except on the security of six reputable men of that Mistery or craft'.

The next King, Edward III, strengthened the power of the Crown but spent much of his long reign in wars against France and Scotland which made him equally dependent on financial backing from London. An Act of Parliament passed at his bidding in 1363 ordered that 'all artificers and people of Misteries shall each choose his own Mistery before the next Candlemas and that, having so chosen it, he shall henceforth use no other'. A later historian, Macaulay, attached so much importance to the constitutional effects of this Act that he commented : 'Here commences the history of the English nation'. Be that as it may, the Act gave legal effect to the exclusive power of control which the gilds asserted over their respective crafts, and it may well have been instrumental in deciding the Founders to set up their own body in 1365.

In 1351, 13 leading Companies gained the right to elect the Common Council of the City from their own members, in the proportion of six each from the Grocers, Mercers, and Fishmongers; four each from the Drapers, Goldsmiths, Woolmongers, Vintners, Skinners, Saddlers, Tailors, Cordwainers, and Butchers; and two from the Ironmongers. This gave the Council a total membership of 56, but allowed no places for the lesser gilds. In 1375, the Common Council passed an act transferring the right of electing the chief City magnates and the City Members of Parliament from the Wards to the trading Companies, and by that time the Council had been expanded to include representatives from many other Companies. A list made in 1376 shows that the membership had then risen to 148 and was drawn from 48 different City Companies.

To illustrate the number and variety of crafts then active, and their ranking order, it may be useful to quote the list of 1376 in full. The Grocers, Mercers, Drapers, Fishmongers, Goldsmiths, Vintners, Tailors, Skinners, and Blacksmiths each had six seats on the Common Council; the Brewers had five; the Saddlers, Weavers, Tapestry Weavers, Chandlers, Fullers, Girdlers, Stainers, Salters, Masons, Ironmongers, Leather Dressers, and Butchers each had four; and the Founders had two seats, as did the Haberdashers, Leathersellers, Joiners, Curriers, Free-masons, Fletchers, Bakers, Cloth Measurers, Braziers, Cappers, Pewterers, Ale-Brewers, Hatters, Horners, Armourers, Cutlers, Spurriers, Plumbers, Wax Chandlers, Barbers, Painters, Tanners, Pouch-Makers, Woodmongers and Pinners.

Both in 1351 and 1376, the list of Companies was headed by the Grocers, but this is a later, and misleading, spelling of their name. They were originally called 'Grossers' and known as such because they were a gild of wholesale merchants dealing in bulk quantities or 'gross', whose operations were not confined to a single commodity or craft, but extended over many other markets. They thus incurred the hostility of many orthodox craft gilds which jealously guarded their particular monopolies, and were violently attacked for raising consumer prices. In fact, the Act of Edward III in 1363 forbidding the members of one 'Mistery' to belong to any other was largely due to pressure from gilds which sought to limit the activities of the 'Grossers'.

6   CITIZENS AND FOUNDERS

This clash of interests arose from a deeper conflict between the simpler medieval pattern of economic life, which gave birth to the craft gild, and the new demands for commercial integration and investment caused by the increasing variety and sophistication of the goods produced. With the support of Mayors and Aldermen, the gilds succeeded for a long time in maintaining their exclusive rights and privileges, but it was the merchant interest which prevailed in the end. The wealth of the City, and the influence it exerted, increasingly fell into the hands of the merchants, as compared with the working craftsmen.

The expulsion of the Jews by Edward I in 1290, pressed upon him by a City of London which envied Jewish wealth and hated Jews as alien competitors, made the King all the more dependent on financial aid from the London merchants and brought them rich rewards. A 'subsidy roll' or list of tax assessments made in 1319 shows that the wealthier citizens were to be found among drapers, mercers, grossers, fishmongers, woolmongers, skinners, and goldsmiths, all belonging to Companies dominated by the merchant class. Some of the older and more powerful Companies had their own tribunals, dating back to early medieval times, which exercised jurisdiction in trade disputes, such as the Weavers' Court and the 'Hallmote' of the Fishmongers. By 1320, the Mercers and the Vintners had gained a leading place in general import and export trade, as well as their own business. They had their agents in the chief European commercial centres, owned their own ships, and formed syndicates to finance trading ventures. The Woolmongers had their 'Staple' or market in Calais which handled the big exports of English wool.

Some of the greater Companies obtained Royal Charters enabling them to impose trade controls and restrictions, in matters such as price-fixing, wages, and working conditions, which served their own interests but were often damaging to the welfare and independence of the lesser gilds. Right up to the end of Edward II's reign in 1327, most of the Ordinances granted to City Companies by the Court of Aldermen were not primarily designed to regulate a particular craft, but to settle a conflict of interests between different gilds in questions such as prices and competition.

The unity which had enabled the gilds to win self-government from kings and feudal magnates was thus broken, and they were divided by their own rivalries and ambitions. Following the example of the great feudal lords, the more powerful Companies obtained coats of arms and paraded in distinctive liveries, hence giving rise to the term of Livery Company. They mustered private armies and formed alliances in the City to uphold their economic claims and their social prestige. Street fighting broke out between opposing groups, and there was a bloody example of it in 1267, when the Goldsmiths, supported by the Clothworkers, clashed with the Tailors, who were joined by the Cordwainers. Over 500 men were said to have been engaged in this combat, some of them being killed and many wounded. A clothworker called Geoffrey de Beverley and 12 others from both sides were hanged for their part in this affray.

Despite these troubles, the London gilds made a remarkable contribution to English social and economic history, and this is described as follows by Professor E. Lipson in his book, *The Growth of English Society* :

THE BEGINNING
7

The fact that masters were recruited from the ranks of the labouring class meant that no impassable gulf separated them from their workmen. We need not idealise early industrial society to recognise that employers and men were on the same economic plane and shared a common fellowship as brethren of the same gild. Nothing is more remarkable in these gild enactments than the rules setting out the duties and responsibilities of the brethren. They demonstrate clearly that the gildsmen cherished high standards by which their conduct, while often selfish, must have been in practice deeply influenced.
In the best days of the gild, its professions of good faith were not a mere cloak concealing a blind attachment to its own narrow interests. They represented a genuine anxiety to uphold the ideals of sound craftsmanship in order to safeguard the consumer against defective commodities and the producer against cheap labour. In medieval times, industry was conceived in the light of a public service carried on for the common profit of the community.

In our own time, a doctrinaire socialist might claim that the nationalised industries are performing the same function, but he would find few people to agree with him.

CHAPTER II

The Spring of Years

FOR A HUNDRED YEARS or more after the Founders were granted their ordinances in 1365, very little is known about them. This is frustrating for their historian, but suggests a quiet domestic life which may have been a blessing at the time. For this was a turbulent period when City Companies, like nations, were happier without having a history to remember. Prudent men kept their heads down, while bolder ones were losing theirs in battle or by the headsman's axe.

The English position in France was restored by Henry V who won at Agincourt in 1415 and recovered Normandy. Supported by the Duke of Burgundy, he went from strength to strength, married a French princess, Catherine, and entered Paris in triumph in 1420, after a peace treaty at Troyes which made him Regent of France and successor to the French throne. But Henry died comparatively young in 1422, the siege of Orléans was raised by Jeanne d'Arc, and by 1455 the English were driven from all their French possessions except Calais. The feudal nobility of England then destroyed itself in the suicidal Wars of the Roses between the houses of York and Lancaster, but the yeomen and bowmen who had mown down the flower of French chivalry at Crécy, Poitiers, and Agincourt returned to their farms and villages with a new sense of pride and skill in arms which powerfully reinforced English liberties.

The latter part of the 14th century was a time of social unrest and revolutionary ferment. John Wycliffe was denouncing the corruption of wealthy churchmen, and Chaucer's poems voiced popular feeling against clerical abuses and Papal extortions. In 1381, a revolt of peasant labourers broke out, sparked off by a ruinous poll tax which fell on rich and poor alike, but basically due to a hatred of feudal dues and services. An army of Kentish men marched on London, led by Wat Tyler, who had served in the French wars. They had friends in the City who opened the gates, and the rebels broke into the Tower of London, where the Archbishop of Canterbury, Sudbury, had taken refuge. They dragged the old man out and beheaded him on Tower Hill. Shortly after, when the young King Richard II rode out to meet Wat Tyler at Smithfield, the rebel leader was stabbed to death by the Mayor of London, William Walworth, and his followers were persuaded to go home by false promises that their grievances would be met.

Throughout this stormy period, the City of London continued to grow in wealth and independence. By 1400, it had gained powers of self-government which made

THE SPRING OF YEARS 9

it virtually a state within a state. The jurisdiction of the Mayor and Aldermen extended to large areas on both sides of the Thames, and was enforced by their own officers. There was trouble in store for any agent of kings or barons who sought to invade these powers or trespass on the rights of a London citizen. Moreover, the City could mobilise and arm its own militia from the Livery Companies, while the Crown had no standing army and civilian police forces were non-existent. More potent still was the financial strength which the City derived from its supremacy in English commerce at home and abroad, and which made even the highest in the land cultivate good relations with the rich City merchants. Edward III himself, a strong king, was quite content to become a member of the Armourers' Company.

By the end of the 14th century, the wealthier merchant companies, such as the Mercers, Grocers, and Drapers, had established a prior claim to the governing posts of Mayor and Aldermen. As early as 1325, a list of 25 'misteries' entitled to elect officers for their own 'government and instruction' consisted almost entirely of mercantile gilds which had already obtained Royal charters or were about to do so. As already noted, however, there was a rapid increase in the number of craft gilds which gained recognition between 1327 and 1377, and it would be quite wrong to think that the liverymen of the City companies were drawn only from the merchant class. On the contrary, a large majority of them were still working masters employing apprentices and journeymen, or hired labour, and selling their goods either on their own premises or through agents.

We pick up the story of the Founders again in 1487, when the Court of Aldermen issued an order forbidding the City Companies to make Ordinances without their consent and approval. The Mayor and Aldermen had always claimed authority over the Companies and their administration, though not always with success. Their new order was apparently prompted by a request from the Tallow Chandlers for larger rights of search, which the Court of Aldermen rejected. Every Company was now required to submit its Ordinances for inspection, and in some cases the Aldermen ordered that pages should be torn out and replaced by new ones.

This seems to have been the case with the Founders, for in April, 1489, their Wardens and other members appeared before the Mayor, William White, and the Aldermen in the Inner Chamber of Guildhall and presented a new set of Ordinances for approval. These were unanimously agreed and entered in the records, and their full text is given in Appendix B. They give some indication of changes which had occurred in the Company since the first Ordinances of 1365. They show that a division of the Company's membership had taken place into three sections, namely 'Brothers of the Clothing', meaning Liverymen; 'Householders not of the Clothing'; and 'Journeymen'. The last two categories both formed part of what came to be known as the 'Yeomanry' of a City company, the 'householders' probably being masters who had their own workshops, and the 'journeymen' being hired craftsmen. This division may be compared unfavourably with the more democratic practice of early medieval times, when no such class distinctions sep-

CITIZENS AND FOUNDERS

arated masters and men, and it is true that the Livery had emerged as a privileged minority.

On the other hand, the Livery was not a 'closed shop'. It was recruited by selection from those of the Yeomanry who had the ability and willingness to accept the heavier burdens of responsibility and expense which promotion to the Livery entailed.

Another point worth noting in the 1489 Ordinances is the allocation of apprentices on a differential scale. The Upper Warden, then equivalent to Master, was allowed four apprentices, a past Warden three, a Liveryman two, and a Yeomanry member only one, which could exceptionally be raised to two if the City Chamberlain gave his consent. All apprentices had to be approved by the Wardens before being bound and a breach of this rule incurred a fine of 3s. 4d.

The origins of the Founders as a religious fraternity were preserved in a clause which made every member of the Company pay 'quarterage' yearly to the Wardens for 'Keeping of Masses, Burying of poor Brethren, and other deed of Alms'. The rate for Liverymen was three pence a quarter, for a 'Householder not of the Clothing' it was two pence, and for 'Journeymen', one penny. Failure to pay quarterage was penalised by a fine of 12 pence, divided equally between the City Chamber and the Company. All members of the Company were required to attend, with the Wardens, at a Solemn Mass held yearly at St. Lawrence church, Jewry, on the Feast of the Assumption of Our Lady on 15 August. This would indicate that the Founders were still using St. Lawrence as their parish church in 1489.

Rules were also laid down for maintaining discipline and good relations between members. All were obliged to turn out and accompany the wardens on ceremonial occasions when the Livery Companies escorted the Mayor and Sheriffs. It was an offence to 'revile, call, or rebuke' a warden or Liveryman. No member was permitted to sue another without leave from the Wardens, and a defendant had the right, established earlier in City custom, to be judged by the Mayor and Aldermen. This right was reserved by the Cutlers, for example, in their Ordinances of 1344, but it did not prevent them from stipulating, in their later Ordinances of 1380, that none could work as a cutler unless he abided by the rules of the Company's 'overseers'. Under another rule in the Founders' Ordinances of 1489, any member taking his wares to a fair for sale had to submit them for inspection by the Wardens before they were packed, so that they could be judged 'able and sufficient for the King's liege people'.

The Mayor and Aldermen were prepared to grant Ordinances, at their own discretion, which gave the Companies considerable powers of self-government, but they were also quick to repress abuses which might cause friction between the Companies themselves and damage the higher interests of the City. Nor did they look with favour on applications for new Royal Charters which would extend to others the larger privileges enjoyed by the greater Companies, to which the Mayor and Aldermen usually belonged. In 1498, and again in 1516, the Founders made efforts to obtain a Charter, as related in later pages, but they failed on both occasions and this must have been due to opposition from Guildhall.

THE SPRING OF YEARS   11

The Court of Aldermen also encouraged mergers whereby a weaker gild, finding it hard to survive under changing economic conditions, was absorbed in a
stronger rival. For example, the Leathersellers had a long series of disputes over
the right of search for defective goods, involving the Tawyers, or leather-dressers,
the Glovers, Pursers, Whittawyers or saddlers, and Pouchmakers. The Tawyers
were merged with the Leathersellers in 1479, as were the Pursers and Glovers in
1502, and the Pouchmakers in 1517. Similarly, the Armourers took over the Bladesmiths and the Braziers, the Blacksmiths swallowed the Spurriers, the Haberdashers
incorporated the Hatters and the Cappers, and the Girdlers took in the Pinners and
the Wiresellers. The Barber-Surgeons joined hands with the Painter-Stainers. The
shrewdest coup was achieved by the Fullers and the Shearmen, who had been losing members to the Drapers, but who joined together to form the Clothworkers
Company in 1528, just in time to secure the last place in the official list of 'The
Twelve Great Companies', which they still retain to this day.

We have now reached a stage where a new and invaluable source of information about the Founders is available in their Wardens' Accounts from 1497 to
1681, which have been admirably edited by Mr. Guy Parsloe. Not only do they
illuminate many obscure aspects of the Company's affairs, but they also provide
many interesting sidelights on the larger history of their times. In the very first year
of these Accounts, 1497-8, we find the earliest recorded list of members which dis-
tinguishes them from the faceless jelly of history and recalls them as living individuals, flesh of our flesh and blood of our blood.

The list shows payments made by the Brethren 'for quarterages and the Mass'
and the names are clearly entered in order of seniority, though not under the headings of 'Livery' or 'Yeomanry' which became the practice in later years. The first
three are the Wardens, Robert Setcole, Edmond Bird and John Parker, otherwise
called John Sena, possibly meaning John Parker, senior. These are followed by
28 others who also belonged to the Livery, judging by their contributions, and
another 48 who can be classed as Yeomanry members from their payments, some
at the quarterage rate prescribed for 'householders not of the Clothing' in the 1489
Ordinances, and others at the rate payable by 'journeymen'. One of these names
has a blank space against it for payment, and another is marked 'forgiven by the
Masters'. The total membership came to 79, of whom 31, including the Wardens,
can be identified as Liverymen, 27 as Yeomanry householders, and 21 as Yeomanry journeymen. The quarterage lists cease to appear in the accounts after
1568, but up to that date there were only three lists containing a hundred names
or more, and only two in which they fell below the 1497 figure of seventy-nine.

The names of those paying quarterage at the Livery rate in 1497 include that
of a woman, 'Mistress Hawke'. She was the widow of Richard Hawke, a benefactor of the Company who gave it a standing cup with a hawk engraved and also
money for a yearly requiem mass in his memory and refreshments for the mourners.
This is the first recorded evidence of women as members of the Company, though
there may well have been others earlier. They were presumably widows of master-
craftsmen who carried on with their late husband's work, and in some later years

the quarterage lists also include widows who received help from the Company. Between 1518 and 1544, the membership lists were usually headed 'Brethren and Sisters of the Company', but in later years this was replaced by 'Names of the Company' and sub-headings for Livery, Yeomanry, 'Strangers', and 'Widows'. The list for 1543-4 gives the names of 12 'widows and sisters', some called 'Mistress', a higher married title, and others described as 'Goodwife', or 'Mother', or simply 'Tanner's Wife'. Of the 12 women in question, five paid quarterage at varying rates and one, Mistress Sewen, paid Mass money as well. She was probably the widow of James Sewen, Master in 1541-2. Another widow, Mistress Ford, paid the Company a rent of 16s. a year for her house.

The book-keeping methods employed in the Wardens' Accounts are so primitive, so full of errors and omissions, that a modern auditor would view them with horror. They must have relied a great deal on the memory of Wardens who were still unable to write, and they may well have been supplemented by notebooks which have since perished. Nevertheless, their entries of receipts and expenditures provide a wealth of information about the business and organisation of the Company. If the amounts involved seem very small when measured in our own terms of galloping inflation, the value of money in 1497 was quite a different matter. To translate those values into modern currency accurately is a difficult task, for there is no true basis for comparison; but in the reign of Henry VII a penny was still worth having, a shilling might be a week's wage, and a pound was a substantial amount.

The largest amount of income in 1497-8 came from the 'fines', or fees, received from nine new Liverymen, who each paid 6s. 8d., and totalling £3. Next came fines paid by 10 brethren, eight of them in the Livery and two in the Yeomanry, for the 'abling and admission' of apprentices. A separate order made that year fixed this fine at 3s. 4d., producing a total sum of 33s. 4d. from this source. The order also directed that the fines for binding apprentices in the Company should be used for alms to needy members, as the Founders were 'poor handicraftsmen not having any lands, tenements, or other livelihood or goods in common to relieve the poor people of the same craft falling into poverty, impotence, and great age'. The third source of revenue, in order of magnitude, was the receipt of payments from the members for quarterage and Mass, which totalled 15s. and 7s. 8d. respectively. It is worth noting that quarterage payments included one from John Ashe, described as a Wax Chandler, which suggests that the Act of 1363 requiring a man to belong to one gild only was no longer being enforced.

Fourthly, the income collected by the Wardens included fines for offences against the Company's rules, such as luring an apprentice away from his master; setting to work a child not bound and abled as an apprentice; reviling another brother; failing to obey a summons to attend on the Wardens; and the historically interesting offence of citing a Warden to appear before the 'Spiritual Court'. This was probably the Archdeacon's Court, one of many ecclesiastical tribunals which then exercised jurisdiction in matters of faith and morals. To summon any fellow-Founder, let alone a Warden, before one of these courts was forbidden under the clause in the 1489 Ordinances which did not allow one member to sue another without leave

THE SPRING OF YEARS

of the Wardens. Moreover, the ecclesiastical courts were a symbol of dictation by the Pope which the new independent temper of the English people fiercely resented. The man responsible, John Banys, was himself hauled before the Mayor and lodged in Newgate prison.

The Company's income was completed by contributions from its members towards the cost of dinners and the hiring of barges when the Company took part in ceremonial processions on the river. On the expenses side in 1497-8, the largest item was the cost of two Company dinners that year, one for the Livery and the other for those outside it, which together amounted to just over £8. William Meriell, described as Clerk to the Company, was paid 16s. 8d. for his year's wages, and a further 13s. 4d. to buy a gown. It seems more likely, however, that Meriell did the manual work of a beadle, because an outsider, Richard Magson, was paid for copying out the accounts and doing other clerical work. Meriell may have been unable to write.

The Company's religious affiliation is shown by payments for wax tapers and torches to celebrate St. Lawrence's day, 10 August, in the parish church, and for the services of two deacons, two parish clerks, a choir led by Robert Holme, and the sexton for 'attending our light' and bell-ringing, during the year. The fact that payments were made to two deacons and parish clerks suggests that, although the Company was still attached to St. Lawrence, Jewry, in 1497, it may already have formed some connection with St. Margaret Church nearby in Lothbury.

Other payments for 1497-8 included a winding-sheet for 'Edward Jordan's wife' and help for 'Mother Campion' for her rent. Fees were paid to two of the Mayor's Yeomen of the Chamber for their services, one of them, referred to simply as 'Hugh', being the officer who arrested John Banys for his offence against a Warden; and the other, Robert Horn, who escorted 'William, apprentice with the Goodwife Sweeting' to Newgate and thence to Guildhall for judgment, although William's offence is not stated. The Company also paid 32s. 4d. to 'the stainer' for making banners used by the Company on ceremonial occasions.

At the end of that year, there was an accumulated balance of £13 which was worth a great deal more then than it is now. Of this amount, £7 was deposited in the Company's chest or 'stock', but £6 was allotted for alms and Mass and handed over to the incoming Wardens, who kept it in a separate petty-cash box. It is clear from later years of the Accounts that this alms money was often diverted to other purposes when there was not enough money in the chest to meet expenses. There appears to have been no audit or check of any kind on the Wardens in these early years, and it would have been easy for them to raid the petty cash in an emergency, or even to put some of the money in their own pockets.

One of the most troublesome and expensive charges on the Livery Companies at this time was the frequency of lawsuits and their attendant costs for legal fees, clerical work, and gifts to persons of influence. Whether this rage for litigation was imported by the Normans, always keen lawyers, or whether it was endemic in the English character is a moot point, but the fact remains that the Founders were

14 CITIZENS AND FOUNDERS

involved in no less than four such suits between 1506 and 1514 which bore hard on their slender resources. These were all internal disputes between Master and Wardens, on one side, and members of the Company on the other, and they provide information about the Company's affairs which makes them worth examining in some detail.

In 1506, one of the Yeomanry, Thomas Bassett, brought an action in the Court of Exchequer against the Wardens for 1505-6, Randolf Austin, Edmond Bird and Robert Setcole. He charged them with fining him illegally for disobeying an order issued by Austin which fixed minimum prices for the sale of founders' wares. Bassett claimed that this order was itself illegal, since it contravened a statute passed under Henry VII in 1503 which required gild ordinances to be approved by the Lord Chancellor, the Lord Treasurer, and the Chief Justices. He also accused Austin of buying goods from other members of the Company at prices below those he had fixed himself and selling them at a profit.

Setcole died before the case came up for trial, but Austin and Bird were found guilty and fined £40, a very large sum in those days. They raised the money by selling the Company's plate and jewels and taking the rest from the 'stock' in the chest. As a result, they were sued in the Star Chamber before the Lord Chancellor in 1507 for misappropriating the Company's property, an action brought by two of the three Wardens that year, Thomas Halifax and John Botland, supported by other members of the Company. Austin and Bird were again found guilty and were ordered to restore the missing property at their own cost.

Justice was done, but at a heavy expense to the Company. This was a time when many holders of high office were paid little or nothing from public funds, but bought their places and counted on a good return from the presents they received for showing favour. Thus the payments for lawsuits in the Accounts were not only for legal fees and copies of writs, pleas, and judgments, but also for influencing the verdict. A man named Pecsall was given money for speaking to one of the Exchequer Court judges, a Lord Chief Baron called Sir William Hody. That great man himself accepted a gift in cash, as did his clerk and his servants. Then there were payments to 'Roger the Sergeant' for warning the jury to attend in Westminster Hall, and to provide drinks for the jurymen; for 'the cloth to hang behind my Lord', presumably referring to the Lord Chancellor when he sat in court; and also for the seal in green wax affixed to the court findings. All this was a severe strain on the Company's modest funds and may explain why the Accounts for 1507-8 show no expenditure on Company dinners or payment of alms.

These lawsuits were a warning to the Company as to the need for ensuring that its Ordinances were approved by the Lord Chancellor and other high officers of the Crown, as required by the Parliamentary Act of 1503 which Thomas Bassett had quoted to justify his action. With the support of the whole membership, 'saving only two or three wayward persons', the Wardens were therefore authorised 'to have our Acts and Rules corrected and ordered according to the aforesaid Parliament, that the Craft might be harmless against the King our Sovereign Lord'. Before they could do so, however, a third lawsuit was brought by John Sandford,

THE SPRING OF YEARS   15

a Yeomanry member, who sued Halifax and Botland, Wardens in 1507-8, in the Exchequer Court on a charge of 'making an act contrary to the Parliament', as Bassett had done previously.

A contemporary note in the Accounts says that Sandford was 'one of the simplest persons of all the fellowship' and acted 'of evil will and malice'. The exact nature of his complaint is not stated, but he coupled the name of another Yeomanry member, Thomas Sweeting, with the Wardens in his indictment, and it looks as if he had some quarrel with Sweeting arising from the Company's Ordinances. The jury acquitted all three defendants, but the case had serious financial repercussions. It not only put the Company to further heavy expense, but also made the Wardens so anxious not to incur any similar charge again that they did not even venture to collect quarterage dues from members in 1507-8.

New Ordinances were duly drawn up, approved by the Lords and Justices, and registered by the Court of Aldermen in March 1508. In that year also, the Lord Mayor, Sir Laurence Aylmer, sat in judgment on 'the great variance and discord' between the Founders' Wardens and others of the Livery, on one side, and Yeomanry members on the other. This is the earliest reference to the use of the word 'Yeomanry' to describe those of the Founders outside the Livery. The causes of discontent were named as being 'the custody of certain plate, napery, money, and other jewels belonging to the said Craft, as for other misdemeanours'. Evidently, the removal and sale of Company property by Austin and Bird in 1506 had prompted a demand for closer supervision of the Wardens and better arrangements for the safe keeping of the plate and other valuables.

Aylmer delivered his 'award' in October 1508. He ordered that the Company's plate, money, jewels, and table linen should be kept in a chest with four locks and keys in St. Clement's chapel in St. Margaret church, Lothbury, 'where the said Craft have yearly their Mass for the Brethren and Sisters of the said Fellowship of Founders'. This suggests that the Company must have transferred its religious base from St. Lawrence, Jewry, to St. Margaret at some date between 1497-8, when the annual service was still held in St. Lawrence, and 1508. Their chapel in St. Margaret was named after their patron saint.

The Lord Mayor also directed that six Yeomanry representatives, chosen by the Wardens as being 'the most notable and convenient', should be present when the retiring Wardens delivered their annual accounts and handed over to their successors. One of these Yeomanry members, again selected by the Wardens, was to hold a key to the Company's chest, the other three being kept by the Wardens. The chest containing the valuables could be removed from St. Clement's chapel at any time, as decided by the Wardens and Fellowship, and the Wardens retained custody of the box with the petty cash.

In order to meet charges against the Wardens of acting illegally and making Ordinances without the knowledge or consent of the Yeomanry, Aylmer further laid down that the retiring Wardens, when presenting their accounts, should 'call all persons of the said Craft afore them and cause the Ordinances granted unto them by the Mayor and Aldermen to be read unto them, so that they shall not run

16   CITIZENS AND FOUNDERS

into no wilful disobedience for lack of information'. Finally, any breaches of the
Mayor's award incurred a fine of 26s. 6d. divided equally between the Company,
for the benefit of its members, and the City Chamber, for the common body of
citizens.

Although Aylmer's judgment gave the Yeomanry a key to the chest and some
right to be kept informed of decisions by the Wardens, it conceded no share in the
management of the Company's affairs. Nor did the Yeomanry ask for one, since
this was an age which respected authority. Even the minor reforms proposed by
Aylmer seem to have been more honoured in the breach than the observance. There
is evidence in the Accounts that the Company chest was often removed from St.
Clement's chapel in later years by Master or Wardens, without any reference to
the general membership. Even in 1508-9, immediately after the Mayor's instructions, the Accounts show a payment made for carrying the chest from the house
of the senior Warden, Thomas Halifax, to that of his successor, Robert Stacy. The
latter did report, however, at the end of his year, that the chest was back in the
chapel where it belonged. In 1514, when Halifax was Master, some members complained that he was keeping the chest at home, and he promised to return it immediately.

Then again, the rule that six Yeomanry members should be called to hear the
Wardens' Accounts read and approved is only on record as having been observed
in three later years, those from 1519 to 1522. In some years, only five or six of the
Livery attended, and in others even that vestigial presence seems to have been
abandoned. The rule that the Ordinances should be read out to the whole membership when the accounts were presented may have been followed for a year or two,
judging by a few vague references, but seems to have been ignored thereafter.

The dissensions between Livery and Yeomanry basically arose from new class
distinctions and divisions created by economic changes which upset the simpler
uniformity and balance of the old gilds. The Yeomanry bodies in the City Companies had their origins in the journeymen and 'serving men' who worked for a
master-craftsman under strict conditions, including a contractual obligation not to
marry. But with the expansion of trade and investment, a widening gulf appeared
between a wealthy minority of merchant-financiers, representing capital, and a
much poorer labouring majority of manual workers which increased with the
growth of population and came to include many master-craftsmen as well as their
journeymen.

It became harder for the manufacturing masters in a gild to survive and pay
their way against mounting outside competition, price-cutting, and rising wages.
Their journeymen, faced by a dwindling prospect of ever becoming masters themselves, became discontented with their working conditions and gild wages. They
also accused their employers of preventing them from becoming masters, so as to
avoid competition, and charging exorbitant fees for proposing them for the City
freedom, which was an essential condition for carrying on a trade. The masters
blamed the journeymen for demanding excessive wages, especially in times of
labour shortage such as occurred after the ravages of the 'Black Death', or bubonic

THE SPRING OF YEARS   17

plague, in 1348. The masters also complained that journeymen went absent without leave, quitted their service without giving proper notice, and were often too drunk to work.

The end result was that many journeymen left their masters and moved outside the City limits, where they married and set up as self-employed traders. They even formed their own gilds which, in 1400 and as defined by George Unwin, could be described as 'a prohibited association of rebellious journeymen'. The masters retaliated by setting up their own pickets who, on more than one occasion, resorted to pole-axes, daggers, and iron-tipped poles. In due course, however, the City Companies made some concession to change by creating a 'Yeomanry' class of membership ranking below the privileged Livery, and by 1500, to quote Unwin again, this had become 'a recognised but subordinate branch of the Livery Company'.

For those Yeomanry members who won promotion to the Livery, there was little cause for complaint, but for the majority which did not, there were good grounds for discontent. Their main grievance in the Founders was that they were subjected to the rule and discipline of Liverymen who no longer worked in the craft themselves, but followed other and more profitable occupations. Personal feelings of envy and malice may well have played a large part, especially among the more incapable and lazier Yeomanry members with no chance of entering the Livery, but it cannot be doubted that the top positions in the companies, as in the City government, were passing into the hands of men no longer engaged in the manufacturing crafts and pursuing other trades. The case already mentioned of the Warden, Randolf Austin, who bought founders' wares below the minimum prices which he himself had fixed, and sold them at a profit, suggests that he was more of a merchant than a craftsman.

It was not a serving Yeomanry member, however, who provoked the next Company crisis, but a Liveryman called John Sonlowe who had been chosen from the Yeomanry in 1510. In 1514, Sonlowe swore an indictment in the Exchequer Court against Thomas Halifax, the senior Warden that year and equivalent to Master, William Knight and David Mills, both Liverymen, and Thomas Bassett, the same Yeomanry member who had sued Austin and Bird in 1506 for abusing their powers. Halifax must by this time have been heartily sick of legal conflicts, after having taken the lead in forcing Austin and Bird to make restitution of the Company's property, and being acquitted himself in Sandford's suit against the Wardens.

Sonlowe charged the four defendants with a breach of the same Act of Parliament cited in 1506 by Thomas Bassett in his own suit, and the latter thus found himself hoist with his own petard. Sonlowe claimed that the four men had acted illegally by making an order that no Founder could take an apprentice without paying a fine of 3s. 4d. A report on his charge in the Wardens' Accounts accuses him of committing perjury, but the defendants were arrested and sent to the Fleet prison to await trial. Thus it was that the senior Warden, or Master of the Company, Thomas Halifax, found himself in durance vile, as Randolf Austin had been before him, and as would happen again in later history (see page 84). Un-

18   CITIZENS AND FOUNDERS

like Austin, however, Halifax and his co-defendants had the full support of the Company, which paid for their release on bail, and they were acquitted when the case was heard.

Nevertheless, there are some curious features of this affair which are hard to fathom. Firstly, nothing is known about Sonlowe's motives for bringing his action and thus, in effect, biting the hand which had raised him from the Yeomanry to the Livery rank. Nor do we know why he waited till 1514 before going to court, although he alleged that the defendants had committed their offence three years earlier, in 1511. Secondly, only one of the defendants, David Mills, was in office at that time, when he was Master, and Bassett was only a Yeomanry member. Thirdly, and one would have thought decisively, the payment of a fine of 3s. 4d. for binding an apprentice was explicitly authorised by a Company order of 1497, which specified that the proceeds were to be used for poor relief. Yet the defence seems to have relied entirely on the fact that three of the four accused were not in office in 1511 and therefore could not have made an 'act', but did not point out that the payment of fines for binding apprentices was an established and properly authorised rule of the Company.

There is one possible clue to Sonlowe's suit, though it can only be a tentative suggestion. The Wardens' Accounts for 1507-8 show that Bassett paid fees that year for taking on two apprentices, and for a third one the year after. This looks like a clear breach of the rule in the 1489 ordinances that a Yeomanry master, such as Bassett, should have only one apprentice, or two if the City Chamberlain gave special permission, of which there is no mention. Sonlowe may have had this in mind when he brought his action, and he did indeed allege that the four defendants had conspired, at a meeting 'in Coleman Street', to bind as many as three apprentices at a time. Such a meeting would probably have taken place in the house of David Mills, as Master in 1511, and Bassett could have paid fines for binding three apprentices contrary to the rules. If this actually happened, it would help to explain why the defence avoided reference to the Ordinances, though it still does not account for Sonlowe's delay in starting proceedings.

Whatever the full story may be, the Company again had to pay a large sum for legal fees and gifts to influential persons. Payments were made to the Warden of the Fleet prison for bail; for a writ of 'Tales' ordering the Sheriff to fill jury vacancies, and a writ of 'Scire Facias' requiring the parties to show cause why judgment should not be executed; for money given to the jurymen in gifts and expenses; for a fee to the City Recorder, Sir Richard Broke, and presents to the Lord Chief Baron and his clerk in the Court of Exchequer. Even if there was any substance in Sonlowe's charges, his chances of winning against such opposition cannot be rated very highly.

At the same time, the position of Master and Wardens was a difficult one which deserves some sympathy. After all, it was the Mayor and Aldermen who insisted on inspecting and approving the Ordinances of the City Companies, and it was primarily their responsibility to detect and correct any errors in them. Yet there was no visible sign of support from Guildhall for the Founders when the Ordi-

THE SPRING OF YEARS   19

nances were challenged in the law courts, though some City influence may have been at work through other channels. The general effect of these legal disputes on the Livery Companies was to make those which did not possess Royal Charters renew their efforts to obtain one, so as to protect their rights more effectively. But here they came up against the dislike felt by the Mayor and Aldermen for increasing the number of Charters and were in a cleft stick. It was not until a century later, when James I badly needed money, that Charters were more freely granted.

After the Sonlowe case, the Founders again sought a Royal Charter and incurred further heavy expense in petitioning the Mayor, preparing drafts, paying lawyers to correct them, and other Companies for leave to examine their Charters. One item was for money paid to a man 'to labour to my Lord Cardinal for our Corporation', the Cardinal being Wolsey, then at the height of power. The Company's finances were so strained by all these demands that money had to be borrowed by pledging the silver and plate. But these efforts came to nothing, and the Company fell back on the familiar course of submitting new Ordinances to the Mayor and Aldermen, who approved them in 1516.

They confirmed the right to charge fines for 'abling' apprentices which Sonlowe had disputed, and dealt with their conditions of entry and service. They also made an interesting change in the structure of the Company by abolishing the previous distinction between 'householders' and 'journeymen' in the Yeomanry in their payment of different rates for quarterage and Mass money. This suggests that a growing number of journeymen had by this time become householders themselves and drawn nearer to Yeomanry masters in social and financial status, but it also tended to widen the gap between a minority in the Livery, increasingly drawn from other trades, and a more unified and cohesive Yeomanry in which the founding craft was still uppermost.

The Livery paid for its privileges by higher cash contributions and a much heavier burden of work and responsibility when serving as Master or Warden. So long as Masters and Wardens were seen to be carrying out their duties honestly and efficiently, and so long as ambitious Yeomanry members could stand a fair chance of being chosen for the Livery, the system worked quite well. But when these conditions were not fulfilled, there was trouble. It is significant, for example, that the internal quarrels and lawsuits here described took place in a short period of time when the Livery membership was reduced from 31 in 1497 to only 15 in 1508, while the Yeomanry strength rose from 48 to 76 in that time. Such a polarisation of extremes was not calculated to promote internal harmony, but encouraged a sense of grievance. For a hundred years or so after Mayor Aylmer's 'Award' of 1508, order and discipline in the Company seem to have been restored, but the underlying conflict between Livery and Yeomanry again broke out in the revolutionary atmosphere of Cromwell's time, as described in a later chapter.

CHAPTER III

Winds of Change

THE ENGLISH PEOPLE have been singularly fortunate in their past history and situation as an island kingdom, enjoying a freedom from foreign invasion which gave them time to work out their social and constitutional development by a process of change which was gradual and, for the most part, peaceful. In our present phase of change which is worldwide and, in the Western sphere, largely destructive, our past advantages make it much harder for us to revise our thinking and to understand how our long-term interests, and those of our children, are best served at a time when our former strengths in defence capacity, Imperial greatness, and pre-eminence as a maritime trading nation have all disappeared. For us, more than for other nations, the problems of coming to terms with a world which is now inter-dependent are exceptionally difficult and painful.

For our predecessors in the Founders, living in times of national growth and expansion, the effects of change were more easily absorbed and digested, however much they fell short of the material improvements in living standards which have since taken place. The transformation of the medieval gild from a closely-knit professional brotherhood of craftsmen into a Livery Company representing much more varied interests was the inevitable result of change, but change spread over a much longer period and blending what was good in the past with the new trends. As Professor Lipson has described it :

> The degeneracy of the gild system was a symptom, rather than a fundamental cause, of its gradual break-up. It was the inevitable result of economic forces. The gilds belonged to a stage of industrial evolution where the master craftsman was an independent producer owning the raw material as well as the instruments of production, and selling the finished product direct to the consumer. The essence was the combination of handicraft and trading functions in the same hands. So long as the market was limited, the gild system answered to the needs of the time.

> When the market widened, the mercantile functions passed to a special class of traders, while the master craftsmen confined to purely manual functions lost their economic independence. Thus production and distribution were separated. The gild system was supplanted by the domestic system whereby a class of employers acting as middlemen thrust itself between the artificer and

WINDS OF CHANGE

the consumer, reducing the former to the status of a wage-earner. A new kind of industrial association emerged in the Livery Company, differing from the craft gild in the appearance of two distinct classes – capitalists who wore the 'Livery' and small masters or yeomanry restricted to the manual parts of their occupation.

This new pattern of economic development was alien in many respects to the democratic spirit of the old craft gild and its pride of quality in workmanship, but the new wealth which it created was used to fertilise many other fields. The moneyed men of the City formed financial and matrimonial alliances with the landed gentry and often ploughed their wealth back into these broader acres. Many country squires sent their younger sons to London to serve as apprentices and take the road to fortune. County families like the Stonors, who were big sheep-farmers in the West Country, exported their wool through the City's market in Calais, until it was lost to France in 1558, and thought it an honour to be styled 'Merchants of the Staple', as the market was called.

The 16th-century story of the Founders gives evidence both of the Company's earlier origins and of changes in its evolution. As already mentioned, the religious link with the Brotherhood of St. Clement remained strong, but the Founders were one of the poorer Companies and they relied on contributions from members and gifts from benefactors to pay for their religious observances and the distribution of alms. The Ordinances of 1516 suggest that the St. Clement's Brotherhood was still, at that date, treated as a separate entity under its own Masters and that it received, at least nominally, the Mass money of one penny a quarter paid by all Company members alike, although the receipts and payments were shown by the Wardens in their accounts.

John Blowbell, a Liveryman, gave the Company an altar-table with an image of St. Clement by his will dated in 1500, and also a silver-gilt cup. The late Dr. Stannus, in a paper dated 1955, established the fact that Blowbell was born at Wassbrook in Suffolk and owned land in that county and in Essex. His will shows that he was a parishioner of St. Lawrence, Jewry, suggesting that the Company may still have been associated with St. Lawrence when he made his gifts. In 1500-1, the Company paid for new wax 'put to the beam light in St. Lawrence church', and the Wardens' Accounts for 1509-11 record payments to the parish priest of St. Lawrence and the deacons for singing Mass. On that evidence, it would seem that the Company was still using St. Lawrence church even after Mayor Aylmer's judgment of 1508, in which he referred to St. Margaret, Lothbury, as the church where the Founders held their yearly Mass and where their chest was to be kept in St. Clement's chapel. Even as late as 1681, the Accounts include small payments for expenses, unspecified, at St. Lawrence church.

Individual members and benefactors of the Company certainly had connections with either one of these two churches. Richard Hawke, for example, whose name has already been mentioned, left the Company money under his will in 1495 for a yearly requiem at St. Margaret, Lothbury, and also a silver-gilt cup known

22   CITIZENS AND FOUNDERS

as 'The Hawk'. His memorial service was celebrated by the Company for many years and known as 'Hawke's Dirge'. Payments for bread, cheese and ale for the mourners appear in the Accounts until 1547, when Henry VIII died, and no doubt the 'Dirge' was then abolished under the Reformation of Edward VI, which suppressed the religious chantries as 'Popish practices' and confiscated their endowments.

Hawke's cup is listed in an inventory of the Company's possessions made in 1497, which gives its weight as 34 ounces. It was pledged in 1550 to a Warden, William Pendred, as security for repayment to him of a debit balance of £6 on the accounts which he took over that year. He gave a receipt and undertook to return the cup when the deficit was made good, which seems to have been quite a common practice. The cup no longer appears in inventories of 1603 and 1610, and may possibly have been forfeited to Pendred or some other Warden earlier, but a much more likely explanation is that it was sold, with other Company silver and plate, to meet some special financial need, such as the cost of obtaining a grant of arms for the Company in 1590. Such forced sales were often necessary to remedy the shortage of income, and they account for the loss of many Founders' heirlooms.

The longest-lasting benefaction to the Company was an annual distribution of coal among 20 poor Founders, known as 'Jordan's Dole' and paid for as part of a legacy of land and tenements by Henry Jordan to the Fishmongers' Company under his will in 1468. Jordan was himself a Fishmonger, but apparently had some family connection with the Founders, perhaps indicated by a later payment made by that Company in 1497-8 for a winding-sheet 'for the wife of Edward Jordan'. His legacy to the Fishmongers was intended to pay for annual requiem Masses and prayers for himself and his family, as well as the distribution of alms for coal, but he included in this distribution 'twenty of the poor householders of the Craft of Founders dwelling within the walls of the City of London'.

This was commuted into a payment of one mark yearly, or 13s. 4d. at that time, paid by the Fishmongers to the Founders, whose Younger Warden saw to its division between 20 recipients who each got 8d. This annual payment was still being made by the Fishmongers in 1925, more than 450 years after the original bequest, but it has since been transferred to local government administration. Gifts such as 'Jordan's Dole' were probably safe from the diversion by the Wardens of alms money for other purposes, since they were protected by a legal deed. It should be added that, when times were easier, the Wardens frequently excused needy members from paying arrears of quarterage, or remitted fines imposed for breaches of the rules.

From very early times, there were three alternative means of gaining admission to the Company one by 'patrimony', being the son of a freeman; the second by 'servitude' as an apprentice to a freeman; and the third by 'redemption' or purchase. In all three cases, however, a new member was enrolled in the Yeomanry and remained there unless chosen for the Livery later on. In 1508-9, for example, three new brethren called John Goter, John Sankey, and Roger Wright were admitted by 'redemption', each paying a fine of 6s. 8d. and another 12d. for 'oath

WINDS OF CHANGE

23

money', but only Goter gained promotion to the Livery. This was in 1517-8, when he and four other Yeomanry members paid an additional fine of 6s. 8d. 'for the livery entering'. Goter went on to serve the offices of Third and Second Warden, and was chosen as Master in 1542 and 1545. In 1574-5, Robert Waldo paid 20s. for admission, and was promoted to the Livery only two years later. He served as Younger Warden in 1578-9, Second Warden in 1582-3, and was four times Master in later years. Promotions from Yeomanry to Livery seem to have taken place every three or four years on average, though there were times when the disproportion in size between a small Livery and large Yeomanry was allowed to rise to a dangerous degree.

In the earlier times of the medieval gilds, when their religious function was stronger, no distinction was made between them in the 'clothing' worn by members on public occasions. They all wore black gowns similar to those worn by monks, with cowls over the head and pieces of fur attached to warm the neck and shoulders. Later, when the Livery Companies took to wearing different colours, the Liverymen of the Founders paid for the making of their gowns, but the Wardens provided free samples of material, or 'scantlings', as they were called.

A striking feature of the Tudor period is the highly important, and mostly beneficial, effect produced by the entry of foreign craftsmen, many of whom came as refugees from religious persecution in their own countries. This influx of foreign immigrants was no new phenomenon, but had long played a creative part in developing new English industries and skills. The London weavers were nearly all foreign immigrants by origin, entirely so in the case of the French silk-weavers who settled in Spitalfields and Shoreditch. Other immigrants from Flanders started the use of hops for brewing ale, while French felt-makers pioneered the making of felt hats which replaced the old caps. Foreign craftsmen also excelled as shoemakers and in the tanning and dressing of leather. The English goldsmiths learned a great deal from the ideas imported by their foreign rivals, but the most influential contribution was made by the Flemish printers who accompanied William Caxton when he set up the first English printing-machine near Westminster Abbey in 1477. Caxton had spent over 30 years in the Low Countries as local Governor of the English Company of Merchant Adventurers. His epoch-making success in printing owed much to the fact that linen for making paper was coming into use and replacing the old, expensive parchment.

But although the arrival of these French Huguenots, Dutch Protestants, and other refugee craftsmen was England's gain, and a loss to their native countries, the London craftsmen hated and feared them as competitors who, in many cases, were the better and more skilful workmen. Not only that, but some of the immigrants were merchants who made money from the import and export trade, and thus kindled fresh jealousy among the London manual workers. In 1514, the City crafts submitted a petition to the King's Council protesting against the freedom allowed to aliens, and in 1516 an anonymous notice was put up in the City accusing the Government of ruining the country by 'favouring foreigners'. On May Day 1517, a London mob attacked the foreigners in an outburst of fury, killing or

24 CITIZENS AND FOUNDERS

wounding many of them and looting their houses before setting them on fire. The rioters discovered that Henry VIII had as short a way with the rabble as he did with redundant wives. A dozen apprentices were hanged in the streets, and 400 other prisoners were sentenced to death but had their lives spared after the rope had been put round their necks.

In 1529, Parliament passed an Act which confirmed a decree by the Star Chamber that 'strangers' coming to London, and setting up shop there as craftsmen, must be enrolled in the City Company representing their particular trade. This applied both to foreign immigrants and to English settlers from other parts of the country, but it was mainly directed at those coming from abroad in rapidly multiplying numbers. As Unwin points out in his book on the London Gilds, licences were granted to 1,800 aliens in 1437, of whom 540 resided in London, mostly in Southwark or the eastern suburbs. In 1563, the aliens living within the old City limits, or in Southwark and Westminster, numbered over 4,500, and by 1583 this had risen to 5,141.

The effect of the 1529 Act on the Founders is shown in the Wardens' Accounts for 1529-30, where the usual list of members is followed by 16 new names under the heading 'Franche [French] Men'. A few, such as 'Tetu' or 'Duprom', have a recognisable French likeness, but most have been put into an English form, either because they adopted English names or perhaps because some were English 'strangers' moving to London. The most interesting name on the list is that of a French 'stranger' called Peter Baude, sometimes written as Balde, who was a gunfounder working in Houndsditch. His enrolment in the Founders links that Company with a major development in British foundry history. Peter Balde was an expert brass founder and was certainly casting brass guns in 1533 at his Houndsditch foundry. He was later called to Buxted, in Sussex by a local iron-master, Ralph Hogg, and employed in an iron-works owned by the Rector of Buxted, the Rev. William Levett, who seems to have been a militant sort of churchman. In Buxted, Peter Balde's special technique was used to produce the first British cast-iron cannon in 1543, making him the creator of the iron gun-founding industry in this country. Many of these guns were exported to Europe, and some were later discovered in Spanish warships, much to the annoyance of Elizabeth's Privy Council.

The London parishes where these 'strangers' lived are listed with their names, and show that nearly all of them resided either in Southwark or Westminster, or in the newer suburbs outside the City proper, where they were beyond the Lord Mayor's jurisdiction. This helps to explain why, although required to pay quarterage and Mass money like ordinary members, only four of the 16 'strangers' concerned actually paid up and the rest defaulted. The four who paid did so at the Livery rate of 12d. yearly for quarterage and 2d. for Mass money, perhaps because they were master-craftsmen who saw an advantage in being associated with the Company. The names of defaulters still continued to appear in membership lists, probably because there was a legal obligation to record the names under the Act of 1529, even if they did not fulfil their obligations.

WINDS OF CHANGE 25

The Founders, like other Livery Companies, continued for many years to experience difficulty in asserting their rights over the 'strangers'. In 1547-8, the Wardens paid one of the Mayor's officers to arrest a stranger, whose name and offence are not mentioned. In 1576, the Wardens were authorised by the Court of Aldermen to commit two strangers to prison, if they persisted in refusing the oath to observe the Company's Ordinances. There was a marked improvement, however in receipts of quarterage and Mass money from this source, and the Accounts for 1568-9, the last to include a membership list, give the names of 29 'strangers', of whom 22 paid varying amounts to the Company. Twelve paid quarterage at the rate prescribed for Liverymen, but were not accorded that rank in the list, nor does any 'stranger' ever seem to have been recognised as a Livery or Yeomanry member, much less have served as a Master or Warden of the Founders. They may have been disqualified by their foreign birth.

Starting in 1557-8, the membership lists give the names of 'strangers' and 'journeymen strangers' under separate headings, thus indicating a difference in status between master-craftsmen and hired workers. A hundred years or so later, in 1673-4, the receipts of income that year included a sum of 7s. 8d. 'when the Dutchmen were made free', but no details are given. In the year following, 1674-5, the expenses listed by the Master, Roger Fisher, include an item for 'a trial with the foreigners' at Hicks Hall, the name given to the Middlesex Sessions House at Clerkenwell because the cost of building it in 1612 was met by Sir Baptist Hicks, one of the magistrates. There is no further mention of 'strangers' in the Founders' records.

It was the apprenticeship system, however, which gave a Livery Company its true character and continuity by supplying new members trained in the craft and identifying their interests with it. This system is thought to have been imported into England from Western Europe in the 13th century, under Henry III. Fines for the 'abling and admission' of apprentices provided a regular source of income for the Founders throughout the whole period of the Wardens' Accounts from 1497 to 1681, and admission by 'servitude' still continues to this present day, though it has long since become a polite fiction.

A distinction was drawn between the apprentice and the journeyman, or hired workman, but it was by no means rigid or exclusive. An apprentice might find, at the end of his service, that he lacked the means to set himself up as a master and must earn his living as a journeyman. Conversely, a journeyman might do well enough to become an independent master. The working conditions for an apprentice were hard by any modern standards. A boy of 11 or 12 and sometimes a little girl, was tied to the employer for a period of seldom less than three years and more often ten or twelve. He worked, lived, and fed in the master's house, sleeping in an attic or basement. He was required to be 'sound in wind and limb' and might need all his strength to stay the course, since a bad master could keep him short of food, beat him, and even cheat on his wages or refuse to propose the apprentice for the freedom of the Company at the end of his contract. A bad mistress could make an even worse employer.

Apprentices were not allowed to marry during their service, a rule upheld by

26   CITIZENS AND FOUNDERS

an Act of Common Council in 1572, and they had to wear distinctive clothing. In 1572-3, an officer from Bridewell prison was called to Founders' Hall to whip an apprentice for being improperly dressed, and in 1614 another apprentice, George Rogers, who had disobeyed the ban on marriage, was forbidden to work for members of the Company. He may have recovered from this setback, as in 1619-20 a man of that name presented the Company with a silver spoon on receiving the freedom, as required under an order made by the Court of Assistants in 1612. Rogers may therefore have survived to complete his apprenticeship as a married man and, it must be hoped, live happy ever after.

The Court often showed kindness and leniency towards offenders, and the cases of misconduct by apprentices mentioned in the Wardens' Accounts are far outnumbered by the penalties imposed for their ill-treatment. Fines were frequently paid by masters, and sometimes by their widows, for such offences as refusing to release an apprentice when his time was up; failing to present him to the Wardens for 'abling' and admission as a freeman; denying him his wages, or making him work at night; or setting a child to work who had not been bound as an apprentice.

The London apprentices were a turbulent breed and often took an active part in street rioting. In 1641, on the eve of civil war between King and Parliament, they petitioned the House of Commons for the relief of their grievances and a better respect 'for the privileges of their order'. They complained that they were always singled out as scapegoats for disorders in the City, and blamed the foreign craftsmen for robbing them of their living. They also protested that, although they were bound to serve only their masters, 'yet of late their mistresses had gotten the predominancy over them also'. Despite all their complaints, however, many an English family sought to apprentice their sons in the City as the start to a brilliant career already made famous by Sir Richard Whittington, three times Mayor of London, who died in 1425.

To secure an apprenticeship in the City, it was obviously necessary to have some family or business connection with a Livery Company, but certain rules also had to be observed. In 1548, two of the Founders, Edward Collingwood and James Winkles, signed an agreement before a public notary which was distinctly unorthodox and led to trouble. Collingwood was a senior Liveryman who had himself started as an apprentice in the Company many years earlier and worked his way up to Third Warden in 1532-3 and Second Warden in 1537-8. Winkles was a Yeomanry member. The two men agreed to co-operate in obtaining an apprenticeship for a young man called Robert Thompson, the son of a weaver who lived in Towcester, Northants, before his death.

Collingwood undertook, at his own cost, to present and 'able' Thompson as an apprentice in the Founders for 12 years of service, but to turn him over immediately to Winkles for his training. Winkles agreed to teach the boy, pay for his keep, and give him a weekly wage of 4d. Collingwood promised to obtain the City freedom for Thompson when the latter had completed his term as apprentice. Both Collingwood and Winkles pledged their executors to honour the agreement, and each put down £10 as security for his undertakings.

WINDS OF CHANGE 27

It is not clear which of the two men was the prime mover in this transaction, but it looks as if they used Collingwood's entitlement, as a past Warden, to more apprentices than Winkles as a cover for getting young Thompson apprenticed to Collingwood in name only, while he actually lived and worked with Winkles. The agreement evidently came to the attention of the Master and Wardens and they did not like it, for they entered the full text in the Wardens' Accounts under the heading: 'A certain false conclusion made between Edward Collingwood and James Winkles under a feigned colour'. In 1548-9, the Company paid 4d. for 'engrossing the matter between Collingwood and Winkles at Mr. Chamberlain's request', from which it would seem that the City Chamberlain had been called in to settle the affair. The Yeomanry list for 1558-9 includes a 'Robert Thomsone' for the first time, but we cannot tell whether this was the same man as the erstwhile apprentice.

So long as the Companies still consisted mainly of craftsmen making and selling their own products, the number of apprentices was strictly limited, with the object of restricting competition from those who set up shop themselves later as masters or self-employed journeymen. As noted already, the Founders' rules of 1489 laid down a fixed scale of apprentices allowed to members according to rank. In some Companies, those seeking to take up the freedom as journeymen were discouraged by having to produce for the approval of Master and Wardens a difficult and expensive 'work of art'.

So long as the crafts were confined to the old City 'within the walls', it was not too difficult for a Company to maintain a 'closed shop' in its own trade by controlling employment and wages, and carrying out searches for defective goods. But when production became more varied and was taken up in the outer suburbs, when merchants and financiers arose whose interests spread beyond the limits of any one trade, then the monopoly powers of the old gilds inevitably decayed. It was not much use for the journeymen in a Company to demand, as they did, that their position should be protected by forbidding their masters to employ outside labour, since their own supply of it was often too scarce and too expensive. Nor did a Livery or Court of Assistants increasingly subject to merchant influences see the same need as before to limit the number of apprentices and forgo the handsome source of Company income in fees which this provided.

Nevertheless, the Livery Companies put up a long and stubborn defence of their old rights and privileges. The Founders continued to retain their limitations on apprentices, a ban on the hawking of Company wares in the streets, and the right of search for defective wares, extended by the Charter in 1614 to an area of three miles 'without the City'. Moreover, the numerous Companies which were formed in the Stuart period, some representing new trades and others a revival of old ones which regained their independence, these also insisted that only their own members should be allowed to pursue the trade of the Company in the City; that freemen of other Companies who followed that trade should be translated from those Companies to the Company directly representing it; and that all persons engaged in a particular trade should bind and make free their apprentices in the Company

28   CITIZENS AND FOUNDERS

associated with it and none other. In principle, the Mayor and Aldermen accepted a Company's right of control over its own trade, and many Acts of Common Council were passed confirming such rights. Sometimes, however, things turned out rather differently.

In 1659, to look ahead for a moment, a joint petition was presented to the Court of Aldermen by the Founders, Scriveners, Upholders, Freemasons, Clockmakers, Carpenters and Gunmakers, in which they claimed that all persons who followed those occupations, but were freemen of other Companies, should bind their apprentices 'to each of those Companies whose Art they exercise'. This petition was referred by the Aldermen to a committee which heard evidence from the Companies concerned, but it was also instructed to consult 'the Twelve Great Companies'. These latter, having widely-spread merchant interests which did not accord with the vesting of control over a trade in the hands of one company, and that not their own, presented arguments against the petition which led the committee to reject it. As a sop to the petitioners, the committee's report added the ambiguous remark :

> Howbeit we think that some expedient as to view and search, and the limitation of persons free of other Companies different from their acts in binding apprentices, be thought on as to the contentment of those Companies as the weal of the City and Citizens.

In practice, however, it was the Great Companies which had the last word, and not surprisingly, since it was they who ruled the City.

Long before this, however, the number of apprentices in the Founders, as in many other Companies, had shown a large increase. Possibly this was the cause of a petition made to the Court of Aldermen by the 'workmen' of the Founders in 1543, and a counter-petition submitted by the Wardens in 1550 against 'certain perverse persons of their Fellowship'. In 1555, the Common Council approved a rule that no apprentice was to be admitted as a freeman, or allowed to set himself up as a householder, until the age of twenty four. And in 1556 the Lord Mayor and Aldermen summoned the wardens of the Founders, and 16 other Companies, 'to take order for the number of their apprentices'. In 1587, Alderman Stephen Slaney, a Skinner, was sent to meet the Wardens and others of the Founders' Company at their Hall to consider whether the Ordinances were being properly kept or not. It was agreed that no Liveryman 'being metal men or workers of metal, and the moulders' should take any new apprentice till the existing ones were diminished, and that no Yeomanry member should take on an apprentice pending such a reduction in numbers.

Although breaches of this rule were punishable by a fine of 20s. and the loss of an unauthorised apprentice, its effects were short-lived. For a few years, the Wardens' Accounts show no receipt of fines for 'abling' new apprentices, but in 1591-2 seven apprentices were admitted, rising to 20 in 1603-4, and no less than 49 in 1625-6. In 1657, the Founders laid down a scale of three apprentices for a Master, Warden or Assistant, past or present, two for a liveryman, and one for any other member who kept house or shop for himself, but excluding journeymen. At the

WINDS OF CHANGE

same time, a minimum term of service lasting seven years was fixed for apprentices, and only those of English birth could be accepted or bound.

After this, the intake of apprentices fell back on a more even keel. In the last five years of the Wardens' Accounts, ending in 1680-1, the average number of bindings annually was 16, and the fine had risen from 3s. 4d. to 5s.

CHAPTER IV

London Pride

THE WARS of the Roses ended in 1485 with the Lancastrian victory at Bosworth and the seizure of the Crown by a Welshman, Henry Tudor, Earl of Richmond. As Henry VII, he founded a Tudor dynasty which consolidated the Royal power and gave England a long period of peace and stability lasting until Elizabeth died childless in 1603 and was followed by the Stuarts. At the same time, English ideas were much influenced by the intellectual ferment of the Renaissance in Europe, which challenged the old institutions and enriched English poetry and music with a new creative vigour, as well as turning the minds of men to exploration overseas and the discovery of unknown lands.

The City of London had continued to flourish during the Wars of the Roses, thanks to its key position in the national scale and a prudent policy of making gifts and loans to whichever side, Yorkist or Lancastrian, had the upper hand. The murderous strife which decimated the feudal chivalry left the City free to increase its own powers of self-government, and Mayors and Aldermen displayed all the pomp and ostentation of the wealthy merchant Companies from which most of them came. The London docks and shipyards were hard at work, and the Thames swarmed with boats and barges carrying private citizens or City magnates about their business. New and imposing public buildings, churches, and private residences appeared in large numbers to bear witness to London's wealth and pre-eminence. As G. M. Trevelyan remarks in his *History of England*, 'Westminster had become the recognised centre of Royal administration, but it was only a village at London's gate'. A contemporary observer, the Scottish poet Dunbar, paid his own famous tribute when he exclaimed: 'London, thou art the flower of cities all'.

Nevertheless, this flower had many seamy sides. The City streets were still a medieval maze of narrow alleys full of filth and garbage thrown out from doors and windows. There were no pavements, which meant that pedestrians were forced into the gutters by carts or riders and 'went to the wall', as this saying was then used. Most of the houses were still made of wood and wattle, but the use of stone was beginning to appear in the richer quarters, and the old thatched roofs were gradually being replaced by red tiles. Much of the ground still consisted of open spaces, such as courtyards, gardens, and allotments, which gave London a rustic flavour, but there was a foul stench in the air from the burning of 'sea coal' shipped to London from Newcastle, which was driving out charcoal. It was strong enough to

LONDON PRIDE

cause fears of infection and make the richer citizens take country villas in Chelsea or Fulham, while poorer people moved out to the eastern suburbs.

Public health and hygiene were primitive in the extreme. The plague of the 'Black Death', which in 1348-9 wiped out nearly half a population of four million, continued to recur, though on a lesser scale, until late in the 17th century. Trevelyan suggests that it finally died out because the black rats which carried the plague-transmitting fleas were driven out by the brown rats.

On the other hand, the 16th century saw some notable advances in education. Many of the grammar schools which have served England so well were founded at this time with endowments given by public-spirited bishops, City Companies, and merchant princes seeking to give poor boys a better chance of making their way in the world. This was all the more welcome because the Reformation under Edward VI closed down the schools maintained by religious bodies and the Crown seized their property endowments, either giving them as rewards to greedy Ministers or selling them to the highest bidder. There were a few happier endings. Trinity College, Cambridge, was founded by Henry VIII largely from his confiscations of monastic lands, and Christ Church, Oxford, was similarly endowed by Cardinal Wolsey from the spoils of the religious houses which fell into his hands.

The Bishop of Ely founded Jesus College, Cambridge, from the revenues of St. Radegund's Nunnery nearby, which he dissolved in 1496, but he gave a different reason. He justified the dissolution by referring to 'the negligence and improvidence and dissolute disposition and incontinence of the religious women of the house, by reason of the vicinity of Cambridge University'.

Although popular feeling ran high against wealthy and corrupt churchmen, religion itself continued to play a large part in the daily lives of ordinary men and women. The rejection of Papal authority by Henry VIII was not forced on him by his people, but was designed, in the first place, to give Henry a free hand in his marriages. But it led to a struggle between different schools of thought as to what kind of church settlement should replace the old Catholic order. The more con-servative churchmen tried to suppress English translations of the Bible, which seemed to them to encourage religious disobedience and the rejection of spiritual authority exercised by bishops. At times when this school was in power, even the possession of an English Bible might be taken as evidence of heresy and punished by death. At other times, when the reformers were on top, they imprisoned and executed parish priests for holding to the old service rituals.

Most people in the Tudor age still lacked the ability to read or write, and there were few of the letters and diaries which later provided so much material for his-torians. It was a robust and self-reliant age which enjoyed the simpler pleasures of life and learned to create its own forms of relaxation and amusement. Music was popular among all classes, and they joined in playing, singing, and dancing. Story-telling was still a living art practised in the family circle and with friends, and hand-written political satires in verse circulated among the more educated public. The first public libraries were being opened, one founded by Whittington at Grey Friars, and another at Guildhall.

32   CITIZENS AND FOUNDERS

Card games were coming into favour, with kings, queens, and knaves dressed in the old Court costumes which they still wear today. People loved great pageants and processions and enjoyed dressing up for them, or watching a brilliant cavalcade go by in a blaze of colour. The Elizabethan theatre was midwife to the universal genius of Shakespeare, and travelling companies of actors were already visiting towns and villages.

In Tudor England, most people were country-dwellers, and even in the towns and cities, men still lived close to woods, fields, and streams. Birds, flowers, and wild life were familiar, everyday sights to most English eyes, and country sports, such as archery, wrestling, and coursing, were widely practised. The family was the binding force in the social structure, and marriage was chiefly a contract designed to advance family interests and ensure the inheritance of estates, farms, or trades. It was a process which treated women as chattels, but also gave them real power in family affairs and the upbringing of children.

The Livery Companies of the City benefited from Tudor policies which avoided foreign wars and provided a more efficiently organised system of government, both national and local, with a stronger rule of law. For the Founders, the 16th century was a period of slowly rising prosperity and progress, but one in which they had to overcome many difficulties. Although the Company's Ordinances of 1516 restored order in its domestic relations, it took longer to recover from the financial strains imposed by the series of lawsuits which plagued the Company between 1506 and 1514. For many years thereafter, the Accounts showed a surplus of only a few pounds after meeting expenses, and it was not until the end of the century that the Company was able to set aside money for investment.

The Company seems to have been exceptionally well served by Robert Wells, who was the senior Warden or Master for two financial years from 1509 to 1511, and was again chosen for the three years from 1515 to 1518. His name appears as one of the Livery in 1497-8, the earliest year recorded in the Accounts. In his first term of office, when he had John Payne and David Mills as his co-Wardens, they started with a cash balance of £6 2s. handed over from the previous year. On the income side, they collected £2 10s. for 'abling' 15 apprentices; £3 13s. 4d. in fines paid by 11 new Liverymen; 9s. 1d. for other fines, after paying a half-share to the City Chamberlain; £3 1s. 7d. for quarterage and Mass money; and £2 6s. 2d. in contributions from members to the cost of the Company's dinner.

Turning to expenses, the dinner was the main item and cost nearly £8, including food, drink, hire of a 'hall', and payments for cook, butler, spit-turners, water-bearers, minstrels, plate and linen and laundry. The bill of fare consisted of brawn, beef, mutton, doves in syrup, geese, plovers, capons and roasted rabbits, followed by 'small birds', pies of meat or fruit covered in broth or milk, and cream of almonds. This modest repast was washed down by copious draughts of strong ale, Gascony wine, and wine from the Canaries called 'Malvoisie' which is still produced there.

Money was also disbursed for helping needy members with their rent, or providing them with medical treatment described as 'leechcraft'. Burial expenses were

LONDON PRIDE   33

paid when, as often happened, the leeches did not save the patient, but hastened
his end. Other expenses were incurred for 'breakfast' and boat hire when the Company escorted the newly-elected Mayor and sheriffs to Westminster to be sworn in;
for joining in a petition to the King by the City Companies, asking for a reduction in imports of foreign wares; for the Beadle's annual wage of 18s. 8d., and
another 6s. 8d. towards his gown; for the clothes worn by the men who represented
the Company in the 'Midsummer Watch', and samples of blue cloth for the gowns
of new Liverymen. Finally, a scrivener was paid 2s. for 'making and writing of our
account'. At the end of his first term in 1511, Robert Wells handed over a surplus
of £7 to his successor as Master, Thomas Halifax.

In his second, and longer term of office, Wells had a harder struggle to make
both ends meet. He began with a balance of £4 in 1515-6, and at the end of that
year was 2s. out of pocket, which the Company owed him. In 1516-7, he achieved
a surplus of just over £2, and when his last year ended in 1518, he and his fellow-
Wardens handed over a surplus of over £6. Even this modest result was only made
possible by cancelling the Company dinners in 1516 and 1517, when the Company
was still suffering financially from the effects of Sonlowe's lawsuit.

The Accounts make no mention of any audit at this time, although in the
earliest year on record, 1497-8, two 'daysmen' are named who acted as witnesses
to the handing-over by one set of Wardens to another. From 1513 to 1519, the
accounts are counter-signed by a small number of senior Liverymen, but in 1526-7
four of the Livery were appointed to act as Auditors, an office now filled by four
Court Assistants. On the other hand, the rule for six of the Yeomanry to be represented when the accounts were presented, as laid down by Mayor Aylmer in 1508,
seems to have been obeyed only in the three financial years from 1518 to 1521.

In 1516, while Wells was the senior Warden, the Company made a renewed
attempt to obtain a Royal Charter. By such incorporation, a Livery Company not
only enhanced its status and reputation, but also secured new sources of revenue
from the rights and privileges conferred by the Charter. Most of the chief Companies had already been granted Charters by this date, but the Founders again
failed in their attempt. It involved them in large additional expenditure which explains the small deficit incurred by Wells in 1515-6, and reflects all the more credit
on his surpluses in the next two years.

In 1522, the Company pledged most of its plate to various Livery or Yeomanry
members, a measure probably taken to forestall a demand by Wolsey for the City
Companies to surrender their plate to him, as Mr. Parsloe suggests in his notes on
the Accounts. Most of the pledges were redeemed by 1527, thus restoring the Company's property. The enrolment of 'strangers' which began in 1528-9 brought in
some useful additional income, but even so the surplus for that year only amounted
to £2 12s. 7d. From 1516 to 1531, there is only one specific mention of a payment
for alms, although money was received by the Wardens from St. Clement's Brotherhood, and paid to it, which may have served that purpose. It was a common practice to reduce alms payments when short of funds, and also to make increases in
fines and other charges. In 1535, for example, the Court decided that every Livery-

34   CITIZENS AND FOUNDERS

man should pay 2s. for dinner at the Master's Feast, 'whether Man and Wife, or the Man alone be there, or not be there, in town or not in town, whether they come or not'.

Despite its financial weakness, the Company now gave a striking proof of confidence in the future by deciding to build its own Hall, instead of renting those of other Companies, such as the Armourers, Brewers, and Leathersellers, for its meetings. Taking a long-term view, the acquisition of a Hall would not only save this expense, but also produce valuable income from letting out parts of the premises not required by the Founders for their own use. In addition, it would bear witness to the Company's standing and help to sustain its claims for a Royal Charter.

In 1531, therefore, the Company bought from the Grocers some land formerly belonging to the Augustine Friars, whose noble church and monastery stood in Broad Street until the Reformation destroyed them. This site for the Hall is believed to have been either the garden or burial ground of the 'Austin Friars', and was situated between St. Margaret, Lothbury, and what is now Moorgate Street. The Founders also bought two houses in Lothbury adjoining the building site.

It was on such occasions that Liverymen were expected to dip into their pockets, and in this hour of need they were not found wanting. Gifts were made by 18 out of 23 Livery members, headed by the Master for 1530-1, William Knight, and between them they raised a sum of £10. 15s. The purchase price, as recorded in the Grocers' books, was £32. It may seem incredible that the ground and houses could be bought for such a trivial amount, but the real value of money was then infinitely greater than it is now, and property could be bought much more cheaply. The deed of sale, dated 29 March 1531, was signed for the Founders by John Wise, who was Third Warden that year and later served three times as Master. The Company also paid a quit-rent of 20s. a year to the Gild or Fraternity of St. Mary in Queenhythe, which may have had an interest as tenants, but this rent was redeemed by purchase in 1550.

Although many of the abbeys and monasteries suppressed by Henry VIII had grown rich and outlived their spiritual purpose, their destruction was a great loss to the English architectural and cultural heritage. The fate of the Augustine Friars' church was a particularly notable example. Henry's Lord Treasurer, the Marquess of Winchester, got possession of it and pulled down much of the fabric to build himself a palatial town house. According to Stow, the old London chronicler, the west end of the church was left standing and let in 1550 as a place of worship for the Dutch Protestant community in London. The rest was used for domestic offices and storing corn and coal.

Winchester's son and heir stripped the lead from the roof, replacing it with tiles, sold off the funeral monuments in the interior, and used the vacant space for stabling his horses. By this time, the east end of the church had been demolished to make way for a new street of houses called Winchester Street, built at a time when the rapidly increasing population of the City created a brisk market for property speculators and developers. The St. Augustine's steeple, described by Stow as one of the rarest and most beautiful sights in the City, was still standing in 1602, but

LONDON PRIDE   35

its condition was so bad that a petition was submitted to the Lord Mayor and
Aldermen, begging them to ask the Lord Winchester of that date for £50 or £60
to save it. This appeal seems to have fallen on deaf ears.

The noble families were now leaving the City for new houses near the seat of
Royal power in Westminster, and most of their old residences were sub-divided into
overcrowded tenements and slums. In some cases, however, these great aristocratic
houses were earlier acquired by wealthy City Companies which used them as their
Halls, adapting and altering the interiors as required, but retaining many old
ideas of feudal splendour. The Merchant Taylors occupied a stately house in
Threadneedle Street formerly belonging to Sir Oliver de Ingham, who served
Edward III as Seneschal of Gascony and defended Bordeaux against French attack,
It contained a chapel, portrait gallery, King's chamber and other reception rooms,
exchequer office and treasury, together with pantry, buttery, kitchen, bakehouse,
brewery, gardener's cottage and stables.

The Grocers had their Hall in a mansion formerly owned by the Fitzwalters
which boasted a 'royal tennis' court and a prolific vine. In 1431, the Grocers issued
orders reserving the use of the tennis court for their 'freemen shopholders'; and
also directing that the grapes taken from the garden were to be left indoors hanging 'still and ripe', so that every Liveryman could send two or three clusters home
daily. Skinners' Hall was originally an old manor called Copped Hall, a name still
preserved as Copthall, and the Pewterers took over a house formerly attached to
the Leadenhall estate of the Nevilles.

The Drapers acquired the palace built in Threadneedle Street by Thomas Cromwell, Henry VIII's ruthless minister, who was eventually dismissed and executed.
The Goldsmiths bought the site for their Hall in 1357 from Sir Nicholas de Segrave,
brother of the Bishop of London. Other companies profited from the confiscations
of religious properties, enabling the Mercers to set up their Hall in the old Hospital
of St. Thomas Aquinas; the Leathersellers to take possession of St. Helen's Priory;
and the Founders themselves, as we have seen, to build their own Hall on ground
which had once belonged to the Augustine Friars.

The decision by the Founders to build their own Hall marked a turning-point
in their history, and it is all the more unfortunate that, just at this moment in time,
the Wardens' Accounts are reduced to skeleton summaries from 1531 to 1539
which give no information on this subject. An old map shows the Hall as a fairly
substantial building approached by an alley from Lothbury and looking out at
the back over market gardens and allotments intersected by the Walbrook stream.
The fuller Accounts resumed in 1539 contain payments for materials and labour
which show that work on the Hall was still in progress at that date. Loads of stone
were arriving from Tower Hill, Garlickhythe, and the storehouse of the 'King's
Great Wardrobe'; payments were made to the 'tiler' for the roof and the 'plumber'
for lead gutters and drainpipes; timber for floors and ceilings was supplied by
'the pewterer', who also provided the wooden wainscoting which lined the principal rooms; and there were bills for lime and sand, for decorating the Hall with
'cloths and painting', and hanging the walls with carpets, as was then a common

36 CITIZENS AND FOUNDERS

practice. As late as 1544-5, there was an item of one penny for 'tenter-hooks', which were used for wall-hangings, and a 'cool-house' was installed in the kitchen. The main building work seems to have been finished that year, judging by payments made to the 'plasterer' and 'for making clean the house and carrying away of rubbish'.

In view of its limited means, the Company probably had the work carried out in stages and took over each section when it was ready for occupation. For example, the Parlour ceiling was fitted in 1539-40, and in the following year the Company received its first income from fees paid for the use of the Hall by three wedding parties. The bridegrooms were all Yeomanry members of the Company, named John Rawlett, Robert Shurlock, and Thomas Pincock, but the first two paid a fee of 12d. for use of the Hall, while Pincock paid only 8d. Shurlock was promoted to the Livery in 1551-2 and served two years as Master from 1567 to 1569.

In 1544-5 and some years later, the Hall was hired by 'players', though it is not stated whether they were actors or musicians, or whether they were rehearsing or giving performances. Also in 1544-5, the Company was paid 16d. 'by a gentleman for making pastime in the Hall', the nature of which is not explained, and on some later occasions the Hall was taken by the Waterbearers for their feast at a fee of 2s.

A close and long-lasting association grew up between the Founders and the Company of Brown Bakers which rented the basement for its meetings and dinners. Their first quarterly payment of rent was made in 1576-7 and continued for over 60 years until 1640, when their lease finally expired and the basement was let to merchants as a warehouse. As a token of their friendly relations, the Brown Bakers regularly presented the Founders with a cup when renewing their lease. They were allowed to use the kitchen in Founders' Hall for their dinners, and in 1594 they 'lovingly' helped to pay for new paving in it.

The first mention of rent received for the two houses in Lothbury appears in 1540-1, when the names of four tenants are given in the Accounts. These were John Brewer, a Yeomanry member, who paid a comparatively high rent of 21s. 8d. a year; William Ford, a senior Liveryman who had twice served as a Warden and paid 16s.; a 'Mr. Predyox' or Priddocks, not of the Company, whose rent was 13s. 4d.; and 'Mother Clifford', widow of Richard Clifford, a Yeomanry member, who paid 9s. 8d. Since only two houses are mentioned in the original purchase, it is possible that they were sub-divided, or that one or two rooms in the Hall were let to tenants. The Company made payments for fitting doors with locks and keys. From 1585, one house was occupied by either the Clerk or Beadle.

The money received for rents and hiring of the Hall had a healthy effect on the Company's finances. In the decade from 1539 to 1549, these sources yielded a net average surplus of 20s. yearly, after deducting the costs of maintenance and repairs, lighting, and heating, and also the quit rent of 20s. later redeemed in 1550. If this seems an insignificant yield in modern terms, it should be noted

LONDON PRIDE   37

that total annual quarterage payments by members seldom rose above £2 10s. in this period and the Company's total annual income varied from £10 to £15. The property income was therefore a useful return on the Company's investment. In the period 1576 to 1586, yearly income averaged nearly £20, an increase almost entirely due to money from rents.

The additional work involved in the management of the Hall led to a redistribution of duties as between Master and Wardens. Up to 1539, the Accounts do not show how their tasks were divided, but in some later years a 'Younger' or 'Renter' Warden is designated for collecting the rents. He also made payments in some years for building work or repairs for the Hall and the Lothbury houses, but there was no clearly defined separation of tasks between Master and Wardens. This must have depended to a large extent on their age, state of health, and general fitness for the job. Having no postal or telephone facilities, they conducted their business entirely by personal contacts and had to be out and about in all weathers, either tramping the City streets or taking boat for Westminster to consult with lawyers or officials. The burdens of office in the Company were real enough, and its privileges were usually well earned.

At this time, early in the 16th century, the offices of Clerk and Beadle were combined in one man. In the first recorded year of the accounts, 1497-8, William Meriell is described as 'Clerk' at a yearly wage of 16s. 8d., but in 1504-5 he is called 'Clerk and Beadle'. In any case, the holder of this post was apparently regarded as one of the family circle. Meriell gave it up in 1508, but his name then appears in the list of members of the Yeomanry class, and in 1510 he was admitted to the Livery. His successor as Beadle, John Preston, is listed as a Yeomanry member from 1479 to 1508. In 1543, the office of clerk was filled by another Yeomanry member, Adam Wood, who wrote the accounts himself and was evidently a well-educated man. There was also a Beadle in that year, not named, but Wood seems to have given up as Clerk after one year, and in 1545-6 he is listed as a Liveryman and so continues till 1556. Not until 1612-3 was there a clear separation of the two offices, when wages were paid to William Liddell as Clerk and Thomas Platt as Beadle.

Successive Masters and Wardens continued to keep a close eye on the interests of the craft. In 1529, discussions took place with the Cordwainers' Company about the Act of Parliament passed that year which compelled immigrant craftsmen to register with a City Company. The Cordwainers were specially concerned with this matter and managed to secure the appointment of an official commission, at the end of 1529, to reduce the number of alien cordwainers in and around London. Their Company was also specifically mentioned in the Star Chamber judgment which gave rise to the Parliamentary Act.

In 1540, the Founders paid 2d. for a copy of another Act passed that year against alien craftsmen. In that year also, the Company paid legal fees for an action which it took in the 'Court of Pie-Powder' against 'a stranger's wife', after she had been found in possession of two defective candlesticks at St. Bartholomew's Fair. This Court dealt with disputes arising at markets and fairs and derived its

38 CITIZENS AND FOUNDERS

curious title from the French name of 'pieds poudrés', or 'dusty feet'.

In 1542 and 1543, the Company went to considerable trouble and expense to promote the passage of an Act through Parliament banning the export of brass and brass alloys, among other metals. Gifts were lavished on Parliamentary officials, high and low, in what was then considered a perfectly normal fashion. Mr. Speaker himself, Sir Thomas Moyle, received two plates 'with balls and cups', two candlesticks, three trencher-plates, a dish with 'foot', and some money. The Recorder of Parliament, Sir Roger Cholmley, got a cash payment. The Common Sergeant, Sir Robert Broke was also given money and two plates 'of new fashion'. The Reader in the Commons collected two candlesticks, several cash payments, and a pint of 'Malmsey', or Madeira wine. Even the Commons doorkeeper and the 'Knight who kept the door at the Lords' drew their plums from this pie. It was lucky for the Master and wardens that all this outlay was not wasted and that the Bill was duly passed, for they might otherwise have faced some awkward questions from their colleagues.

These expenses, coming as they did so soon after the building of the Hall, imposed a need for strict economy and probably explain why there is no mention of any 'Choice Dinner' being held between 1531 and 1545. This was the main annual function of the Company, sometimes called the 'Master's Feast', which usually took place in late August or early September to celebrate the election of a new Master and Wardens, and it was attended by Yeomanry, as well as Livery, members. In Tudor times, 'dinner' was taken in mid-afternoon, and the Company often re-assembled for 'breakfast' at noon next day.

Tudor appetites were a great deal heartier than ours, and were well served by the way in which the wealthier Livery Companies strove to excel each other in splendid entertainment. So much so, indeed, that in 1544 the Common Council of the City passed an act 'for retrenching the extravagant method of living by the Lord Mayor, Aldermen, Sheriffs, and City Companies'. As an example of Tudor ideas about 'retrenchment', the Act bears fuller quotation :

Thenceforth they [Lord Mayors] should have no more than one course, either at dinner or supper; and that on a festival being a flesh day, they should have no more than seven dishes, whether hot or cold; and on every festival being a fish day, eight dishes exclusive of brawn, collops with eggs, salads, pottage, butter, cheese, eggs, herrings, sprats, and shrimps, together with all sorts of shellfish and fruits.

That the Aldermen and Sheriffs should have one dish less than the Lord Mayor, and all the City Companies, at their several entertainments, the same number of dishes as the Aldermen and Sheriffs, but with this restriction, to have neither swan, crane, nor bustard, provided always that no other entertainment be given after dinner than hippocras (spiced wine) and wafers.

It was also enacted, in consideration of the great and annual expense the

LONDON PRIDE 39

Mayor and Sheriffs were at in providing a sumptuous entertainment every
Lord Mayor's day at the Guildhall for the honour of the City and regaling
persons of the greatest distinction, that every subsequent Mayor, as an allevia-
tion of that charge, should be paid out of the Chamber of the City the sum
of One Hundred Pounds.

If this was the rule laid down for 'retrenchment', the Founders probably thought
they were showing considerable self-restraint in the bill of fare for the 'Master's
Dinner' on 29 August 1563. This is worth quoting in detail, as it also gives prices
and provides some idea of the purchasing power of Tudor money. The list reads
as follows:

	s.	d.
6½ dozen of bread	10	6
2 stands of ale and beer	10	3
100 eggs	3	0
4 gallons of cream	3	8
9 dishes of butter	3	0
8 lbs. of suet, 4 long marrowbones	3	4
150 pears	1	0
11 capons, to boil and roast	17	0
A turkey-hen	2	0
A bushel of fine flour	2	8
Salt, herbs, onions, sauce, parsley	2	2
11 stone and 3 lbs of beef	11	4
1 stone and 2lbs more of beef	1	2
5 legs of mutton and a neck	3	6
6 gallons of wine, and a quart of 'moscadyn' [muscatel]	7	10
6 geese	10	0
14 rabbits	4	4
2 dozen pigeons	2	4
9 ounces of pepper	1	8
6 lbs of currants	2	6
2 ounces of cloves and mace	1	10
4 lbs of prunes		8
2 lbs of dates	2	8
1 ounce of nutmegs		4
Half-ounce of ginger		2
4 lbs, 3 ounces of sugar	3	6
2 lbs of 'great raisins'		4
Biscuits and caraways, ¾ lb.		10
Saffron		5

	s.	d.
The minstrel	2	4
The Cook and his men	6	0
The Butler	2	6
A pint of rose-water		6
Water		4
Fox's Wife 'for her paynes in the kitchen'	1	0
Candles and broom		6
The porter	1	0
Hiring 2 'garnish of vessel'	1	8

These charges add up to a total cost of £6 9s. 10d. for the Company's dinner in 1563, whereas the expense of a Livery dinner in 1975, of much more modest proportions, but catering for perhaps an additional 60 people, may be roughly estimated at £1,500 to £2000. By this yardstick, the English pound in 1563 was worth about 200 times its value, in real terms, at the level of 1975. It is a somewhat sobering thought.

It should be noted, however, that inflation is no new thing in English history, but a frequently recurring scourge. In Tudor times, one of its main causes was the frequent debasing of the coinage by the Crown to raise money, and in 1559-60, when Elizabeth was calling in the coinage to reform it, the Founders had to repay their Master, John Jackson, for the loss he incurred on the transaction.

A list of 48 Livery Companies made in 1515, and in order of precedence, puts the Founders in 33rd place, between the Innholders and the Poulters, and the Company still holds that place. Like other Companies, the Founders were required to turn out at the summons of the Lord Mayor on great ceremonial occasions. In 1538, Henry VIII's third wife, Jane Seymour, died after presenting him with an heir, the future Edward VI, and there was an elaborate display of public mourning. The following order was issued by the Mayor and Aldermen :

At this Court it was agreed that a solemn hearse shall be made in Paul's with four great candlesticks with four great tapers, and the hearse to be garnished with thirty other great tapers with two branches of virgin wax and the same to be garnished with black cloth and the Queens Arms. And upon Monday next at afternoon the great bells in every church at one of the clock to be rung and so continue till three, and then all the bells in every church to ring till six of the clock. And my Lord Mayor and Sheriffs to continue [in mourning?] by the space of fourteen days. And also agreed that all the Aldermen shall go in black.

And agreed that at two of the clock in the afternoon to assemble here upon Monday next, and that afternoon a solemn obit to be kept at Paul's, and on the morrow the Mass, and that of every church two priests shall give attendance, every one in their surplices, and the said priests to be divided in five places, in our Lady Chapel, St. George's Chapel and St. Dunstan's, the great Chapels on the North and South part. And that warning be given by the clerk

LONDON PRIDE 41

of every church to the churchwardens of every church, and officer of my Lord Mayor's to go West and another East.

Also to give warning to the churchwardens that the bells of every church upon Tuesday next shall begin at nine of the clock and continue until eleven of the clock aforenoon, and then the great bells of every church to ring alone till twelve of the clock by-stricken, and that my Lord for his officers eight black gowns shall have, and every one of the Sheriffs to have four apiece at the cost of this City, and that Mr. Recorder shall have thirty-three shillings and fourpence; the Chamberlain, Under-Chamberlain, and the Town Clerk, every one of them twenty shillings apiece by the commandment of the Lord Mayor.

Perhaps it was lucky for the Founders that they could not foresee the extent of Henry's neurotic furies. In August 1540, Jane Seymour's successor in Henry's bed, Catherine Howard, celebrated the 'triumph' of her marriage to the King, and recognition as Queen, by a river pageant. The Founders hired a barge for this occasion and paid 'drinking money' to rowers and steersman. The party refreshed themselves with oysters, fresh fish, salted salmon and cod, bread and butter, and strong ale, while the Clerk entertained them by playing a musical instrument, for which he received fourpence. Two years later Catherine was beheaded in the Tower, yet another victim in the deadly dance of Tudor power politics.

One of the oldest City observances was the parading of armed 'watches' formed by men from the various gilds. In 1469, when the Mayor summoned a 'muster of crafts', the Founders supplied 30 men. In addition to the 'standing watch' in each of the City wards, there were special occasions, such as Royal visits, when the Companies provided armed guards in the streets. In 1475, as noted in the Guild-hall records, 'a Watch was made by the Aldermen and Mysteries when the King [Edward IV] went through the City by night from the palace of the Bishop of London through Chepe to the Bridge and from thence to Greenwich'. The Founders were posted in the Poultry on that occasion, together with the Armourers, Tallow Chandlers, Patternmakers, and Poulters. In 1483, the Mayor ordered a nightly watch to assemble in Cheapside and stay on duty from eight at night till six in the morning, but for this purpose the Founders only sent two men.

It was in the yearly 'Midsummer Night's Watch' or 'Marching Watch' that the power and pomp of London were most splendidly displayed. The London chronicler, Stow, has left us a stirring description of this ceremony in 1548. The long route followed by the procession was lined by 700 men holding 'cressets', or torches mounted in iron cradles, which needed two men to support them and a third carrying a bag of lights. These bearers were 'poor men' hired for the occasion, 500 being paid for by the City Companies and 200 by the Chamber of London. They wore straw hats with a painted badge, and the Founders' Accounts show payments in many years for their wages and hats, and for the 'cresset lights'. In addition, more than 240 London 'constables' or watchmen paraded with attendants carrying torches, and there were English archers in the military procession. The Founders supplied two of them in 1548.

The scene is best pictured in Stow's own words:

42 CITIZENS AND FOUNDERS

The marching watch contained in number about 2,000 men, part of them being old soldiers of skill, to be captains, lieutenants, serjeants, corporals, etc., whifflers, drummers and fifes, standard and ensign bearers, sword players, trumpeters on horseback, demi-lances on great horses, gunners with hand guns or half-hakes, archers in coats of white fustian signed on the breast and back with the arms of the City, their bows bent in their hands with sheaves of arrows by their sides, pikemen in bright corselets, burganets, etc., halberds, the light billmen in almaine [German] rivets and aprons of mail in great number.

There were also divers pageants, morris dancers, constables, the one half which was 120 on St. John's Eve, the other half on St. Peter's Eve, in bright harness, some overgilt, and every one a jornet of scarlet thereupon and a chain of gold, his henchman following him, his minstrels before him, and his cresset light passing by him, the waits [watchmen] of the City, the Mayor's officers for his guard before him, all in a livery of worsted or jackets party-coloured, the Mayor himself well mounted on horseback, the sword-bearer before him in fair armour well mounted also, the Mayor's footmen, and the like torch-bearers about him, henchmen twain upon great stirring horses following him.

The Sheriffs' watches came one after the other in like order, but not so large in number as the Mayor's; for where the Mayor had, beside his giant, three pageants, each of the Sheriffs had beside their giants but two pageants, each their morris dance and one henchman, their officers in jacket of worsted or party-coloured differing from the Mayor's and each from other, but having harnessed men a great many.

In Stow's disjointed rush of words, we catch the moving ranks of men, the long column of horsemen, archers, gunners and pikemen, the torchlight dancing on banners and steel, and the great river beyond, lying dark and silent. The splendour of that Midsummer Night Watch has long faded, but the Founders can still feel glad that their forbears were a part of it.

CHAPTER V

The Sun Queen

IN 1544, Henry VIII raised an expeditionary force and led it across the Channel to France. This was more of an armed raid or show of strength than a serious invasion, and its only success, the capture of Boulogne, was short-lived. For the Founders' Company, however, it did have an important result later on, because the Venetian painted goblet presented to the Company by Richard Weoley in 1643 was originally part of the plunder brought back from Boulogne. This gift is more fully described in a later chapter. The costs of mounting such expeditions were now being borne by taxation, since the feudal armies which previously fought in the French wars no longer existed. The Wars of the Roses, followed by a Tudor policy of taming the few great lords who survived, had effectively put an end to the existence of private armies.

Although Henry was the founder of the Royal Navy, he had no standing army and therefore had to find money for soldiers and supplies from financial charges on his subjects. The wealth of London naturally singled it out for the largest contribution. In May, 1544 the Common Council of the City agreed to provide 500 or 600 soldiers for Henry's French expedition as a first instalment, and added two further contingents a few months later. Each Livery Company had to contribute its quota, the Founders being required to supply four 'sowgears', or soldiers, with their arms and equipment. The Wardens' Accounts contain many items of military expenditure at this time.

Each soldier was paid a shilling on enlistment, giving rise to the later description of 'the King's shilling', but in 1544 the term 'prest money' was used, suggesting that there were more pressed men or conscripts than volunteers. They were armed with swords, daggers and 'bills', which were curved blades on a long pole. The Company also provided 'harness' or light body armour, boots, sword-belts, doublets made of canvas and 'fustian', a mixture of cotton and flax, coats of yellow cloth, and stockings made from 'kersey', a coarsely-woven wool. Some of these garments were second-hand, as money was paid for their 'new translation' and adapting.

It was not only in military matters that Henry found himself short of cash. His reign coincided with a new era of rising public expenditure in many departments which the Crown revenues could no longer meet, still less with a king like Henry VIII who was extravagant and soon dissipated the reserves carefully built up by

44   CITIZENS AND FOUNDERS

his father, Henry VII, the first of the Tudors. Thus the Crown became more dependent than before on subsidies granted by Parliament, and the two Houses, Lords and Commons, which had previously functioned respectively as an extension of Court factions and a tribunal for legal appeals, now began to acquire a new power of the purse. This commanded respect even from a king like Henry VIII who wielded absolute power, and it was to have far-reaching political and constitutional effects on later British history.

Parliament granted Henry a subsidy in 1540, when the Founders paid 20d. for the 'King's money', as it was called. In 1545-6, taxation made heavier demands. The Company paid an old tax of 'one-fifteenth' assessed on land and moveable goods and, in addition, a much larger subsidy based on the same method of assessment, but greatly increased under the Tudors by frequent revaluations. In that year also, the Founders had to pay 'two-fifteenths' towards another Parliamentary subsidy for the King, and yet another 'two-fifteenths' under a tax levied by the Common Council for bringing fresh water into the City from Hackney. In all, the Company's tax payments for 1545-6 came to just over £1, which means nothing to us today, but more at a time when the Company's total income was just under £12.

Taxes for local government purposes, such as the water supply already mentioned, now figured more often in the Wardens' Accounts, though they were still imposed for a specific object and had not yet become regular annual payments. In 1520, already, as in some later years, the Mayor demanded 'corn money' from the Livery Companies to build up reserves of wheat for the City in a granary called 'Bridge House', at the Southwark end of London Bridge. This was a sensible and forward-looking measure which enabled wheat to be bought cheaply in times of plenty and sold below market prices when there was a shortage, thus helping to prevent sudden and excessive rises in the price of bread. In later years, the Founders' Company sometimes commissioned one of its own members to buy corn and store it in readiness for the next demand from the Mayor. In 1590-1, when the cost of buying corn rose in the accounts to over £14, a relatively large sum, a number of Liverymen lent money to the Company for this purpose and were repaid by the auditors.

Henry VIII died in 1547, his bloated body rotten with venereal disease, a wreck of the handsome and gifted young prince who had mounted the throne 38 years earlier. Yet Henry, despite his bloody matrimonial troubles, ruled with a firm hand and was strong enough to hold rival parties and passions in check. Under his next two successors, Edward VI and Mary Tudor, England became a battleground for religious and social conflicts. Edward was a sickly boy who died before he was 16 and the country was then ruled by a Regency Council headed first by Jane Seymour's brother, Edward, who made himself Duke of Somerset and Protector of the realm; and after him by John Dudley, the equally self-made Duke of Northumberland. A new and unholy compact was formed between Protestant fanatics bent on destroying the last vestiges of Catholic ritual and a new class of upstart political adventurers, nobles, and courtiers only interested in seizing church lands for themselves.

THE SUN QUEEN   45

Many Englishmen were sickened by the violence and intolerance of religious persecution and angered by demands for social revolution which included legalised polygamy and the common ownership of all property. The old religion still had widespread support, particularly in the North and West of England and the Midlands. London was always a Protestant stronghold, but in Devon, Cornwall, and Oxfordshire, there were popular risings which were savagely repressed with the aid of German and Italian mercenaries.

Much discontent and suffering was caused by the high prices and fall in the value of money which followed the debasing of the coinage by Henry VIII. A peasant rising broke out in Norfolk, partly in protest against sheep-farming by landlords encroaching on common land, and partly demanding the freeing of 'villeins' from the feudal ties which still bound them to their landlords. It was one of those chaotic periods of history which benefits only the profiteers and political agitators, and it also bred that singularly repulsive specimen, the paid informer who denounced innocent people on trumped-up charges of religious misconduct.

As has already been mentioned, the confiscation of religious endowments by the Protestant Reformation put an end to the Founders' 'Brotherhood of Saint Clement', and also abolished, as a 'Popish practice', the annual celebration of Mass by the Company with priests, choir and bell-ringer. The more extreme reformers looked upon such services as the work of the Devil. In 1548, Royal Commissioners called 'the King's Visitors' sat in judgment on the City chantries, or religious endowments, and the Founders paid a legal expert to represent them at the hearing. The last mention of the Company's attendance at 'Mass' is in the Wardens' Accounts for 1558-9, though services of a Protestant kind continued, and in 1559-60 a 'Master Verone' was paid 5s. by the Company for preaching. Mr. Parsloe has suggested that this man was probably John Veron, or Viron, Prebendary of Mora, who held several City livings and died in 1563. In 1559-60 he was Rector of St. Martin, Ludgate.

The closure of schools, hospitals, and almshouses supported by religious endowments naturally created a bigger demand for the provision of such services by local authorities with money which could only be raised by taxation. In 1548, the Common Council of London levied a tax of 500 marks a year, or about £330 at that time, on the Livery Companies for the support of St. Bartholomew's Hospital. The Founders paid 26s. 8d. annually for this tax up to and including 1553-4, and in 1556-7 they made a further contribution to the relief of the poor in the City's new workhouse at Bridewell. In years when such taxes had to be met, the Company collected money 'for the poor' from its members, both Livery and Yeomanry, at the same time as quarterage. The old payments of 'Mass money' no longer appear in the Accounts after 1546.

With the suppression of St. Clement's Brotherhood and the abolition of contributions in 'Mass money', the responsibility for looking after members in need fell directly on the Company, and there are some grounds for thinking that this obligation was no longer carried out as faithfully as it had been in the past. The Accounts from 1546 to 1586 contain few references to either the collection or distribution of alms money for the poor of the Company, except for 'Jordan's dole' under his legacy, and even the rare entries on alms are sometimes vague and contradictory. In four years of account, those of 1566-7, 1570-1, 1571-2 and 1572-3, the Younger Warden is shown as looking after the 'poor's money' and he also, in one or two of those years, recorded the collection of quarterage 'for the poor', as called for by the Ordinances of 1516. Yet in most years no such collection is mentioned, and even when the distribution of alms is recorded, they are not properly balanced against the money received for that purpose.

This does not necessarily mean that the Company had abandoned its primary and long-standing concern for members in distress, for there may have been separate books of account for alms which would fill the gaps if they still existed. It does seem reasonable to conclude, however, that the destruction of the Company's Brotherhood of St. Clement, which had its own Masters and kept its own accounts, made it much easier for the Wardens to use the alms money for other purposes, or even to put it in their own pockets if so inclined. We know for a fact that dissension arose in the Company about the handling of alms, because in 1578 a petition was presented to the Court of Aldermen by 'certain persons free of the Company of Founders' upon causes of variance among the Freemen and 'touching a certain relief to be gathered towards the aid of the poor of the same Company and the order and distribution of the same'.

The Aldermen appointed a committee consisting of Sir John Rivers, Mr. Dixie, and Mr. Bowyer to hear this petition. After hearing evidence from the petitioners, the Wardens, and others of the Founders, the committee issued its report on 28 January 1579, and made certain proposals which were approved by the Mayor and Aldermen. The Wardens and Liverymen of the Company were required in future to make quarterly payments of 3d. towards the aid and relief of the Company's poor, and the Yeomanry members were to pay 2d. for that purpose. Refusal to pay incurred a forfeit of 5d. for each such offence by a Warden or Liveryman, and 4d. for the Yeomanry. In accordance with custom, half these fines went to the Chamber of London and the other half to the Company for the use of its poor. The Wardens were authorised to enforce these penalties, if necessary, by taking 'distress' or seizing goods from defaulters.

The task of collecting the quarterly payments for the poor from the Wardens and Livery was given to the Younger Warden, confirming an arrangement which, as we have seen, was already operating in one or two years of the Accounts. In addition, however, the Yeomanry were to elect two of their own members as 'collectors' after the Wardens and Livery had nominated as candidates four persons from the Yeomanry whom they considered suitable for such service. These nominations were to be made 'without any feasting, drinking, or other charges'. Refusal to act as a 'collector' incurred a forfeit of 6s. 8d. equally divided between the City and the Company. The money collected for alms was to be lodged in a box in Founders' Hall with three locks and keys, one held by the Younger Warden and the other two by the Yeomanry collectors. The three of them were authorised to distribute this money to those in need according to their discretion, and any difference of opinion among them was to be decided by the other two Wardens.

THE SUN QUEEN 47

The main object of these proposals seems to have been to bring back into force old rules for providing money for alms which had fallen into disuse, rather than to create a whole new system, but the question is largely academic. In practice, the committee findings of 1579 were as little observed as the 'award' by Mayor Aylmer in 1508 calling for the Yeomanry to be properly represented when the Wardens presented their accounts. In other words, while lip service was paid to the rights which all members ought to enjoy in common, the situation in practice was that the power of the Wardens, and the Livery which elected them, were not diminished. In the accounts which followed the arbitration of 1579, there is no mention of any collection or distribution of money for alms except Henry Jordan's 'dole' or bequest of payments to poor Founders for buying coal. A formula was found to reconcile the differences in the Company superficially, but the underlying sense of grievance must have persisted only to break out again later in the revolutionary age of Cromwell.

Meanwhile, however, the chequered pattern of Tudor history continued to unfold. While the young Edward VI lived, Dudley, as Duke of Northumberland, was the most powerful man in the country and he ruled in the King's name. But when Edward was dying in 1553, Dudley sought to maintain his own position and that of his family by making Edward sign a will excluding Henry VIII's daughters, Mary and Elizabeth, from the throne and leaving it to Lady Jane Grey, a granddaughter of Henry VII. Dudley claimed to be guarding against the dangers of a Catholic revival under Mary, which were real enough, but he showed his true purpose by marrying Lady Jane Grey to his own son. The plot failed, partly because Northumberland had made himself detested by Protestants and Catholics alike, and partly because most ordinary people still regarded Mary as the lawful successor and were angered by such a brazen attempt to deprive her of her rights. Northumberland was defeated and beheaded in the Tower, a fate also shared by his innocent pawn, Lady Jane Grey, and by her husband and her uncles.

In September 1553, Mary went in procession through the City to celebrate her coronation. The Founders turned out with the other Livery Companies to greet her, and paid 24s. 5d. for setting up their 'stand' and railings. The scene is described as follows in a passage from the *Pictorial History of England* which William M. Williams quotes in his *Annals of the Founders Company* :

On the last day of September, the Queen rode in great state from the Tower through the City of London towards Westminster, sitting in a chariot covered with cloth of gold. Before her rode the Lord Mayor of London clad in crimson velvet, bearing the sceptre of gold. After the Queen's chariot, Sir Edward Hastings led her horse in hand; and then came another chariot covered all over with white silver cloth, wherein sat the Princess Elizabeth and our old fair-complexioned and contented Lady Anne of Cleves. The enumeration of the rest of the train would excite little interest, but there were two other chariots covered with red satin, with hosts of gentlemen and gentlewomen riding on horseback in crimson satin, and there was much wine running in the streets,

48   CITIZENS AND FOUNDERS

and there were pageants and conjurings at certain stages all the way from Cornhill and Cheap to Charing Cross, where the Queen took leave of the Lord Mayor, giving him gracious thanks for his pains and the City for their cost and loyalty.

At this coronation, the Princess Elizabeth carried the Crown. It is said that she whispered to the French Ambassador, Noailles, that it was very heavy, and that he replied : 'Be patient, it will seem lighter when it is on your own head !'

As things turned out, Elizabeth was lucky to keep her head on her shoulders and survive to wear the Crown. Public support for Mary as Queen soon changed to opposition when she revealed her intention of marrying Philip of Spain and restoring the Papal supremacy in England. In 1554, Sir Thomas Wyatt led a revolt in Kent and marched on London, but Mary showed her Tudor spirit in this crisis by riding to Guildhall and personally appealing for help from the City. The London 'train-bands' or militia were sent to join the forces opposing Wyatt and, although many of them went over to his side, he found the City gates closed against him and was prevented from crossing the river at Southwark.

The Founders played their part in Wyatt's defeat. The Wardens' Accounts for 1553-4 show payments for 'two strange men to go against Mr. Wyatt', and the Company also sent four of its Yeomanry members to serve in the force guarding the City gates. Their names were Francis Boyes, Robert Hunt, Peter Spencer, and Robert Croft. The Company armed them with swords, daggers, bills and body armour.

Wyatt was captured and executed in the Tower, where the young Elizabeth also lay for some months under the shadow of death, having become the unwilling symbol of Protestant resistance. Mary was married to Philip at Winchester in July 1554, and rode through London with him a month later, when the Founders again joined with the other Livery Companies in saluting her. But now came the unleashing of the Catholic terror which sent Bishops Latimer and Ridley to the stake with many other humbler victims. The English Cardinal Pole returned from exile as Papal legate and received the submission of the Lords and Commons on their bended knees. In a short space of time, the earlier sympathy felt for Mary as the legal heir turned into anger and hatred, intensified by the sense of national humiliation suffered by the loss of Calais, the last English foothold in France, in January 1558.

The threat of a French invasion was answered by a muster of an English defence force at Leadenhall, in the City, and its transport by the Thames to Queenborough in the Isle of Sheppey. The Founders sent three of their Yeomanry to join this force, namely Thomas Stepney, Richard Wilson and Richard Hill, and gave them 'prest money', travel expenses, food and drink, and a 'reward'. Two other men, Harry Fisher and John Wilson, were also enlisted by the Company for this service, but they do not appear in the list of members. The five men were provided with swords, daggers, light helmets known as 'sallets', harquebuses or hand-guns with powder and lead shot, and 'morris pikes', probably so-called because they were of

THE SUN QUEEN   49

Moorish pattern. The Company also paid money to 'Goodman Nicolls' for going
with the soldiers, perhaps as a kind of 'batman' or servant.

Two of the Founders who served on this occasion, Richard Hill and Thomas
Stepney, were men of some distinction in the Company. Hill was a Master of the
Yeomanry in 1557-8 and hired the Hall that year for a 'wedding party', presumably his own, though it is not clear whether he got married before leaving for
Queenborough or on his return. Stepney was chosen as a Master of the Yeomanry
in 1559-60 and promoted to the Livery in 1568-9. He served as Third Warden in
1579-80 and his name continues to appear in the Accounts until 1583-4, 25 years
after his military expedition. He and Hill no doubt had stories to tell their children which improved with each repetition, but in fact neither of them fired a
shot. The French stayed on their own side of the Channel and the English defence
force saw no action.

By this time, England was on the verge of armed rebellion against Mary's religious persecution, but it was she who broke under the strain of trying to enforce
obedience and died, childless, shortly after the loss of Calais. Elizabeth succeeded
to the throne in an atmosphere of great public relief and rejoicing. On 12 January
1559, she went in state by the river from Westminster to the Tower of London,
where she had once so narrowly escaped execution but now awaited her own
coronation procession through the City.

The Founders hired a barge for the river pageant and paid 'singing men' to
entertain them, as well as providing breakfast for the singers and the bargemen.
Two days later, the Company manned its stand and railings for Elizabeth's tri-
umphal progress through the City streets. The Master in that memorable year was
John Jackson and his colleagues as Wardens were Robert Falconer and Uryan
Daniell. The Company then consisted of 19 Liverymen each paying 3d. a quarter,
three Masters of the Yeomanry and 51 other Yeomanry members all paying 2d.,
11 'strangers' paying 3d., and 11 'journeymen strangers' paying 2d., making a
total membership of ninety-five.

The City's welcome is described in the rather florid prose of the *Pictorial History
of England* as follows:

> The Lord Mayor and Citizens had been lavish of their loyalty and their
> money, and all the streets through which the procession passed on its way to
> Westminster were furnished with stately pageants, sumptuous shows, and
> cunning devices. The figures of the Queen's grandfather and grandmother,
> father and mother, were brought upon the stage, and Henry VIII and Anne
> Boleyn, with a glorious forgetfulness of the past, were seen walking lovingly
> together. In another pageant, Time led forth his daughter Truth, and Truth
> greeting Her Majesty, presented to her an English Bible, which the Queen
> accepted with a gracious countenance, and reverently kissing it and pressing
> it to her bosom, said that she would oft-times read that Holy Book. 'Be ye
> assured', said Elizabeth to the people, 'I shall stand your good Queen' – a
> promise which on the whole was gloriously kept.

There were three areas of policy in which Elizabeth's character and ideas were

50   CITIZENS AND FOUNDERS

admirably suited to the needs and temper of her country. First, she was not a religious fanatic, like Mary Tudor, but a sophisticated and tolerant daughter of the Renaissance who spoke fluent French and Italian, addressed the universities of Oxford and Cambridge in Greek and Latin, and could talk to many foreign envoys and distinguished visitors in their own tongues. She enjoyed talking to scholars and poets as much as she liked music, dancing, and flirting. She was not only offended by religious bigotry, but found it boring. When listening to a long-winded sermon by Dean Nowell, in which he attacked the use of images, she cried out : 'Stick to your text, Master Dean, leave that alone'. On another occasion, she complained that 'every merchant of London must have his schoolmaster and nightly conventicles, expounding scriptures and catechising their servants and maids'.

Elizabeth was as much opposed to a restoration of Papal authority as were most of her subjects. She approved the restoration by Parliament of the Royal supremacy over the Church, the abolition of Mary's laws against heretics, the re-adoption of Edward VI's Prayer Book, and the reversal of Mary's decree forcing some private looters of monastic property to disgorge it. But for most of her reign, she tried to restrain Protestant reprisals against Catholics, and it was only towards the end that she resorted to savage measures herself, when she had been excommunicated and outlawed by the Pope, when Philip of Spain was massing his forces for invasion, when the St. Bartholomew's Day massacre of French Huguenots, and the Duke of Alva's butchery of Dutch Protestants, had deeply stirred English feelings, and when Elizabeth's own life was in danger from Catholic plots. The fact remains that England was spared the far worse horrors of religious war suffered by other countries in Europe, and when Elizabeth died in 1603 the Protestant settlement was established firmly enough not to become a major issue in the civil war between King and Parliament.

Secondly, Elizabeth ruled with a strong hand and soon put a stop to the anarchy caused by the greed of upstart fortune-hunters and the ambitions of political bishops under Edward VI and Mary Tudor. Her attitude could be summed up in her own remark when refusing to allow one of her courtiers to accept a foreign decoration : 'My dogges shall wear no collar but mine own'. She herself had no scruples about looting church property for her own benefit or to reward ministers and favourites. The Cecil family estates were formed from the confiscated lands of the Peterborough diocese which Elizabeth gave to Burleigh. The bishopric of Ely was plundered to enrich Elizabeth's Treasurer, the dashing Sir Christopher Hatton, and when the Bishop dared to protest, the Queen wrote to him : 'Proud prelate, you know what you were before I made you what you are. If you do not immediately comply with my request, by God I will unfrock you'.

But she never let pleasure interfere with business. Those who thought they could use her as a tool to pave their own way to power were rudely disillusioned, and Essex paid with his head for that mistake. The Queen chose good men for her service, worked them hard, and often treated them abominably. There were times when her delaying tactics and refusal to make up her mind nearly drove her Privy Council mad, but her mastery of State business earned their respect as well as their loyalty. The Privy Council governed England well in the Queen's name, and made its

THE SUN QUEEN   51

orders obeyed through the local Justices of the Peace who were appointed by the
Crown, but unpaid, an economy which Elizabeth no doubt appreciated. The rule
of law was upheld by free juries whose verdicts were secure from pressure by rich
and powerful neighbours.

A notable Elizabethan reform, and one which did much to relieve the misery
underlying the popular revolts of earlier times, was a new system of aid for the
poor, administered by the Justices of the Peace in each parish. Funds were raised
by a compulsory rate for poor relief, and 'overseers of the poor' were appointed who
bought flax, hemp, wool, thread, iron and other materials to provide work and
wages for the unemployed. The Privy Council also used the local justices to control the price of grain and arrange for wheat to be imported and distributed in
case of need. G. M. Trevelyan has remarked that these social welfare measures
were not only a great improvement on any previously adopted in England, but
also in advance of anything done in other European countries for a long time after.

Elizabeth's third major achievement was her support for the great English sea
captains and explorers such as Drake, Frobisher, Raleigh and Hawkins, whose
voyages and discoveries set England on the path to world power in terms of naval
supremacy, overseas trade, and colonial empire. The Queen did her utmost to
avoid being drawn into European rivalries and coalitions, using even her own
marriage proposals as a diplomatic card, but she allowed her captains to carry on
a naval guerrilla warfare which sometimes amounted to piracy on the high seas.
She herself took a keen business interest in these commerce-raiding expeditions,
charging their organisers for the loan of her ships and demanding the lion's share
of the profits, but this was not wholly inspired by personal gain. Despite her popu-
larity, Elizabeth often had to contend with a Parliament which refused to provide
adequate subsidies. Even in the year of the Spanish Armada, 1588-9, the Queen's
total revenue for meeting all national expenditure amounted to only £485,000, of
which £360,000 came from standing sources, such as customs duties, and only
£125,000 from Parliamentary grants. Lack of finance was a constant factor in
her foreign policy.

The maritime thrust of English seamen and explorers into distant lands and
oceans greatly encouraged the development of new markets overseas by English
merchants. Trade did not only follow the flag, but sometimes preceded it, and a
commercial agent might find himself acting as a temporary diplomat in countries
where no resident embassy had yet been established. The first Englishmen to represent their country in Moscow and in India were merchants, simply because they
got there before anyone else. Commerce and high adventure went hand in hand,
for the 'merchant-venturing' companies did not sail their ships in convoy with
naval escorts, but had to rely on their own defence against enemy warships, free-
booting privateers, and Moorish pirates.

The Founders are linked with this stirring story by the fact that their Hall was
rented by some of the great overseas trading Companies, which seem to have used
it mainly for their Court meetings and sometimes for dinners. The first of these
tenants was the Merchant Adventurers of England, trading with the Low Countries,
France, and Spain, who received a grant of privileges from the Crown in 1407 and

52   CITIZENS AND FOUNDERS

a Charter in 1505. They started paying rent in 1554 at £4 yearly and were still recorded as tenants of the Founders in 1680-1, the last year in the Wardens' Accounts, when their rent had risen to £8.

Next came the Muscovy Merchants, or Russia Company, inaugurated in 1553, who paid a year's rent of £2 in 1576-7 but then vanished from the Accounts till 1653-4, when they reappeared as tenants and so continued until the destruction of Founders' Hall in the Great Fire of 1666. The Barbary Merchants, who were granted trade monopoly rights in 1585 for 12 years, paid rent for the Hall in 1585-6 but did not renew it. The Eastland Company, incorporated in 1579 for trade with the Baltic countries, became tenants in 1589 and so remained nearly a hundred years later, in 1681, the last year recorded in the Accounts. Greatest of them all, the East India Company paid rent for using the Hall from 1603 to 1608, after receiving its Charter from Elizabeth in 1600.

In 1607, the colony of Virginia was re-settled by the Virginia Company, after an earlier attempt by Raleigh had failed. The Founders were among 56 Livery Companies which shared in this new venture, looking for profits from Virginian tobacco plantations. Cheap labour was supplied by shipping workers, apprentices, and servants from England, many of whom were only boys and girls. The Wardens' Accounts show payments to the parish poor rate between 1617 and 1622 for 'the setting-out of children to Virginia'.

The total population of Elizabethan England was only about five million, living in a green and pleasant land unscarred by industrial slums. The poorer folk still lived in primitive wooden cottages with thatched roofs, gables, and walls made of clay, loam, rubble or wooden laths. The manufacture of glass was introduced from Europe early in Elizabeth's reign, providing windows which let light and fresh air into the dark, unhealthy interiors.

A Scottish observer, Fynes Morison, had this to say about Elizabethan food:

The English have abundance of white meats, of all kinds of flesh, fowl, and fish, and all things good for food. In the seasons of the year, the English eat fallow deer plentifully, as bucks in summer and does in winter, which they bake in pasties, and this venison pasty is a dainty rarely found in any other kingdom. No kingdom in the world hath so many dove-houses. Likewise brawn is a proper meat to the English, not known to others.

English cooks, in comparison with other nations, are most commended for roast meats. English beef and mutton are the best in Europe, and the bacon better than any except Westphalian. The English eat almost no flesh commoner than hens, and for geese they eat them in two seasons, when they are fatted upon the stubble after harvest and when they are green about Whitsuntide. And howsoever hares are thought to nourish melancholy, yet they are eaten as venison both roast and boiled. They have also great plenty of conies [rabbits] the flesh whereof is fat, tender, and more delicate than any I have eaten in other parts. The German conies are more like roasted cats than the English conies.

THE SUN QUEEN   53

Trevelyan remarks that wheat and bread were the staple English foods. Vegetables were seldom eaten with meat and cabbages were mainly used for making soup. Potatoes were just starting to be grown in garden plots, but not yet as a field crop. Puddings and stewed fruit were not as popular as they later became. In an age when people rose early to start the day's work, and went early to bed, the chief meal was a late breakfast or dinner served between 11 in the morning and midday, followed by supper at 4 or 5 in the afternoon.

The payments for dinners in the Wardens' Accounts of the Founders show that sub-tropical fruits and spices were already being imported before Elizabethan days. They include purchases of dates, 'raisins of Corinth', cloves, and pepper, in 1498, cinnamon and ginger in 1509, and nutmeg in 1562. In order to help the fishermen from whom the Navy chiefly drew its seamen, the Privy Council appointed regular 'fish days' when only fish could be eaten, and restricted the consumption of beef and mutton, which not only competed with fish as food, but also caused too much arable land to be converted to pasture.

Elizabeth hated war, chiefly because it was so expensive, but there were times when she had to raise troops either to help the Protestant cause in Europe or to guard against an invasion of England. In 1562, the Livery Companies of London were required to contribute soldiers, and their arms, for an English expeditionary force to aid the French Huguenot rebels. The Founders recruited six men, five of whom were members of their Yeomanry, namely Davy Monk, Leonard Sewen, Martin Wheatley, Thomas Brewer and Harry Higginson. The sixth man, Nicholas Nell, seems to have been found elsewhere. Once again, the prosaic pages of the Wardens' Accounts resound with entries for swords, daggers, pikes, helmets and gunpowder. In 1572, the Company mustered 10 men, unnamed, to serve in a defence force raised and equipped by the City Companies which was reviewed by Elizabeth at Greenwich on May Day that year. The Founders paid their men and armed them with calivers, or light muskets, powder-flasks, tinder-boxes, gunpowder, swords, helmets and breastplates. Again, in 1579-80, when another muster of troops was held at Mile End, the Company paid and armed three of its Yeomanry members to take part, their names being Benet Bishop, George Lester and William Simpson.

After the assassination in 1584 of the Dutch Protestant leader, William the Silent and Elizabeth's expulsion of the Spanish Ambassador in London, Mendoza, the threat of invasion rapidly drew nearer. In 1584, the Privy Council revived the military parades, or Midsummer Night watches, formerly held in the City on the Feast of St. John Baptist, 24 June and that of St. Peter, 29 June. The Founders were represented by three of their Livery, William Glover, Walter Hunt and John Bond, who paid the Company 3s. 'for lending of the armour'. Glover served as Third Warden in 1586-7 and Second Warden in 1590-1. Walter Hunt was Third Warden in 1588-9 and Second Warden in 1594-5. John Bond was Third Warden in 1602-3.

In April and May 1585, there were further musters of troops at Greenwich, when the Founders hired and armed two gunners and four other soldiers for these

54 CITIZENS AND FOUNDERS

occasions. In August 1585, in answer to Dutch appeals for English reinforcements to fight the Spaniards, Elizabeth reluctantly agreed to despatch an expeditionary force to Flanders commanded by her favourite, Robert Dudley, the Earl of Leicester, a glib courtier with no military experience. The Founders paid and armed a soldier called Robert Weller for this service, but Antwerp had already fallen into Spanish hands by the time Leicester arrived, and he fought a losing battle at Zutphen in which his nephew, Sir Philip Sidney, died.

In May 1586, the City Companies were ordered to keep stores of gunpowder in reserve, which cost the Founders £2 for buying 48 pounds of gunpowder and another 8d. for a cask to hold it. Elizabeth had gained much valuable time by playing on the rivalry between Spain and France for supremacy in Europe, and by using English neutrality as a bargaining counter with King Philip. Moreover, while Mary Stuart, Queen of Scots, still lived Philip could have some hopes of a Catholic successor to the throne of England, for Mary was the next legal heir and a staunch Catholic believer. In 1587, however, Elizabeth's Privy Council felt strong enough to challenge Philip openly by persuading Elizabeth to sign the warrant for Mary's execution, though they must have known that they were, in effect, giving the signal for invasion. Before Mary died, she assigned her rights to the English Crown to Philip, and he now resolved to assert them by force of arms.

The Spanish Armada sailed in 1588 and the story of its defeat by English seamanship and gunnery, followed by its destruction by shipwreck round the coasts of Britain, is too well known to need repetition here. It is enough to say that Elizabethan England was saved by a Royal Navy starved of ships and men, just as Hitler's threat of German invasion in 1940 was smashed by a Royal Air Force which had for years been denied by 'appeasement' the aircraft and pilots which it desperately needed. In 1588, as in 1940, the home defence forces on land were not engaged in action, and this was fortunate. Although the Livery Companies kept stocks of arms in their Halls, they remained there for years on end without proper care and maintenance. The Wardens' Accounts for Elizabeth's reign abound in payments for repairing broken swords, fitting new springs and cocks to old handguns, and mending breastplates or helmets. The raw London levies of 1588 would have faced the invader with the same stubborn courage as the Home Guard of 1940, but their chances of victory against the veteran Spanish infantry would have been as slim as those of 'Dad's Army' against the Nazi armoured divisions.

On 18 November 1588, Elizabeth came in great state from Somerset House to old St. Paul's to attend a service of national thanksgiving for the defeat of the Armada. She had to listen to another sermon, but must have been in a better mood to bear it, and was fortified, one hopes, by the welcome she received from the City. The Lord Mayor issued detailed instructions to the Livery Companies for the occasion. All Liverymen were ordered to appear in their best robes and hoods, and their stands were to be strong, well-railed and 'covered with a fair blue cloth'. Standards and streamers were to be displayed all along the route of the procession. Each company paraded with at least 10 'whifflers' or ushers preceding it, wearing velvet coats and ceremonial gold chains. The Companies took up their positions

THE SUN QUEEN   55

lining the roadway from Temple Bar to the old cathedral of St. Paul's and each
of them fell in behind the Queen's procession as it reached them.

During the service, the Companies occupied their stands and benches outside St.
Paul's, which had been guarded by six of their Yeomanry in each case since six
o'clock that morning. Masters and Wardens took their places in a special stand,
carrying their staves of office.

And so it was that the Founders made their appearance in history on that great
day, to thank God and salute a Queen whose personal leadership and example in
the hour of need was only surpassed in our own time by Winston Churchill.

CHAPTER VI

Matters of Weight

ELIZABETH'S long reign of 44 years was probably the most eventful and creative period in our history, and one which also brought many benefits to the Founders' Company. For a few more years after the defeat of the Spanish Armada, however, the Livery Companies were still required to make their contributions to national defence. In 1591, for example, the Common Council agreed to equip six ships and a pinnace for the Queen's service, and the Founders contributed £20 to this fund. As they still lacked any capital reserve, the money had to be raised from the members, though it is not clear whether this took the form of a compulsory levy or consisted of voluntary gifts. Again, in 1598, the City Corporation made an interest-free loan of £20,000 to the Queen for suppressing rebellion in Ireland, and the Founders were assessed to pay £30.

The Merchant Taylors paid the highest rate of assessment for this loan, contributing the large sum of £1,800, while at the lower end of the scale the Bowyers, Fletchers, Woolmen and Minstrels each paid £10.

Through all the high drama of the Elizabethan age, the Founders quietly pursued their ways, working for the day and planning for the morrow. We may therefore pause at this point to consider changes which took place in the 16th century in the Company's internal organisation, beginning with the Court of Assistants. The first of the City Companies to establish a Court, in the sense of a permanent governing body, was the Grocers, who decided in 1379 that six members should be chosen yearly to give aid and counsel to the Wardens. The Shearmen appointed 12 members for that purpose in 1452. In 1487, the Carpenters initiated weekly meetings in their Hall between the Master and Wardens and such members as they thought fit, in order to discuss business and maintain 'the good rules and ordering of the Craft'.

The Mercers at one time held informal meetings between their Wardens, past and present, and Aldermen free of the Company, to consider special matters, such as the drafting of new Ordinances, which were then submitted to a general meeting for approval. In 1463, however, the Mercers decided that 'it was tedious and grievous to call so many courts and congregations of the Fellowship for matters of no great effect', and ordered that 12 persons should in future be chosen yearly as assistants to the Wardens, and that majority decisions by that body should be binding on the Company. These assistants were called 'the Assembly', and in 1479

MATTERS OF WEIGHT   57

they began to exercise the right of nominating candidates from whom the Wardens chose their successors. In 1504, those eligible for choice as assistants were defined as 'sad and discreet persons' who had served as Wardens, and a quorum of seven assistants was laid down. The Assembly was also forbidden to put the common seal of the Mercers to any document without reference to a general court.

The evolution of 'the Court of Assistants' in the Founders' Company shows many similarities with these examples. In 1497-8, the first year recorded in the Wardens' Accounts, the Company made payments for 'two days assembling' in Brewers' Hall and another two days in Armourers' Hall. It is not clear whether these gatherings were general meetings of the whole Fellowship, both Livery and Yeomanry, or a more limited 'assembly' of Master, Wardens, and assistants like that of the Mercers. It would certainly have been natural, from the earliest times, for the Wardens to seek advice and support from a small group of colleagues, especially those who had already served in office, but such meetings would have been only informal consultations.

The first mention of 'courts', so-called, in the Founders' case is found in the Accounts for 1509-11, when payments were made 'to keep in Cortis at divers times and seasons', but similar entries in other years suggest that the word 'court' was still being used to denote small, informal meetings between Master, Wardens, and a few others which took place either in a tavern or in the house of a Master, Warden, or senior Liveryman. There is so far no mention of the 'Court' as a permanent body.

In 1516, however, the new Ordinances adopted by the Company that year laid down that new Wardens were to be chosen from 'the Wardens and their associates and assistants', suggesting that some kind of standing committee was in existence. The late Mr. W. M. Williams deduced in his *Annals* that the appointment of assistants originated in the Founders with the ruling given in 1508 by Mayor Aylmer that six Yeomanry members should attend when the outgoing Wardens presented their accounts, and Hibbert copies this in his later edition of the *Annals*. It is quite clear, however, from the wording of Aylmer's 'award', that he never intended to give the Yeomanry an equal share with the Livery in the Company's management, but only a right to be kept informed of what was going on. From the earliest mention of 'assistants' as office-holders, they were invariably drawn from the Livery.

It was probably the increasing amount and variety of work involved in looking after the Company's interests that gradually transformed what had been a small panel of advisers with whom the Wardens took counsel into a fully fledged Court of Assistants. There is some evidence of such a process at work in a few contemporary notes included in the Wardens' Accounts. In 1532, for example, a meeting took place in the Hall to settle a dispute with William Abbot, a Liveryman and later Master, over the fee payable by him for binding an apprentice. This meeting was attended by Master, Wardens, and all the Livery members save one. In 1535, four senior Livery members sat with the Master and Wardens in a 'court' to fix the payments required from Liverymen for the Master's Feast. And in 1540, the Wardens had a meeting 'with the Assistants' to settle a debt owed by a Yeomanry member, Richard Gray, to a Liveryman, William Baker. It was agreed that

58   CITIZENS AND FOUNDERS

Richard should turn over to William 'nine small lamps every week' until the debt was fully discharged.

In the Wardens' Accounts for 1550-1, mention is made of 'the elder Clothing' in connection with payments for dinners. This must refer to senior liverymen who clearly had a special status and may have already served as Wardens. It was from such men that the nucleus of a Court of Assistants was probably drawn. Its meetings became more frequent in course of time, and in 1571-2 the Wardens' Accounts include expenses 'for drink' at no less than five 'Cort days'. The position of the Court as a permanent body was first recognised officially in the charter granted to the Founders by James I in 1614 and its supplementary Ordinances, which are more fully examined in a later chapter.

The Court of Assistants in a Livery Company was a self-perpetuating oligarchy drawn from a minority class of Liverymen, and this may offend some modern concepts of liberty, equality, and fraternity. Past history must be judged, however, not by the changes which have since occurred, but by the conditions prevailing at the time. As George Unwin has pointed out in his study of the gilds, the government of a Livery Company followed the general rule prevailing in Elizabethan institutions, including the colleges of universities, the borough corporations, and the Inns of Court. To some extent, indeed, the practice of the City Companies was more liberal, since the Livery itself was recruited from the Yeomanry.

The offices of Master and Wardens were no sinecures, but made strenuous demands on physical stamina, leisure time, and private purses which made men think twice before accepting them. This may be illustrated by some examples which have survived in the Founders' records of the duties undertaken by Masters and Wardens in Elizabethan and Stuart times. In 1553, the Founders' Wardens lodged a complaint with the Court of Aldermen against 'certain alien-born that of late hath brought certain andirons and other things made of latten into this City to be sold, contrary to the form of Parliament made in the time of King Edward the Fourth'. The Wardens reported that the King's Attorney was already informed on this subject and that the offenders 'were committed to the common law for the same'.

In 1556-7, fines were imposed by the Wardens on two of the Yeomanry, Alexander Metcalfe and James Jeny, for 'turning a pewterer's mould contrary to the orders of the house'. Jeny was one of the three Masters of the Yeomanry that year, and Metcalfe held the same office in 1559-60. In 1561-2, fines were collected from 'certain men for carrying of naughty wares to Bartolomew Fair'. In 1567, the Company paid 40s. to the first public lottery in London, organised under the patronage of Queen Elizabeth to raise funds for public works. Payments were made in 1571 to carpenters for timber and work on the Company's stand when Elizabeth visited the City that year, probably on the occasion when she opened the Royal Exchange and dined with its founder, Sir Thomas Gresham. Gresham was one of her most trusted and able financial advisers, and he was chiefly responsible for reforming the coinage debased by Henry VIII.

The fixing of wages by Justices of the Peace, acting for the Queen's Privy Council, is illustrated by an order issued by the Lord Mayor in 1586 dealing with

MATTERS OF WEIGHT 59

wages in the City. The rate of pay which he allotted to 'the best and most skilful workmen who are journeymen of the Founders' Company' was five pounds a year, including meat and drink, or 16d. by the day without subsistence. As a measure of comparison in money values at that time, an annual house rent of 23s. 4d. was paid to the Company by one of its tenants, Richard Fabott. Fabott was a Master of the Yeomanry in 1560-1 and was elected to the Livery in 1568-9, later serving as Younger Warden in 1572-3 and Second Warden in 1579-80. He was presumably a man of some means and paid a higher rent than a journeyman of the Company would have done.

A pleasant interlude in the working day is mentioned in the Wardens' Accounts for 1598-9, when the Second Warden, William Glover, was allowed a refund of 3s. 4d. 'for baking of pies when they went a swan-hopping'. This refers to the ancient custom of 'swan-upping' on the Thames, when the City Companies took part in the notching of swans on their beaks with different marks to identify their owners. Swans and cygnets not marked in this way were Crown property and therefore liable to seizure. The 'swan-upping' expedition on the river is still carried out every year by the Queen's Swan Master in conjunction with the Vintners and Dyers Companies, and the Master and Wardens of the Founders are kindly invited by the Dyers to join them on their launch and receive their generous hospitality.

Another City tradition, but one which has long died out, was instituted in 1556 when Alderman Draper, of the Cordwainers' Ward, appointed a 'bellman' whose duty it was 'to go about the Ward by night and, ringing his bell at certain places, exhort the inhabitants with an audible voice to take care of their lives and lights, to help the poor, and to pray for the dead'. This example was soon followed in all the City Wards.

In addition to the daily tasks of looking after the Company's affairs, the thoughts of the Founders' Masters, Wardens, and Liverymen during the Elizabethan period must have been increasingly occupied with the future role of the Company and its adaptation to the demands of change. The Founders, like many other City Companies, had reached a stage of evolution which posed new problems and called for new solutions. By this time, their membership no longer consisted solely of craftsmen working as founders, but already contained a new element of merchants, strongly represented in the Livery, whose business interests extended to many other trades. The old edict of 1363 which ordained that all craftsmen should choose one 'mistery' or gild, and join no other, was no longer enforced. Men could, and did, become members of more than one City Company and have remained free to do so to this day.

The Founders' own membership lists of the 16th century include one or two names of men shown as belonging to another Company as well. Nor was the old rule maintained that members of a City Company must be citizens of London who lived and worked there. For example, the Wardens and Assistants of the Founders agreed in 1587 that Richard Dixon, a freeman of the Company who had moved to Shrewsbury, should pay 2s. a year to cover all his quarterage dues for the future and a lump sum of 20s. for his arrears.

60 CITIZENS AND FOUNDERS

The growing complexity and inter-locking of trade and industry undermined the original concept of the gild as a 'closed shop' of craftsmen who alone had the right to manufacture and sell their particular products within the City limits. The influx of population into new London suburbs brought with it new competitors who were not bound by craft rules and were free to sell inferior goods at cut prices. This was a serious threat to the Yeomanry members of the Founders who were still mainly engaged in manufacture and dependent on it for their living.

The City Companies now began to look around them for new and more profitable means of exercising control over their trades by obtaining monopoly rights of inspection and licensing in the supply of raw materials, components, and retail outlets. In this they were sometimes aided, and sometimes challenged, by a new class of 'patentees' who were professional middlemen or speculators mainly concerned with buying and selling exclusive rights of this kind. These agents were already at work in the later years of Elizabeth's reign and multiplied under the Stuarts. They had contacts in ruling circles and were favoured by the Crown, which gained a lucrative source of revenue from the sale of patents, and by courtiers and officials who were well rewarded for their services as intermediaries. It was claimed for these monopolies that they served the public interest by eliminating unscrupulous traders and ensuring a regular supply of goods for the consumer, but more often they kept prices artificially high, lowered standards of quality for lack of competition, and aroused bitter resentment.

In 1576, the Tallow Chandlers obtained a patent from Elizabeth which authorised them to search and examine all soap, vinegar, butter, hops and oils, not only within the old City limits, but also in Southwark, Whitechapel, Westminster, and other outlying suburbs. The merchants dealing in these articles had to pay levies on them for inspection and were forbidden to sell them until the Tallow Chandlers had given their approval. The Vintners' Company was granted a monopoly of the retail sales of wine.

We do not know how far the Founders were influenced by such examples, but their thoughts were evidently running on similar lines. In 1584-5, they submitted a petition to the Lord Mayor and Aldermen asking for exclusive powers of 'assizing' all brass weights in the City, meaning the right to compel all sellers or users of such weights to present them for testing at Founders' Hall, where they would either be certified as accurate by the Company's mark, or broken up if found defective.

The Court of Aldermen did not as a rule look kindly on projects of this nature, which might trespass on their own rights of licensing and taxation in the City, but the use of false weights was a widespread abuse at this time and provided the Founders with a genuine case for action. We may be sure that they made the most of it and said less about the fees which the Company would collect for its services. They were no doubt also prepared for some arduous negotiations to establish their claim, but they could not have foreseen that one of their own officers would cheat them in the process.

The Company appointed two of its senior members, Edward Falconer and William Lester or Leicester, to act on its behalf in pursuing the suit about weights.

MATTERS OF WEIGHT   61

Falconer was Master in 1584-5 when the petition was submitted, and Lester was a former Master of the Yeomanry who served as Second Warden in 1586-7. On 5 April 1587, a Court was held at Founders' Hall to consider charges against Lester of abusing his trust. He was accused of having exploited his function as a negotiator to get a grant from the Lord Mayor to undertake the assize of weights for his own profit and not for the Company. The Court of Aldermen had appointed one of its members, Alderman Stephen Slaney of the Skinners' Company, to look into these charges and he presided at the meeting in Founders' Hall.

A full report of this meeting was inserted in the Wardens' Accounts. It notes that Lester informed the Court of his transaction, but adds that 'the Company thought themselves very evil dealt with, for that he, being Warden and put in trust by them, should get the office to himself'. It was also pointed out at the meeting that Lester was old and partly blind, and lacked the knowledge to carry out the assize of weights as efficiently as the Company desired. If there were other arguments in his favour, they are not recorded. Lester himself admitted the charge, but claimed that he had done nothing wrong.

Slaney's position as arbitrator was not an easy one, for the Lord Mayor's action in granting the assize to Lester without the knowledge or consent of the Company was very much open to question. This may explain why Slaney proposed a compromise whereby the Company would pay Lester his expenses in the negotiations, and something more for two or three years, in return for an acknowledgment by Lester that he was acting on the Company's behalf and not for himself. The Court accepted these terms and offered to pay Lester, in addition to his expenses, a sum of £4 a year or one-third of the profits from assizing weights during his lifetime.

This was a generous offer, and Alderman Slaney was well satisfied with it, but Lester told the Court 'that he thought it was nothing, but that he had deserved a great deal more'. He asked for a few days in which to consider the Company's offer and this was granted, after Lester had promised not to intervene with the Lord Treasurer or anybody else so as to prevent the Company from gaining its rights. Two days later, however, Lester called a 'court' of his own choosing at the house of a 'Father Croft', who was not a priest but an ale-house keeper. This meeting was attended by about 20 'of the worst sort and poorest of the Company', according to the report in the accounts, and Lester got them to sign a paper, presumably endorsing his own claim, which he said had already been signed by a former Warden, Nicholas Roberts, and several of the Assistants.

On hearing of this, the Master, Uryan Daniell, and the Third Warden, William Glover, summoned a proper 'Court of Assistance' at which Roberts declared that he had never signed anything for Lester, and the 'poor men' who had put their names or marks to Lester's paper pleaded that they had done so without knowing what was in it. When Lester was asked to produce the paper, he refused and merely said 'that he would do it again'. The Court then committed him to prison, where he cooled his heels for a while and then appealed to the indulgent Alderman Slaney to arrange matters with the Company.

Slaney, who throughout this business showed a partiality for Lester which is

62 CITIZENS AND FOUNDERS

hard to explain unless he was acting on the Lord Mayor's instructions, then called a meeting at his own house attended by the Master, Third Warden, and several Assistants. He also had Lester brought to it from prison. After a long discussion in which Slaney put further pressure on the Company, a settlement was reached on terms much more favourable for Lester than he can have deserved or expected. In return for his promise 'to be quiet and live amongst them as a brother ought to do', the Company agreed to refund all the expenses he had already incurred as a negotiator, or alternatively to pay him £4 for his expenses when the Company had won its suit for assizing weights. Thereafter, Lester was to do the work and receive one-half of the profit, instead of the one-third share first proposed, but he also agreed to pay half the working costs.

Shortly after, in May 1587, a formal agreement was registered in Guildhall which specified that no weights were to be offered for sale in the City until they had been 'sized' at Founders' Hall, stamped with the Company's mark, sealed by the Keeper of the Guildhall, and approved by the Company. A scale of fees was laid down at rates of 4d. for an eight-pound weight, 2d. for a four-pound weight, 1d. for a two-pound weight, and the same for smaller ones. The Company was to have no more than the Guildhall Keeper received for sealing weights, and fines for selling unauthorised weights were to be divided equally between the Founders and the City Chamberlain. This was followed by an order from the Lord Mayor that the Founders should 'set and stamp' their Arms on every brass weight which they assized. A grant of Arms was made in October 1590, by Robert Cooke, Clarenceux King of Arms, and the Company paid him a fee of £3 2s. 8d. through the Norroy Herald. The document making the grant reads as follows:

> The field azure, a Laver-Pot between two Candlesticks gold. And to the Crest upon the Helm on a wreath gold and azure a fiery Furnace proper, out of the clouds proper two Arms the hands carnat, the sleeves azure holding a pair of Closing-Tongs sables taking hold of a Melting-Pot proper mantled gules doubled silver as more plainly appeareth in the margin.

> To have and to hold the said Arms and Crest to Robert Waldo, James Lambert, and Thomas Jackson, now Wardens of the said Company, and to their successors in like place and office, and to all the Commonalty of the Founders of the City of London, and they the same to use, bear, and show forth for ever in all places for the credit of the same Company in shield, standard, banner, pennon or otherways at their liberty and pleasure according to the ancient Laws of Arms, without impediment, let, or interruption of any person or persons'.

The Founders must have been cheered by their success in obtaining the assize of brass weights, despite having to share the proceeds with Lester, and in 1590 they tried to push matters further by petitioning the Queen's Privy Council for an order that all weights under two pounds and made of lead should be replaced by brass. The petition complained of the 'wrong' done to the Company and others of the

MATTERS OF WEIGHT

63

Queen's subjects by the use of lead weights which wore out and became defective more quickly than those made of brass. This was no doubt true enough, but the real point was that the Company, as workers in brass, stood to gain substantially from such a change. In this case, however, the Founders were rebuffed.

The Privy Council had larger matters of state on their minds and naturally referred the petition back to the Lord Mayor and Aldermen for their opinion, which was hostile. They advised the Privy Council in 1591 that the conversion of smaller lead weights into brass was 'very inconvenient to be yielded unto', and they gave three reasons.

First, they said, although leaden weights might wear out quicker than brass, a change would not prevent dishonest users from continuing to practise frauds. The remedy lay in the wisdom and energy of the officers charged with searching and examining weights, without which a change from lead to brass would serve little purpose. Secondly, the leaden weights had always been used by the shopmen and sellers of small wares, except for the finer kinds such as sewing silk and gold lace, and a change would involve them in great expense which, being mostly poor men, they could not afford. Conversely, the Founders were hoping to make great gains purely for themselves. Thirdly, the Lord Mayor and Aldermen asked by what right could they force men to buy brass weights when others such as the Plumbers, who made lead weights and were mostly very poor, would complain that their living was being taken from them and given to the Founders.

In a cutting parting shot, the City governors told the Privy Council that they had already made their answer to the Founders 'and therefore marvel the more they would trouble your Lordships with so partial a request that respecteth nothing else but their own profit. If they importune your Lordships any further hereafter, we leave it to your Lordships' wisdom and discretion what is meet to be said unto them touching their request'.

The disagreement between the Founders and the City Corporation on this subject was not surprising, for they approached it from different angles. For the Company, the replacement of lead weights by brass would have created more work for the Yeomanry members, who were still mainly engaged in manufacturing and suffering most from new trading conditions and competition. For the Court of Aldermen, however, dominated as it was by the 'Great Companies' and their mercantile interests, the larger question was the effect of changes in weights on the 'shopmen' and, to a lesser extent, the anger which would be felt among other metal-workers if lead weights were replaced by brass. Moreover, the 'Twelve Great Companies' possessed a chartered right of search and inspection over weights and measures in the City, and an enlargement of the Founders' powers in this field might have been regarded as an invasion of those privileges.

A few years later, however, in 1599, the Founders received a substantial vindication which must have pleased them. The Lord Mayor appointed a committee to consider the reform of abuses in unlawful weights and measures used in buying and selling gold and silver. Its members included not only seven aldermen headed by Sir Stephen Soame, but also three representatives of the Founders' Company,

64

CITIZENS AND FOUNDERS

namely Robert Waldo, John Storer or Storey, and William Baker. This committee recommended that only 'troy' weights should in future be used for gold and silver, and only 'avoirdupois' for other goods. It referred to 'great and manifold abuses daily committed by such as use false and unlawful weights and balances', and proposed a scale of fines to punish offenders.

The committee did not revive the idea of replacing lead weights by brass, but it did agree that 'all leaden weights within a very small time after the use thereof do wear and become lighter, and so consequently false'. It proposed that all weights made and used in the City should be made of iron, lead or brass, and be sealed on the top; that those of iron should be made to a standard pattern laid down; and that all weights taken from owners should be sealed and delivered back to them.

The committee was less well disposed to the Plumbers than the Court of Aldermen in 1591. It considered that the Plumbers' fee of 3s. per hundredweight for 'sizing' defective lead weights was excessive, and that the reform and amendment of these weights should be carried out under the direction of the Keeper of the Guildhall, James Harman. He should be assisted by George Lester and Robert Thompson, both belonging to the Founders, who had undertaken to size and amend defective lead weights for a reasonable consideration. Lester may have been related to the man who had given the Company so much trouble over the sizing of brass weights, while Thompson was a senior Liveryman and a 'moulder'. Finally, the committee proposed that, if any of the Twelve Great Companies neglected their charter right of searching for false weights and measures, then others should be appointed for that purpose. The Founders were not designated as incumbents, but they were clearly regarded as having the right qualifications.

As things turned out, the Company's monopoly of searching and sizing brass weights was never extended beyond those of 14 pounds and under. Moreover, the agreement whereby the Company had to share the profits equally with William Lester, and also the costs, lasted much longer than could have been expected in view of his advanced age and poor health. The first entries for receipts and payments arising from the assize of weights appear in the Accounts for 1587-8, when the Second Warden received £8 8s. 6d. from this source and paid out £5 17s. 1d., which presumably covered Lester's half-share of the fees and a refund of half his working expenses.

Also in 1587-8, when the sizing of weights started at Founders' Hall, the Company made a grant of the 'melting-house' to William Lester and Thomas Palmer, a Yeomanry member who seems to have been employed by Lester to help him. Whatever his faults and lack of scruples, Lester must have been a tough old man, for in 1592-3 he was still getting half the money from sizing. There is then a gap in the records, except for brief summaries, but in 1607-8 the Second Warden, Edward Parnell, received £8 11s. 5d. from Thomas Platt, who had taken over the sizing of weights, and paid out 1s. 6d. for the mending of a pair of scales.

Platt succeeded Henry Jewdrey as Beadle when the latter died in 1612 and was paid by allowing him to keep a half-share of the profits from weights. He was also given the use of the Company house formerly occupied by the Clerk, Henry Fend-

MATTERS OF WEIGHT

rey, who died in 1612, like Jewdrey, and was replaced by William Liddell, a founder. Platt and Liddell were both members of the Company, and their appointments as Beadle and Clerk suggest that the Company preferred to employ men of its own in these posts, or perhaps could find no suitable candidates elsewhere. However, Platt also died shortly after his appointment as Beadle, and it was the Clerk, Liddell, who then took over the sizing of weights and kept a half-share of the profits. This continued to be a perquisite of the Clerk under Liddell's successors, John Falkener, William Basspoole, Francis Lambert, and James Dickinson extending over the whole remaining period covered by the Accounts up to 1681, and for an uncertain period of time thereafter. In 1680-1, the Company's income from weights was £15, as compared with £8 in 1609-10. This showed a substantial increase, but the practice of leaving the Clerk to do the sizing gave the Company serious trouble in 1699 and 1700, as will be related in due course.

Few benefactions to the Company are on record in the 16th century, and such information as we have is therefore all the more of interest. In 1564, Roger Taylor, who died on 12 November that year, left the Company 13s. 4d. 'for divers years to come' and a silver-gilt goblet weighing 22 ounces. Taylor had a long and distinguished career in the Company. He was bound as an apprentice in 1508-9 and admitted to the Company in 1516-7 as a Yeomanry member. He was elected to the Livery in 1529-30, serving as Third Warden in 1537-8 and Second Warden in 1543-4 and 1548-9. His standing in the Company is shown by the fact that he was chosen as Master four times, in 1551-2, 1552-3, 1554-5 and 1560-1. His cup was brought to the Hall by his widow, and the Livery paid tribute to his memory by giving a 'breakfast' for her on this occasion. These are the kind of intimate glimpses which make history live and turn printed names into real people.

In 1594, the Company received another gift from one of its members, Robert Thompson, but with strings attached which seem to have caused trouble. Robert Thompson gave the Founders five marks equal to £3 6s. 8d., with the proviso that the Company should add 20 nobles, or £6 13s. 4d. and the combined total of £10 should then be put out at interest. The yearly income was to be distributed among the poor people of the Company at the discretion of the Wardens for the time being. The Court accepted this proposition, and also agreed that Thompson himself should have the use of the £10 for the next five years on giving a pledge of repayment and paying interest at 10 per cent on the money. Thompson duly handed over his five marks and presumably got it back with the sum advanced by the Company, but he only made one payment of interest so far as the records show, which was in 1597-8. In 1602-3, he and his surety, Richard Walker, are shown as debtors to the Company for £3 13s. 4d. in cash and another £3 on his bond. There is no evidence that these debts were ever repaid.

In 1585-6, the Founders made another attempt to obtain a Royal Charter. Payments were made to Cutts, a scrivener, for engrossing the draft on to parchment, and to Dawes, another scrivener, for engrossing a petition to the Queen. Money was also paid to 'Mr. Chapman', clerk to the Attorney-General, Sir John Popham, to induce his master to sign the Company's application. These efforts came to noth-

66   CITIZENS AND FOUNDERS

ing, and indeed Mr. Parsloe remarks, in a note on the Wardens' Accounts, that there appears to be no trace of this petition for a Charter either in the Public Records or those of the City Corporation.

Nevertheless, the Founders had reason to feel satisfied with their progress as the 16th century drew to its end. They were well settled in their new Hall, which brought them added status and new income from rents. Their sizing of weights was also producing a good return, even if the Company did not get the full benefit. They must have known in their hearts, as Elizabeth lay dying in 1603, that a great era had come to an end, but none could have foreseen that her Stuart successors would so soon cast away the splendid legacy of a united country which she left them.

CHAPTER VII

Royal Charter

IF ELIZABETH had married and left an heir to the throne, the course of English history in the next century would have been very different, and the relationship between Crown and Parliament might have been settled peacefully instead of erupting into civil war. There is some doubt, however, as to whether she was capable of bearing children, and she may have known or suspected this when the Privy Council was urging her to take a husband. Such knowledge would have made her doubly conscious of the ironical twist of fate by which the Crown passed to James VI of Scotland, son of Mary Stuart by Darnley, and thus made amends for Mary's long imprisonment by Elizabeth and her final execution.

James was neither a fool nor a fanatic, but a self-conceited and pedantic man who had no liking or understanding for his English subjects. Worse still, he was a firm believer in the divine right of kings, a concept alien to an English people which, though it still retained a mystical sense of union with the Crown, was certainly not prepared to agree that kings could do as they pleased and stood above the law. Parliament was already flexing its muscles under Elizabeth, but she had handled it with a political insight which warned her when she must bend or be broken. James took the bull by the horns, and in the end it was the bull that won.

James began his reign with a fund of goodwill from a country which had feared that his succession might cause a renewal of internal conflict, but was reassured by his acceptance of the Protestant settlement and the existing order. Among the Catholics, however, the persecution which they continued to suffer aroused fierce anger and desperation. In 1604, a group of Catholic gentlemen led by Robert Catesby organised the Gunpowder Plot and chose a professional soldier called Sir Guy Fawkes to blow up both Parliament and King James when he went to open it. The failure of the plot is usually attributed to a warning letter sent by one of the conspirators, Tresham, to his friend Lord Monteagle, but it is possible that the highly efficient secret service which James inherited from Elizabeth succeeded in penetrating the plot at an early stage and used Tresham's letter as cover when it was sure of arresting all those involved.

As might have been expected, or was even planned behind the scenes, the effect of the plot was to revive all the old Protestant fears and stir up popular fury against innocent Catholics, many of whom were killed or imprisoned. A day of national thanksgiving was appointed for the escape of King and Parliament which has

68   CITIZENS AND FOUNDERS

delighted many generations of children ever since, and the Founders joined in these celebrations. In October 1606, the Wardens and Assistants issued the following order :

> That the fifth day of November, being a day observed as a holiday for the King's Majesty and the rest of the whole estate of this land, their deliverance from the grievous treason pretended against them and the Parliament House, at which day the Company is to use to assemble at Poules [St. Paul's] and after to dine together. There shall be allowed by the Hall towards that dinner thirty shillings, and that every person of the Livery shall pay towards the said dinner, and every one of the said Livery that shall make default and come not to the service then shall pay twelve pence whether he come to the dinner or not, except sickness or other reasonable cause.

A year earlier, in 1605, similar arrangements had already been instituted for a service at St. Paul's, followed by a dinner, to celebrate James's escape from the Gowrie conspiracy in Scotland in 1600, before he came to England. The last mention of 'Gowrie's Day' occurs in the Wardens' Accounts for 1622-3, but the Company's dinner in memory of the 'Great Powder Treason' was still taking place in 1681, the last year of account on record.

The early sympathies which the City Companies felt for James were alienated by the way he acted, or failed to act, in later years. English commerce and the City merchants suffered heavy losses because he allowed the small, but efficient, Elizabethan navy to sink into decay, so much so that pirates operated freely even in the English Channel. Englishmen were thus hurt both in their pride and their pockets, a dangerous combination. The City also had to endure a mounting burden of taxation. Although James I shunned foreign wars, neglected the navy, and kept much less luxury at court than Elizabeth, he was always short of money to meet the rising demands of public expenditure. Englishmen in the past had been willing to render services in kind, such as work on local roads, drains, bridges, city walls and military duty in emergencies, but they had none of our present spirit of submission to paying exorbitant taxes in hard cash. James had to deal with a House of Commons which was already using its power of the purse to seek fresh concessions from the Crown as the price of subsidies, and he replied by simply dissolving Parliament and muddling on as best he could.

In 1604, within a year of coming to the throne, James raised a loan of £20,000 from the City of London, to which the Founders had to contribute £22 10s., or just over half their balance in hand at the end of the previous accounting year. This was repaid in 1606-7. In 1607-8, the Company paid traditional levies to the Crown of 'one-fifteenth' and 'three-fifteenths' assessed on its fixed assets, as well as additional subsidies to the King that year and in the two which followed. In 1608-9, James received a gift of money from the City, in accordance with feudal custom, when his eldest son, Prince Henry, came of age and was knighted. A similar gift was made in 1612, when James's daughter, Princess Elizabeth, was married to Frederick, Elector of the Palatinate in Germany.

ROYAL CHARTER

In 1609, James and his advisers resorted to a new method of raising money by selling lands in Ulster forfeited to the Crown by Irish rebels, and bringing in Protestant settlers, mainly Presbyterian Scots, to take their place. It was a decision which has since caused much tragedy and bloodshed, as we know to our cost today. The Lord Mayor issued a 'precept' calling on the City companies to contribute a sum of £20,000 for the 'plantation' of Ulster and the establishment there of settlers from London. The various companies were assessed at different rates for this purpose, the Founders being required to pay £34. The money was raised by making a levy of £1 on each member of the Livery and asking the Yeomanry members to make voluntary contributions. Any further sum needed to make up the balance was to be provided from the common fund.

This was followed, in July 1609, by a further summons from the Lord Mayor requiring the Livery Companies to take land in Ulster and 'build and plant the same' at their own cost and charges. The Founders were allotted land in Derry and Coleraine, and also the fishing rights and other privileges attached to 7,000 acres of common land in that area. The Company evidently had doubts about accepting this demand, for it was not until February 1610, that the Court agreed to it, 'having better considered thereof'. In July 1611, the Court decided that whatever charges should arise from these lands, over and above the contributions already made by members of the Company, should be borne by the common stock in the Hall and not met by a further poll tax on individuals. The Court also directed that any profit arising from the Ulster lands should go into the common stock and not be used to repay members of the Company, or their heirs and executors, for their personal contributions. Doubts were clearly felt as to whether any profit would in fact be seen, as the minutes added : 'When it shall please God to send it'.

In 1614, a body called the Irish Society was set up to buy the Irish estates from the Crown at a cost of £60,000, a very large sum at that time. The money was raised by compelling each of the 'Twelve Great Companies' of London to invest £5,000 and draw lots for the land distributed among them. They in turn formed 'syndicates' with lesser Companies which subscribed part of the purchase money and received a share of the estates. The Founders, together with the Wax Chandlers and the Turners, were linked with the Haberdashers in this business, probably against their will and better judgment, but submitting to orders from a Lord Mayor who himself had to answer to the King for the City's obedience. In the ensuing years, the Founders' Wardens had frequent meetings with those of the Wax Chandlers and Turners to discuss their Irish problems.

The part played by the City of London in the 'plantation' of Ulster is still visibly recalled by the old cannons supplied by Companies such as the Fishmongers, Vintners and Merchant Taylors, for the defence of the settlement in Londonderry, which bear their arms. As for the Founders, they got little but trouble and expense from this business. The Wardens' Accounts show that the Company paid at least £90 in contributions up to the end of 1616, and a further £10 between 1616 and 1634. In return it received rents totalling just over £31.

In 1634, Charles I revoked the charter of the Irish Society and the City's Irish

70   CITIZENS AND FOUNDERS

lands were declared forfeit to the Crown. The 'Great Companies' set up a committee to negotiate for the City, and the Founders lent it £100 at the end of 1642. In 1654, under Cromwell, the Company authorised the committee to sell enough of its lands in Ireland to pay off this loan, and in the same year it received £7 from special commissioners sitting at Goldsmiths' Hall to consider claims.

The Ulster lands were given back by Charles II after his restoration in 1660, but the only further payment to the Founders recorded in their Accounts is one for £144 in 1686, when they sold all further interest in their Irish holdings. The Court of Assistants authorised the Master to sign this agreement after 'taking into consideration that they have nothing to show for the land, nor having received any rent or profits for above fifty years past'. It must have been a relief to the Founders to wind up this business, but the Irish fishing rights were apparently retained until 1730, when their sale to the Haberdashers was negotiated. This was a loss which some present Founders may well regret.

The Company had to meet other heavy charges in the early years of James I's reign. There were constant expenses for repairs or alterations to the Hall, suggesting that the original building work may not have been very well done. In one year alone, 1605-6, the Company spent nearly £52, probably equivalent to several thousand pounds in modern terms, on 'new covering the Hall and trimming within' and building the kitchen chimney. The effect on the Company's finances was to turn what would have been a net surplus of about £32 for that year into a deficit of nearly £20. This was made up by the retiring Master, or Upper Warden as he was called at that time, and refunded to him by his successor, Richard Rowdinge. In the next two or three years, payments were made for repairing glass windows in the 'sizing-house' and parlour, mending the kitchen door and range, and restoring the 'hand pace' of the stairs, referring perhaps to a landing between two flights or else the balustrade.

The Company was then receiving about £18 a year from rents and another £8 or £9 from the sizing of weights, over and above the income from quarterage dues, fines, and fees paid by members. The Loriners' Company paid a rent of £4 yearly for the use of Founders' Hall from 1606 to 1608. The Founders received a gift of money from Dorcas Greathead, wife of Oswald Greathead, Second Warden in 1605-6, and her daughter, Elizabeth, for a new carpet 'for the table in the parlour'. It was then customary to use carpets for covering walls or tables, and to strew rushes or sawdust on the floors.

Another burden laid on the Companies was the provision of corn to build up reserves which could be sold in hard times to bring down the price of bread, as noted in an earlier chapter. For many years, the Livery Companies were assessed at varying rates for payment of 'corn money' to the City Corporation, which stored the grain in the City granary in Bridge House at the Southwark end of London Bridge. In Stuart times, however, the Companies had to buy the corn themselves and keep it in store for delivery when needed. This was more expensive, not only because agents had to be employed and paid, but also because the corn might go mouldy and need to be replaced.

ROYAL CHARTER

The Livery Companies were subjected to heavy demands for purchases of corn early in James I's reign. In 1605, they were required by the Lord Mayor to buy 10,000 quarters of wheat and charged 'to have special care thereof so as the price of corn in the market be not thereby increased'. The quota for the Founders was 25 quarters. In 1608, the Company made an agreement with Gregory Hobbs, one of its Livery members who later served as Third Warden, whereby Hobbs was to keep corn in store at Queenhythe for delivery at four or five days' notice. He was paid 40s. a year for this service, reduced to 30s. if his expenses were less than 10s.

In 1612, the Lord Mayor ordered the companies to provide another 10,000 quarters of corn, but this time the Founders rebelled and the Court resolved : 'That we do rest and *not* provide, referring it to the next precept which shall be sent from the Lord Mayor touching the same, and we do stand to the hazard of the price of the same'. This was a bold refusal in an age when authority was not so easily flouted as it is today. In 1621-2, however, the Company arranged for a corn merchant called Humphrey Dovey to supply 10 quarters of wheat whenever required at an annual charge of £2, and he continued to do so till 1645-6. In 1631, the Founders recorded a loss of over £9 from corn, and the Grocers noted that they had lost at least £400 in supplying the City markets and Wards with corn 'agreeably to the direction of the Privy Council'. It must therefore be concluded that the Lord Mayor and Aldermen were acting on government instructions.

The corn assessments were fixed by an Act of Common Council, and in 1600 the same rating method was used to collect a tax of £500 from the Livery Companies for the City workhouse at Bridewell. The purpose of the tax, as described by the Court of Aldermen, was to set to work 'the great numbers of idle, lewd, and wicked persons flocking and resorting hither from all quarters of this realm, which do live here and maintain themselves by robbing and stealing'.

The mounting burden of taxes imposed by the Crown and the City Corporation caused much discontent among the Livery Companies, and was manifested in resistance which shows that the idea of a 'taxpayers' strike' is no new invention. In February 1604, the Wardens of the Brewers, Lawrence Tristram and John Clarke, were committed to prison in Wood Street for refusing to pay a sum of £50 demanded from their Company towards the expenses of pageants and shows to welcome James I when he visited the City. As already noted, the Founders refused to provide corn, though the Master and Wardens managed to keep out of gaol on this occasion. In October 1604, the Court of Aldermen heard complaints from various Companies that 'they have of late been over-rated and assessed at higher rates for loans of money, provisions of corn, going and precedence of companies, and other grievances, than in right they ought'. The Aldermen appointed a committee consisting of two members from each of the 'Great Companies' and one from others of lesser rank to 'rate and proportion' every Company with a grievance. This seems to have had little effect, however, and the constant demands for money continued.

In 1606, for example, the Lord Mayor raised £1,000 from the City companies to pay for the pomp and pageantry of a Royal visit by James I and the King of

CITIZENS AND FOUNDERS

Denmark, whose daughter, Anne, was James's Queen. In 1621, the Lord Mayor transmitted a demand from the Privy Council for contributions from the Livery Companies to help James's son-in-law, the Elector Palatine, who was at war in Germany. The Founders paid £7 10s. for this purpose which they could ill afford.

The wording of this particular demand was more diplomatically expressed than the usual brusque orders, perhaps because it was at last dawning on the Privy Council that the golden goose was turning rather nasty. It spoke of 'desiring contributions of some reasonable sums of money towards the Palatinate already invaded by the enemy, being the ancient inheritance of His Majesty's son-in-law, which is to descend to His Majesty's posterity. A matter of that importance which every good subject is sensible of, and how much it doth and may concern His Majesty himself, his children and posterity, and the welfare of his kingdom and the state of religion'. This wording tactfully combined both James's dynastic interest and English obligations to the German Protestant cause, since the Elector Frederick had chosen that side and stood to lose his domains if it turned out that he had backed the wrong horse. James had no intention of being drawn into the war himself, but he probably saw no reason why the Protestant majority of his own subjects should not help to pay for it. A few English volunteers also fought for Frederick.

The Wardens' Accounts of the Founders give clear indications of the financial strains endured by the Company in this period. In 1611, the Court ordered that every Liveryman should pay 1s. for the dinners held on quarter-days, whether he attended or not, and the same for the 'thanksgiving' dinners held on 5 August and 5 November to celebrate James's escape from the Gowrie conspiracy and the Gunpowder Plot. Fines were imposed on Liverymen who failed to attend the quarter-day meetings at the Hall, when members paid their quarterage, or absented themselves on Court days or arrived late, or failed to take part in the burial of members. The 'Ancients' of the Company, meaning those who had served as Master or Upper Warden, only had to pay half the charge for dinners and nothing for failing to attend Courts and quarter-day meetings.

In August 1612, the Court decided that the usual Michaelmas dinner held late in September to mark the election of new Wardens should be cancelled for that year and the one after. The new Wardens were to make some provision to celebrate the occasion, but no charge was to fall on the Hall. In October 1612, a further Court order was issued reading as follows:

> That forasmuch as the Company is greatly impoverished by reason of the daily wages and taxes levied both for His Majesty's service and for the service of the City, we think it fitting for the good of the said Society, and for the increase of the stock of the same, that no man having served his full time of years, or otherwise to be made a new brother of the fraternity, but first, before he be sworn a brother of the same, he shall give for the benefit of the said Company one silver spoon, being in value at the least of six shillings and eightpence, be he ever so poor.

ROYAL CHARTER   73

A year later, the Court raised the minimum value of these spoons to 13s. 4d., double the initial amount, but discontinued the old practice whereby newly-admitted members were required to give a dinner for the Master, Wardens, senior Assistants, and their wives. New members who failed to give spoons had to pay a fine equal to the minimum value laid down.

Voluntary gifts of spoons were an old custom of the Company and helped to build up a stock of silver and plate which served as a capital reserve fund in times of crisis. Between 1617 and 1624, under James I, the Company was forced to sell no less than 85 of its silver spoons, each marked with the initials of the donor, which realised a total sum of about £45. In 1635, under Charles I, the Company was again so hard pressed that it sold off all its remaining spoons, then numbering 51, except for one presented by Humphrey Bowen on his admission in 1624-5. The spoons were bought by members of the Company, chiefly by the Master that year, Francis Curwen, and his Renter Warden, Leonard Lambart. The Bowen spoon probably owed its preservation to the charming inscription on each side of the handle reading: 'If You Love Me, Keep Me Ever. That's My Desire and Your Endeavour'. It has remained a treasured possession of the Founders, and a replica was presented to every member when the Company celebrated its 600th anniversary in 1965. Bowen must have been a man of some means, as he rented two houses in Founders' Court from the Company from 1627 until his death in 1636, paying £8 a year. The custom of presenting silver spoons on admission to the Company continued for many years after the sale of spoons in 1635 and is last recorded in 1661-2. None of these later spoons has survived, and they must have been sold, like the others, in times of crisis, unless they were destroyed in the Great Fire of 1666.

To set against its financial difficulties, the Founders' Company could rejoice in having at last achieved success in its long quest for a Royal Charter. In 1613, the Company sought leave from the Lord Mayor, Sir Thomas Middleton, to petition the Crown for a Charter, and it appointed John Rawlings, then Second Warden, and Robert Thompson to argue the case with the Court of Aldermen. This must have been a different man from the Robert Thompson whose unfortunate financial dealings with the Company were referred to in the previous chapter.

Middleton set up a committee under his own chairmanship which heard the views of other interested parties in the City and then approved the Founders' application. The committee also recommended that 'all Melters and Workers of Molten Brasses and Copper Metals' in the City and within a compass of three miles should be subject to the Ordinances of the Founders. It made only one exception by exempting those members of the Pewterers' Company who had been accustomed to work for 10 years in copper or brass for their own trade. The committee also upheld the right of the Founders to inspect and mark all brass weights within the three-mile limit.

The Royal Charter was issued on 18 September 1614, and signed by James I as 'King of England, France, and Ireland and Scotland'. The full text is reproduced in Appendix C, but some of the main points should be mentioned here.

74   CITIZENS AND FOUNDERS

The Charter gave the Founders corporate rights to hold lands not exceeding £40 a year, to sue and be sued, and to have a common seal. The governing body was to consist of a Master and two Wardens elected annually and 15 Assistants elected for life unless removed or dismissed. The Master was to be chosen from nominations of two persons who had served as the senior Warden and were reputed the senior Assistants. The two Wardens were to be chosen from six nominations of Assistants or of persons from the Livery. The Master, Wardens, and Assistants were given full powers to elect officers, hold Courts, and make statutes or laws.

The Charter laid down that all brass weights within the three-mile City limit must be brought to Founders' Hall to be sized and stamped with the Company's mark on payment of a fee 'as heretofore'. Failure to do so was punishable by fines, which the Master, Wardens and Assistants were authorised to enforce by 'distress' or seizure of goods. The Company was to appoint 'discreet persons' under its common seal to search all shops, warehouses, and other places for 'deceitful works and weights', and they could call on the aid of the Lord Mayor and Sheriffs and the Justices of the Peace.

Supplementing the Charter, new Ordinances dated 15 January 1615, were granted to the Founders by the Lord Chancellor, Lord Ellesmere, and two Chief Justices, Sir Edward Coke and Sir Henry Hobart (See Appendix D). They confirmed the Company's right of search and stipulated that every person 'working brass or copper wares' within the three-mile limit must identify them by a maker's mark allowed by the Master, Wardens and Assistants of the Founders.

These Ordinances called for 'Courts of Master and Wardens' to be held every Monday, and for 'Courts of Assistants' to be convened by Master and Wardens as often as business demanded. In addition, 'General Courts' attended by the Livery and the 'general body or fellowship' were to be held quarterly in February, May, August and on 29 October, which was then observed as Lord Mayor's Day.

In most other respects, the 1615 Ordinances confirmed rules already in existence. Thus, fines were specified for various offences of long standing, such as reviling a brother-member, failing to attend the funeral of a brother Liveryman or his wife, defaulting on quarterage payments, or refusing to pay any 'just and reasonable assessment' made by the Court for the service of the King or the City. Any Master, Warden, Assistant or Liveryman attending a Court without his gown was to forfeit 12d. Any Liveryman failing to attend on the King 'by horse or foot' when he visited the City, or neglecting 'any reasonable service' appointed by the Master, was to pay a fine of 20s. A refusal to accept the office of Master incurred a fine of £10, and refusal to serve as an Assistant resulted in a fine of 20s. Every new Master Warden, Assistant, Liveryman and Freeman of the Company had to swear allegiance to the Crown, as well as take his oath to the Company, and this also applied to the Auditors, Sizers, Searchers, Clerks and Beadles. Any Master, Warden or other person concerned with receipts or payments, or with the money and goods of the Company, was obliged to account for them to the Auditors and bind himself with sureties to make good any default.

The grant of the Charter bore witness to the Company's rising reputation and

ROYAL CHARTER

75

was a fitting reward for the labours of earlier Founders, but it also involved a good deal of extra expenditure. The preparatory work called for payments to Rawlings and Thompson for their expenses in attending the Lord Mayor's committee; to the Cutlers' Company for consulting their Charter; to the cost of providing the Pewterers and the Ironmongers with copies of the Founders' proposals; and to the Company's Clerk, William Liddell, for his extra work and expenses.

The Charter itself required a heavy outlay for legal advice, gifts to influential people at court and in the City, and fees for the 'scriveners' who wrote and engrossed the final text. Cash payments were made to Mr. Young, Clerk to the Attorney-General, who was none other than Sir Francis Bacon; to a Mr. Bassett, Secretary to the Chancellor of the Exchequer, who rejoiced in the name of Sir Julius Caesar; to Mr. Locke, Clerk to the King's Commissioners; and to the City Recorder, Sir Henry Montague. But by far the largest payment went to the City Remembrancer, William Dyos or Diss, whose services cost the Founders £100. Diss seems to have had a keen eye for the pickings from his office, for when he gave it up in 1619 he complained to the King that he had not been allowed to sell it. He also protested that the City Chamber had given him £400 less for quitting his office than he had paid for it, although the truth was that the City had cancelled a debt of £700 which he owed it and made him a gift of £300.

The Founders were in no position to pay these costs out of capital or income, but had to rely on assistance from their members. It is of interest to note that in May 1614, when the Charter application was under consideration, some Yeomanry members urged the Court of Assistants to press on with it and offered to pay £20 towards the cost. They also agreed to pay the interest on a loan of £100 for the next two years, if the Company had to borrow money outside. The Yeomanry had a special interest in a Charter which would incorporate valuable privileges for the founding craft, but their offer of help still makes a pleasant contrast with the disputes between Livery and Yeomanry which had broken out in the past and would do so again.

The main contribution to the Charter expenses was made by Richard Rowdinge, one of the Company's most senior members, who advanced £150 against a promise of repayment at some future date left open. He received interest on this loan, which the Company repaid in three instalments of £50 in 1616-17, 1619-20 and 1624-5. Rowdinge died before the last repayment was made and it went to his executors. He had already, in 1609, given the Company the reversion of two houses which he owned in Lothbury.

Richard Rowdinge had a long and distinguished record of service in the Founders' Company which deserves special mention. He was admitted to the Livery in 1575-6, served as Third Warden in 1584-5, and was Second Warden in 1588-9. During the 17 years from 1598 to 1615, he was chosen as Upper Warden or Master no less than six times. He was also for many years an Auditor of the Company, and in his later age the senior among them. Rowdinge lived through the vintage years of Elizabeth's reign into the lean years of James I. He must have taken pride in the exploits of Drake, Frobisher, Grenville and Hawkins, and been

76   CITIZENS AND FOUNDERS

present when Elizabeth came to St. Paul's for the thanksgiving after the defeat of the Armada. He may even have gone across the river to the Globe theatre at Southwark to see one of the plays written by an obscure actor-manager called William Shakespeare. And he died only a year or so after Raleigh was executed in the Tower by James as a sop to Spain.

A happy postscript to Rowdinge's many services was recorded in 1647, when the Court ordered that his memory should be honoured by a purchase of plate with his name on each piece. Sad to relate, these have all vanished without trace and may have been sold when the Company was pressed for money.

Once safely in possession of their Charter, the Founders lost no time in asserting their rights. In March 1615, the Master and Wardens were instructed to take 'distress' against freemen of other Companies who made brass or copper wares without having a mark allowed them at Founders' Hall. At the same time, the Clerk was ordered to provide 'beams and scales and standards, as other things fitting for the trying and sizing of Troy weights for the use of this Company, and also any other provision for the going abroad to search, to be had or needful to be made'. Two beams and scales for sizing Troy weights were bought for £4, a pile of weights for 16s. and a complete set of bell weights for £5 12s.

In April 1617, the Court ordered that 'view and search should be made of all Shops and Warehouses within the City of London or elsewhere'. A month later, it was decided that the Company would petition the Lord Mayor for the 'turning-over' to the Company of all apprentices of all workers of brass or copper wares, and their presentation at Founders' Hall. In September 1617, the Court ruled that 'no old weights of any kind should be sealed or allowed of, by reason that there are many defaced or bottomed with lead'. In 1628, the Court called for a report on the number and value of weights and wares seized by the Company.

Naturally enough, these activities were not popular with some other Companies whose interest in weights overlapped with those of the Founders. The Braziers, in particular, put up a stubborn resistance against the rights given to the Founders by their Charter over all makers of brass and copper wares in the City, and they were supported by the Armourers. In 1617, an Armourer called Gauntlett started proceedings in the King's Bench against the Founders, and the dispute between the two Companies was submitted to the Court of Aldermen. The Aldermen suspended their hearing of the case after Gauntlett had promised to withdraw his suit in the King's Bench, and apparently the Founders managed to establish their claims. In 1619-20, they received £2 'for the oath of eight Braziers' at a fee of 5s. each, plus 2s. from another Brazier, and in 1623-4 four more Braziers each paid 1s. for their 'oath'. It is not clear whether these payments were made for admission to the freedom of the Founders, or for having brass weights marked at Founders' Hall, or for presenting apprentices to the Founders' Company instead of the Braziers. In any case, the Founders made a bad financial bargain, for they had to pay about £50 in legal costs and received under £3 from fees paid by Braziers.

The grant of a Charter not only gave the Founders' Company legally enforceable rights of control over brass weights and wares, but also authorised the raising

ROYAL CHARTER 77

of additional revenue from its own members. For example, the Ordinances of 1615 imposed on Livery and Yeomanry alike a uniform quarterage payment of 12d. a quarter, whereas a Court order issued in October 1614, had laid down a differential scale of 5d. for the Livery quarterage, plus another 3d. for the poor of the Company, totalling 8d.; and 4d. for Yeomanry quarterage, plus another 2d. for the poor, making 6d. Moreover, the fines for many old offences against Company rules were increased in 1615 and new ones were added, such as the penalties for refusing to serve as Master, Assistant or Steward.

Such refusals were no doubt influenced by the increasing burden of work and responsibility falling on Masters and Wardens whose tasks now included the collection of rents, the supervision of maintenance and repairs for the Hall, and the exercise of the Company's rights over weights and measures, as well as defending the Company's interests in its dealings with the Lord Mayor and Aldermen and maintaining good order and harmony among the members. Authority for imposing fines for refusal of office was first given in the Ordinances of 1592, when they were applied to those who declined to serve as Warden or to accept election to the Livery. There seems to have been no case of enforcement until 1608-9, when Robert Dyer was fined £1, and Richard Jeffrey 10s., for refusing election to the Livery. Both men were presumably Yeomanry members who preferred to stay there. Dyer made another payment of £5 in 1614-5 'given not to be of the Livery', which suggests that he again refused an invitation to join the Livery, and either paid a lump sum to secure immunity or paid a much larger fine. He evidently remained on good terms with the Company, as he left it a small legacy of £1 in 1632-3.

The office of Steward was filled by selection from the Livery, and it proved to be an expensive honour as time went on. It is first mentioned in the Accounts for 1557-8, when the duties were shared by the Third Warden, Robert Shurlock, and a Liveryman, Robert Couche. They paid 10s. between them for the cost of the Company's contribution to the 'Mayor's Feast', which was the annual banquet in Guildhall at which the Mayor entertained distinguished guests.

Under a Court order made in October 1614, the Master, Wardens, Assistants and Liverymen were each obliged to pay the Stewards 2s. towards the cost of providing the 'Master's Feast', and a further 2s. for a guest other than a wife. In addition, the Master and Wardens were to pay for meals taken when the Company met on quarter-days, and also for the dinners on 'thanksgiving days' to celebrate James I's escape from the Gowrie conspiracy and the Gunpowder Plot, but a payment of 12d. from each Liveryman had to be made for these dinners under an order issued in September 1611. The Master and Wardens were to be allowed 20s. from the 'common stock' for the annual 'audit dinner', but the dinner usually held in the Hall after the choice of a new Master and Wardens, and attended by Liverymen and their wives, was discontinued. Instead, the Master and Wardens might have 'some small banquet' at their own cost. This may have been a temporary economy measure dictated by the heavy burden of taxes on the Company at this time.

78   CITIZENS AND FOUNDERS

The order of October 1614, names the Stewards for that year as being John Bower, Under Warden, and F. Darwin, a Liveryman and Assistant, and notes that they were the first Stewards appointed after the grant of the Charter. Under the Ordinances of 1615, the cost of providing a dinner for the Master, Wardens, and Assistants on Lord Mayor's Day was to be met by two Stewards chosen on the same day as the new Master and Wardens. This clause also ruled that no Liveryman could be chosen as a Court Assistant unless he had first served as a Steward or paid a fine of £5 for refusing that office, but it specified that nobody could be called on to serve twice as a Steward.

In 1634, a Court order made further changes in the arrangements for dinners. The Stewards were no longer required to provide the food and drink, but had to make a payment of £7 each 'to discharge them of their two dinners', presumably referring to those held on Lord Mayor's Day and to mark the election of a new Master and Wardens. The charges for these dinners were to be borne by the Company, but not exceeding £6 for the Lord Mayor's Day dinner and £2 for the Court dinner.

It is clear from the Company's records that many difficulties arose in balancing the financial demands on the Stewards against the services they provided, and the rules on this subject were frequently changed. The Stewards apparently found that they could save themselves money by supplying the food and drink, rather than make a cash payment to the Company, and they continued to do so despite the Court order of 1634 substituting a payment from them of £7 each. In 1647, the Court again prohibited the Stewards from buying the provisions themselves and reaffirmed that they must pay £7 each instead, but in 1655 the policy changed again and the Court ordered that the charges for the feast on Lord Mayor's Day should always be borne by the Stewards. In 1658, the Court repeated this order and also directed that a 'bill of fare' should be given to the Stewards to ensure that they provided dinner 'in a comely and decent sort'.

The Court had evidently realised that the Stewards were tempted to cut their own expense by economising on dinners and failing to satisfy the heartier appetites of the Founders in those days. In fact, this is what probably happened, for in 1669 the Court reverted to a cash payment from the Stewards to discharge their obligations and raised it to £7 13s. 4d. In 1674, this was again raised to £10, but the Stewards were given the option of providing dinner on Lord Mayor's Day.

In 1631, the fine for refusing the office of Steward was raised from £5 to £10, and the Court also reserved the right to dismiss those who refused to serve from the Livery. In 1646, the weights belonging to William Lambert were seized to pay for his fine as Steward, and in 1666 John White was sued for the same default. In 1669, Thomas Pope was arrested for not paying his fines for serving as a Steward and being elected to the Livery, but he then paid up. In 1697, Samuel Kerrison and John Apthorpe were prosecuted and dismissed from the Livery for not paying their fines as Stewards and failing to provide a dinner for the Company. In 1702, the Stewards for that year were summoned before the Lord Mayor for refusing 'to treat the Assistants, Livery, and Yeomanry, or to pay their fines'.

In 1774, however, the Company ran into trouble when it took legal action

ROYAL CHARTER 79

against James Sims for refusing the office of Steward. Sims had the suit thrown out on the grounds that there was no evidence of the bye-law justifying his prosecution, and the Company had to pay costs amounting to nearly £100. There had been similar occasions in the past when the Company suffered because it could not produce evidence from the Ordinances to sustain its demands on members, but relied on traditional custom. Here was another example, but it still seems odd that the Court of Assistants failed to support its suit by quoting the Ordinances. It is true that the Company was often at fault in not looking after its records properly, but copies of the Ordinances should have been available in Guildhall.

Fortunately for the historian, enough material has survived in the Founders' records to conclude this chapter with some references to other aspects of the Company's affairs in the early Stuart period. In 1605, John Tiffin was appointed as 'Cook' to the Company at a wage of 26s. 8d. a year, subject to the condition that they might remove him and choose another 'if they shall mislike of the said Cook'. His predecessor, Richard Kemp, was paid a yearly wage of only 13s. 4d. Tiffin's wife took his place in 1617 and was followed in 1630 by Anthony Dixon. From 1635 to 1645, the duties of cook were carried out by the clerk, John Falkener, and his wife, who received payments for 'dressing of dinners'.

From very early times, the Founders hired a 'Butler' for their dinners, but the first mention of a standing engagement for this task occurs in 1605-6, when John King was paid a yearly wage of 12s. as 'Butler and Carver'. In 1609-10, the Company also employed William Thompson as 'Under-Butler' at a yearly fee of 3s. 4d., later raised to 5s., and in 1615 Thompson succeeded King as Butler. From 1621 to 1633, the Butler was John Trott, who was paid 12s. in most years, but received £1 in his last year. From that date up to 1644, the duties of Butler were taken over by the Clerk, John Falkener, who got into debt with the Company and took on all the extra work and fees he could find. The Accounts contain only two further references to the employment of a Butler, one being in 1645-6, when a payment of 5s. was made 'for a Butler supplying the place all the year round', and another in 1658-9, when the same amount was given to the Butler 'when he lay a-dying'.

The annual celebration by the Founders of 'Hawke's Dirge' and other memorial services for benefactors had been abolished by the Protestant Reformation, but the old medieval custom of escorting fellow-members to their graves, dating back to the origins of the gilds as parish fraternities, was still maintained. In 1609, for example, six Liverymen were chosen to attend the funeral of Richard Pearce in their gowns. Pearce was Second Warden in 1607-8. In 1614, after the burial of Oswald Greathead, three times a Warden, the mourners from the Company took supper together and left a debit balance which was made up from the common fund. The Company's Ordinances of 1615 renewed the obligation for all Livery members to attend the funeral of a brother-Liveryman or his wife, or pay a fine of 10s. In 1623-4, money was again paid from the common fund to make up the expenses of a Company supper after the burial of Edward Parnell, who had twice been Master.

The Company's rules for good behaviour, both in professional matters and in

80   CITIZENS AND FOUNDERS

personal relations between members, continued to be enforced, with some later variations. In 1604, a Liveryman called John Hull was taken into custody by one of the Lord Mayor's officers for offences 'contrary to his oath' which are not specified, but this clearly left no hard feelings, as Hull was Third Warden in 1606-7, Second Warden in 1610-11, and Master in 1613-14, 1616-17 and 1627-8. Incidents of this kind seem to have been almost as common in City Companies as beatings in the Victorian public school, and as lightly regarded. In 1605, John Falkener was given permission to keep on for a few months a servant not apprenticed to the Company, on condition that the man did no work which might 'hinder' any poor brother of the Company and only went on errands or did 'drudgery'.

In 1607, Maurice Austin was fined 20s. for confining John Springham 'to work in a Buckle Caster's house in filing Gynner Rings', presumably meaning 'gunner rings'. Springham himself was in trouble because he was five years in arrears with his quarterage dues, and Austin was ordered to bring him before the Wardens or commit him to prison. A few months later, Springham agreed to clear off his quarterage dues by paying 3d. a week. In 1608, an apprentice called William Collins was ordered by the Court to give an undertaking to his master, Robert Thompson, that he would not in future 'play at bowls, bet at bowls or cards, dice and tables, shovelboard, or any other unlawful game to the value of twopence a game'. If he did so, Thompson was instructed to take legal action against him. This did not prevent Collins from being admitted to the Livery in 1621-2 and serving as Third Warden 10 years later. In 1635, however, he was fined 5s. for 'misbehaving himself in the face of this Court' and threatened with dismissal from his position as an Assistant if he refused to pay.

In 1613, a Founder called Edmund Clapham was ordered to pay a fine of 20s., or be committed to prison, for having 'contrary to his oath, molested and troubled Thomas Houlton without leave of the Wardens, he being a brother of the said Society'. Clapham was sent to prison for not paying this fine, but he soon produced it. The Wardens gave it back to him, 'considering his poor estate and his submission for this offence'. There are many such examples of leniency in the Company's records. But then the wives of Clapham and Houlton took a hand in the quarrel, and the Second Warden, Edward Parnell, was instructed to hear their arguments and make unity between them, failing which both the husbands and wives would be summoned to the Hall to appear before the whole membership. This apparently settled the matter, as there is no further mention of it.

The Wardens' Accounts for 1618-9 show a payment of £3 15s. 4d. made for 80 pounds of gunpowder and 9s. 6d. for a bundle of 'matches'. The City Companies were first ordered to hold reserves of gunpowder by Elizabeth's Privy Council, through the Lord Mayor, in 1574, as a measure of defence against the threat of invasion. This fresh demand under James I may have been due to pressure on James by Parliament and public opinion to give help to the ill-fated Elector Frederick, his son-in-law, who was now King of Bohemia and the German Protestant leader against a Catholic league backed by Spanish troops. A room with a

ROYAL CHARTER 81

new door was made in Founders' Hall for the gunpowder and the Company also paid for its transport by boat from Rotherhithe, for a barrel to keep it in, and a padlock for the storeroom door.

In 1642-3, when the Civil War broke out, the Company paid for 'new hooping' of the powder. Its condition by that time can hardly have been very satisfactory, but in 1652, under Cromwell, the Company was ordered to deliver it and received £4. The Court must have been mightily relieved to see the last of this gunpowder, and would have been more so had they known that Founders' Hall would be burned down in the Great Fire only 14 years later.

In 1625-6, the year in which James I died, the Founders bought lengths of crimson and blue 'taffety sarsenet', a fine silk material, to make new banners and streamers for the Company, together with fustian, or coarse cotton, silk, and string for the covers, and poles. The men who made the banners, 'Mr. Ball and Mr. Tresham', were paid £13 10s., a handsome sum in those days. Nevertheless, the Company's finances remained precariously balanced between annual surpluses and deficits.

This was largely due to the heavy tax demands by the Crown and City, but it also reflected the ravages of inflation in pushing up costs and prices. As Mr. Parsloe points out in his notes on the Accounts, the Company's expenditure on wages and Hall expenses in heating, repairs, and maintenance roughly doubled between 1585 and 1607, while the average cost of dinners rose from £5 to £12 and parish rates and taxes rose from under 9s. to over £3. The income from sizing weights and rents for the Hall, coupled with increases in fines for refusing office or election to the Livery, produced a rise in annual revenue from an average of £49 yearly from 1612 to 1616 to £59 from 1616 to 1620, but over the same periods the annual average expenditure rose from £40 to £72.

The Company was only able to pay its way by selling plate and spoons, borrowing money from the more prosperous Liverymen, and dipping into the 'poor box'. In 1615-16, over £13 was taken from the 'poor box' to help in paying for the costs of the Charter. In the 10 years from 1620 to 1630, the 'poor box' was called into contribution no less than nine times. In four such cases, the withdrawals were used to assist in repaying the loan made by Richard Rowdinge for the Charter expenses in 1614. On another occasion, money from the 'poor box' was applied towards the cost of repairs to the Hall, and in four other years it was used to supplement the ordinary income when it fell short of expenditure. The shortage of income was largely due to members defaulting on their quarterage payments, especially after the increased rates laid down in the Ordinances of 1615. These arrears mounted to such an extent that in 1623 all members who owed quarterage were summoned to the Hall to discharge their debts, on pain of being brought before the Lord Mayor. This seems to have been effective, as the Accounts for 1623-4 show a number of payments by members for arrears.

One cannot rule out the possibility of a dishonest Warden taking money from the 'poor box' for his own gain, but there is no positive evidence of such cases in the records. The Accounts do show, however, that the checks on Masters and

82 CITIZENS AND FOUNDERS

Wardens became stronger as time went on. From 1526 onwards, their annual accounts were examined by four 'Auditors' drawn from senior Assistants who had held office themselves. From 1556, the Master and Wardens listed their receipts and payments separately, instead of jointly as before, and the Auditors usually added a statement of the cash in hand and debts owing to the Company which were 'charged' to the incoming Master and Wardens. From 1565, this certificate also included the Company's silver and plate, though not in every year.

Beginning in 1576-7, a new Master had to provide a 'bond' or guarantee taken by the Auditors for his liabilities. The amount recoverable by the Company under this bond stood at £40 in 1591, but was raised to £60 in 1599 and £100 in 1601. From 1586-7, a new Master also provided a 'surety' or friend who backed his guarantee. These sureties were often found from personal contacts in other City Companies. For example, in 1588-9 the Upper Warden, Robert Waldo, as the Master was then called, was joined in his bond by Lawrence Waldo, Grocer, who was probably his brother. A Cutler called Thomas Hatfield stood surety for Nicholas Roberts, Upper Warden in 1601-2. The Master for 1613-14, John Hull, named 'Mr. Broderick, Embroiderer' as his surety. The Company's records show only one case of the Master's bond being invoked against him, in 1666, when Clement Dawes was Master and was sued 'for his not paying the money that came into his hands'. Dawes settled his account in full shortly after and was again elected Master for 1675-6, but he died in office.

When one considers the risks and burdens of office carried by Masters and Wardens in many a troubled period of the Founders' history, it is fitting to remember the long succession of men whose services to the Company far outweighed the few who failed. We are now coming to a period of national crisis in which the strengths and weaknesses of those in authority were to be rigorously tested.

CHAPTER VIII

Civil War

IF THE FOUNDERS nourished any hopes of reduced taxation after the death of James I in 1625, they were soon disillusioned. His successor, Charles I, did not share James's reluctance to undertake English military intervention in Europe and he was encouraged to do so by the incapable and spendthrift George Villiers, Duke of Buckingham, who was as much of a favourite with Charles as he had been with James. Buckingham was allowed to lead expeditions for the relief of the French Huguenots in La Rochelle and a descent on the Spanish coast at Cadiz which not only failed, but were very expensive.

Parliament demanded Buckingham's dismissal in vain and refused to grant subsidies to Charles, while insisting in the famous 'Petition of Right' that it was illegal for the Crown to levy taxes without the consent of the Lords and Commons. But Charles was as obstinate and headstrong in his assertion of Royal supremacy as James had been before him, and he proceeded to impose taxes without Parliamentary approval. This caused widespread indignation, even among the Crown's most loyal supporters, and it was aggravated by the waste and shame of Buckingham's military failures. It might be added that, when the American colonists invoked the same right of 'no taxation without representation' 150 years later, the British Parliament backed George III and Lord North in fighting and losing the American War of Independence. Sauce for the English goose was viewed as sedition when claimed by the American gander.

In 1627, the Founders were ordered by the Lord Mayor to contribute £90 towards a forced loan of £120,000 demanded by Charles I from the City. This loan was secured on the Crown lands and carried interest at six per cent. It was to be repaid from money obtained by the City Corporation from selling Crown lands. Half the loan proceeds were earmarked for paying off debts already owed to the City by the Crown, and the other half was repayable at six months' notice. The City Companies thus paid out with one hand what they recovered with the other, but the King's security proved good on this occasion, as shown by the fact that in 1630 the Wardens of the Grocers received repayment of £6,000 in loan capital and £750 for interest.

For a small and relatively poor Company like the Founders, however, the demand for £90 far exceeded their resources. A second and more peremptory order for payment was received a fortnight later, and a worried Court then persuaded

84   CITIZENS AND FOUNDERS

Ezekiel Major, who had served three times as Master, to intercede with the Lord Mayor. They promised to give him aid and assistance and to bear all charges which he or the Wardens might incur. A week later, however, the Court of Aldermen sent Ezekiel Major, Henry Carless, and Joseph Parratt to Newgate prison for failing to supply the money required of the Founders. The three men are described in the Guildhall records as 'Wardens of the Company of Founders', but this is not strictly accurate. The Master in 1627-8 was John Hull and in 1626-7 it was Abraham Woodall. Major had already served his last term as Master in 1623-4 and was the senior Auditor at the time of the King's loan. Henry Carless was Third Warden in 1625-6. Parratt was Third Warden in 1627-8, serving under John Hull. To add to the confusion, in the Accounts presented for 1627-8 by John Hull as Master, he includes a payment of £3 15s. made by him for the Company 'being committed to Newgate by the Court of Aldermen for that we paid not the loan money to the King'.

Whoever had the honour of going to Newgate for the Company, they were among friends, for the Masters and Wardens of the Saddlers, Glaziers, Plumbers and Joiners all shared the same fate. In the case of the Founders, at least, their confinement seems to have been soon ended, for a few days later the Lord Mayor agreed to pay the Company's loan assessment of £90 to the City Chamberlain himself, in return for a cash payment of £20 and the sole use and benefit of the capital repayment, interest, and profit accruing from the Founders' quota of £90. One suspects that the Lord Mayor was not inspired by purely charitable motives, but probably felt pretty sure that he would not lose on the deal.

In 1625, the Court of Aldermen ordered the City Companies to provide the very large sum of £4,300 to pay for the costs of 'pageants and other solemnities, shows, and work for beautifying the City' for the coronation procession of Charles I. The Companies were assessed at the rates used for their contributions of corn, the highest charges falling on the Merchant Taylors, who paid £225 and the Grocers, who paid £215. The Founders were charged £3 4s. 6d. equivalent to 15 quarters of corn, but they were among a number of Companies which delayed payment and were again summoned 10 months later to provide the money at once. By that time, the sum demanded of the Founders had risen to £6 9s., and this was finally handed over to the Chamber of London in 1631-2, when Richard Weoley was Master.

In October 1634, Charles made his first levy for 'ship money', which was very properly aimed at restoring English naval strength after its neglect by James I. The Founders paid £12 for 'ship money' in 1634-5, another £5 in 1635-6, and a third sum of £4 in 1636-7. In 1639, Charles led an army into Scotland against the rebel 'Covenanters', but was forced to withdraw to York, pursued by the Scots, who captured Newcastle. As Parliament opposed the war and refused to give subsidies for it, Charles had to raise money elsewhere and he called on the City of London for a loan of £200,000. The Founders had to pay £5 towards it, which was taken from the 'stock' and not by contributions from members. In 1642, after a rebellion broke out in Ireland in which thousands of English and Scottish settlers were massacred, Parliament raised a loan of £100,000 from the City for which the

CIVIL WAR
85

Founders paid £100. This had to be borrowed at interest on the seal of the Company.

At this point, the struggle between King and Parliament erupted into civil war. London was on the side of Parliament, so much so that the City gave shelter to five leading rebel Members, Pym, Hampden, Hazlerigg, Holles and Strode, when Charles tried to arrest them in the Commons and they made their escape by river. Charles went to Guildhall next day to demand their surrender, but the Sheriffs ignored the warrants. Four days later, when the five Members returned to Westminster in triumph, they were escorted by the London watermen and the City train-bands or militia.

The possession of London gave Parliament a secure base and an overwhelming advantage in money, manpower and arms. By contrast, Charles was dependent on the loyalty of country squires whose sales of family lands and silver for the King were no match for the City coffers, and whose dash and courage could not prevail against the highly disciplined, and regularly paid, 'New Model' army which Cromwell raised for Parliament. The Parliamentary forces also had the advantage of strategic mobility and the capacity to concentrate where they chose, while the King's men were dispersed in widely separated areas and prevented from uniting. The Navy, which Charles had tried to help, turned against him, and the greater nobles mostly backed Parliament as the winning side, or remained neutral.

It is not necessary here to follow the course of this tragic conflict in which divided loyalties and power politics were equally mixed and ending with Cromwell's triumph and his cold-blooded execution of Charles I. We need only concern ourselves with its effects on the City Companies and the Founders in particular. The rule of Parliament brought no relief from the burden of taxation, and the City soon found that it was expected to back its defence of the new republic with hard cash. The Wardens' Accounts of the Founders illustrate this very clearly.

In 1642-3, the House of Commons instituted a regular annual collection of taxes for which the Founders paid £12 yearly. In the following year, Parliament also demanded the subsidies formerly paid by the Companies to the Crown, but multiplied the old basis of assessment by fifty. In addition, the Founders had to pay £4 for 'the advancing of the Earl of Essex', a Parliamentary general, and in 1644-5 they paid £9 10s. to support the operations of another Parliamentary commander, Sir Thomas Fairfax, and for 'fortifications in Ireland'. In that year, the Auditors had to take all the remaining money in the chest, about £19, to clear the Company's ordinary debts. In the next 12 years, special payments had to be made again for the support of Fairfax, for taxes to maintain the Army and militia, and for the City entertaining Cromwell, as Lord Protector, at Grocers' Hall.

These demands, enforced by Cromwell with an iron hand, rapidly created havoc in the Company's finances. By 1648-9, when the civil war was virtually over, there was a deficit of over £38 which was met by selling silver spoons and disposing of a lease bought by 'Captain' John Jones. Jones was a wealthy Grocer, an active Presbyterian, a member of the City's Common Council, and a Member of Parliament for the City. His military duties evidently left him plenty of time for

86 CITIZENS AND FOUNDERS

politics and business. By 1653, the Founders were owed £422 for money which they had lent to 'the State', first to Charles and then to Parliament. The Company made several attempts to recover this loss, but there is no indication that it was ever repaid. In 1647, the Merchant Taylors noted that they had lent over £26,000 to Parliament, a vast sum at that time, and the Ironmongers claimed that Parliament owed them £7,000, but both Companies had recovered only a trifling amount.

The revolutionary temper of the period also produced a serious conflict within the body of the Founders. A division had long existed between the minority of Livery members, who led the Company, and the more numerous Yeomanry, which filled vacancies in the Livery but had no share in management. The expansion and diversification of trade and manufacturing, coupled with new demands for capital investment, had created a new class of merchants who prospered, while the craftsmen and journeymen in the Yeomanry tended to get left behind. The latent sense of jealousy and resentment thus generated was inflamed by the Parliamentary challenge to the rule of Kings, and by the Puritan reaction against all forms of temporal power.

Evidence of this internal unrest appeared in February 1651, when a petition bearing no signatures, but claiming to speak for the 'Commonalty' of the Founders, was addressed to the Master, Wardens, and Assistants. It presented a curious mixture of injured innocence and dumb insolence, and its wording showed the influence of the many religious fanatics and popular agitators who were then active in London. The text reads more like a bad sermon than anything else and ran as follows:

> That whereas it is most falsely and unjustly reported that we are those whose design it is to overthrow and bring into confusion the government of the Company, for the vindication of ourselves we greet you with this brief account of our desires, if you will be pleased to take cognisance of them. We do for our parts declare that we are so tender of the reputation of you, our Governors, that we are in no wise willing to do anything of a disparaging reflection upon you, but to attend the providence of God for a reducement of ourselves to our primitive rights and privileges, and this we know is justifiable both by the law of God, of Nature, and of Nations. The motive being the consideration of the engagements that lie upon you to preserve the liberties of those people over whom you rule, for very sensible we are of many things done in the exercise of your power over us altogether inconsistent with the laws of righteousness, the rules of safety, and our public good.

> Therefore seeing men in all ages have, through their supine carelessness, degenerated from the righteousness of their first principles, and if your ancestors have been guilty of anything of this nature, we entreat that it may be to your sorrow and not your sin, and suffer us to persuade you to a recollection of all those things that are held up on corrupt customs. Examine them by the Law and by the Testimony, so shall you make good that you have spoken in the

CIVIL WAR

87

ears of the Lord when you vowed to reform all things so far as in you lay according to His words. This our addressment presenteth you with an opportunity of being seen in the best of your glory, if you will make your names to be the repairers of the great breach and restorers of paths to dwell in through many generations.

Now we humbly desire you would let us have the Charter of the Company read, without which we are in no rational capacity to know our privileges, but we shall be led in a way of ignorance and blindness as we have been hitherto all our days, doing things we know not why, for ends we know not what. These things we pray you to consider and return us a positive answer, and so you shall engage our hearts to be willing to serve you in any Christian service.

The Court accepted the request for a general meeting to hear the Charter read over, but the minutes record that 'there were many unseemly speeches claiming an equal power with the Court of Assistants in government and authority, without distinction of persons, to the great disturbance of the said Court'. The Charter was duly read by the Clerk, William Basspoole, but a heated debate then broke out. Some of the leading rebels left the Hall with threats to pay no more quarterage in future 'except the Company would keep better their Charter and let them have those privileges unto which they were born, for they had been made slaves long enough by the Company'.

These threats did not deter the Master and Wardens from carrying out their duties. In July 1652, they made a search of several workshops kept by Company members and gave strict orders 'that no brass work should be filled with lead to deceive and cozen any people of the nation, and that all kinds of brass ware be made of good strong metal without any deceit'. In the house of Abel Hodges, a Yeomanry member, of whom many complaints had already been made, they found 'one great stopcock so thin that it would be of no service, and another stopcock filled with lead'. On the premises of Evan Evans, they found 'other great stillcocks filled with lead and so basely wrought that they were at once taken and defaced'. Evans was summoned to the next Court and fined 20s., but he paid the fine, confessed his fault, and promised to mend his ways. The Court then gave him back the larger part of his fine and the rest of his broken ware.

Abel Hodges 'sternly refused to yield obedience' or pay a fine. The Court then ordered the Master and Wardens to take a 'distress' on his goods to the value of 43s. 4d. to pay his fine and the costs of the search, with 10 groats added 'for unseemly speeches uttered unto the said Company'. The Master and Wardens were also ordered to seize goods to the value of 5s. from men who had refused to pay quarterage and had incited others not to pay. This penalty of distraint on an offender's goods was allowed by the Company's Ordinances, and the Lord Mayor's officers could be called on to give assistance if required.

The distraint on Abel Hodges was carried out with no trouble, and also in the case of Thomas Brown and John Lucas, two of the quarterage defaulters. Another defaulter, John Reynolds, submitted and paid his fine when visited. But when the

88 CITIZENS AND FOUNDERS

Master and Wardens tried to seize goods from three other quarterage defaulters, William Nicholls, Philip Thomas and Daniel Baker, they were opposed. The Court records state that Thomas 'resisted them with many threatening words and taking up tools in his hand and bid them look to themselves if they but touch anything there'. Nicholls and Baker 'would yield no obedience, but kept them forth of their doors by violence'. Baker later submitted and paid his fine of 5s. Nicholls and Thomas were brought to trial, but the verdict is not stated. The goods seized from Hodges, Brown, and Lucas were sold for £2 12s. 7d.

It may well have been the challenge by disaffected Yeomanry members which prompted the Court, in October 1652, to apply to the Parliamentary Committee for Corporations for a renewal of the Charter. This petition also asked for the incorporation into the Company of all founders of brass and copper in and about London within the three-mile limit, and an extension of those limits to 7 or 10 miles. These proposals were clearly directed against competition from unlicensed craftsmen working in the new suburbs and outside the City's jurisdiction. If adopted, they would have mainly served the Yeomanry interest, but no more is heard of them.

We do know, however, that the Court's petition for a renewal of the Charter was immediately followed by a counter-petition to the Committee for Corporations from five of the Yeomanry rebels. They complained that they had been 'for many years extremely trodden and kept under foot by the power and will of the Master and Wardens and Assistants'. They asked the Committee to send for the Charter and renew it 'with alterations of such things as are destructive to the Commonwealth', and to fix a day for hearing their grievances. It is significant that two of the men who signed this counter-petition were William Nicholls and Philip Thomas, the men who had forcibly resisted the attempt to distrain on their goods, and two of the others were Brown and Lucas, who had also been in trouble for refusing to pay quarterage. These four men clearly had a personal grudge against the Company.

The Committee for Corporations ordered the rebel petitioners to submit their grievances in writing, and this they did shortly after with a covering letter signed by 16 men. In it, they claimed that their complaints arose from 'the perpetuity of these persons being our rulers who are not able to judge of anything relating to the trade, for that they being men of other callings of which three-thirds [sic] part of the Assistants do consist'. This bears witness to the division, already noted in these pages, between a minority of more prosperous Liverymen who were for the most part no longer pursuing the founding trade, and a poorer majority of Yeomanry masters and hired men who continued to manufacture and sell their own wares.

It is also interesting to note that the letter from the rebel petitioners repeated the request in the Court's own petition for 'all melters and workers of brass' to be reduced into one corporation, meaning the Founders' Company, and argued that many evils would thus be prevented. In effect, both the Court and the Yeomanry rebels were asking for the maintenance and extension of monopoly rights for the Company which the changes in economic conditions had rendered obsolete. The

CIVIL WAR

89

real cause of their dispute was the demand by some Yeomanry members for worker-participation in management.

The accompanying statement of rebel grievances submitted to the Committee for Corporations was drawn up in a style which showed signs of legal advice, but also resorted to some crude political blackmail and religious propaganda. The complaints were set out under 11 headings and may be summed up as follows:

1. The Master and Wardens imposed fines on members of the 'Commonalty' for disobeying rules which had not been made known to them. They ignored the obligation to have the Charter and Ordinances read out to the Yeomanry at least once a year.
2. The Charter had not been properly read at the Hall meeting in 1652, and the Clerk had wilfully omitted the parts dealing with the Yeomanry privileges. The petitioners claimed to have verified this by obtaining a copy of the Charter.
3. The Master, Wardens and Assistants conducted the Company's affairs privately and without the consent of the Commonalty, contrary to the Charter.
4. They had 'misapplied' the gifts and charities of the Company.
5. The office-holders 'do things contrary to the Charter'. No examples were given.
6. They fined men unreasonably 'for doing things which themselves do usually practise', again without examples.
7. They wasted the stock and revenue of the Company and had threatened to sell the Hall and its contents.
8. The major part of the Master, Wardens and Assistants 'were notoriously disaffected to the present Government and upon all opportunities have manifested their malignity in words and deeds, particularly in choosing one Mr. Pilchard Upper Warden this year, being a man twice sequestered for delinquency and served the late King at Oxford during the times of the war. Not much good to be expected from men so qualified'.
9. Six of the Commonalty had been fined 5s. each in August 1652, before being acquainted with their offence, and their goods distrained, whereby the Master, Wardens and Assistants had shown themselves 'instead of nourishers of the members of their Company, to be destroyers'.
10. The Master, Wardens and Assistants 'do countenance the Clerk of the Company [William Basspoole] who is a mocker and scoffer of all manner of godliness and holiness and goodness, in conniving at and passing over his unfaithfulness without any controlment at all, and also counterfeiteth the Goldsmiths' mark to seal Troy weights'.
11. When the Commonalty were summoned to the Hall on quarter-days, they had to wait until called for separately into a 'close parlour' where the Court sat, whereas other Companies kept open Court in the Halls for every member to be heard and make his complaint known.

The Court gave a prompt and vigorous reply in writing to the Committee for Corporations, rejecting what they called 'the scandals and false reports put upon, and can be no way proved, against the Master, Wardens and Assistants'. Dealing with each of the charges in turn, they began by declaring that they 'never yet did use either will or power over or against any of the false pretending complainers, but entreated them as brethren in love when they would level the government and orders of the Company according to their own perverse, proud, and peevish minds'. Whenever the Commonalty desired anything to be read over to them, that had been done, but the Court knew 'right well' that such a request was not made for instruction, but for what the complainants could 'catch at to enlarge their levelling minds and proud imperous wills, and for no other purpose than to quarrel with the Company'.

The Court stated that it could fully prove that nothing had been done except what the Charter allowed and according to precedent and custom for over 60 years. The legacies to poor and unfortunate members had always been properly paid, though they had sometimes been misapplied by being given to 'these scandalous and black-mouthed people', the rebel petitioners and their parents. The Court challenged them to prove which of the Assistants had misapplied money for alms.

Far from wasting the Company's resources, the Court had in love and unity helped several Princes in their reigns, paid their taxes in the City, and fulfilled their obligations to the parish, to the poor of the Company, and to 'this happy and glorious Government in these times', meaning Cromwell. And they still had a reserve in hand. At this point, the Court's reply refers to the Company as having begun in 1472 'with 24 poor honest men', ignoring the earlier grant of Ordinances in 1365.

Replying to the potentially lethal charge of disloyalty to the Cromwellian Commonwealth, the Court wrote: 'There is not a man amongst the Assistants that hath not given and lent unto this Parliament, that hath not willingly subscribed unto every command and order of Parliament. Or let them show any one man that hath been imprisoned, sequestered, or bore arms against the Parliament, then shall we give these slanderous people further answer'.

The charge of conniving in misconduct by the Clerk was rejected, and the Court added that it did not believe that he sized or sealed any brass weights made of base and adulterate metals. 'He is old enough, and we hope honest enough. Let him answer the complaint himself, if he hath so offended'.

Finally, the Court's reply flatly dismissed the claim by the petitioners that the government of the Company should be shared equally between all its members. 'These men show forth their violent and proud spirits by desiring admittance equal with a Court of Assistants. Where was it ever known to have all to hear and determine alike in any nation or body corporate, or that the people which should be ruled should seem to instruct their rulers? We have a cloud of witnesses to prove these mens' private contrivings and mischievous threatenings of the Company, and they never yet would prove anything but their own wills to level all alike without

CIVIL WAR 91

any needless distinctions between member and member, as they please to set forth in their peremptory demands. We will leave God to judge, and this Honourable Committee, unto whom they have falsely accused us'.

In verbal exchanges of this sort, the hard facts tend to be ignored or overlooked, and this was no exception. For example, the Court was fully justified in demanding fines for refusal to pay quarterage. Such fines were authorised by the Company's Ordinances of 1489 and renewed in later years. The Ordinances of 1516 gave the Wardens the right of 'distraint' for refusals to pay, and this also was later renewed. In 1614, the Charter itself confirmed that all offenders against the rules were liable for fines at the discretion of Master, Wardens and Assistants and 'by distress or otherwise'. Why did the Court make so little mention of these precedents and rely instead on traditional custom? One can only conclude that in this dispute, as in some others, the Court brought trouble on its own head by ignorance of the Company's Ordinances and a failure to keep proper records.

Next, the Court's total denial of any abuse in the handling of charitable funds was no doubt sincere and understandable, but it did not go to the root of the matter. As we have seen, the Company's 'poor box' was often drawn on to meet other pressing demands and help to meet a deficit when annual expenditure exceeded ordinary income. The Court might have argued, with some reason, that it was no crime to draw on the poor box when the survival of the Company depended on it. Their omission to do so could have been due to an uneasy knowledge that the rules laid down by the Aldermen in 1579 for Yeomanry participation in the collection of quarterage, and the safe custody of the petty-cash box, had long been disregarded.

Although there were many years when the Wardens' Accounts show no distribution of alms from the poor box, there were others when such obligations were fulfilled. The money received from the Fishmongers since 1517 for 'Jordan's Dole' of coals continued to be paid regularly, and so was a legacy of £6 a year given by John Rawlings, Master in 1618-9, for distribution among six poor brethren. Likewise, a legacy of £2 a year for the Company's poor left by Abraham Woodall, three times Master between 1626 and 1635, was regularly paid out. Woodall left property on trust to the Churchwardens of St. Bride's to provide this annual payment and it was still being distributed in 1680-1, the last year on record in the Accounts, as was 'Jordan's Dole'.

Starting in 1645, quarterly payments were made from Company income to eight 'pensioners', mostly widows of members. These were small sums distributed by the Renter Warden. The number of pensioners rose to 14 in 1664-5, but it varied in different years and in 1669-70 it fell to seven. In some years, the Renter Warden noted that details of these payments were entered in 'the Poor's book', which has not been preserved. It is therefore possible that the Wardens' Accounts do not give a full statement of the alms distributed, especially in those earlier years when payments for alms do not appear in the Accounts. It is also worth noting that in some years the Master, and occasionally the Clerk, include payments for alms in their own accounts which may have come from their own pockets. In 1647-8, for example, the Renter Warden for that year, Edmund Clapham, neither collected

92 CITIZENS AND FOUNDERS

nor paid the money for pensions, and the Master, Thomas Stead, did it for him. Clapham was the same man who was involved in domestic quarrels with other members of the Company, as noted in the previous chapter, and he seems to have given a lot of trouble. In 1650-1, the money collected by the Renter Warden, Clement Dawes, from quarterage for the poor fell short of the distributions to pensioners by over £5, and this was made up by the Master, Joseph Parratt, and the Clerk, William Basspoole.

To return to the dispute between the Court and the Yeomanry rebels which was referred to the Committee for Corporations in 1652, the Court was accused of denying the Yeomanry privileges which it had been granted by the Charter in 1614, but the Charter itself does not support this charge. The Ordinances of 1615, supplementing the Charter, specified that 'General Courts for the appearance of Livery and general body of fellowship' should be called four times a year on 'quarter-days', namely on Lord Mayor's Day, 29 October; and on the Mondays following Lammas Day, 1 August; Candlemas Day, 2 February and May Day. The Ordinances added that 'every person under the government of this Company' should 'then and there pay for quarterage 12 pence in money for the use of the Company, or in default thereof, or not performing such other rights and duties as may be required of him, shall forfeit 5 shillings'. Neither in the Charter nor the Ordinances are these 'General Courts' given any powers of decision, or even discussion, in the daily administration of the Company.

The Wardens' Accounts show that these quarter-day meetings were held regularly. It may well be true, as the rebels alleged, that Yeomanry members had to wait outside the Court room and were called in one by one to pay their quarterage or make excuses and complaints. This procedure could have been interpreted as a wrong application of the rule calling for 'General Courts', and the claim that other Companies admitted all their members together in 'open Court' may have had some substance. But it is still open to doubt whether many peace-loving Yeomanry members would have been willing to discuss their personal affairs and finances in front of all their neighbours. It should also be noted that many other Livery Companies were faced with similar demands from discontented Yeomanry members for a share in the management, including the Goldsmiths, Merchant Taylors, Clothworkers, Saddlers, Weavers, Stationers and Clockmakers.

Looking at these distant quarrels from the viewpoint of our own far more advanced ideas of democracy, it may seem only right and proper that all members of a City Company should have had equal status and representation in it. Ours is a very different age, however, and we must take into account the state of society prevailing in Stuart times, when few people had even the simplest education to qualify them for positions of responsibility. Nobody could have been more opposed to the idea of democratic equality than the Lord Protector himself, Oliver Cromwell, the man who invaded the House of Commons with his troopers and told them to 'take away that bauble', the Speaker's mace.

Nor can we tell how far the Yeomanry protests were a genuine and spontaneous outbreak supported by all their members, or a revolt worked up by a minority of

The Weoley Cup

St. Lawrence, Jewry, 1798

The Hall in 1848, when occupied by the Electric Telegraph Company

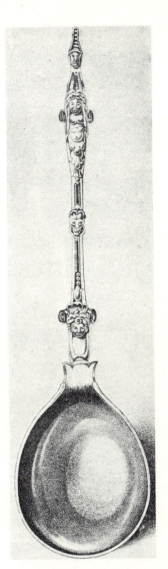
Bowen's Spoon, 1625

Poor's Box. Gift of Stephen Pilchard

Grant of Arms to the Founders' Company
by Robert Cooke, Clarenceux, 1590

asswell Nobles and gentiz as others to whome these presentes shall ...
... vnderstood Robert Cooke Esquier alias Clarencieulx Kinge of Armes
the East west and Southe partes of this Realme of England Sending ...
... Auncientlie from the begynninge the valient and vertuous actes of ...
... to the world with sondrey monumentes and remembraunces of their ...
... chiefest and most especiall hath ben the bearinge of signes and tokens
other thinges then euidences and demonstrations of prowes and ...
... to the qualities and desartes of the persons. So the entent that suche ...
... their prince or Countrey either in warre or peace or otherwise by the
... or proceedinges of any person or persons in the augmentacion of the ...
... or Countrey, myght therby bothe receaue due honor in their liues ...
... their posteritie and successoures after them, **And whereas** the
... the ffounders of the Citie of London are Incorporated by the name of three ...
... they shall haue a perpetuall succession, they haue therefore required me
... assigne vnto them suche Armes and Creast as they may lawfully ...
... person or persons, Wheruppon consideringe their request to be reason...
... orders of the Lawes of Armes, I haue thought by vertue of my Office ...
... Creast hereafter followinge. **That is to saye** the field azure a ...
... stickes gold. And to the Creast vppon the healme on a wreathe gold ...
... of the cloudes pro... two Armes the handes carnat the sleeues ...
... sables inbre... ... of a mestwt vppon proper manteled gules ...
... depicted in the margent. **To haue and to holde** the sayd ...
... James Lambert and Thomas Jackson now wardens of the sayd ...
... place and Office, And to all the Cominaltie of the ffounders of the ...
... for the credite of the same Company in shield standard Banner ...
... of Armes, without vnpediment lett or interrupcion of any ...
... haue sett hereunto my hande and Seale of Office the viij day of ...
... gracious Soueraigne Lady Elizabeth by the grace of god Queene

Rob Cooke Alias Clarencieulx
Roy Darmes

Founders' Company Window, West Crypt, Guildhall

8. FOUNDERS' HALL.

1 Armorers' Hall.
2 Leather Sellers' Hall.
3 Carpenters' Hall.
4 Allhallows in the Wall.
5 St. Peter's le Poor.
6 Drapers' Hall.
7 St. Margaret's, Lothbury.
9 St. Stephen's, Coleman Street
10 Grocers' Hall.
11 St. Mildred's, Poultry.
12 St. Christopher's Stocks.
13 St. Bartholomew's.
14 St. Benet Fink.
15 Merchant Tailors' Hall.

Sketch plan of the old City, showing Founders' Hall

St. Margaret Church, Lothbury, *circa* 1815

CIVIL WAR 93

extremists whose aims and methods went far beyond the views of their more moderate, or cautious, colleagues. The Court's petition in 1652 for a renewal of the Charter was signed by the Master, Wardens 'and 45 others', while the counter-petition from Yeomanry members bore 16 signatures. There must have been many abstentions in both cases, but the figures suggest a majority of about two-thirds of all members who supported the Court and one-third against it.

The Parliamentary Committee for Corporations directed the Master and Wardens of the Founders to submit their order books and accounts for inspection, and summoned both sides to a hearing on 18 November 1652, but the Committee's findings are not on record and we do not know which side they favoured. Judging by entries in the Wardens' Accounts, things went on much as before and the trouble with the Yeomanry died out. One of the five men who signed the first protest in 1652, Philip Thomas, paid his quarterage for 1652-3, while two more, Thomas Brown and Richard Smith, paid money in 1654-5, apparently for fines or costs resulting from a suit by the Company against them.

The Court's petition for a renewal of the Charter was apparently shelved or rejected, as no more is heard of it. The Clerk, William Basspoole, denounced by the rebels as a 'mocker and scoffer' of religion, was dismissed by the Court in 1658 'after mature consideration of several complaints against him'. Nevertheless, he continued to serve as Clerk until his death five years later. He was presumably able to clear himself of the charges, and he may have had support among the Assistants.

In 1642-3, the Company acquired what is now its most treasured possession, the Weoley Cup, given by Richard Weoley, Master in 1631-2 and again in 1640-1. Williams assumes in his *Annals*, and Hibbert copies him, that Richard Weoley left the cup to the Company in his will, but this is not correct. A privately printed monograph on Weoley, written by Dr. Hugh Stannus, Master of the Company in 1930, shows that he died in August 1644, and gives the full text of his will, which makes no mention of the cup. Moreover, it is recorded in the Wardens' Accounts for 1642-3 that the cup was delivered to the Hall 'by Mr. Weoley's man' during that year. Weoley must therefore have made a deed of gift before he died, and it is this document, with its moving and eloquent message, which is still read out when the Court elects the new Master, and the retiring Master drinks to him from the cup. It runs as follows:

And whereas I, the said Richard Weoley, for 34 years have been a member of the Livery of the Company of Founders of the City of London, from whom I always have good respect and observation ever showed to me in that time aforesaid, in requital whereof I give and bequeath unto the said Company my painted drinking glass with the silver and gilt foot, which by relation was brought from Bullen [Boulogne] out of France, at the time when Henry the Eighth, King of England, had that place yielded unto him; this glass being part of the pillage then taken by a Yeoman of the Crown, and hath remained in one and the same family to this day.

Which glass I bought for a valuable consideration and do desire this glass

94   CITIZENS AND FOUNDERS

may be used in the Founders' Hall only upon the Election Day, when the
Master and Wardens are to be elected and chosen according to the ancient
custom of the Company, the old Master presenting to the new Master a cup
of hippocras, drinking unto him by the name of Master, which I desire may
be in this glass. And I do hereby wish that my means were agreeable to my
will, then should they record me a better benefactor. And I shall ever wish the
whole Body may ever live in unity, concord, and brotherly love which is pleas-
ing to God and Man. Even thus the God of Heaven bless them all – Amen.

The cup is a very rare specimen of a Venetian drinking goblet in glass with a
painted decoration in fine enamelled colours. Its original glass base was later broken
and replaced by a silver-gilt foot which, from its plate marks, was apparently made
in England in 1607. Expert opinion differs as to the identity of the figures shown
in the painted design. Williams suggests in his *Annals*, without naming his source,
that it depicts the marine goddess, Tethys, wife of Oceanus, riding a sea-horse on
the ocean bed with two of her daughters. The sea-bed is described as being carpeted
with seaweed and shells from which a sacrificial altar rises with a human skull on
each side. On the other hand, a note by R. J. Charleston, of the Victoria and Albert
Museum, undated but probably written in about 1960, claims that the figures are
those of a king wearing a blue robe and two boys naked except for boots, and that
they are riding on land over grass and flowers. He concludes that the Weoley Cup
is a Venetian enamelled glass made within a few years of 1500, probably just after
that year.

Thanks to the work done by the late Dr. Stannus, we know more about Richard
Weoley's personal background than we do of other Masters. He was born in 1584
at Chipping Campden in Gloucestershire and was the second son of Thomas
Weoley. The family was descended from Cotswold wool merchants and country
gentry whose old coat of arms was confirmed to Thomas Weoley by the College of
Heralds. Thomas Weoley died when Richard was 10, and the boy was later sent
to London to make his way. He seems to have been financially independent, holding a plot of Crown land in Kennington on lease and a house in Hackney which
he bought from an aunt. He also leased a house and ground from the hospitals or
hostels of Bridewell and Bethlehem, and built two brick houses on that site.

Weoley was Parish Clerk at the church of St. Botolph-without-Bishopsgate from
1618 until his death in 1644, and a member of the Parish Clerks' Company as
well as the Founders. He served as a Warden of the Parish Clerks and was their
Master in 1629. His example confirms that the Livery of the Founders already
contained, in early Stuart times, men no longer following the craft of founding,
but it also shows that such men could render outstanding services to the Company,
despite the Yeomanry complaints that they knew nothing of the manufacturing side.

Richard Weoley married in London and had 12 children, but it was an un-
happy match. Weoley complains in his will that he got no benefit from the houses
he built, because his wife, Mary, took possession of one house and disposed of the
other as she pleased. She, for her part, brought a petition for maintenance against

CIVIL WAR 95

her husband, alleging that he ill-treated her and that his property was bought with her money. In his will, Weoley welcomes death as a release 'from the matrimonial discontent wherein and whereby I have so feelingly and bitterly suffered for many years past'.

Despite the Yeomanry complaint that the Company's governors were no longer men qualified in the craft, the Court continued to keep a watchful eye on those standards of workmanship and quality on which the Company's welfare and reputation so much depended. Nor was it true, as the Yeomanry rebels maintained, that it was only they who were punished, while Liverymen did the same things with impunity.

In 1645, a complaint was made to the Court against a Liveryman called Thomas Embrey for 'trimming and making up brass works for persons not free of the Company'. He admitted this, but pleaded that he did not know it was a breach of his oath, and he was apparently excused. He served as a Steward in 1647-8, paying his fine of £7 for that office, and in 1658-9 he was Renter Warden. The Court issued an order confirming that no freeman of the Company working in brass should thereafter trim or make any brass or copper works except for Company members. It also ordered that no founder belonging to the Company should 'fill or stop with lead any brass works made up by them, whereby the King's liege people may be damnified or any private person cheated in buying the same again for brass'. A fine of 20s. was imposed for such an offence. In 1646, the weights belonging to another Liveryman, William Lambert, were seized and sold to discharge his Steward's fine for the previous year.

In 1647, the Court heard complaints against four members named John Falkener, Abel Hodges, Anthony Green and Robert Haselton. Falkener was probably the same man as the former Clerk of that name who was succeeded by Basspoole in 1644. He was accused of 'hawking and proffering' his wares at cut prices and casting his weights from base metal, but promised to mend his ways and was forgiven. Haselton admitted that he hawked his wares 'by his wife' and said he would do it again, 'with many other unseemly speeches'. He was unable to pay his fine and a City officer was sent for to arrest him, but the Court again relented and he was discharged. He owed his release partly to 'the earnest entreaty of Mr. Parratt, whom he had most offended', and partly to the fact that he was in no fit state to go to prison. Joseph Parratt was Master in 1638-9 and again in 1643-4 and 1650-1. He left the Company £20 in his will and £4 a year for poor members.

Anthony Green, like Haselton, was a Yeomanry member at this time. He was charged with keeping a boy to work for him, as well as the apprentice allowed him by the Company's rules. He excused himself on the grounds that he was old and needed extra help because his apprentice was lame, and protested 'how he aimed at nothing but the good of the Company'. Once more, the Court showed kindness and gave him permission to bind the boy as well as the apprentice. Green was admitted to the Livery in the following year. Although he had pleaded age as an excuse for his offence, he went on to serve as Third Warden in 1661-2 and Second Warden in 1669-70.

96 CITIZENS AND FOUNDERS

Abel Hodges was the man who, as already described, defied the Court in 1652. On this earlier occasion, he 'had many things proved against him' but denied them all. He was fined 10s., but in view of his plea of poverty and the 'simplicity of the man', the Court reduced the fine to 10 groats, or 3s. 4d., to be paid within seven days. This leniency seems to have been wasted on Hodges, judging by his renewed misconduct five years later, when defective wares were found in his house and he refused to pay a fine. It is a remarkable fact that, despite these offences, he was admitted to the Livery from the Yeomanry in 1662-3, served as a Warden in two later years, and finally rose to be Master in 1678-9. His record hardly qualified him for that honour, but perhaps he turned out better as a gamekeeper than a poacher.

When hearing these cases in 1647, the Court reaffirmed an order prohibiting members of the Company from hawking their wares in the streets which had figured in the Company's Ordinances since 1515. It also ordered that brass weights cast by members should have no pot brass or lead in them, or be made of any worse brass than 'yellow metal as of former times'. Under no pretence whatever was any founder to 'bottom' weights in such a way that only another founder could detect it. No brass weights were to be cast, made up, and offered for sale unless the maker stamped them with his mark within seven days.

In 1648, a Yeomanry member called James Maltby was prosecuted by the Company at the Old Bailey for dishonestly causing two 'stamps' to be made of steel and used for counterfeiting and sealing brass weights. He was fined £20, but begged the Company to pardon him and not to pursue him further, promising not to repeat the offence. All his stamps and the weights he had sealed were taken away, broken, and defaced. In 1653, a general search for 'deceited and base work' was made by the Master, Wardens and Assistants at Bartholomew Fair. Defective wares were seized from 14 persons, who were summoned before the Lord Mayor and punished according to law.

While the 'sizing' of weights was done at Founders' Hall, they also had to be 'sealed' by the Keeper of the Guildhall. In 1652, the Court directed that the Company's 'sizer', then the Clerk, William Basspoole, should not return weights to their owners until the latter had paid in full both the fees due for sizing and those for the sealing at Guildhall, which were divided equally between the City and the Company. Shortly after, the Court decided that the sealer of the troy weights sized at Founders' Hall should have those profits for his own use, provided that he took no more than what was formerly given by the Company.

In 1657, the Court ordered that any Founder who took his weights to Guildhall before bringing them to the sizers at Founders' Hall should forfeit 20s. for the use of the Company's poor. In addition, every member making brass weights had to mark them with his own authorised stamp before having them sealed at Guildhall, or pay a fine of 10s. Owners of weights were to pay the Clerk the fees for sealing weights, as well as for sizing, when their weights were returned to them. The Clerk was to bear any loss to the City and the Company which might arise if he let owners of weights have them back on trust when they had not paid for sealing as well as sizing. This may possibly have had something to do with the com-

CIVIL WAR 97

plaints against Basspoole in 1658, but he would hardly have been reinstated if they had been proved.

In 1640, the Court prohibited the installation of any furnace or 'annealing' by a founder within the three-mile limit of the City unless it had been approved by the Master, Wardens and Assistants. The reason given was to ensure that a furnace 'be free from firing the place where it standeth', but offenders who 'melted' in a furnace without leave incurred fines of 20s. for the first occasion and £5 for the second. No doubt the Court hoped that this would provide a useful addition to income, but they must have been disappointed. The only recorded example of such a fine occurred much earlier, in 1622-3, when a freeman of the Company, Michael Draper, had to pay 2s. for using his furnace without permission. The right of inspecting and licensing furnaces was granted to the Company under the Ordinances of 1592, but was omitted from both the Charter in 1614 and the supplementary Ordinances of 1615. This must have made it difficult to enforce the Company's jurisdiction over furnaces, although it did not deter the Court from repeating its ban on unauthorised furnaces in 1649.

In 1617, the Company petitioned the Lord Mayor and Aldermen for the 'turning-over' and presentation at Founders' Hall of all apprentices bound to workers of brass and copper wares in the City. This seems to have been refused, possibly due to opposition from the Braziers. In 1658, the Founders renewed their demand on a wider front, when they joined with the Carpenters, Scriveners, Upholders, Clockmakers, Gunmakers and Freemasons in a petition to the Lord Mayor and Common Council which asked that members of Companies other than those representing these particular trades, but themselves pursuing them, should bind their apprentices to the Company which embodied the craft or 'art' concerned. This did not suit the 'Great Companies', which had larger numbers of Liverymen in different occupations, and they made objections which caused the petition to be rejected.

The Founders themselves were willing to practise what they preached by allowing their own apprentices to be bound to other Companies in similar circumstances. In 1640-1, for example, they allowed Henry Carless to 'turn over' his son, Thomas, to the Woodmongers instead of being apprenticed to his father in the Founders. This suggests that Carless himself was a timber merchant and not a founder by trade. He was Master of the Founders in 1636-7, and 1642-3, and he gave the Company 'a white cup weighing 12 ounces' when his son was transferred to the Woodmongers.

In 1656, another Liveryman, John Cook, was permitted to transfer his son, John, to the Brewers' Company and paid the Founders a sum of £30 for it. Here again, we may infer that the father was a brewer and that his son worked for him in that trade, but there was another and more remarkable feature of this family connection. Both father and son were admitted to the Founders' Livery together in 1652-3, a case unique in the Company's own records and probably rare in any others. The explanation is given in a Court minute written at the time. This points out that John Cook, senior, was bound as an apprentice in the Founders in 1616,

98 CITIZENS AND FOUNDERS

and became a freeman in 1625, but since then he had 'lived unknown to the Company that he was free thereof', and this was only discovered when he obtained the freedom of the City in 1652. He was then admitted to the Livery, and his son with him, and the other Liverymen, 'in regard of his age and want of such men', gave him precedence over them. John Cook, senior, paid an office fine of £7 10s. for serving as a Steward in 1652-3 and was chosen as Renter Warden the year after, but excused himself, probably on account of age, and paid instead a fine of £7 13s. 4d.

A somewhat similar case occurred in 1657, when John Beauchamp was chosen as Renter Warden. He asked that his son, John, should be brought into the Livery and allowed to help him because of his own age and infirmity. He promised that his son would pay all the usual fines, and his request was granted.

In 1661, a freeman of the Founders called Anthony Barnard was translated into the Woodmongers' Company and paid £3. A Court minute noted that his livelihood as a 'carman' depended on permission from the Woodmongers to do that work, and that he had been in trouble with them three times for that reason.

As already noted, the Court was prepared to enforce discipline on its own members and the other Liverymen as well as on the Yeomanry, and sometimes more strictly. In 1638, a newly elected Younger Warden, John Major, was summarily dismissed from that office for reasons not stated. In 1655, the Second Warden, Marmaduke Almond, was sued for non-payment of his office fine, but paid up and went on to serve as Master in 1660-1 and 1663-4. Assistants were fined for not attending Court when summoned, arriving late, or being improperly dressed by coming to meetings without their gowns. When eight new Livery members were called to the Hall in 1658, they received a command in the traditional form:

> You are required by the Master, Wardens, and Assistants of the Company of Founders whereof you are free to appear at Founders Hall the next 29th October, 1659, in a Livery gown and hood and decent good apparel, according unto the custom of the City and order of the Company. And that you be there by nine of the clock in the morning to give your attendance with the rest of the Livery, as you will answer the same at your peril.

The increasing burden of office fines and other charges borne by Masters, Wardens and Assistants, imposed by the need to meet tax demands and higher costs generally, reached a point where many Liverymen preferred to pay fines for refusing office rather than face the expense of accepting it. These burdens were already recognised by a Court order in 1623 which exempted those who had served as Master or Warden six times, or had done so five times and once been Stewards, from doing so again; or alternatively allowed them to have all their charges paid from Company funds if they were still willing to accept office.

In 1634, a rule was made that the Master and Wardens should each pay £6 to clear them of their charges for all dinners except a supper when a new Master and Wardens were chosen. In 1647, however, the Court ordered that every new Master or Warden should pay their £6 for dinners on the day they were sworn and, in

CIVIL WAR   99

addition, the Wardens were to pay 6s. 8d. and 13s. 4d. respectively towards the
Livery dinner on Lord Mayor's Day. Both Masters and Wardens were also to pay
three nobles, or about £1, towards the cost of quarter-day dinners. In 1659, the
Court suspended these dinners, 'finding that it is to the charge and loss of the
Company, and not any profit or quiet' and attributing this measure to the fact
that 'the times are very bad and great charge is like to fall upon the Hall'.

Although the Company's finances were so badly strained by taxation and inflation, causing deficits in many years which had to be met by borrowing, or selling
silver and plate, there were some years in which it was possible to set aside money
for investment from gifts or legacies. In 1638-9, a legacy of £6 was received from
John Keely, a Saddler, who also left four white 'wine cups' to the Company. In
1637-8, a legacy of £10 bequeathed by Francis Curwen, Master in 1625-6, 1628-9
and 1633-4, was handed over by his son. In 1639-40, the Company began to receive
interest at six per cent on a loan of £300 which it made to one of its tenants, the
Merchant Adventurers' Company. Of this loan, £100 was provided by the legacy
already mentioned earlier from John Rawlings, and the £6 of interest on it was
regularly paid to 'six poor Founders', as he had directed. In 1647, the amount of
this loan was increased to £500, partly provided by the receipt of £100 when the
leases of the two houses in Lothbury assigned to the Company by Richard Rowdinge expired.

The Wardens' Accounts show annual receipts of interest on the Merchant
Adventurers loan up to the end of 1665, and their bond was still listed by the
Auditors in May 1666, as one of the assets held 'in the great trunk in the inner
buttery'. There is no further mention of either the bond or the receipt of interest on
the loan, and the Company may have called it in to help to meet the costs of
rebuilding Founders' Hall after the Great Fire in September 1666. The bond itself
may have been destroyed in the Fire.

Local taxes and rates increased after 1600. In 1607-8, the Company started
paying an annual rate of 17s. 4d. for the poor of the parish, raised to £1 6s. in
1641. In 1636, a special payment of £2 8s. 8d, 'forced by the Lord Mayor', was
made for the relief of the poor in the 'out-parishes' or suburbs, which had suffered
a severe outbreak of plague. Occasional payments are also recorded for 'warding'
or sealing off infected houses. Payments of tithe to the Rector of St. Margaret, Lothbury, began in 1640-1 at a rate of 6s. collected by the Parish Clerk, and the Company also made small annual contributions to his stipend. The Founders made
various payments towards repairs in St. Margaret's at a rate fixed in 1607, when
the vestry decided to assess parishioners for repairs on the same basis as the poor
rate. In 1658-9, a sum of £1 4s. was paid for 'the river water' which was then laid
on to the hall.

The cost of repairs to the Hall rose rapidly during this period. In 1655-6, when
the building was well over a hundred years old, major repairs were carried out by
the Master, Stephen Pilchard, at a cost of £22. The Auditors disallowed his claim
for these expenses on the grounds that they had been 'laid forth without consent
of a Court of Assistants and to the great inconveniency and prejudice of the Hall

and the Company'. It will be recalled that Pilchard was denounced by the Yeomanry rebels in 1652, when he was Upper Warden, as a 'malignant Royalist', and it is possible that the Auditors were influenced by republican sentiments. In any event, they called on Pilchard to pay the costs of repairs from his own pocket, which he did without protest. Not only that, but he also made a gift of £50 towards the building of the new Hall after the Great Fire of 1666.

Stephen Pilchard was a conspicuous example in the long list of Founders whose gifts bore witness to their devotion to the Company. He lived on to see the restoration of Charles II in 1660, when Pilchard was the senior Auditor in the Company. He died in 1672 or 1673, having lived through the Civil War, the last great slaughter of the Plague in 1665, and the Great Fire which destroyed the old City of London, and Founders' Hall with it, in 1666.

CHAPTER IX

Ordeal by Fire

THE RESTORATION of monarchy in 1660 was welcomed by an English nation which had been subjected to a harsher form of republican tyranny under Cromwell than anything experienced under the two Stuart kings who ruled before him. Cromwell was a great Englishman who made his country a leading naval power respected and feared in Europe, but at home, as Lord Protector, he was a dictator who ruled without Parliament and depended on the New Model Army for his exercise of power. As his own letters and speeches make abundantly clear, he believed himself to be God's chosen instrument on earth, and those who opposed him must therefore be agents of the Devil to be destroyed by fire and sword. His political philosophy did not differ very much from the divine right of kings claimed by Charles I, and indeed Cromwell seriously considered putting the Crown on his own head.

Under his rule, England was divided into 10 regional military governments, each commanded by a Major-General with powers to disarm 'all Papists and Royalists' and arrest all suspicious persons. Taxes were levied by Cromwell solely on his own authority, without Parliamentary sanction, and enforced by the seizure of property and goods. There was a rigorous press censorship, and even a critical remark made in the family circle might be reported by informers and used as evidence of treason.

Cromwell's England also suffered from the excesses of Puritan fanatics whose abuses of power he was either unwilling or unable to prevent. These men, many of whom were totally without education, were self-appointed preachers and keepers of their neighbours' conscience. Like fanatics in all ages, they believed that they alone knew the way to salvation and that it must be forced on others whether they liked it or not. These Puritan inquisitors not only condemned all forms of tradition and ritual in religious worship, but also regarded all popular entertainment or private amusement as works of Satan. They sent Roundhead troopers into houses to see whether the Sabbath was being strictly observed with prayers and fasting, and dragged off to prison anybody found singing, dancing, playing games or reading books other than the Bible. Like makers of revolutions in all ages, they were not only killers on a large scale, but kill-joys as well.

Under Cromwell, the traditional English family celebration of Christmas with holly, ivy and Yule log was banned as a 'pagan superstition'. The old country

102   CITIZENS AND FOUNDERS

pursuits of dancing round the Maypole on village greens, cock-fighting, wrestling
and horse-racing were prohibited as sins against the spirit. All theatres were closed.
The Episcopalian clergy, those who still clung to the traditional form and celebration of religious services, were forbidden to serve as ministers or tutors and expelled
from their livings. The churches were invaded by Puritan vandals who smashed
stained-glass windows, destroyed figures of saints, and burned altar-pieces and
vestments. At its best, the Puritan creed was nobly expressed in Milton's poetry
and John Bunyan's *Pilgrim's Progress*. At its worst, it was a sterile doctrine of
religious hatred and intolerance.

In London, many of the City merchants had backed Parliament against King
with their money, but the new ideas of social and religious revolution found their
main support among the small traders, craftsmen, and apprentices of the Livery
Companies. It was this ferment which played such a large part in the conflict between the Founders' Livery and Yeomanry described in the last chapter. The process of disillusion began with the execution of Charles I in 1649, which struck a
great many English people of all classes as a savage and horrifying act of revenge.
It was followed by drastic measures against those who had fought for the King,
including the confiscation or forced sale of their property and their exclusion from
voting for Parliament. These reprisals wrecked the hopes of moderate men for a
national reconciliation which would heal the wounds of the Civil War.

The City of London also felt the heavy hand of Puritan repression. Humphrey
Tabor, Rector of St. Margaret, Lothbury, since 1627, was among the clergymen
expelled and imprisoned. A Puritan pamphlet entitled *A Succinct Traiterologie*,
written in the crude ideological jargon of the sectarian fanatics, said that he was
sequestered 'for being a most popishly affected ceremony-monger, a proud ponti-
fical enemy to frequent preaching, and a most desperate malignant against the
Parliament'. Conversely, a church pamphlet entitled *A General Bill of Mortality
of the Clergie of London* referred to him as 'Mr. Tabor of Margaret, Lothbury,
imprisoned in the King's Bench, his wife and children turned out of doors at midnight, and he sequestered'. His successor, Leonard Cooke, signed himself as 'pastor'.

In 1643, the ancient 'Paul's Cross' which stood outside the old Cathedral was
demolished by order of Parliament, together with all other similar Crosses in London and Westminster. The old London chronicler, Stow, described Paul's Cross as
'a pulpit or cross of timber mounted upon steps of stone and covered with lead'. It
had been for centuries a place where the people assembled to voice their grievances,
discuss civic affairs, and listen to sermons. Such Crosses were regarded by the
Puritan zealots as a Popish form of superstition, but their destruction was a bad
omen for the maintenance of constitutional liberty under republican rule.

In 1645, Parliament issued orders forbidding 'all Popish images', and the City
Companies were forced to burn the 'hearse cloths' which they had used since medieval times to cover the coffin of a dead member when it was carried in procession
to the grave. Many of these 'hearse cloths' were magnificent pieces of workmanship made from silk and velvet of different colours and decorated with pictures in
gold or silver thread of the Company's patron saint surrounded by angels. The
silver on the Founders' cloth was saved and sold for 16s.

ORDEAL BY FIRE

Cromwellian rule also frowned on the lavish City pageants which had long been mounted to mark the appointment of a new Lord Mayor or a Royal visit. It is significant that the Wardens' Accounts of the Founders from 1642 to 1657 contain no payments for the 'whifflers', meaning whistlers or ushers, who preceded the Company when it paraded on these occasions. The City pageants reached their peak in the reigns of James I and Charles I, when the Twelve Great Companies were keen rivals for the honour of putting on the best and biggest show and went to great expense. George Unwin, in his book on the London gilds, gives a graphic picture of their splendid and colourful displays.

The Fishmongers' pageant in 1616 consisted of six separate tableaux, starting with the Company's traditional 'Fishing Buss' manned by three fishermen, one of them casting a net and the others throwing live fish to the spectators. Another float showed the 'King of the Moors' mounted on a golden leopard and throwing gold and silver all round him, followed by six vassal kings. Next came a large lemon tree representing the Lord Mayor and a pelican feeding her young with her blood 'to symbolise the cherishing love borne by the Mayor to the citizens'. The final scene was 'a goodly bower shaped in form of a flowery arbour and adorned with the scutcheons of arms of so many worthy men of the Fishmongers' Company as have been Lord Mayors'.

In 1629, the dramatist, John Webster, designed a set of pageants for the Merchant Taylors in which actors portrayed famous English seamen such as Drake and Hawkins, the rivers Thames and Medway, and the renowned English mercenary soldier, Sir John Hawkwood. Hawkwood was mobilised on this occasion because he started in life as an apprentice in the Merchant Taylors before becoming a soldier and fighting under the Black Prince in France. Also in 1629, the Ironmongers staged a pageant prepared by another dramatist and poet, Thomas Dekker, who sang the praises of iron in verse which was prophetic though scarcely immortal, including these lines:

> Iron, best of metals! Pride of Minerals,
> Heart of the earth! Hand of the world! Which falls
> Heavy when it strikes home . . .
> Iron, that main hinge on which the world doth turn!

In the years after the Restoration, Thomas Jordan presented a pageant for the Grocers which included 'a proper masculine woman with a tawny face, raven-black long hair, several pearl necklaces, aurora-coloured silk stockings, silver buskins laced up to the calf with gold ribbons, bearing a banner with the Lord Mayor's family coat of arms'. This Amazon identified herself with the words:

> That I the better may attention draw,
> Be pleased to know I am America!

These flights of fancy became still more elaborate as time went on. In 1671, the Skinners produced a group of satyrs dancing to the music of Orpheus and a bear performing on a rope. The Haberdashers presented their patron saint, Catherine, in a silver chariot with golden wheels drawn by two large Indian goats. They

104 CITIZENS AND FOUNDERS

followed this in 1699 by depicting 'Commerce' seated on a rich throne with milliners shops for her footstool, while screws of tobacco were thrown to the crowd. By that time, however, the pageants had become little more than attempts to keep alive by artificial respiration an old City spirit of popular revelry which was dying out.

In 1650, the Master and Wardens of the Founders, like those of other Companies, took the 'Engagement' or oath of loyalty to the Commonwealth state which was imposed on all office-holders under a government order issued in 1649. This was followed by an order from the Council of State which noted that the Royal Arms and pictures 'of the late King' were still displayed in some Company Halls and demanded their immediate removal and destruction, with a certificate confirming that this had been done. In 1651-2, the Founders paid 18s. for putting 'the State's Arms in the glass window'.

The King's return in 1660 was celebrated with an enthusiasm redoubled by relief at the end of Puritan austerity, but at considerable expense to the City Companies. In May 1660, the Lord Mayor and Aldermen authorised a gift of £10,000 to Charles II from the City, and another £2,000 to be shared by his brothers, the Dukes of York and Gloucester. Perhaps mindful of past experience and the large debts owed to the City by Crown and Parliament, the Lord Mayor added that this gift was not intended as a precedent for the future. In July that year, the City entertained Charles, together with the Lords and Commons, at a great banquet in Guildhall and the streets were adorned with costly pageants.

In April 1661, the Court of Aldermen voted a loan of £60,000 to the King, a gift to him of £1,000 in gold, and £9,000 to pay for the street decorations and shows when Charles went in procession through the City from the Tower to Westminster Abbey for his coronation. The Livery Companies were assessed for contributions to these expenses according to their quotas for the supply of corn, and the Founders paid £53 in 1660-1, a heavy charge. The Company had to borrow money at interest of six per cent to make good this amount. In 1664, the City granted another loan to the King and this time the Founders had to provide £200. In 1665-6, they contributed £12 8s. 6d. to the building of a ship for the Royal Navy called the 'Loyal London'.

It may have been the need to raise more money from fines, as well as concern for the craft, which led the Master and Wardens to carry out a search in 1660 of all workshops kept by founders and coppersmiths in Lothbury and Bartholomew Lane. In the house of John Lucas, a Liveryman of the Company, they discovered 'one cock of brass filled in with 20 ounces of lead and one 4lb weight unsealed, unsized, and unmarked with the maker's stamp, which work was brought into the Hall'. As a Yeomanry member in 1652, before being promoted to the Livery, Lucas had already been in trouble for refusing to pay quarterage, and he was also one of the five men who signed a petition that year to the Parliamentary Committee for Corporations asking it to hear the complaints of the Yeomanry.

His promotion to the Livery was clearly ill-merited, for he denied the Court's authority to search his premises in 1660 and said 'that they were a Company of

ORDEAL BY FIRE

knaves and fools, and that one knave searched another'. He was dismissed from the Livery on this occasion, but submitted to a fine of 20s., and a long-suffering Court not only remitted this fine, after taking 5s. from it for the 'Poor's Box', but also restored Lucas to the Livery in 1663. This was yet another example of forgiveness by the Court, even when the financial situation was precarious, but whether it served the best interests of the Company is another question.

Far greater troubles were about to descend on the City. In 1665, the last major outbreak of the Black Death, or bubonic plague, broke out in London and is said to have killed 100,000 people in six months. This was followed, in September 1666, by the Great Fire of London, which wiped out houses, churches, halls, monuments and warehouses alike. It may be thought that the Fire at least destroyed the dark maze of slums and alleys in which the plague infection flourished, but much of the City was rebuilt in its old, congested form and the decline of the plague seems to have been due to other causes.

The Great Fire started in the early hours of Sunday, 2 September 1666, in a baker's house in Pudding Lane. A spell of warm, dry weather had made the mass of overhanging wooden houses a tinder-box, and there was a wind which fanned the flames. Even so, they might easily have been brought under control in the first few hours if the danger had been appreciated in time. As it was, being a Sunday morning, few people were up and about and many who saw the smoke from a distance thought little of it and went back to bed. Once it had gained a foothold, the fire spread with terrifying speed. Among the eye-witness accounts, one of the most vivid was recorded by the diarist, John Evelyn, who served on various Royal Commissions and was a member of the Royal Society founded in 1662 by Charles II for the improvement of natural science by experiment. Evelyn watched the scene from Southwark on the Sunday and returned there next day. He writes:

I went on foot to the same place, whence I saw the whole south part of the City burning from Cheapside to the Thames and all along Cornhill. For it likewise kindled back against the wind as well as forward. It burnt through Tower Street, Fenchurch Street, and Gracechurch Street, and so along to Baynard's Castle, and was now taking hold of St. Paul's Cathedral, to which the scaffolding contributed exceedingly. The conflagration was so universal, and the people so astonished, that from the beginning, I know not by what desponding or fate, they hardly stirred to quench it. There was nothing seen or heard but crying out and lamentation and running about like distracted creatures without at all attempting to save even their goods. Such a strange consternation there was upon them that the fire burned, both in breadth and length, the churches, public halls, Exchange, hospitals, monuments, and ornaments, leaping from house to house and street to street after a prodigious manner.

Here we saw the Thames covered with floating goods, all the barges and boats laden with what some had courage and time to save, and the carts

106   CITIZENS AND FOUNDERS

carrying goods out to the fields which, for many miles, were strewn with moveables of all sorts and tents erected to shelter both people and what goods they could get away. O the miserable and calamitous spectacle, such as perhaps the whole world had not seen its like since the foundation of it, nor is it to be outdone until the world's universal conflagration! All the sky was of a fiery aspect like the top of a burning oven, and the light was seen for above forty miles round about for many nights. God grant my eyes may never behold the like, who now saw above ten thousand houses all in one flame. The noise, crackling, and thunder of the impetuous flames, the shrieking of women and children, the hurry of people, and the fall of towers, houses, and churches was like an hideous storm. And the air all about was so hot and inflamed that, at the last, one was not able to approach it, so that they were forced to stand still and let the flames consume on, which they did for nearly two miles in length and one in breadth. The clouds of smoke also were dismal and reached, upon computation, nearly fifty miles in length. Thus I left it this afternoon burning, a resemblance of Sodom or the Last Day. London was, but is no more.

Next day, Evelyn went on horseback as far as the Inner Temple and found the fire still raging. He continues:

All Fleet Street, Ludgate Hill, Warwick Lane, Newgate, and the Old Bailey was now flaming and most of it reduced to ashes. The stones of St. Paul's flew like grenades and the lead melted down the streets in a stream. The very pavements glowed with fiery redness and neither horse nor man was able to tread on them, and the demolitions had stopped all the passages, so that no help could be applied . . . On the 5th, the fire crossed towards Whitehall, but oh the confusion that was then at that Court! It pleased His Majesty to command me, among the rest, to look after the quenching of Fetter Lane and to preserve, if possible, that part of Holborn. The rest of the gentlemen took their several posts, some at one part, some at another, for now they began to bestir themselves and not till now, who had stood as men restrained with their arms crossed.

Now they began to realise that nothing was likely to put a stop but the blowing up of so many houses as might make a wider gap than any that had yet been made by the ordinary method of pulling them down with engines. Some stout seamen had proposed this early enough to have saved the whole city, but some tenacious and avaricious Aldermen did not permit it, because their houses would have been among the first to be demolished.

Evelyn returned again on foot on 7 September, 'clambering over mountains of yet smoking rubbish and frequently mistaking where I was, the ground under my feet being so hot that it made me not only sweat, but burnt the soles of my shoes'. Old St. Paul's lay in ruins, its massive stonework split and calcined by the intense heat. The fountains were dried up and ruined, while the well waters were still

ORDEAL BY FIRE

boiling. Dark clouds of smoke belched from cellars and warehouses and the air stank of death. Evelyn went on towards Islington and Highgate, 'where one might have seen two hundred thousand people of all ranks and degrees dispersed and lying alongside their heaps of what they could save from the Incendium, deploring their loss and yet, though ready to perish for hunger and destitution, not asking one penny for relief'.

The rebuilding of the City offered a unique opportunity for town-planning on new and healthier lines, but the chance was missed. Some new streets were opened and others widened. Brick and stone replaced wood in many new houses, and splendid new churches, halls and public buildings rose from the ashes. The genius of Christopher Wren raised the new St. Paul's Cathedral. But the old medley of narrow passages, crowded houses, courtyards and small gardens reappeared over a large area much as it was before. Indeed, living conditions in London may have grown worse, because the increase of population in the outer suburbs, which had escaped the Fire, made them the more overcrowded.

For the Founders, the destruction of their Hall was a shattering blow, since it not only deprived them of their chief capital asset, but also cut off the income from rents and sizing of weights. From 1666 to 1670, only £1 was received in rental income, but some money still came in from sizing. The Accounts show that this work was carried on in a rented shed nearby, and the equipment was presumably either salvaged from the Hall in time or found elsewhere. The Clerk, Francis Lambert, lived on the premises or in Founders' Court nearby, and in 1669-70 he was given £7 'for his charges in saving the plate and other things belonging to the Hall'. In 1672, when Lambert owed the Company £36, he asked for compensation for his charges in renting accommodation after the Fire and the Court replied by cancelling his debt.

The task of rebuilding Founders' Hall was tackled with vigour and determination. It took some time to clear away the ruins and make a new survey, but a rebuilding committee was appointed and the work began early in 1670. A list was opened for subscriptions towards the cost, and George Dixon, Master in 1668-9 and again in 1669-70, was chosen to act as treasurer. It seems that all Liverymen were compelled to subscribe, as the Court ordered in December 1670, that 'a course of law' should be taken against those who had not paid, and also against office-holders who had not paid their fines.

The building contract was given to Thomas Beauchamp, a Liveryman of the Company who served as Second Warden in 1666-7, but this seems to have been an unfortunate choice. The Company paid bills from Beauchamp for £778, but he claimed more and summoned the Master and Wardens before the Lord Mayor. The Accounts for 1671-2 show that they were arrested and the Company paid bail for their release. The City Surveyor, Mr. Oliver, was called in as arbitrator and awarded Beauchamp another £138. The Company paid up, but Beauchamp's name does not appear again in the Accounts and he may have been dismissed from the Company or resigned.

The total cost of rebuilding came to £1,037, of which £500 was raised by

108   CITIZENS AND FOUNDERS

borrowing money on the security of the new Hall, £335 came from subscriptions and gifts by members, £69 from the sale of the Company's plate, and the rest either from loans from members or from the 'stock' in hand. William Burroughes, Master in 1657-8 and 1659-60, paid for fixing the Hall window over the entrance and all the brass work for the water supply, as well as subscribing £10 10s.

Very little information has come down to us about the layout of the rebuilt Hall and its interior fittings. The new Hall must have been built of brick, as this was required by the Rebuilding Act of 1667, and we also know that the Court ordered in 1669 that the front 'should be beautified with stone work'. A rough sketch of the elevation made much later in 1835, when the rebuilt Hall was still standing, shows a substantial edifice with two main floors, attics and basement, together with houses belonging to the Company in Founders Alley. An inventory of the contents made in 1680 by the Wardens that year, John Underwood and Richard Meakins, reads as follows:

In the Parlour: 1 King's Arms, 1 table, 1 green carpet, 3 forms, 1 pair of andirons, shovel and tongs of brass, 1 pair of iron dogs.

In the Sizing Room: 4 beams and scales, 1 set of bell weights, from the half-hundred to the pound, 1 set of flat weight from the stone to the dram.

In the Yard: 1 leaden cistern, pipes and cocks, and 1 'pising' cistern.

In the Kitchen: 1 range, 1 jack, pulleys, cord and weight, 1 pair of iron spit racks, 12 large butter dishes, 6 two-quart pots, 3 salts, 9 dozen and three plates, 1 leaden sink pipe and cock, 1 table cloth, 16 diaper [linen] napkins, 1 dozen of knives and case, 4 silk trophies [probably Company banners], 1 King's Arms, 1 City Arms, Tubal Cain and Founders Arms, 7 dozen trenchers.

This is not an impressive list, even allowing for losses in the Great Fire and the sale of the Company's plate to help in paying for the new Hall. The Weoley Cup must have survived and we know that there were 'other things' which the Clerk, Lambert, was able to save. Perhaps the inventory excluded the Company's chest and other objects of value, or they were kept elsewhere after the Fire. The Company was probably too short of money to provide anything more than basic equipment for the new Hall.

As a means of securing badly needed income, the Court resorted to the time-honoured method of raising office fees and fines. In 1669, the fine paid by a new Master or Warden was increased from £6 to £8. The Stewards' fines went up £6 to £7 13s. 4d. and to £10 in 1674. The fine for admission to the Livery rose from £3 6s. 8d. to £6, and the fine paid by new freemen was raised from 14s. 4d. to 25s., of which the Clerk received 2s. 6d. and the Beadle got 1s. The fee for binding an apprentice was doubled from 5s. to 10s., of which the Clerk took 4s. 6d. and the Beadle 1s. In 1678, the fine for refusing office as Master was increased to £12, and the fine for refusing office as Warden went up to £10. No doubt the Court had a shrewd idea of the Liverymen who might be unwilling to take office for reasons of

ORDEAL BY FIRE   109

health or age, and who were therefore a profitable source of income from fines for refusal.

As a result of these increases, the receipts from office fines in 1669-70 showed a rise of £121, as compared with an annual average of only £30 from 1661 to 1666 and £55 from 1666 to 1669. In 1673-4, when the Company's regular income from all sources exceeded £200 for the first time, the office fines provided £139. On the other hand, the receipts from quarterage and sizing of weights yielded less in the five years after the Fire than in the five years before it.

In September 1672, the Court celebrated this recovery by issuing the following order, here reproduced in the original spelling :

> It was taken into consideration and debated and found by the Court then sitting : That many good Laws and Ordinances, Orders, Customs, and Usages of the Company of Founders hath bin of late very much neglected and omitted, by reason of the great trouble and distractions that have befallen the sayd Company in general as well as the particular Members, occasioned by the late dreadful fyer in London, which wholly consumed the Hall and all the Lands and Tenements and many of the movables, books and papers belonging to the sayd Company.
>
> And now seeing it hath pleased God to bless the sayd Company soe well as to enable them to procure the rebuilding of their Hall and Tenements again; Therefore it is ordered by this Court of Assistants that all those Laws, Ordinances, Orders, Customs, and Usages of the sayd Company shall be put in practice again and be observed as formerly, and that an Abstract or Memorandum of them shall be fairly written by the Clerk and be delivered to every Master soe soon as he shall be sworne into his office, that he may better understand and know what his office of Master requires him to observe, and see it be done for the best government and management of the good welfare and honour of the Company.

With the completion of the new Hall, income was again forthcoming from some old tenants who returned and some new ones. The Eastland Company started using the Hall again in 1672 at an annual rent of £6, and in that year the Woolwinders' Company were given leave to meet at Founders' Hall for two days in the year and keep a chest or trunk there for their papers. They made an annual payment of £2. The Merchant Adventurers resumed their tenancy in 1675 at a rent of £8, and in 1683 they also rented the Sizing Room and Gown Room for £16 yearly. The Gunmakers' Company, which received a charter from Charles I in 1637, paid £2 3s. for meeting in the Hall in 1682, and in 1702 the Clockmakers, also incorporated under Charles I, were allowed the use of the Parlour for their meetings at an annual rent of £10. Looking further ahead, the Tackle and Ticket Porters were granted the use of the Court Room for one day monthly in 1759 for a rent of £6 a year, and in 1767 the Loriners' Company paid a rent of £10 to use the Hall for their monthly Courts and annual dinner.

CITIZENS AND FOUNDERS

The new Hall was also hired for many other purposes. In 1678, the Court decided that a fee of 20s. should be paid 'for every funeral that shall be brought out of the Hall', and it also required 'the same service to be given to the Master and Wardens as to the people that are invited'. The Clerk was to receive 10s. of this fee, and the Beadle 5s. while the remaining 5s. went into the Poor Box. No fee was charged if the deceased was a member of the Company, but only the cost of cleaning the Hall. In 1690, the Company received £7 as a half-year's rent 'for dancing in the Hall', and in 1700 the Parlour was let to a dancing-master for three days a week at a half-yearly fee of £6.

An interesting new development was the use of the Hall and Parlour by 'dissenters' and Nonconformist congregations for their meetings and services. In his *Manners and Customs of London*, Malcolm remarks, somewhat unkindly :

> The Halls of the different Companies appear, at this period, to have been used for almost every public purpose, but particularly for the sighings and groanings of grace and over-righteousness, and to reverberate in thrice-dissonant thunder the voices of the elect, who saved themselves and dealt universal misery to all around them.

> Sunday, a world of women with green aprons get on their pattens after eight, reach Brewers' Hall and White Hart Court by nine, are ready to burst with the spirit a minute or two after, and are delivered of it by ten. Much sighing at Salters' Hall about the same hour. Great frowning at St. Paul's while the service is singing, a tolerable attention to the sermon, but no respect at all is paid to the sacrament.

In April 1672, the Founders appointed a committee to arrange for the letting of the Hall and Parlour 'to such persons as will desire to have them for a public place to preach in'. In June that year, according to an article by the Rev. Philip Williams in the *Journal of the Presbyterian Historical Society of England* for May 1922, as quoted by Mr. Parsloe in his introduction to the Wardens' Accounts, the Hall was let to a Scottish Presbyterian congregation whose first minister, Alexander Carmichael, died in 1677 and was succeeded by Jeremiah Marsden. In his *Annals of the Founders' Company*, W. M. Williams refers to a passage from a book called *Wilson's Dissenting Churches* which describes the Scots church 'formerly meeting at Founders' Hall' as the oldest of its kind in London.

The first mention in the Wardens' Accounts of the use of the Hall by religious dissenters does not appear until 1676-7, when a part payment of £6 10s. was received for rent from 'Dr. Singleton'. This was John Singleton, pastor of a London Nonconformist congregation from which, as noted by Mr. Parsloe, he was dismissed in 1688. There is no evidence in the Accounts that the Hall was rented by the Scottish Presbyterians in 1672. A rent of £14 a year was still being received from 'the Minister' in 1680-1, the last year recorded in the Accounts, but this presumably refers to the Nonconformist congregation already mentioned. In 1687, the lease for religious meetings was apparently vacated, as in that year the Master

ORDEAL BY FIRE

and Wardens were authorised to let the Hall or Parlour again for preaching or prayers at a rent of not less than £20 paid in advance. The Company's records show that a rent of £30 was in fact received that same year from an unnamed congregation.

The first positive identification of the Scottish Presbyterians as tenants appears only in 1699, when an agreement was signed with 'Mr. Fleming's Congregation' for the lease of the Hall and Parlour, presumably on Sundays, for 41 years. This is confirmed in an extract from *Wilson's Dissenting Churches* quoted by Williams in his *Annals*, and it adds that Fleming had been recalled by the Scots church from Rotterdam to London. In 1700, the Court agreed that the Scots congregation could make alterations to the Hall, at its own expense, by 'removing the windows backwards into the yard' and making a skylight into the room 'belonging to the Hamburg Merchants', who were apparently the same as the Eastland Company, a long-standing tenant.

The Founders' lease to the Scottish Presbyterians was renewed in 1738 for 21 years at a rent of £20 a year, plus a 'fine' of £100 and all charges. In 1764, however, they found the accommodation too small and moved to London Wall. A fresh lease of the Hall 'with the pews, galleries, and other things therein' was granted in 1765 for 31 years to a group of dissenting Scottish Presbyterians led by Thomas Uffington. They paid a rent of £28 a year and agreed to spend £300 or £400 on repairs and improvements. In 1763, the Society for Promoting Religious Knowledge paid £4 for using the Parlour once a month and the Court Room on four evenings that year.

After the Scottish Presbyterian lease expired in 1796, a congregation of Scottish Independents, led by a Scots pastor called Anthony Crole, rented the Hall as their meeting-house. In 1821, the Hall was rented for one year by Dr. Collyer and Mr. Pearce for meetings of the Salters' Hall congregation, and the Court allowed one quarter's rent towards repairs.

In the earlier years after the Restoration, the religious dissenters suffered harsh treatment from a Royalist Parliament, although Charles II, whose sympathies lay with the Catholics, favoured a more tolerant attitude to the dissenters as well. But he was dependent on Parliament for funds to carry on the government and to satisfy the demands of his numerous mistresses and provide for his equally numerous bastards. Finding, however, that even the Cavalier Parliament kept a tight hand on the purse-strings, Charles concluded the secret Treaty of Dover with Louis XIV in 1670, a typically cynical operation which gave him a large French subsidy in return for his promise to prevent English forces from joining a European alliance against France and to work for a Catholic restoration in England. The subsidy was renewed in 1680 and then denounced by the radical Earl of Shaftesbury, Anthony Ashley Cooper, who fought in the Civil War first for the King, and then against him, and later led the Whig opposition in Parliament.

Shaftesbury exploited anti-Catholic feeling for his own political purposes and employed Titus Oates, a renegade Catholic turned Baptist minister and a hired informer, to spread rumours of Catholic plots to kill the King and restore Catholic

112   CITIZENS AND FOUNDERS

supremacy. This agitation stirred up so much public fury and hysteria that many innocent Catholics were murdered or imprisoned. In London, a Puritan stronghold, all Catholics were ordered by the Lord Mayor to leave the City, the train-bands were called to arms, and the streets were patrolled to guard against a Catholic rising. Between 1670 and 1681, the last year covered in the Wardens' Accounts, the Founders made various payments for soldiers to take part in the musters of train-bands. In 1679, the Clerk, James Dickinson, bought a cudgel to defend himself in case rioting broke out in the streets when the 'Gunpowder Treason' anniversary was celebrated that year.

Amid these alarms and excursions, the Company was busy settling into its new Hall. In 1671-2, a payment was made for 'laying in the water' and the Company started paying the 'hearth tax' imposed in 1662. In March 1672, there was a meeting between the Founders and the Paviors' Company, probably to discuss the paving of Founders Alley, following an Act on street-paving passed by the Common Council in October 1671. In August 1669, there were expenses for meetings 'about the coppersmiths', and in 1678 similar expenses arose for meetings with 'the pewterers founders'. These meetings may have been held to discuss the position of coppersmiths whose affiliation was claimed both by the Founders' Company and the Pewterers.

The searches by Master and Wardens for defective wares in brass or copper had naturally lapsed after the destruction of the City in the Great Fire and it seems that they were not resumed until 1677-8, when the Wardens' Accounts show the receipt of 'several fines for defective goods'. In that year also, fees of a shilling each were received from '17 persons for striking their marks'. The Accounts for 1671-2 contain a payment for 'making an alphabet for the names of the members of the Company', this being the first mention on record of such a list. In 1675-6, the Court made a contribution 'to the slaves', which was probably paid to a City fund for ransoming Christian slaves from the Barbary pirates. New banners were ordered for the Company in 1677-8 and the 'painters' received £30 for them, which was well over twice the amount paid for banners in 1626 and gives some indication of the rise in prices. Starting in 1672-3, payments were made for 'tobacco, pipes and candles' for smoking at Court or other meetings.

In January 1684, the Thames was frozen solid. The Master and Upper Warden 'played at ninepins' on the ice and saw a coach and horses come trotting from one side to the other. Describing the scene in his diary, John Evelyn remarks that coaches plied for hire on the river from Westminster to the Temple. A printing press was set up on the ice where people paid to have their names set down with the date, and Evelyn adds that there were horse and coach races, bull baiting, puppet plays, cook-shops, tippling and 'other lewd places, so that it seemed a Bacchanalian triumph or carnival on the water, whilst it was a severe judgment on the land'.

Although Evelyn was a staunch Royalist, he also had strong religious feelings which made him condemn, like many others, the promiscuous morals of Charles II and his Court. But in 1684 the Livery Companies had other reasons for feeling that

ORDEAL BY FIRE

the Merry Monarch was behaving badly. Charles had been forced to make some major concessions to Shaftesbury's demands for reform and his campaign against the Catholics. He accepted the Habeas Corpus Act passed in 1679 and a relaxation of censorship. He also reluctantly accepted an Act of Parliament banning Catholics from sitting as members, which was only repealed in 1829 by the Duke of Wellington. But the King got the upper hand again, partly because of public reaction against the savage persecution of Catholics, and partly because the Whigs, led by Shaftesbury, pushed their demands for social reform to such extremes that they aroused fears of revolution and a renewal of civil war. Charles showed great skill in turning these feelings to his own advantage.

Tory supporters of the King regained control of local government in many parts of the country, and even in London, which supported Shaftesbury and gave him shelter after his downfall, two Tory-Sheriffs were elected in 1682. The King's party then revived an old legal device known as 'Quo Warranto', which required all corporations to justify their privileges, surrender their charters, and provide proofs of loyalty to get them renewed. In April 1684, a Court meeting of the Founders learned that a writ of 'Quo Warranto' was to be issued against the Company for the Crown.

The Court decided that a petition to the King should be drawn up with legal advice, to prevent the writ from being served and to obtain a new Charter. A committee consisting of the Master, Wardens and some others was set up for this purpose. A month later, the Master reported that the committee 'had petitioned the King and been graciously received by His Majesty'. The Court ordered that money should be raised to meet the costs of a new Charter, and that a list of the Livery and Assistants should be given to the King. In June 1684, the Court agreed that the Company's seal should be affixed to a deed surrendering the Charter which was to be delivered to the Attorney-General with the list of the Livery and Assistants. The committee was instructed to consult with counsel so as to get as many advantages as possible written into the new Charter. The City Corporation surrendered its own ancient Charter to the King, and this example was followed by almost all the Livery Companies which had one.

In October 1684, the King appointed a Royalist cavalry officer called Colonel Theophilus Oglethorpe as Master of the Founders, with John White as Deputy-Master and Anthony Giles and John Attwick as Wardens. John White had served as Master in 1677-8 and Anthony Giles as Third Warden in 1679-80, while Attwick was a Livery member. These Company men were presumably chosen because they were politically reliable and also had the experience to do the work for Oglethorpe, the Royal nominee as Master. Three other Royalist supporters, namely Colonel Edmund Mayne, Captain Charles Adderley, and Mr. John Pey, were admitted to the Founders' Livery at the same time, clearly under compulsion.

Early in 1685, however, Charles died with a characteristic apology for 'being so unconscionably long a-dying' and a whispered request to his brother James, heir to the throne, not to let 'poor Nelly' starve, meaning Nell Gwyn. It was an appeal which fell on deaf ears. So much attention has been focussed on Charles's

CITIZENS AND FOUNDERS

sexual exploits that his more serious side is often overlooked. He was a man spiritually impotent, but possessed by an excess of sensuality which made a variety of women as necessary to him as changes of wine or linen. He had resolved 'never to go on his travels again', and his policies at home and abroad were dominated by this self-interested motive. Yet his reign saw a new upsurge of scientific enquiry and rational thought in England which Charles himself did much to encourage, and a continuing expansion of English commerce overseas.

The Restoration period saw the foundation of the Royal Society by Charles II, and of the Greenwich Observatory, a landmark in astronomy. Woodward was formulating the science of mineralogy and Boyle's air pump was breaking new ground in the study of pneumatics. Above all, this was the age of Isaac Newton, Professor of Mathematics at Cambridge and pioneer in the laws of gravity. At the same time, the great trading companies of merchant venturers were extending their markets overseas, and many leading men in government and politics were glad to be associated with them. Charles's brother and heir, James, Duke of York, was Governor of the Royal Africa Company and a shareholder in the East India Company, whose stock rose in 1685 to five times its par value and showed annual returns of between 20 and 40 per cent for 30 years after the Restoration. James also succeeded Prince Rupert as Governor of the Hudson's Bay Company, and was followed in that office by the great Duke of Marlborough.

There was still a great deal of poverty in England, and in 1688 a contemporary observer, Gregory King, estimated that one million people, nearly a fifth of the population at that time, were periodically in receipt of alms. A much improved system of parish relief helped to meet these needs but often caused hardship, because its cost was so high that a family which moved to a new parish might be refused admission or sent back to their old parish if they looked like becoming a charge on the local rates.

The City of London remained the greatest port and trading centre in the kingdom, or even in the world. By 1700, its population had risen to more than half a million, or well over one-tenth of the national figure. Its wealthy merchant princes were courted and flattered by men in high office. Samuel Pepys, Secretary of the Navy, was a well-known and popular figure in the City, and his diary mentions many visits to it. He was elected Master of the Clothworkers' Company and presented them with a handsome cup. Political control of the City and its immense resources was the prize sought by Charles II when he launched his threat of 'Quo Warranto' against the City Corporation and the Livery Companies. His successor, James II, adopted the same policy, but he lacked the political insight and sense of realities which enabled Charles to weather the storms of his own reign, and in a few short years he destroyed the Stuart dynasty.

CHAPTER X

False Colours

CHARLES having died without legal issue, the Crown passed to his brother, James, Duke of York, and this immediately revived the explosive question of the King's religion. Charles was reconciled to the Catholic Church on his deathbed, but during his lifetime his shrewd political sense, coupled with his own easy-going habits of tolerance, made him let sleeping dogs lie, and he avoided a confrontation with his own people which he knew could very easily cost him his throne. At the same time, although James was an avowed Catholic, Charles stoutly defended his right of succession and managed, at considerable risk to himself, to block the passage of an Act of Parliament introduced by Shaftesbury to exclude James from his inheritance. The fact that James was known to be an ardent Catholic was serious enough, but his stiff and stubborn assertion of divine right did even more to precipitate that ruin of Stuart fortunes which Charles had striven to prevent.

James immediately pushed on with the use of Quo Warranto writs initiated by Charles to impose the King's will on the City of London, but in a much rougher fashion. Immediately after his accession in 1685, he ordered the Lord Mayor to issue instructions to the Livery Companies requiring them to choose only 'loyal and worthy members' to elect the City representatives in Parliament. The Masters, Wardens and Assistants were compelled to surrender all their rights, titles or interests so that their offices could be filled by men on whom the King could rely. The names of Wardens and Clerks were first to be submitted to the King, and only if they were approved under the Sign Manual or Privy Signet could they then proceed to take their oaths of allegiance. If they were rejected, the Court of Assistants had to go on proposing others until the King was satisfied.

James also reserved the right to remove by an order of the Privy Council any Warden, Assistant or Clerk who displeased him. All elections of officers by the Companies was subject to approval by a Lord Mayor and Court of Aldermen with Royalist sympathies. These were acts of despotism which trampled underfoot the self-governing rights so long enjoyed by the City, but when the Lord Mayor and Aldermen submitted to them, the Livery Companies could hardly do otherwise than follow suit.

The Master, Wardens and Assistants of the Founders surrendered their offices to the new King in March 1685. In May that year, the Company submitted a list of nominations for the Livery which the Lord Mayor and Aldermen approved,

116   CITIZENS AND FOUNDERS

but with a warning that they were to be informed if any Liveryman omitted to take the oath of allegiance. The list was headed by Oglethorpe, the Royalist officer imposed on the Company as Master before Charles II died. He had previously commanded the new King's troop of Horse Guards when James was Duke of York. He was a cavalry leader in the Royal army under John Churchill, later Duke of Marlborough, which routed the Protestant Duke of Monmouth at Sedgemoor in July 1685. Unlike John Churchill, Oglethorpe remained loyal to James after the King's abdication and flight in 1688, and he had to go into hiding to escape arrest. He was eventually reconciled with William and Mary, served as Deputy-Lieutenant for Surrey, sat in the Commons as member for Haslemere, and died in 1701, being buried in St. James's church, Piccadilly.

The other names on the Company's list were obviously those of its members who were considered politically reliable as supporters of James. The full list was as follows :

Master: Colonel Hon. Theophilus Oglethorpe.

Wardens: Richard Meakins, Henry Warren.

Assistants: John White, Thomas Aylward, John Underwood, Henry Hemings, William Rutter, John Prince, Thomas Hawgood, Thomas Watson, Edmund Read, William Walmsley.

Livery: Owen Humphries, Daniel Sturmer, Matthew Beaver, James Bartlett, Nathaniel Stringer, Richard Plaister, John Bugden, Lawrence Pinder, William Rogers, Richard Symons, George Clarke, Ezekiel Gibbs.

Except for Oglethorpe, nearly all these men are mentioned in the closing years of the Wardens' Accounts as members of the Founders' Company, and a few had served as Master or Warden. It is significant, however, that the names on the list are much fewer in number than the normal strength of the Court and Livery. They do not include the Masters for 1679-80 and 1680-1, Daniel Houghton and Peter Causton, nor the names of 13 out of 14 men who are recorded in the Accounts as having been elected to the Livery in those two years. Some may have died before 1685, but the omissions are sufficiently numerous to suggest that a fair number of Assistants and Liverymen were either rejected because their loyalty to James was suspect, or themselves refused to bow the knee. Some of these missing names reappear with distinction in later years, notably that of Noah Delaunay, and their exclusion did not last long.

On the other hand, several of the men who agreed to serve under Oglethorpe later proved unworthy of their trust, as we shall see in due course. Owen Humphries was an ale-house keeper whose misconduct later did serious damage to the Company. Thomas Aylward, Master in 1700-1, was dismissed by the Court of Assistants for abusing his office. John White cheated the Company by pocketing fees he received when he was Master, and so did Henry Hemings. These men were later the cause of a crisis in the Company's affairs which nearly wrecked it.

FALSE COLOURS

In supporting James II, however, they backed a born loser. James set about his work with a reckless arrogance which was his own undoing. He made it clear that he was determined to restore Catholic supremacy in England and crush all opposition. He turned to the Irish Catholics for support and maintained a standing army camped at Hounslow to threaten London. He revenged himself for Monmouth's rebellion not only by executing its leader, but by inflicting on his deluded followers all the bloody savagery and mockery of justice handed out by the infamous Judge Jeffreys. In short, he made treason not only respectable, but a patriotic duty, and achieved the almost impossible task of uniting both Tories and Whigs against him.

A group of influential English magnates invited the Dutch Protestant leader, Prince William of Orange, to mount an invasion. William, who had married James's daughter and heiress, Mary, was chiefly interested in mobilising English resources for his struggle against Catholic domination in Europe, and he answered the call. He landed at Torbay in November 1688, with a large army and met no serious resistance. The 'Glorious Revolution' was accomplished with very little bloodshed. James was deserted by almost all around him, but was sensibly allowed to make his escape to France, where he found refuge with Louis XIV. As William refused to act merely as Regent, and Mary would not accept the Crown unless she shared it with William, they both pledged themselves to maintain English liberties and ruled as joint sovereigns. But it was William who held the real power.

The news of William's preparations for invasion had already persuaded James to try and save himself at the last moment by revoking his most oppressive measures, and the Corporation of London received its Charter back in triumph before William landed. The City Companies regained their own Charters, but they had paid a heavy price. The Founders spent £280 in their efforts to get a new Charter from Charles II in 1684. They paid a fee of £50 to a lawyer called 'Mr. Burton' and gave him another £165 to pay for the Charter, which was presumably the King's price for granting it. The Attorney-General received £16 for his fees and the Common Sergeant's advice cost the Company £2 2s. Another £26 was spent, unsuccessfully, on 'getting some additions to the Charter', and a visit to the King at Windsor by Master and Wardens cost £8, of which £2 10s. was for hiring a coach. All the Company had to show for it when the crisis ended was the restoration of its old Charter and a new set of Ordinances approved by the Lord Chancellor at a further cost of nearly £66.

Oglethorpe's brief reign as a usurping Master was also expensive. In September 1687, the Wardens were ordered to pay him their office fines of £8 a piece, and it was further ordered that Oglethorpe, and not the Wardens, was to keep 'all payments and reckonings'. A month later, perhaps as a result of protests, he agreed to refund part of a Warden's office fine if he dismissed him, but even this concession shows that Oglethorpe had taken such dismissals into his own hands. Such treatment can hardly have encouraged the Wardens to carry out their duties cheerfully or efficiently, and it may well have caused a neglect on their part in collecting Company dues and fines which added to the financial strain.

A curious episode occurred in February 1685, when the Court ordered that 'all

118   CITIZENS AND FOUNDERS

the four persons now chosen Assistants', before being admitted, should give a pair
of Cordovan gloves, made of fine Spanish leather, to the Master, Wardens, Assistants and Clerk of the Company. This was described as 'a token of brotherly love
and friendship', and the same rule was to apply to all who were thereafter chosen
as Assistants. But it was an expensive present and the Company's records show no
earlier precedent for it. The order was issued only a month or so before the legally-
elected Court was forced to hand over all offices to James II's nominees, and the
four new Assistants mentioned in it may well have been the four King's men
forcibly admitted to the Livery in October 1684, namely Oglethorpe himself,
Colonel Mayne, Captain Adderley and John Pey. If so, it was a pleasant stroke
of irony and malice for the Court to demand these costly gifts of gloves from the
intruders, even though the chances of their producing them must have been small.

The Company got its Charter back, but it emerged from these troubles heavily
in debt and divided within itself. There were wounds which needed healing and
injuries to the Company not easily forgotten or forgiven. This helps to explain why,
during the reign of William and Mary from 1689 to 1702, the Founders went
through a period of internal trouble, largely self-inflicted, which could have proved
fatal to their continued existence. Unhappily for the historian, the termination of
the Wardens' Accounts in 1681 removed the most detailed and fruitful source of
information about the Company's affairs, and the story of later years can only be
pieced together from scattered entries in such Court books and Guildhall references as have survived. The extracts made by Williams in his *Annals* are of great
value in helping us to reconstruct the main sequence of events.

An indication of the Company's financial problems is given in a Court order of
September 1689, which instructed the Master to 'treat with Mr. Skinner, a member of this Company, or any other person, for them to fine for all offices and to
raise so much money for the Company's use as he shall reasonably think fit'. The
intention here was that the Master should obtain more cash by asking Liverymen
to pay fines in return for their exemption from being chosen for office, or possibly
as advance payments if they later agreed to serve. It was not the first time such
methods had been used, and its success depended on a careful choice of the more
prosperous Liverymen who might be able and willing to pay the fine. In 1673-4,
two Liverymen called Gregory and Ducke, or Duke, paid £21 10s. and £10
respectively for exemption from all offices, and a year later another Liveryman
called Munt, or Mount, paid £10 to be excused. A 'Mr. Skinner' appears in the
Wardens' Accounts for 1673 to 1675 as a tenant paying a yearly rent of £15 'for
the use of the Hall', which suggests that he was a man of some means. He may
well have been the Liveryman named in the Court's order as a likely target.

Despite its financial difficulties, the Company made a payment of £9 10s. in
1693 to 'the Church Warden for pewing St. Margaret Church and all differences',
which may also refer to a settlement of arrears in parish rates. In 1695, however,
the Master informed the Court that, on account of the debts owed by the Company, he had cancelled the dinners usually held on quarter-days. He also advised
the Court to make an order against 'feasting' except on Lord Mayor's Day. The
Court decided that the 'usual diet' should be provided on Lord Mayor's Day, but

FALSE COLOURS 119

that no Master or Warden should spend more than 10s. on quarter-days or any other occasion, and that not more than 20s. should be spent on the Audit dinner. It also ordered that 'the usual manner of bread, butter, cheese, drink, and other things that hath been at the Hall for breakfast at Quarter or other days shall be paid by the Master as formerly, and not reckoned part of the 10 shillings; and that three pounds yearly be paid to the Clerk, and one pound ten shillings to the Beadle, in lieu of money that used to be given at Candlemas'.

In July 1690, the Lord Mayor called on the Livery Companies to provide money for raising 'one Regiment of Horse and one Regiment of Dragoons' for the service of William and Mary. William was then mustering troops at Hounslow to reinforce the English expeditionary force which had been sent to Flanders under John Churchill, whose later campaigns were to win him fame and fortune as Marlborough. This was a time of great danger on several different fronts. The exiled King, James II, had landed in Ireland with French troops, and the Irish Catholics were again butchering the Protestant settlers. The siege of Londonderry was beaten off by a heroic defence, and in July 1690, William defeated James at the Battle of the Boyne, forcing him to escape again to France.

In William's absence from England, a French fleet under Tourville appeared off the coast of Devon and landed sailors who burned Teignmouth. A French army of invasion was assembled in Normandy, but this threat was ended by an English naval victory at La Hogue. In Scotland, the Highland clansmen took up arms for James, but were crushed by Scottish Lowland forces which took William's side and slaughtered the Macdonalds in the Glencoe massacre in 1692.

The Founders were too poor to make much of a contribution to the Lord Mayor's call for military aid, but did what little they could, as recorded in a Court minute:

It was taken into consideration that the Company having no stock, but being six hundred pounds in debt, yet nevertheless considering the imminent danger that may ensue, it is ordered that the Master shall provide a good and able horse and man to serve in Their Majesties' service, according to the order of the Common Council dated the 10th of this instant July.

To add to the Company's financial difficulties, a storm was now brewing over its head from within its own midst. Its immediate cause was misconduct by the Clerk, James Dickinson, and the Beadle, John Martin, which was not exposed until they were both dismissed by the Court in 1696, as will be related hereafter. Much of the trouble, however, seems to have been due to neglect and mismanagement by the Court in earlier years. This was largely due to the change from the past, when most Masters and Wardens were working founders experienced in the craft and the Clerk and the Beadle played a relatively small part, to a new order in which the men who governed the Company were mainly, if not entirely, engaged in other occupations and therefore more inclined to delegate Company business to the Clerk or Beadle. To see this process at work, we must go back some way in time.

The Company has had many loyal and devoted Clerks and Beadles in its long history. The only man referred to affectionately by his Christian name in the

CITIZENS AND FOUNDERS

Wardens' Accounts from 1497 to 1681 is Charles Campion, who succeeded John Bradley as Beadle in 1640-1, when Richard Weoley was Master, and served until his death in 1668-9. But a notable change occurred in the Clerk's position in 1640, when that office was held by John Falkener. Up to that time, the yearly receipts and payments were accounted for to the Auditors by the Master and Wardens, according to the way their work was divided, but from thereon the Clerk rendered a separate account. Falkener's accounts shown not only his receipts from the sizing of weights, previously listed by the Master, but also a wide range of additional items which, in some years, included payment of taxes and parish rates, costs of Hall repairs and maintenance, income from rents, receipts from fees for binding apprentices, and fines paid by Stewards and by freemen for election to the Livery.

Falkener had a long innings as Clerk, and William Basspoole, who followed him in 1645, also rendered a separate account covering much the same tasks, as did Francis Lambert, who replaced Basspoole as Clerk in 1662-3. There is no evidence in the Accounts to justify any charge of dishonesty on their part, but it seems fairly clear that an increasing amount of work was transferred over these years from the Master and Wardens to the Clerk, and that this created potential opportunities for defrauding the Company with a good chance of avoiding detection.

This was the situation when James Dickinson was appointed as Clerk in 1679 in place of Lambert, and it was Dickinson who triggered the time-bomb which blew up in the Company's face. The first hint of uneasiness appears in 1692, when the Court reappointed Dickinson as Clerk, but with the condition that neither he nor his family should live in the Hall. Sarah Shurley was confirmed as 'housekeeper' to the Company, giving security for the Hall goods and chattels, and she was allowed the money 'which is given by the Meeting and Dancing quarterly'. This presumably referred to small payments made by Hall users for cleaning, and not to the rents they paid.

Four years later, in December 1696, the Court suspended Dickinson from his duties 'until such time as he can discharge himself of the crimes laid to his charge', and the Beadle, John Martin, was dismissed outright. At the same time, the Court agreed that 'the Master and Wardens be indemnified and kept harmless, and their charges and expenses that they shall expend on behalf of the Company paid, provided they act by the advice of this Court'. No further details were given, but the Court was obviously expecting trouble.

They did not have long to wait. In April 1697, the Court of Aldermen ordered the Master, Wardens and Assistants of the Founders not to proceed with the election of a new Clerk until the Lord Mayor and Aldermen had received the report of a committee set up to examine 'some irregularities' in the Company. The Company submitted answers to the charges which were examined by the Guildhall committee, but they evidently made no impression. On 25 November 1697, a black day for the Founders, the committee issued a damning report which not only condemned Dickinson, but also made grave accusations against the governors of the Company. It read as follows:

FALSE COLOURS

We whose names are under-written have further examined into the several disorders of the Company of Founders and the mismanagement of the government of the said Company, and do find : That the Master, Wardens, and Court of Assistants have in no way regarded the end and institution of the said Company, that is of so great influence to the good or mischief of the public weal as they are entrusted with the examination, sizing, and marking of all brass weights and of brass and copper works made within three miles compass, and of all brass weights made beyond the seas and brought into the City of London or three miles compass. But the said Master and Wardens have filled their Court of Assistants chiefly with unskilful members that have not been bred to the art and mystery of the Founders, and with great partiality have kept out those that have been bred to the trade, and who by seniority ought to have been admitted.

That the late Master, Owen Humphries, was an ale-house keeper and not only cheated the City of his own freedom, but made several others free who had not served him, and bought false weights of a foreigner; and notwithstanding diligent search should be made in all shops and warehouses, the Master and Wardens have greatly neglected their duty therein.

And further, we find many false weights have been sold which are marked with the Founders' mark; and so greatly negligent have the Court been that persons altogether unfaithful and unskilful have been entrusted to size and seal the weights, so that several thousands of weights have been marked that never were sized or examined.

We also find that the late Clerk, Dickinson, hath been guilty of many enormous practices, entering persons bound long before he came to be Clerk, helping to give surreptitious freedoms, as well of the City as of the said Company, for which he stands indicted but could not be brought to justice, the Court of Assistants sheltering him. And further we find by their books that several of the late Masters have cheated the Company. In 1685, one White made free twenty-one and accounted only for nine; bound forty-one and accounted for twenty-two. In 1691, one Hemings bound forty-six and accounted only for fourteen, and several others of the like nature. The same persons that have thus cheated and defrauded the Company are still continued upon the Court of Assistants, etc.

Further we find that they have admitted persons of their Livery who were never free of the City, restraining some as to the number of their apprentices and granting exorbitant liberty to others : so that one person hath bound ten in ten years, etc. All which abuses of the Company, of the City, with the high contempt and insolence offered to this Court, we do with all submission represent for remedy, as this honourable Court in their grave wisdom shall think fit.

Thomas Lane   William Hedges
Owen Buckingham Ric. Levett

122 CITIZENS AND FOUNDERS

Although this report describes Owen Humphries as 'late Master', he does not appear as such in the Company's records, and he may have died or resigned soon after taking office. In pointing out that the Founders had filled their Court of Assistants with men not bred to the Company's trade, the Aldermen's committee correctly diagnosed the root cause of the trouble. As noted earlier, the exclusion of working founders from the Livery was one of the main grievances voiced by the Yeomanry rebels in 1652. It was the failure of later Courts to heed this warning, and their neglect of adequate supervision over the work of the Clerk and Beadle, that invited disaster. The fact that other City Companies were suffering from the same errors did not excuse the Founders, nor could it disguise the fact that their own Masters and Wardens had been found corrupt.

After reading the committee's report, the Court of Aldermen summoned the 'complainants' and the Master, Wardens and all the Assistants to appear before them, together with their former Clerk, Dickinson, and to bring their Court books and other records. At a meeting in December 1697, the Aldermen found the case against the Master, Wardens and Assistants 'fully proved' and ordered them to appear shortly after to answer the charges. Apparently they simply ignored this summons, as, in October 1698, the Aldermen resumed 'the debate of the many abuses and mismanagement of this Company', when they ordered that no person should receive the freedom of the City as a member of the Founders, and that those entitled to it should be admitted to some other Company. Faced with this ultimatum, the Court of Assistants at last came to its senses and humbly petitioned the Aldermen for the return of the Company's books, promising that no further misdemeanours would take place so far as lay in their power. The Court also decided to intercede with the Aldermen through the Common Sergeant or such other Counsel as might be deemed advisable.

On 10 November 1698, the Court of Aldermen was informed that the Master and Wardens of the Founders were resolved to make their humble submission, 'being at last sensible of their many frauds and abuses in their trade, as well as of their contempt and misdemeanour to this Court'. But this was still not the end of the matter. The Aldermen also had a petition from 'several of the Livery and others of the trade' praying them not to receive the Master and Wardens until the grievances laid against them were redressed. This led to further hearings attended by both sides which continued until the end of July 1699, when the Aldermen adopted a further report by their committee of enquiry, containing the following proposals which had been agreed by all concerned :

1. That all bindings and making free should be done as of ancient custom at the monthly Court in the presence of the Master, Wardens, and Assistants, and nowhere else.
2. That such fines as were recognised by ancient usage and by the bye-laws, and no other, should be taken.
3. That all brass weights should be sized according to the Charter etc., and

FALSE COLOURS
123

that honest and able men should be deputed for that trust, fees to be taken according to ancient usage.

4. That the accounts should be 'fairly entered in a book' and audited at least once a year.

5. That £5 should be paid from the Company's stock to refund expenses incurred by Livery and Yeomanry members in the dispute.

The Aldermen then ordered that the Company's books should be returned to the Master.

Although these proposals called for nothing more than the observance of rules which the Court had flagrantly ignored, they produced no improvement. The Master, Wardens, and Assistants had got off so lightly that it seems to have encouraged them to persist in bad habits. Only three months later, in October 1699, they issued a Court order granting the new Clerk, John Humphries (not to be confused with Owen Humphries, but perhaps related to him) a fee of 4s. for every binding of an apprentice and half the money received for sizing weights, while awarding the Beadle a shilling for every binding and making free. The order added that, if the Clerk bound any apprentice out of Court, he should be paid for his 'extraordinary trouble'. This order showed a total disregard for the ruling of the Aldermen that all bindings and admissions to the freedom should be performed at the monthly Court meeting in the presence of the Master, Wardens and Assistants, but it seems to have passed without comment or objection either in the Company or the Court of Aldermen. Only a month later, in November 1699, the Aldermen lifted their ban on admissions to the City Freedom through membership of the Founders.

The new Clerk, John Humphries, turned out to be a rogue like his predecessor, Dickinson. He started off virtuously enough by going to Guildhall in February 1700 with several members of the Company who laid information before the Court of Aldermen against Dickinson. They accused him of practising 'fraud and collusion' by making Roger Fleming and many others free of the City illegally. The Aldermen decided that Dickinson should be prosecuted at the City's expense. A year later, Humphries was dismissed by the Court of Assistants for 'evil practices', unspecified, in which the Master for 1700-1, Thomas Aylward, and the Upper Warden that year, Timothy Lee, were also involved. This fresh scandal is described in the Court minutes made at the time.

The affair started harmlessly enough when Aylward, who had apparently lent the Company some money on behalf of his daughter, Mrs. Evans, offered to advance a further £150 at five per cent interest in her name. The Court agreed and gave the Company's bond for this amount, in addition to what had already been borrowed, but only a part of the money was forthcoming. Several of the Company's creditors then started complaining, upon which 'Mr. Aylward grew weary and shy of meeting any of the old Masters'. He and the Upper Warden and the Clerk 'bound and made free of themselves and ordered the Company as they thought

CITIZENS AND FOUNDERS

fit. And the Master having done ill himself, as much as in him lay protected the Clerk in his evil practices, who had very much wronged the Company'. At the quarter-day Court in May 1701, Aylward declared that Humphries should be Clerk while he was Master, and that he would keep no more Courts in his year of office.

No Court was held on the first Monday in June, as was the usual custom, and as there were some requests for persons to be bound as apprentices or to be made freemen, several of the old Masters consulted together and wrote to the Master, Aylward. He then came to the Hall and promised that in future he would keep Court in the normal manner. He also asked for a written statement of the charges against the Clerk. Matters came to a head at the Court meeting on Midsummer Day in July.

Humphries, the Clerk, was asked at that meeting what he had to say in his own defence, but he asked for his case to be put by a lawyer whom he had brought with him. The majority of the Court wanted him to answer personally, and somebody remarked that 'the Court were all tradesmen, and he an attorney-at-law'. The Master and Wardens insisted on hearing the legal adviser brought by Humphries, but this was not much help to his defence, as the lawyer only said that the Clerk should 'ask all their pardons and promise to be good for the future'. The Court wanted to proceed with the case against Humphries, but the Master, Aylward, then adjourned the meeting. The Assistants protested and themselves consulted counsel, who told them that they might turn the Master and Clerk out and choose others. They decided to wait until the election-day Court, which was not far off.

That meeting was attended by the Master, Wardens, and 13 Assistants. Two nominations for the choice of a new Master were put forward, one being an Assistant called Rogers and the other being Noah Delaunay. Aylward objected to Delaunay's nomination and threatened to adjourn the Court unless it was withdrawn. A senior Assistant then got up and called on all those in favour of proposing Delaunay, as well as Rogers, to raise their hands, whereupon all 13 assistants did so. The Master and Wardens then withdrew to the *King's Head* Tavern, but not before the same senior Assistant had called for a vote, which was unanimously in favour of Delaunay as the new Master. John Humphries, the Clerk, who walked out with Aylward and the Wardens, was sent for but refused to come, 'for which neglect and contempt, and for other crimes, he was dismissed from his office of Clerk for ever'.

Before Aylward's year as Master was up, a further Court meeting took place at which the Master-elect, Delaunay, asked for the books and Charter to be laid on the table, according to custom, so that the choice of Stewards and other offices could be settled. Aylward replied that the Clerk had them and refused to ask Humphries for them unless he was reinstated. The Court then gave notice to the Company's tenants not to pay any rents till further notice, and Delaunay summoned Aylward and Humphries before the Lord Mayor, who left it to the Company to reach agreement. Aylward still refused to hand over the books and declared that he would destroy the Charter. He did not attend the 'swearing-in' Court which confirmed Delaunay as Master for 1701-2.

FALSE COLOURS

The records do not specify the charges against Humphries, as Clerk, nor do they mention any arguments which Aylward and Humphries may have advanced in their own defence. It is clear, however, that the Assistants felt that the charges against them were justified and were equally convinced that Delaunay was the best man to put matters right. He had already been Master in 1698-9. Three days after he again took office, the Court unanimously agreed that it would endeavour to maintain the rights and privileges of the Company; and that if any action or charge was brought against any member of the Company by the late Master, Thomas Aylward, the Upper Warden, Timothy Lee, or John Humphries, the former Clerk, the Court would 'defend and keep harmless every such member at the expense of the Company'.

Noah Delaunay was again re-elected as Master in 1702-3 and thus bore the main responsibility for nursing the Company back to health and strength. He received the key of the chest from Aylward at a Court meeting in November 1701, when Aylward also handed over his accounts for the previous year to the senior Auditor. A paper making allegations about several members of the Court and drawn up by Humphries was shown to Aylward, who was asked if they were true. He declared that most of them were false. The old trouble reappeared in March 1702, when the Court of Aldermen held another meeting to hear complaints of 'fraudulent practices used in the Company of Founders, and particularly in obtaining freedoms for several persons by deceits'. The Company's books were called in by the Aldermen for inspection and afterwards returned to the late Master, Aylward, who seems to have still held on to them at that time. Why they were given back to him, and not to the new Master, Delaunay, is a mystery, but the Aldermen seem to have taken no further action.

There are entries in the Court extracts at this time which indicate that Delaunay set about restoring order with a firm hand and was a man who stood no nonsense. His payments as Master in 1702 included the costs of taking out warrants against Aylward and Humphries; summonses to bring the Stewards before the Lord Mayor for refusing to provide a dinner or to pay their fines; money spent at the Lord Mayor's court to oblige the Wardens to pay their fines; a payment to the officers at the Poultry prison; and another payment made 'for obliging Mr. Turner to come on the Livery'. Delaunay also paid money for the arrest of five men who broke into the Hall. In lighter vein, he bought for the Company five legs of pork and a sirloin and ribs of beef for a Company breakfast on Lord Mayor's Day; and another item in his accounts was for 'music, three Trumpets, and a Kettle Drum'.

Under Delaunay's leadership, the Court took steps to enforce obedience to the Company's rules. In August 1702, an order was issued summoning every member to pay the statutory sum of 12d. quarterly for his dues, and all Masters and Wardens were required to pay their fines of £8 each before being sworn. Every Master, before being sworn, was to 'give and sign a bond and give security to the Company according to custom'. The Court added a new rule whereby any person chosen as Clerk must in future give a bond for £200 and 'security for his good service', as well as a written undertaking to resign and quit the Hall within 14 days if the Court so ordered.

126   CITIZENS AND FOUNDERS

In September 1702, the Court fixed a salary of £12 for the next Clerk and his successors, supplemented by a fee of 2s. 6d. for binding an apprentice and the same for making a member free. Later that month, they interviewed 12 candidates for the post of Clerk made vacant by the dismissal of Humphries, and appointed Joshua Hadfield. In August 1703, the Court resolved to 'stand and act by and fully maintain the Charter and Ordinances'. The Court also declared that Thomas Aylward, Timothy Lee, and others, had been 'enemies to the Court' and should not be nominated for any office in future.

In September 1703, the Clerk who had been dismissed, John Humphries, appeared before the Court, having been brought there from the Fleet prison to which he had been committed. Humphries acknowledged his 'former crimes and misdemeanours' and begged pardon of the Master, Wardens and Assistants. The Court then ordered his release from prison on the understanding that he was to pay all the fees. There was another echo of the past in 1706, when Timothy Lee, who had been Upper Warden under Aylward, was dismissed from the Court of Assistants. He, and others, were charged with having been 'consenting and accessory to the carrying away of the Company's books etc. to the great prejudice of the Company'. Lee was also charged with 'having scandalously reflected upon several members of the Company when summoned before the Lord Mayor for non-payment of his quarterage'. Another Assistant, Downton Bridges, was alleged to have been a party to the removal of the books, but pleaded that he had acted 'not wilfully but innocently'. He was allowed to remain an Assistant, but was excluded from nomination for Master or any other office.

This seems to have been the end of the Aylward affair, but it left the Company in poor shape financially. So much so that in February 1703, the Court offered to admit as Assistants any four members of the Company willing to serve and to pay their fees in advance. At the same time, when Delaunay was Master, the Court took steps to tighten up its own discipline and to enforce the principle of collective responsibility for its decisions. In March 1703, it was resolved that some Assistants who had failed to attend a Court meeting should 'pay the forfeitures for not appearing this day according to the laws and ordinances of the Company, and shall not be admitted to sit any more in this Court until they shall have paid the same'. The Court also decided that 'what order or orders shall for the future be made by the Court of Assistants of this Company shall be entered in the book of orders of this Company, and the next Court day may be read by the Clerk to the said Court; which said order or orders shall be as binding as if the Assistants had set their hands to the said order, as formerly hath been used by them'.

In October 1703, when Delaunay's two-year tenure of office was nearly ended, the Court ordered that every Assistant should have a free choice in electing a Master. It also issued a further order which has a touch of Delaunay about it and ran as follows:

This Court having taken into consideration the affairs of the Company, and how easy it is to run into debt but hard to get out, and the Company being

FALSE COLOURS

willing to do what in them lieth to preserve and maintain not only the Hall, but also all the rights and privileges for the future, one good expedient, they think, will be to take care that the Company shall not run into debt for the future. They therefore order that if any Master or Warden or others shall lay out or expend, without special order, more moneys than the Company's income will pay, such expense shall not be allowed them, but they shall pay the same out of their own private stock.

The last Court order recorded before Delaunay finished his third term as Master, and dated 18 October 1703, imposed a forfeit of 6d. to the Poor Box 'if any member shall presume to speak or give his opinion in Court upon any matter without leave of the Master, or shall interrupt any person or persons of the Assistants speaking'. There may well be occasions, even in our own permissive society, when such an order could be usefully revived.

The Auditors recorded a warm acknowledgment of Delaunay's services in the following terms:

We, the Auditors elected and chosen by the Worshipful Company of Founders to audit the accounts of Mr. Noah Delaunay, Master of the said Company, have read and perused the whole accounts, receipts, and disbursements, and do not only allow and approve the said accounts to be just and reasonable, but do highly commend his good husbanding, industry, and diligence; and who, notwithstanding the charge in law, hath bought a handsome carpet for the Parlour table, a new Cloth for the Stand in Cheapside, paid off all the Company's old debts, which come to £105 2s. 6d., and paid off Underwood's bond of £23 6s. 9d. of thirteen years standing, and left the Company out of debt.

Delaunay served a fourth and final year as Master in 1708-9, and the Company has had few Masters who guided it so well through stormy weather. It was largely due to his efforts that the Founders could now move more easily into the calmer waters of the Georgian era.

CHAPTER XI

A Georgian Summer

IF HUMAN HAPPINESS is measured in terms of motor-cars, television sets, refrigerators, and other mechanical aids to living, then 18th-century England must suffer by comparison with our own age, but it had many compensations which have since been lost. The vast majority of ordinary men and women were untouched by war, which passed them by, and free from the nightmare of nuclear extermination. They lived in a green and pleasant land where the air was clean, the rivers unpolluted, and the balance between man and his natural environment still harmonious. It was a century of reform and progress in many fields, but change was effected by consent, not coercion, and it was slow enough for new ideas and methods to be adopted without throwing away what was good in the older order. English political liberties were far more restricted than they are today, but Parliamentary government was held in far higher respect and the feudal baron had not yet reappeared in the shape of our powerful trade union leaders who can hold governments up to ransom and break them if they show resistance.

The Georgian period was the first to show a serious concern for public education. Although some of the old grammar schools fell into decay, new independent schools were founded which provided secondary education at modest fees for pupils of all classes, and which taught modern languages and science as well as Latin and Greek studies. The Church of England founded many 'charity schools' for poor children where they received a simple primary education and were later apprenticed to trades which gave them a decent living. These schools did not depend on a few wealthy patrons, but collected subscriptions from small shopkeepers and artisans who were expected to take a parental interest in the school and take part in its affairs. They were the pioneers of that 'parent participation' which is now a leading educational issue.

Education had not yet become a function of local government, and there were no parish schools. At Oxford and Cambridge, higher education went through a period of decay, becoming so bad and expensive that the number of university students fell to less than half those in residence a century earlier. By 1773, Oxford degrees were being awarded without any serious examination, while at Cambridge no Regius Professor of History delivered a lecture between 1725 and 1773. Nevertheless, comparing Georgian education with our own far more lavish facilities, G. M. Trevelyan remarks in his *History of England* : 'The product of genius per

A GEORGIAN SUMMER

head of population in Eighteenth Century England seems, by comparison with our own day, to have been in inverse proportion to the amount of education supplied'.

Public health was neglected by Georgian governments and parliaments, but medical science improved and many new hospitals were founded by private endowments, among them being Guy's, Westminster, St. George's, London and Middlesex, which all began between 1725 and 1773. Efforts were made to check the appalling rate of infant mortality, and Coram's Foundling Hospital was endowed in 1745. The Black Death or bubonic plague died out for reasons variously described, but probably due more than anything else to an improvement in housing and public health. Smallpox continued to take a heavy toll and accounted for one death in every 13 until Jenner's discovery of vaccination at the end of the 18th century.

A new scourge arose in the sale of cheap gin, vividly depicted by Hogarth's drawings, which led medical opinion to attribute one death in eight in London to drinking raw spirits. This evil was checked by putting high taxes on spirits and by the import of tea, a softer option which soon became popular among all classes. Between 1756 and 1821, the population of greater London rose from 674,000 to over one and a quarter million, helped by a small rise in the birth rate but much more by a halving of the death rate.

A common hazard of daily life was the spread of violent crime. Armed robbery, murder, and prostitution flourished, and in London the notorious Jonathan Wild for many years led a double life both as a thief-catcher and as an organiser of crime and receiver of stolen goods until his execution in 1725. The roads were infested by highwaymen and in 1775, when seven of them held up the coach from London to Norwich, the guard killed three with his blunderbuss before being killed himself. No less than 400 Acts for building new roads were passed between 1700 and 1750, but this was also a great age for canals which provided cheap transport both for industry and agriculture.

In the more rational atmosphere of Georgian England, the long and deadly feud between Catholics and Protestants gave way to a milder climate of religious toleration, but the Puritan tradition still asserted itself in the horrors of the English Sunday. A German visitor to London in 1710 noted that all he could do on a Sunday afternoon was to join the crowds walking in St. James's Park. No public entertainments or games were allowed, all public-houses were closed, and his landlady would not even let a flute be played in her house for fear of prosecution. He remarked that Sunday observance was the only visible sign that the English were Christians.

London was spreading far beyond the old City limits and expanding also in wealth and commerce. The London docks handled not only cargoes of saltpetre, spices, and silks from China and India, but new imports of tea, porcelain, and woven cloth. The London merchants and bankers also bought and sold human flesh in the barbarous traffic of the slave trade. In one year alone, 1771, 58 slave-trading ships sailed from London, 23 from Bristol, and 107 from Liverpool, carry-

130   CITIZENS AND FOUNDERS

ing Lancashire cotton goods and other cheap manufactures to Africa, where they were exchanged for 50,000 negro slaves who were transported to the West Indies and the American colonies. There the ships loaded cargoes of raw cotton, tobacco and sugar before returning home. The present writer well remembers, as a young man working in the Bank of England, coming across old ledgers giving details of slave-trading by Sir John Houblon, an 18th-century Governor of the Bank, with entries showing the profits from each voyage and the number of slaves who died and were thrown overboard.

The old City of London continued to enjoy its rights of self-government in a democratic form which, though limited in modern terms, were still ahead of their times. The Lord Mayor and Aldermen who controlled the administration and the Common Council were elected by 12,000 rate-paying householders who were nearly all Liverymen of the City Companies, but included many small shopkeepers and craftsmen as well as the more prosperous merchants. The Lord Mayor's authority as 'Conservator' of the Thames ran as far as Gravesend, Tilbury and the bridge at Staines. The jurisdiction of the City magistrates extended to Southwark and Middlesex. The Tower of London was no longer a fortress from which kings could threaten London, but was used as an arsenal supplying cannon and gun-powder for Marlborough's campaigns in Europe, and housing the Royal Mint, which had a famous scientist, Sir Isaac Newton, as its Master.

The City was the most densely populated plot of earth in England, where merchants and artisans still slept 'over the shop' in their houses, with attics and basements where apprentices were lodged and also used as dormitories and warehouses for goods, porters and messengers. The more affluent merchants bought country villas in Dulwich, Richmond and Twickenham for their leisure hours, but in London they met to do business and gather information about shipping movements in the new 'Coffee Houses' which started late in the 17th century and soon became popular resorts for combining work with pleasure. One of the best known was the coffee-house in Lombard Street kept by Edward Lloyd, who gave his name to the great headquarters of insurance. Printed newspapers now replaced the old hand-written broadsheets and devoted most of their space to reporting debates in Parliament and foreign affairs. Although their readers were far fewer in number than in our own age of mass circulations, they exercised considerable political influence, and so did celebrated writers of essays and pamphlets such as Dr. Samuel Johnson and Joseph Addison.

London was still the main manufacturing centre in Queen Anne's reign, but industrial change and development moved fast as the century went on, bringing with it Arkwright's invention of a spinning-machine in 1768 and James Watt's steam-engine in 1765. London excelled in the production of hand-made luxury goods, such as the work of the Georgian silversmiths and furniture-makers, which found a ready market in the expansion of private wealth. They also benefited greatly from the influx of skilled foreign craftsmen, notably the French Huguenots who had fled from persecution after the revocation of the Edict of Nantes in 1685.

Economic changes had varying effects on the Livery Companies in the City. The

A GEORGIAN SUMMER

Pewterers, for example, suffered from the introduction of earthenware plates and utensils which replaced pewter in the 18th century. Generally speaking, however, the admission to a City company and the City freedom became much more important in terms of social status and influence than as a commercial asset. This is illustrated by D. V. Glass in the essay on *Status and Occupations in London* which he contributed to *Studies in London History*, edited by Dr. Hollaender and William Kellaway and published by Hodder and Stoughton in 1969. He quotes figures showing that the yearly intake of apprentices by the Livery Companies, meaning those who joined to learn a trade, fell from 1,590 in 1690 to 1,306 in 1725 and only 546 in 1800. Over the same period, the number of admissions by patrimony rose from 137 to 182, while admissions by 'redemption', or purchase, went up from 123 to 301. The total number of admissions from all three sources fell from 1,850 to 1,029.

The apprentices bound in 1690 were drawn from a wide variety of social backgrounds. The fathers included 177 'gentlemen or squires', 150 husbandmen or working farmers, 241 yeomen or freehold farmers, 26 labourers, and two knights. So far as the Founders are concerned, we have no means of knowing where their apprentices came from, and can only fall back on a few scattered entries in the 18th-century records dealing with membership and administration. In 1708, one of the apprentices who received his freedom that year was Stephen Dumarosq, son of Richard Dumarosq, a former minister of the French Huguenot church in the Savoy.

In 1763, the quarterage payments for journeymen and porters in the Company were halved from 4s. to 2s. a year, but this new economic grading evidently implied no exclusion from promotion in the Company from the Yeomanry to the Livery. This is apparent from a Court order in 1781 that 'journeymen who are not upon the Livery, on account of their ill behaviour, particularly on last Lord Mayor's day, be not admitted into the Hall on Lord Mayor's day next'. It is clear from this order that, if some journeymen misbehaved, others were gaining admission to the Livery and thus becoming eligible for election as Master or Warden. The 'ill behaviour' referred to in the order is not further described, but it may possibly have been a legacy of the Gordon Riots in 1780, when a mob led by a mentally unbalanced nobleman called Lord George Gordon terrorised London for several days, looting and burning, while the Lord Mayor and Aldermen, and even the Government, did nothing to stop them. It was this experience which led to the nightly posting of a Guards detachment in the Bank of England.

Fortunately, the violent quarrels between Yeomanry and Livery which did so much harm to the Founders in the 17th century seem to have subsided in the Georgian age. Moreover, at some date before 1800, the old division between Yeomanry and Livery members disappeared, though the records do not show exactly how or when this occurred. The word 'Commonalty', long used to denote the Yeomanry, was still being used in 1777, when a General Court was held to hear the Charter and Ordinances read out, followed by a reading of proposed new bye-laws. That meeting was attended by the Master and Wardens, 12 Assistants, 29 Livery-

CITIZENS AND FOUNDERS

men and 59 of the 'commonalty', making a total attendance of 103 members. But in 1785, when the Company held its customary dinner on Lord Mayor's day at the *New London* tavern in Cheapside, the landlord, Mr. Lewis, was asked to provide for 'seventy of the Livery', with no mention of any 'commonalty'. And again, in 1794, when the Company dined at the *Horns* tavern in Doctors Commons, provision was made for 'eighty of the Livery' with no mention of 'commonalty'. These figures suggest that the Yeomanry members were merged with the Livery at some date between 1777 and 1785.

From other entries in the Court journals, it is clear that the Court made strenuous efforts to expand the Livery and thus secure additional income in fines for admission. The Master in 1705-6, Richard Nevill, was highly commended by the four Auditors that year, one of whom was our old friend Noah Delaunay, for 'having found and brought into the Livery of the Company three-and-thirty new members, some of whose names were not in the Company's books'. This suggests that many of those who became freemen of the Founders after serving as apprentices dropped out of sight and were either unwilling or unable to remain active members.

The Company still insisted, however, that nobody working as a founder should be allowed to take up the City freedom except through the Founders' Company. In 1727, the Court set up a committee to enquire about persons who worked as founders but had no right to do so because they did not belong to the Company, and ordered their prosecution. In 1750, the Company submitted a petition to this effect to the Court of Common Council, which passed an Act in 1753 upholding the Company's claims as follows :

> From the 29th September, 1753, all and every person and persons not being free of the said City, occupying, using, or exercising the art, trade, or manual occupation of a founder within the City of London or liberties thereof, shall take upon himself the freedom, and be made a freeman, of the said Company of Founders.

The Company sometimes took strong action to compel freemen eligible to join the Livery to fulfil this obligation. In 1736, eight freemen who 'were thought proper persons to be chosen on the Livery' were summoned before the Lord Mayor for this purpose. In 1782, when two freemen called John Mullins and Thomas Boston were chosen for the Livery, but did not attend, the Clerk was instructed to inform them that he had orders to proceed against them if they did not appear and take up their Livery at the next Court meeting. In 1785, 16 freemen were summoned for the Livery, but apparently all complied.

There were other times when the Court used gentler methods of persuasion. In 1755, it resolved that all persons exercising the trade of a founder, but who were freemen of another Company, should be invited to join the Founders as 'Love Brothers', without any payment except 2s. 'for the King's duty'. Nor would they be asked to fill any office in the Company. In 1767, Edward Warner, a member of the Drapers, applied for admission to the Founders as a 'Love Brother' and was duly sworn in, but paid a fine of one guinea and the fees of the Clerk and the Beadle.

A GEORGIAN SUMMER

He initiated a long family connection with the Company which has left a permanent memorial in the Robert Warner Trust. (See Chapter XIII)

There were undoubtedly many cases in which freemen of the Company welcomed admission to the Livery as an honour and privilege. One such example was that of John Cole, who was called to the Livery in 1773. He made a request through the Beadle that he should be clothed in his Livery gown and hood in open Court, as he felt that he was not properly a Liveryman without that ceremony. He was duly received at the Hall by the two Wardens, who robed him and escorted him into the Court Room, preceded by the Beadle wearing his gown and carrying the Company's staff. The Wardens then introduced Cole to the Master and Assistants, after which they all rose and the Master, taking the new Liveryman by the hand, pronounced 'Brother Cole' to be elected. The Master invited Cole to dine with the Court that day, but he 'very genteelly excused himself, alleging that he was engaged in parish business or he should gladly have accepted the invitation'. He then took his leave, after giving 2s. 6d. to the Beadle and the same to the Poor Box. Cole evidently made a good impression, as he was elected Master only four years later for 1777-8.

While the Founders insisted that all who pursued their trade should be freemen of the Company, they continued to allow transfers of their own members in special cases. Robert Goadby was turned over to the Stationers' Company at his own request in 1757, paying a fine of £20 in addition to the fees for the Clerk and the Beadle, and also money which he owed for quarterage. Samuel Smith obtained his transfer to the Fishmongers in 1767 for a fine of £24, and in 1772 a Mr. Lotall was granted a refund of the fine paid by him when he became a freeman of the Founders. He was a clockmaker by trade and the City Chamberlain would only accept him as a freeman of the Clockmakers' Company, which had obtained an Act of Common Council, like the Founders, giving them exclusive rights over freemen engaged in their trade.

The ending of the Wardens' Accounts in 1681 makes it impossible to form any clear idea of the Company's financial performance thereafter. As related in the previous chapter, Noah Delaunay did much to restore the Company's position from 1701 to 1703, and Richard Nevill, Master in 1705-6, received even higher praise from the Auditors for his good management. They noted that 'over and above his paying the usual yearly debt and expenses of the Company, he has treated the Company genteelly and respectably, and paid off £200 of their old debt, and also several other debts amounting to £108 6s. 9d., and has paid to the Auditors to be delivered to the next Master a balance of £39 9s. 11d.' The Auditors also recognised Nevill's services by having his name put up 'in the glass window between the two Parlours'.

The financial demands on the Company for loans and taxes after 1701 must have been much less than those imposed by the Stuart Kings and Cromwell, and taxation in general was a long way removed from its present exorbitant and destructive level. The Jacobite risings in 1715 and 1745 pass without mention in the existing records, and the only echoes of war are heard in 1775, when the

134   CITIZENS AND FOUNDERS

Founders gave 20 guineas to a fund for the use of the British soldiers serving in
the American War of Independence and the relief of the widows and orphans of
those who had fallen 'in defending the constitutional government of this country',
an odd way of describing the causes of that war and the issues at stake.

Rents for the use of the Hall continued to provide the Company with useful income, the main tenants being the Scots Presbyterian and other dissenting congregations whose connection with the Hall has already been described. The Hall was
still being used for funeral parties in 1764, when a fee of £2 12s. 6d. was fixed for
the hire of the Court Room and Parlour on such occasions. In 1772, the Court
allowed Mr. John Wood, a 'broker' of Noble Street, to use the Court Room for
displaying plate, jewellery, toys and other goods on such days as he wished at a
fee of one guinea each time.

For the Founders, as for the whole country, this Georgian age was a period of
relative stability and progress after the rough centuries before, but changes were
germinating beneath the surface, especially in the pattern of industrial development and labour relations, which were the prelude to a new era of social conflct.
Few people saw this at the time, and the Founders were no doubt content to pursue
their own affairs in conventional fashion. It is noticeable, however, that the Court
book entries in the 18th century are more concerned with matters of internal ad-
ministraton and discipline than with the protection of craft standards and rights
which had long been the Company's main concern. The old economic function of
membership as a means of preserving a 'closed shop' was rapidly giving way to a
more limited and formal kind of social grouping which relied far more on traditional status than adaptation to changing needs. There were signs of a new challenge to the old order.

In 1705, an Assistant called Drury was dismissed from the Court for binding
his son as an apprentice to the Drapers and setting him up in trade when the young
man had neither served his time with the Founders nor been made free. Drury was
accused of 'endeavouring to destroy and overturn the Company', a serious charge
which is not further explained. In 1706, two members of the Company were summoned before the Court for 'speaking opprobrious words' against the Master and
were each fined 10s. A Liveryman called Withan was sued in 1708 for non-payment
of a note for £6 which he had given for his admission fee, and in the same year
the Master and Wardens were fined for sitting in Court without their gowns. Also
in 1708, the Livery fine was raised to £8, together with fees of 5s. and 2s. 6d. to
the Clerk and Beadle, and the fine for not serving as Master was fixed at £10. A
year later, this fine was raised to £12, but a Master who agreed to serve still paid
£3 as before.

A fine of £10 for each Warden was laid down in 1708 whether he served or not,
but in 1710 this was changed to £12 for not serving or £10 for accepting the office.
In 1716, the Court decided that all who served as Master should in future be excused from paying any fine. In 1725, the Wardens were each fined 1s. 'for not
having the keys of the Company's chest'.

Another sign of the times was the increasing difficulty of getting a sufficient num-

A GEORGIAN SUMMER

135

ber of Assistants to attend Court meetings. This may have been due to the fact that more of them were living at some distance from London and would not make the journey, but it could also have arisen from a feeling that the problems which came before the Court were no longer so important or urgent as those which had faced it in the past. In 1708, the Master and Wardens were instructed to prosecute some Assistants who had not attended for several previous Courts, and in 1720 three Assistants called Newman, Meakins, and Brooks, possibly the same men as those involved in 1708, were dismissed from the Court for this neglect. In 1795, the annual election of Master and Wardens had to be postponed because there was not a sufficient quorum of Assistants, and at the next Court meeting neither the retiring Master nor his Wardens were present.

Three of the Assistants were each fined 2d. in 1714 for 'departing from the Court without leave', and in 1717 an Assistant called John Brooks, presumably the same man who was dismissed in 1720, was fined £1 for using abusive language in Court and excluded from its meetings until he paid up. On this occasion, he apologised and was excused on his paying 5s. to the Poor Box. A rule was made in 1717 imposing a fine for any disclosure of the business done in Court or its discussions.

Efforts to recall absentee Assistants to a proper sense of their duties by penalties were supplemented by other methods. In 1726, the Court decided that any Assistant who came to a meeting within one hour after the time appointed, and stayed till the end, should receive 1s. In 1736, the Master refunded quarterage payments which had been paid by 22 Assistants. In 1740, the Court decided to enlist four new Assistants 'to defray the expenses of the Company', and in 1746 six Liverymen were called on to serve as Assistants, paying fines of £12 each. The increasing number of Assistants who lived outside London led the Court to agree, in 1764, that 'all members of the Court residing beyond the distance of a twelve-penny stage coach fare be excused attendance on Court days'. This must have made it even harder to get a satisfactory attendance.

In 1769, the Court ordered that the Charter should be read out every year at its meeting on the first Monday in May, but if this was done in the hope of chastening naughty Assistants, it seems to have had little success. In 1780, the Clerk was instructed to visit Mr. Benjamin Smith and ask for his resignation, as he had failed to attend Court meetings and also owed the Company arrears of his quarterage payments. Apparently this request was ignored, as in 1790 Smith, and another Assistant called George Cooke, were both asked to resign because their absence from London made it difficult to secure a proper attendance at Court meetings. Smith lived in the Isle of Wight and Cooke in Lincoln. Cooke was nevertheless elected Master in 1782, but refused office and paid a fine of £12.

In 1753, the Court resolved that its quarterly meeting on 29 October should in future be held on 9 November, so as to conform with an Act of Parliament passed in 1751 which adopted the Gregorian calendar already operating in many European countries.

There have been many occasions in the long history of the Founders when the evil hour produced the right man or men to save the situation, and others when

136   CITIZENS AND FOUNDERS

mediocrity and weakness flourished. With the relaxation of pressures on the Company in the Georgian age, one has the impression that old standards of discipline and service also declined. As already noted, there were Assistants who failed in their duties and enjoyed the privileges of office while refusing to accept its obligations. There were other signs of negligence, small but perhaps worth noting. In 1706, the Court found it necessary to order that the Master should not in future 'lend the Company's linen, pewter, knives, forks, brass, nor any other thing that is now moveable in the Hall to any person without an order from this Court'. In 1708, the Master and Wardens were forbidden to 'carry away any victuals out of the Hall upon any day that the Company treats'. The Master for 1728-9, Mr. North, was dismissed by the Court while still in office after he reported that he was unable to make up his accounts, and a substitute was appointed in his place.

The liability attached to a Master under his bond was fixed at £100 in 1758. In 1778, however, the Company owed the retiring Master £77 and the new Master gave him a note of hand for it. In the following year, when John Jenkin was Master, the Court had to sell £500 of 'reduced 3 per cent Bank Annuities' to pay him the balance due on his accounts. In 1790, an Assistant called William Kinsman either resigned or was dismissed after going bankrupt and was replaced on the Court by William Borradaile.

Despite the Charter provision that the Court should consist of Master, Wardens, and 15 assistants, it is on record that there were 29 Assistants in 1736 and 35 in 1764. This increase in numbers may well have been due to the failure of some Assistants to attend meetings. In 1777, when new bye-laws were being drafted, one of the clauses proposed that no Court meeting should consist of less than nine members attending, including the Master and one of the Wardens. The Court also decided at that time to take legal advice as to the precise definition of the Charter rule for 15 Assistants. The Court took this to mean that they were obliged to have *not less* than 15 but were not confined to that number and no more.

Another bye-law drafted in 1777 stated that any decision to dismiss one of its members for improper conduct or disobedience to the rules and ordinances must be carried by a two-thirds majority of the members present, and at three separate Courts. A third clause stipulated that any Liveryman who had served as Under Warden or paid a fine for refusing it, and was later elected an Assistant, should be admitted to the Court without paying any fine, but otherwise he would pay the Assistant's fine of £10 and be chosen as Under Warden. A General Court, or meeting attended by the Livery and the 'commonalty', was called to hear these draft bye-laws read out, and they were left at the Hall for three months so that any member could examine them. It seems, however, that they were either held up for lengthy revision or replaced by new rules, for it was not until 1782 that the Company paid a fee to the Lord Chief Justice of the Common Pleas, Lord Loughborough, for 'looking over and settling the draft of the intended bye-laws'. They were signed in 1783 'by all the members present', after being approved by Lord Loughborough and Lord Mansfield.

We are reminded of the place allotted to women in the Company by an interest-

A GEORGIAN SUMMER

ing entry in the Court minutes for 1729. This states that 'Ann Story, having served Mrs. Ann Kemp seven years, was made free'. As early as 1497-8, the Wardens' Accounts show the names of widows of members who paid dues for quarterage and the 'Mass', presumably because they carried on with the work of their late husbands and took their place in the Company on the same equal footing. Some examples have already been given in an earlier chapter. In 1519 and some later years, the annual membership lists are headed 'Brethren and Sisters', and the list of 1568-9, the last of its kind in the Accounts, gives the names of six widows, four of whom were paying quarterage and therefore ranked as members of the Company in their own right.

The entry for 1729 quoted above shows that women were still in business as founders at that time, and that girls could be taken on as apprentices entitled to the freedom of the Company. This shows an early regard for women's rights by the Founders, but they were well earned. A Court entry made in 1764 reports: 'An apprentice having applied for his freedom, his master objected that he had not served him faithfully, having refused to work longer than from six o'clock in the morning until eight o'clock in the evening, whereas he ought to have worked until nine o'clock'. The Court ruled that the normal hours were from six in the morning till eight at night, and gave the apprentice his freedom. In 1729, sad to relate, the year of Ann Story's freedom, the Court also found it necessary to order: 'That the Master shall make no entertainment for the women, neither should any other Master for the future without an order from this Court'. We are not told what provoked this expulsion of Eve from the Founders' garden, but perhaps it is just as well.

In 1758, the Court decided that only widows of Liverymen should in future be admitted as pensioners of the Company, and that they should be paid out of the 'poor's money', not from Company funds. In 1766, the pensions were raised from 3s. 4d. a quarter to 5s. 3d., still a pittance by any standards but probably the best the Company could do at the time. In 1736, a widow called Mrs. Wood gave the Company £200 in return for an annuity of £20 during her lifetime. In 1756, another widow, Mrs. Ann Cannon of Romford, also paid £200 to the Company for an annuity, but it was reduced to £15.

The Company's dinners in any period have usually been a good guide to its financial condition. In Georgian days, Livery dinners were held in the early afternoon and there was a 'breakfast' on Lord Mayor's Day at 11 o'clock in the morning. In 1778, the Court decided that the Master could invite two friends to dinner on quarterly Court days and election day. Each Warden was allowed one guest, and an Assistant could invite a friend on payment of 5s. In 1795, when England was at war with revolutionary France, the dinners on Lord Mayor's Day and quarter-days were cancelled because of the high cost of provisions, and in 1796 the Lord Mayor's Day dinner was again omitted because two properly qualified Stewards could not be found.

As this shows, there were continuing difficulties in getting Liverymen to serve as Stewards. In 1705, the Master reported that he had received £4 in cash from

138 CITIZENS AND FOUNDERS

Henry Sherwin for his Steward's fine, but had found it necessary to take his bond for the remaining £8 which was to be paid 'at the said Sherwin's return from Jamaica'. In 1707, promissory notes were again taken for the Stewards' fines. The records show that in 1710 the Stewards were allowed 'the use of the Company's linen, pewter, etc. for Lord Mayor's day, they giving an undertaking to return the same clean, whole, and entire within six days'. In 1749, John Watkins was dismissed from the Livery and fined £5 for refusing to serve as a Steward.

In 1774, however, when another Liveryman called James Sims was prosecuted for refusing service as Steward, he obtained a 'non-suit' on the grounds that there was no documentary evidence of a bye-law to support the charge against him. The Company had to pay legal costs of nearly £100, and it may well have been this episode which led to the drafting of new bye-laws which, as already noted, were finally adopted in 1785. The fact remains that there was ample documentary material to sustain the case against Sims, and the apparent failure of the Court to produce it seems strange.

It is true that the Charter itself said nothing about Stewards, but the Ordinances of 1615 clearly stated that two Liverymen should be appointed as Stewards for the Court dinner on Lord Mayor's Day, or for such other day as the Court might decide, and that anyone refusing or omitting this duty would incur a fine of £5. Furthermore, a Court order issued in 1631 not only raised the fine for refusal to £10, but also authorised the added penalty of dismissal from the Livery. In addition, it laid down that nobody should be taken on to the Court unless he had first served the office of Steward and paid his fine.

It looks as if the Court was unable to produce evidence of these Ordinances and relied on a plea of ancient custom which was rejected. It is also possible that Sims pleaded ignorance of the rules, a familiar complaint in times past, and blamed the Court for failure to inform the Liverymen of their obligations. This would help to explain the care taken by the Court in 1777 to make the draft new bye-laws available to all members for inspection. In any event, the Court does not emerge from the Sims case with much credit, and it only shows that old institutions do not merely have change thrust upon them, but often provoke it by their own failure to adapt to new conditions.

The Company may have had similar difficulties in maintaining its authority over weights, but the Georgian records, such as they are, throw little light on this subject. There is a Court book entry in 1739 directing the Master 'to employ some person to buy such weights of the makers as are not stamped at the Hall according to the Charter, in order to proceed against such makers', but no indication of further action. This use of a hired agent suggests that the Company's old right of 'search' may already have been curtailed or fallen into disuse. 'Searchers' were chosen and sworn in 1746 and a warrant was executed with them 'according to custom', but there is nothing to show that they visited houses and workshops as the Master and Wardens had previously done.

In 1743, the Court apparently got wind of proposals for new legislation affecting the Company's interests in weights, for it appointed a committee to draw up a petition to Parliament on the sealing and sizing of weights, and this was shown to

A GEORGIAN SUMMER 139

'some of the Gentlemen of the Royal Society' and City Members of Parliament. The Court had the petition engrossed and sealed and instructed the committee to proceed with it as they thought best, while the Master was authorised to borrow £100 to meet the expenses.

In 1744, the Court petitioned the Lord Mayor and Court of Aldermen to join with the Founders in an 'advertisement' concerning the making and sizing of brass weights, presumably with the intention of issuing a public warning against unmarked or defective weights, but there is no further mention of it. In 1753, however, a woman called Mrs. Jacombe was summoned for selling brass weights without first having them stamped at Founders' Hall and with counterfeiting the Company's mark. She replied that 'the Company might do their worst' and was then prosecuted, but she settled the matter by paying £50 towards the Company's expenses and the prosecution was withdrawn.

In 1758, the Clerk informed the Court that he had attended a House of Commons committee meeting in connection with the sizing and marking of brass weights, armed with a copy of the Charter and bye-laws. In 1774, the Clerk reported that a Bill had been introduced in the Commons for regulating the weights of gold and silver coinage which, he said, 'would entirely take away the rights and privileges of the Company'. This danger was averted after conferences with City Members of Parliament and the insertion of a clause in the Bill safeguarding the Company's position. The Company continued for many more years to fight a stubborn rearguard action to retain its control over weights, but it clearly came under increasing pressure as time went on.

When the Company first began sizing weights back in 1587, the receipts from fees were equally shared with the Keeper at Guildhall. In 1756, the Company decided to ask him to contribute in future to the expense of the files, stamps, scales, and other equipment used, and this was agreed. The Company paid a 'scale-maker' an annual fee for cleaning the scales and keeping them in order which was fixed at one and a half guineas in 1745 but rose to £2 10s. in 1779, when Mr. Charles Delwave was appointed to do this work in place of Mr. Read. In 1763, the Court resolved that brass weights mixed with lead should not be sealed, as they could not properly be called true weights and were an imposition on the public.

The Court agreed in 1773 that the Beadle should be permitted to size and mark weights of one guinea, half-guinea, and quarter-guinea at a price of 6d. per dozen. In 1800, the Court granted a petition by the Beadle that he should be allowed 1s. 6d. per dozen 'for adjusting and sizing the quarter and half-hundred weights'. At the start of the century, in 1704, the Company had to pay £3 5s. to redeem the 'Staff Head', which had been pawned by John Martin, the Beadle dismissed in 1696. In 1729, the Beadle was required 'to give security by bond with two good persons in the sum of £50', and in 1765 the Court issued an order as to the Beadle's duties and remuneration, reading as follows:

The two late Beadles of the Company having been paid a yearly salary of £6 for what it appears they never did anything, they charging in their bills for everything they did : It was ordered that for the future the Beadle should

140   CITIZENS AND FOUNDERS

deliver all summonses and attend upon all occasions as Beadle of the Company.

That the allowance of ten shillings a year for winding the clock be discontinued, the Beadle living in the Hall, and having the benefit thereof, ought to do it without making any charge for so doing.

That the Beadle be allowed yearly for washing the linen £1 10s. and no more, which we think is very sufficient for that purpose.

That the Beadle shall be allowed yearly for cleaning the knives, forks, and brasses £1 10s. and no more, and fifteen shillings for scouring and cleaning the pewter.

That ten shillings and sixpence be allowed yearly for charwomen for cleaning the Hall and other places. That one shilling and sixpence per annum be allowed for sawdust, oil, and trimming the lamps. One shilling yearly for porters.

That the Beadle be paid for sizing the weights one shilling per gross as at present, and also for collecting the quarterage. That the fees remain as at present and that he shall have lodging and rooms in the Hall. And we are of opinion that upon a moderate calculation the Beadle's place of this Company, according to the above allowances, will be upwards of £60 per annum.

If this strikes a modern reader as shabby treatment, we must again recall the vast difference in the value of money at that time, and it is also worth noting that in 1769 a member of the Court, William Phillips, resigned from it to fill the place of Beadle. In 1773, the Beadle's salary was increased by eight guineas, and in 1790 it was fixed at £15 yearly, with a condition that he was not to do outside work as a journeyman. He was also allowed one 'chaldron' of coals yearly, equivalent to just over a quarter of a ton.

In earlier times, the duties of Clerk and Beadle often overlapped and were combined in one man, but they had long been separated by the 18th century, when the Clerk's responsibilities covered new problems, notably the rising tide of intervention by central and local government in civic affairs. In 1702, the Clerk's salary was only £12 a year, plus his fees of 2s. 6d. for binding an apprentice and the same for making a member free. The Clerk's salary went up to £20 in 1771, and he retained his fees. If the Company had been unlucky in one or two of its earlier choices of a Clerk, it was well rewarded by the appointment of Thomas King to that office. The date when he took over is not stated, but his affection for the Founders was proved by his actions. In October 1784, the Court recorded its thanks to him for a gift of 'six China bowls with the Company's coat of arms thereon'. These bowls are believed to be the work of the Lowestoft pottery which was opened in 1757 and closed in 1802. They are rare and exceptionally fine specimens of their kind and remain one of the Company's most treasured possessions.

In February 1785, at the Court's request, King lent the Company £200 at five

A GEORGIAN SUMMER

141

per cent interest to pay off some of its bills not specified, but which may have been legal charges for the new bye-laws adopted that year. After his death in 1802, the Company received a legacy of £50 from Thomas King to be divided among 10 of its poor widows, and he also left gifts of £2 to each member of the Court with which to buy a ring in his memory.

The memory of an earlier benefactor is preserved by three silver tankards bought by the Company in 1708 with a legacy of £50 from Thomas Fisher, and inscribed with his name as 'Merchant and Founder'. These tankards are still used at the Company's Livery dinners for the ancient ceremony of the 'loving cup' which members pass from hand to hand and drink from in turn.

The old pomp and pageantry displayed by the Livery Companies when they appeared in public steadily declined in Georgian times. In 1704, the Founders were still issuing orders for 'the Whifflers, Music and Trophies, and other usual Ornaments of the Company' to appear on 'Thanksgiving Day' for the Lord Mayor's procession. It was also left to the Master's discretion to decide 'what sort and quantity of wine should be provided for the Stand', and a supper was provided for the Company after its members returned from the parade. In 1747, an agreement was made with 'Mr. Walker, Carpenter', whereby he was to 'keep the Stand and Music place in good repair, and to take it down and to put it up once a year on Lord Mayor's Day, and keep the Stand in a convenient place, dry, and provide proper servants to attend the Stand when put up, during the term of seven years at £7 per year'.

In 1761, when the City was preparing for a state visit by the new King, George III, on Lord Mayor's day, the Founders' stand was in such bad condition that the Court got an estimate of £70 for building a new one. After this visit, a complaint was made against the Master for having introduced his wife into the stand, but the Court decided that he had a right to do so, as it had always been customary for a Master to invite his wife or a friend if he wished. On the other hand, a Liveryman who introduced two friends into the stand was judged to have broken the rules and fined £1.

In 1780, the Court resolved that 'the six Ushers be allowed two shillings and sixpence each for their attendance, instead of being supplied with ribbons as usual'. Gone were the days when the old 'whifflers' made way for the Company when it went in procession, with their whistles, staves, white coats of silk or velvet, gold chains, feathered caps and gloves.

By 1800, the long Georgian summer was over. The English character had lost the colourful joy in life of Elizabethan times and was moving towards the strict conventions and concealment of emotions of the Victorian age. The older England, so long self-sufficient and protected by its moat, was giving way to a great era of industrial expansion and world empire, but in that process much of the gentler simplicity and intimacy of English life would be lost beyond recall.

CHAPTER XII

Imperial Crown

THE 19TH CENTURY saw the emergence of Great Britain as a world power possessing a great colonial empire, naval supremacy and strategic control of every ocean, and the wealth of a great trading nation reinforced by leadership in the industrial revolution. In 1870, the external trade of the United Kingdom was greater in volume than that of France, Germany and Italy combined, and between three and four times greater than the foreign trade of the United States. The English sea-captains, merchant-venturers and colonists who opened up new lands and markets in Elizabethan and Stuart times had paved the way for this imperial destiny, but beneath that glittering surface the seeds were being sown of a bitter harvest in social conflict and industrial strife. Human nature being what it is, the quickening pace of scientific and technical achievement was not matched by an equal understanding of the effects which economic change would have on the lives and expectations of a rapidly expanding population, most of whom were still living under primitive conditions in overcrowded cities and slums when Queen Victoria died in 1901.

The strength and stability of the Victorian age was preceded by a period of great stresses and strains which made many Englishmen afraid of what the future might hold. The loss of the American colonies in the war of 1775 to 1777 was an early blow to British national pride and self-confidence. It was followed by the long struggle against Napoleon's domination of Europe which, though won decisively in the end, caused great hardship in Britain and generated new social tensions. By cutting off supplies of corn from Europe, the Napoleonic wars led to a rise in the price of wheat from 43s. a quarter in 1792 to 126s. in 1812, and the high cost of bread inflicted much suffering. Many farmers in England who increased their production of wheat during the wars were hard hit by the fall in wheat prices when peace came, but the big farming and landed interests were strong enough in Parliament to maintain high prices for wheat which protected agriculture at the expense of the consumer until the repeal of the Corn Laws in 1846. This bred conflict between towns and country, and between rich and poor. At the same time, there was mounting agitation for political reform and a redistribution of seats in the House of Commons to enable the new industrial and urban centres to be properly represented. This grew into a threat of revolution only narrowly averted by the Reform Bill of 1832.

IMPERIAL CROWN 143

The tensions created by industrial development were manifested in events such as the smashing of new machinery in 1811-12 by the 'Luddites', craftsmen who feared that they would be thrown out of work. They were savagely dealt with, but in 1824-5 Parliament legalised trade unions, many of which today show the same hostility as the Luddites did to mechanisation and new technical processes, from the same fear of unemployment.

There are few traces of these restless years in the records of the Founders. The Company dinner on Lord Mayor's Day was cancelled in 1800 because of 'the very high price of provisions', as it had been in 1795. In 1798, when Napoleon was threatening to invade England, the Court considered making a contribution to 'the subscription for the defence of the country', but there were too few Assistants present to make a quorum and the matter was postponed without further mention. The Company's income in 1799 was estimated at £120 and so stated to the Revenue Commissioners. In 1806, the Court discussed whether the Company's plate should be sold 'for the use of the poor', but the outcome is not on record.

The difficulties caused by Assistants who failed to attend Court meetings still persisted, though it is hard to say whether this was solely due to apathy and neglect of duty, or partly because Assistants living some distance from London lacked our modern facilities for travel by road or rail. In 1805, a forfeit of 2s. 6d. payable to the Company's poor box was levied on Assistants living in London for each failure to attend a quarterly Court, and in 1815 this was extended to cover General Courts as well, but members who appeared on time were allowed 5s. for coach hire. In 1825, four Assistants called Barnes, Thornhill, Hornsby, and Mayor were asked to resign from the Court because their failure to attend meetings was making it very difficult to muster a quorum and the business of the Company was seriously hindered. Joseph Mayor evidently took no notice, as he was finally dismissed in 1831 for having failed to attend any Company meetings since 1822.

In 1828, the Court decided that those of its members who arrived after one o'clock for a meeting should not receive the payment of 5s. allowed for coach hire, and should also be fined 2s. 6d. if they came after that time or were absent for the whole meeting. In 1842, an Assistant called Jeremiah Barratt was questioned about his failure to appear for Court meetings or to pay his fines, but he then resigned and the fines were remitted.

While the Court was thus plagued with absentee Assistants, it also had to deal with challenges to its authority which were certainly no novelty in the Company's history, but which were harder to handle when times had changed. In 1807, a Freeman of the Company, F. J. Bouchet, was summoned to take up his Livery, but threw the summons at the Beadle 'and behaved with great indecency and insolence to the Court'. He was then warned that legal action would be taken against him, but he submitted himself to the Court's judgment, pleading that he was unable to take up the Livery and asking that the proceedings against him should be dropped. The Court agreed to this, with the proviso that Bouchet would pay the legal expenses.

A more serious situation arose in 1830, when the Clerk informed the Court that

144 CITIZENS AND FOUNDERS

he had served summonses on two members to appear before the Kingsgate Court of Requests and the City Court of Requests respectively for non-payment of quarterage. One of the men was called Pontifex and the other was that same Frederick Thornhill who had been asked to resign from the Court in 1825 for refusing to attend its meetings. The Clerk reported that the Kingsgate Court had called for the production of the Company's Charter in support of its case, while the City Court had requested evidence 'that the rightful expenditure of the Company required such a contribution'. The Clerk had then waived the two summonses to seek the Founders Court's opinion.

Yet again, as in similar cases mentioned earlier, the Court was apparently unable or unwilling to produce documentary evidence, although such evidence did exist. It is true that the Charter does not mention quarterage, but the Ordinances of 1615 spell out that obligation in clear terms. Either the Company had no copy of those Ordinances, perhaps even no knowledge of them, or it failed to get any help from Guildhall where such records were kept. It is also possible, of course, that the Court preferred to drop the matter rather than go on with legal action which might be prolonged and expensive. In any event, the Company was bluffing and paid the price.

After this experience, the Court set up a committee to examine the Charter 'as regards the power of the Company to compel persons carrying on the trade of founders to take up their freedom in this Company, they being freemen or not of another Company; and to examine also whether the Company had the power to compel persons who were freemen of the Founders, and at the same time free or not free of another Company, to pay up all fines due to the Founders'.

The committee reported in May 1831, when it took the view that quarterage could be recovered for the general purposes of the Company, but that it did not appear by the Charter that the Court could compel persons trading as founders to take up their freedom in the Founders' Company. In this instance, the committee seems to have overlooked the Order of Common Council enacted in 1753, and referred to in the previous chapter, by which 'every person and persons not being free of the said City, occupying, using, or exercising the art, trade, or manual occupation of a founder within the City of London or liberties thereof shall take upon himself the freedom, and be made a freeman, of the said Company of Founders'.

It looks as if the City Chamberlain had overlooked this Order as well, but not the Clerk of the Founders' Company, Michael Tovey. In November, 1831, he entered a case at the City Chamberlain's office against the admission of one Robert Williams to the City freedom through any other Company than the Founders. He followed this up in 1832 by issuing a notice repeating the Common Council Order of 1753 and getting it hung up in the City Chamberlain's office, including a warning that an offence against this rule incurred a fine of £5.

In 1841, the Court appointed another committee 'to examine the Register of Freemen to be elected Liverymen', and a month later letters were sent to 16 of them to take up their Livery. Four persons carrying on the trade of a founder were summoned to take up their freedom in the Company. These tenacious efforts to main-

IMPERIAL CROWN   145

tain the Company's rights thus brought their reward, but have long been super-
seded by the removal of any restrictions on the number of Companies to which a
man may belong, regardless of his occupation.

Some steps were also taken at this time to improve the Company's internal administration. In 1822, the Court ordered that the cash in hand should be kept
with Messrs. Ladbroke and Co., one of the new banking firms then making their
appearance, and authorised the Master to draw on the account as required. A
printed list of the Livery was ordered in 1824, but no copy seems to have survived.
Further Court orders issued in 1828 laid down that the business transacted at
monthly or quarterly Courts should be recorded in the minutes; that no such business should be conducted except in the Court; and that an iron chest should be
bought to hold the books and papers. One key was to be kept by the Master, the
other by the Clerk, and the chest was never to be removed from the Court. Also in
1828, the Court held a meeting to 'examine and arrange the books and records etc.
of the Company, on account of many of them being much neglected and exposed'.
The Court also decided that an inventory of the Company's property should be
inserted in a book kept for that purpose. A modern historian can only regret that
such measures were not taken earlier.

A notable name in the Company's list of benefactors appeared in 1824, when the
Clerk, William Bond, died and gave the Company £1,000 in his will on condition
that the interest of £50 should be paid to his executors, Sophia and Charlotte
Woodcock, during their lifetimes. Thereafter, £40 of the interest was to be equally
divided between four young men who had served their time as apprentices in the
Company, and the remaining £10 was to be applied 'towards refreshments on the
day of opening the Poor Box, or on any other day the Court may appoint'. Like
his predecessor, Thomas King, Bond also left rings to the Master, Wardens and
Assistants. 'Bond's Legacy' still provides gifts of money to young men joining the
Founders by 'servitude', or apprenticeship, although the term has become merely a
polite formality.

Charles Hollier followed William Bond as Clerk in 1824 and was given the
freedom of the Company, but he died within a year. It was probably his illness
which led the Court to appoint one of its members, William Borradaile, a solicitor
of King's Arms Yard, as Assistant Clerk for the time being. It seems unlikely that
this was the William Borradaile elected to the Court in 1790, but it may have been
his son. Michael Tovey succeeded Hollier as Clerk in 1825, when the salary was
doubled from £20 to £40, and Tovey seems to have earned it.

Some changes in the Company's fines and fees should be noted here. In 1826,
the fine for admission to the Livery was raised from £8 to 15 guineas. The fine for
joining the Company by 'redemption' or purchase rose from 13s. 4d. in 1720 to
£2 10s. in 1867, plus £3 for stamp and 7s. 6d. for the fees of the Clerk and the
Beadle. The fine for becoming a freeman by service or patrimony was fixed at
£1 12s. 6d. in 1826, plus stamp and office fees making it up to £3. In 1867, the
Livery fine was reduced from 15 guineas to £10 7s. 6d., including office fees, but
raised again to £15 7s. 6d. in 1869. The fine for election as Upper or Under War-

146   CITIZENS AND FOUNDERS

den went up in 1826 from £10 to £15 and remained so in 1867, exclusive of office fees. The fine for election to the Court of Assistants also rose in 1826 from £10 to £15, but in 1857 it was doubled to 30 guineas. The fine for serving as Steward is not mentioned in the 1826 figures, but in 1867 it was £5 7s. 6d.

In 1829, the fine for 'turning over' an apprentice was laid down as one guinea, of which the Company took 13s. 6d. and 7s. 6d. was paid to the Clerk and the Beadle, and this was still unchanged in 1867. Also in 1829, the Court authorised a payment of one guinea to any person who brought in another person wishing to take up his freedom in the Company. This sum was given to the Ward Beadle of Bishopsgate in 1831, when he introduced a Mr. Soward who attended and took up his freedom.

In 1830, the Court resolved :

> That in future, should it be requisite to elect any gentleman of the Court who has not served the offices of Upper and Under Warden, before he can take his seat as a Member of the Court he must pay the fines attached to those offices, as well as the fine for coming on the Court; such gentlemen to be entitled to the same privileges as if they had served the offices.

Such a case arose in the same year, 1830, when John Moxon was elected to the Court and paid office fines for Under Warden, Upper Warden, and Assistant totalling £46 2s. 6d.

The Company maintained its long tradition of hospitality at dinners so far as its means allowed. In 1829, the Court resolved that the quarterly Court dinner and the Livery dinner should continue to be held at the *Albion* tavern, an old haunt of the Company, as long as the Court approved of its treatment there. It looks as if the Hall had long ceased to be used for full Company meals, perhaps because it had been converted into a 'meeting-house' for the dissenting congregations whose rents were a valuable source of income. Court dinners were still taking place in the Court Room in 1831, but in that year it was decided that the Court would only dine there on 18 October and for the quarterly Court in May. The Court dinner in August was to be held 'at Blackwall' and the Livery dinner was to take place yearly on 9 November, the place not being specified.

The Court also decided in 1831 that the expense of the 'Oyster Feast' should be paid by the Master that year and by the Wardens on the next occasion. This suggests that an 'Oyster Feast' was a regular fixture, but no details are on record. Scattered references to the purchase of oysters are to be found in the Wardens' Accounts from 1497 to 1681, and they were probably served at some dinners.

The food provided for the Company's dinners became much more elaborate and varied in the Victorian age. The proof copy of a menu for the Livery dinner in 1867 has survived. It is printed in the French style which seems to have come into fashion in Victorian times. The edges are cut out in a frilly pattern like lace and the courses are listed in French under Potages, Poissons, Entrées, Relevés, Rotis and Dessert. The dinner began with a choice of soups from 'A la Reine', 'Printanière' and 'Giblet', and these were followed by a selection of fish from

IMPERIAL CROWN 147

salmon, trout, lobster rissoles, sole, red mullet, turbot, eels, and whitebait. The 'entrées' offered filleted duck, veal or lamb cutlets and croquettes of capon. Then there were 'relevés' of braised tongue, roast chicken, York ham, lamb and venison, followed by 'rotis' of duck or goose. After this came meringues, pastries, jellies or iced pudding, and a tail-piece of ice-creams in strawberry, lemon, or vanilla. It would have been interesting to know how all this food was washed down, but the wine-list has not been saved.

The modern mind, or perhaps one should say the stomach, boggles at such profusion, but it is fair to add that the Court cancelled two of its dinners in 1876 and gave £40 towards the relief of people in Bulgaria suffering from Turkish oppression, while in the following year a Company dinner was cancelled and a gift of £30 made to the Indian famine relief fund.

The splendid City pageants in honour of Lord Mayors and visiting sovereigns were now a thing of the past, but in 1837, when the young Queen Victoria visited Guildhall, some members of the Founders paid for a new pair of Company colours costing £45. When the Queen opened the new Royal Exchange in 1844, the Livery went in procession to take up its old 'standing' in Poultry in front of St. Mildred's church. There were not enough Livery gowns to go round, but the Company got leave from the Court of Aldermen to wear blue and yellow rosettes instead. In 1863, when the Danish Princess Alexandra came by sea for her marriage to the future Edward VII and went through the City, the Dean and Chapter of St. Paul's offered the Livery Companies space for putting up stands inside the churchyard railings, on condition that each Company paid its own building expenses. Enquiries showed that a considerable sum was needed and the Founders declined the offer. Instead, a dinner for the Court and Livery was held at the *Albion* tavern to celebrate the Royal wedding. The Master and Upper Warden represented the Company at a thanksgiving service in St. Paul's in 1872 for the recovery of the Prince of Wales from a nearly fatal illness.

The Company's old rules for breaches of discipline, such as 'reviling another Brother', had long been abandoned, but an echo of the past was heard in 1858, when the Court resolved :

> That inasmuch as Mr. [blank], a Liveryman of this Company, has pertinaciously continued annoyance of a very obnoxious character, after great forbearance shown by those he annoyed, the Clerk be, and he is hereby, instructed to see that no invitation to future Livery Dinners be sent to Mr. [blank], and that the Beadle do not again call upon him for quarterage.

The Court refrained from naming the culprit or stating the nature of his offence. Perhaps it was a case of 'drunk and disorderly' several times repeated.

Five years earlier, in 1853, the Beadle was dismissed after leaving the Hall unoccupied for a whole night and appearing before the sitting magistrate at Guildhall, Sir F. G. Moon, on a charge of getting drunk and behaving violently. He was replaced by Edward Vaughan. This coincided with more serious misconduct by the Clerk, John Gray. In December 1852, the Master called a special Court to

148   CITIZENS AND FOUNDERS

enquire into the affairs of the Company and reported that, from a cursory examination of the books, it appeared that there were considerable errors in the accounts. The Court set up a committee to investigate and requested the Master and Wardens to take charge of the premises and property of the Company. The findings of the committee are not recorded, but it reported a month later, and the Clerk was then asked to resign, which he did. His place was filled by Algernon Wells, who served with distinction as Clerk for many years.

The Master who had to deal with these troubles was W. M. Williams, who rendered such great service to the Company by compiling its *Annals*. He was also clearly a Master who showed exceptional ability in dealing with the problems which arose in his term of office. In August 1853, the Court recorded its satisfaction with his arrangements, as Master, for a 'water excursion', and in September that year he was re-elected as Master for a second year. The Court expressed its appreciation of his work in the following minute :

> It was reminded by Mr. Hems that the year of office of the present Master had been a remarkable one in the history of the Company; that difficulties of no common order had been discovered to exist, out of which it had been extricated; and that obstacles to its prosperity had been met and overcome; that to this fortunate result and the present satisfactory position of the Company, William M. Williams Esq., the present Master, had by his business-like conduct and attention to the duties of his office, mainly contributed.

The Company's removal from Lothbury to St. Swithin's Lane took place in 1854, during Williams' second year as Master, and he made an important contribution to it which will be described later in this chapter.

The motion for re-electing Williams as Master was seconded by George Mears, who stood next in line for that office by seniority. During his second term, Williams made proposals for the future management of the Company which were no doubt prompted by the trouble experienced with the former Clerk, and these were adopted by the Court. They called for an inventory of all the goods and effects of the Company to be prepared by the Clerk in future under the direction of the Master and Wardens. One copy was to be kept by the Clerk for the information of the Court, and another given to every new Master, who was required to give a receipt to the retiring Master confirming its correctness. The Clerk was also instructed to provide every new Master with a list of rents and gifts belonging to the Company, with the dates when they fell due.

When Williams ended his second year as Master, the Court again paid a warm tribute to 'his great skill in the management of its affairs and uniform courtesy towards the Members of this Court'. A copy of this resolution was presented to him as a permanent record of esteem from his colleagues.

The Company seems to have been in low water financially in earlier years of that century. This probably explains the various increases in fines and fees already noted, and may account for the Court's rejection in 1826 of a petition for assistance received from the Company of Tobacco Pipe Makers. In 1831, the Court ap-

IMPERIAL CROWN 149

pointed a committee 'to ascertain as nearly as possible the income of the Company and to consider the best means of reducing the expenditure to meet the exigencies of the times'. The fact that the Court did not even know what income the Company possessed may help to explain those 'errors in the accounts' which were discovered in 1852 and remedied by Williams. It would seem, not for the first time in the Company's history, that the Court failed to exercise proper supervision, and that earlier Masters and Wardens left too much to Clerks and Beadles who were usually, but not always, above suspicion.

Company income probably suffered from a decline in the receipts for sizing weights at Founders' Hall, due to changing conditions and lack of enforcement. The costs of maintaining the Hall, rebuilt after the Great Fire in 1666, must also have been substantial, even though tenants were sometimes called on to pay for repairs and alterations. The means available for the relief of poor members and dependents must therefore have been affected. Although quarterage was still being paid by members in 1831 and 1853, there is no mention after 1800 of any part being allotted for poor relief. This would have left only the meagre contents of the Poor Box, which relied on small voluntary contributions occasionally supplemented from Company funds when possible.

Nevertheless, the Founders had always acknowledged a special duty to help their poor, as befitting a Company which had its origins in a medieval parish association of lay brethren providing mutual aid and spiritual comfort, and it remained conscious of this obligation. What had changed was the mental attitude of those who gave the aid and those who received it. In medieval times, the word 'charity' was applied in its Latin derivation from 'caritas', meaning caring or loving-kindness. The man who gave aid did not feel a moral sense of superiority, and the man who received help was not ashamed of it. In the Victorian age of industrial change, however, wealth was replacing land or birth as the main status symbol. The wealthy did not stop giving aid, far from it, but they did it more as a favour than from a sense of compassion, while those in need felt that poverty was something to be ashamed of and hidden by men and women whose pride and self-respect often made them suffer in silence.

Both before and after Queen Victoria's accession in 1837, the Founders did what they could within their limitations, but there is little information on this subject. In 1814, a yearly allowance of 10 guineas was granted to Sarah Bruce, widow of a Beadle, which she received until her death in 1854. In 1825, the Court directed that the fees for all bindings of apprentices should include a payment of 2s. 6d. to the 'Orphan Fund', which is not mentioned elsewhere. In the same year, the Court resolved : 'That the money received in the Poor's Box be made up by the Master, out of the funds in his hands, to make the sum of £2 each for the ten poor women who have applied for their pension'.

There was a major change of policy in 1829, when Thomas Mears, a member of the Court and a Past Master, proposed the creation of a 'Charitable Fund' and suggested that a subscription list should be opened for this purpose. The Court agreed and a sum of £326 was given by 12 of its members, while a further £160

150   CITIZENS AND FOUNDERS

came in from Liverymen, making nearly £500. It was also suggested to members of the Company that they might remember the fund in their wills. The Court passed a warm vote of thanks to Thomas Mears for his initiative. He resigned from it in 1847 on account of ill health and absence from London, but it is pleasant to record that his son, Charles Mears, took his place on the Court, and was Master in 1849-50. Another member of the family, George Mears, was Master in 1854-5.

Under the rules laid down for the Charitable Fund, all sums collected for it were free from subjection to the 'debts or contingencies' of the Company, and were to be applied solely to the objects of the fund. This in itself was a great change from past practice. The capital was to be invested in Bank Consols and the interest used to provide pensions for needy members, or their widows, in order of seniority and initially at a rate of only £3 a year. Certain conditions were made for admission as a pensioner. Members of the Court were not eligible if they continued to hold that office, but otherwise they, and their widows, if in need, were given preference when vacancies occurred in the list of pensioners. They were also to be granted twice the amount of pension given to Liverymen, as soon as the funds allowed. Liverymen who had served any office in the Company received priority over those who had refused to serve.

No Liveryman or widow under 60 could qualify for a pension, unless totally disabled, nor were they eligible if their quarterage payments were unpaid, or if they were in receipt of parish relief, or if they remained on the 'poor's list' of the Company, and therefore might claim other relief. Their incomes must not exceed £20 a year and widows who remarried could not receive a pension.

In 1842, the Court appointed 'a deputation to enquire as to terms etc. with reference to the purchase of the Dyers Alms Houses in the City Road, in reference to the Charitable Fund', but apparently nothing came of this idea. In 1849, the Company advertised in the *Times* and *Morning Chronicle* for applications from 'decayed Liverymen and their Widows as Pensioners on the Charitable Fund', with results which are not stated. An application for aid from the fund was made in 1861 by William Prince, described as having been a freeman of the Company since 1795 and a Liveryman since 1797, who by that reckoning must have been a very old man. Noting that he had paid his quarterage regularly, the Court gave him an 'interim' sum of £10. In 1862, a weekly allowance of £1 was granted to the senior Liveryman, Mr. Bruce, owing to his feeble health and advanced age. In that year also, the widow of Thomas Baxter applied for relief, but the Court decided that she could not be given an annuity because her husband had not paid quarterage and granted her £1. The Master's accounts for 1860-1 showed Company receipts for the year of £1,140 and expenditure of £1,128, leaving a surplus of only £12.

The growth of official intervention was shown in 1854, when the Charity Commissioners requested information about the Founders' Charitable Fund. The Court sent them a copy of the last printed statement and offered to supply any further assistance needed. In 1865, when the Commissioners proposed to hold an enquiry into the Company's charities, the Court appointed two of its members, William Christie and Mark E. Marsden, to attend and provide any details required.

IMPERIAL CROWN   151

In 1876, the Court decided that the original terms of 'Bond's Legacy', referred
to earlier in this chapter, had become obsolete, presumably because the number of
working founders in the Company had fallen to a point where there were not
enough apprentices being taken on to qualify for the gifts left to them by Bond in
his scheme. Instead, a plan was submitted to the Charity Commissioners whereby
the income, then amounting to £27 a year, would be made up to £50 by the
Company and spent on annual prizes for the best workers in brass, copper, or
bronze. They had to submit models of any period chosen from an original nude
figure, an ornamental bell, or a brass door-lock and hinge. In addition, the Freedom
and Livery of the Company were to be presented to the author of the best essay on
the history and art of founding in brass, copper, and bronze, but only persons employed in founding or carrying on that business were eligible to compete.

These prizes were advertised in the press in 1880 and notice of them was sent to
leading firms in the industry and schools of art. Prizes were awarded in 1881 but
later discontinued, either because the response was disappointing or because the
Company thought it could find a better way to encourage young talent. The income from 'Bond's Legacy' has since reverted to its original purpose of making
gifts to young men joining the Founders by apprenticeship, though this is now a
purely nominal term.

The freehold ownership of the Hall in Lothbury, rebuilt after the Great Fire of
1666, was the Company's chief asset, but by 1800 it was in poor condition. The
great merchant-venturing Companies which had been such valued tenants in the
past were no longer renewing their leases, and the later use of the Hall by religious
dissenters was declining. As early as 1789, the Court resolved : 'In consequence of
the great expense incurred by keeping the Hall for doing the Company's business,
to repair the Company's premises adjoining the Hall in order to do the business
there, instead of the Hall, and that a surveyor be engaged to take an account of
the necessary repairs'. The premises in question were the two houses acquired by
the Company in 1531 with the site of the original Hall and probably rebuilt after
the Great Fire.

There is no further mention of this scheme, but in 1799, as noted in earlier
pages, the Hall was rented by an Independent congregation led by Anthony Crole
for 21 years at £30 a year clear of all taxes. They also agreed to spend £100 on
repairs. When Crole died in 1804, his successor, John Thomas, was ordained in
the Hall. In 1810, the Court got a report from another surveyor on making use of
some part of the Hall for the Company's purposes and as a residence for the Beadle,
while converting part of the ground floor into offices. The cost was estimated at
£688 and an annual income of £100 was expected from the office rents. Here
again, nothing more is known about this plan or whether it was carried out. The
Hall was rented in 1821 for one year by the Salters' Hall congregation, and then
let to 'Messrs. Martyr', whose business is not stated. They agreed to pay a rent of
£105 yearly, to meet all rates and taxes, to keep the premises in proper repair, and
to insure them for £3,500.

This must have been a considerable relief to the Company, but it was next faced
with the rising demands of property developers and town-planners. In 1839, notice

152   CITIZENS AND FOUNDERS

was received of an intended application to Parliament 'to alter the present streets etc. in and near Lothbury, and proposing to take the Hall and houses in Founders' Court'. The Court appointed a deputation to act on its behalf, and the Master was able to report shortly after that the Company's property had been withdrawn from the Bill. A vote of thanks was given to William Christie, a member of the Court, 'for his earnest attention to the interests of the Company in the Court of Common Council'.

In 1841, a Mr. Hudson proposed to erect new buildings on the frontage ground in Lothbury adjoining the Company's premises, a site which he held on lease from the Corporation of London. The Founders gave him notice that they would oppose any encroachment on light, air, and access affecting their own premises. When negotiation failed to reach agreement, legal action was taken against Hudson which ended in May 1842 with judgment in favour of the Company on all points. In October that year, Hudson's solicitor handed over £675 for damages and costs.

Martyr's lease of the Hall ended in 1843, when the Company was again faced with the problems of maintenance costs and finding a new tenant. In 1844, in anticipation of a Metropolitan Buildings Bill, the Court decided to pull down the Company's two houses in Founders' Court and build a new Hall on that site. This was to provide offices for renting on the ground and first floors, four rooms for the Beadle's accommodation on the third floor, and a kitchen and scullery in the basement. In April 1845, the Master, John Sexton, reported that he had paid £213 for redemption of land tax on the old Hall and another £152 in respect of the two houses. The new Hall was opened in July 1845 and was built at a cost of £1,854 by a 'Mr. Burton' who was possibly William Samuel Burton, Upper Warden in 1854.

The old Hall was let on a building lease in 1844 to the Electric Telegraph Company, a pioneer in modern communications, which by 1854 had opened 17 offices in London, eight of them in the main railway stations. In 1853, they sought and obtained a lease of the new Founders' Hall in addition to their tenancy of the old Hall which they had rebuilt. They paid an annual rent of £400 for the new Hall, which the Court described as 'very liberal' but which graphically illustrates the soaring rise of City property values and fall in the purchasing power of money in more recent years.

It must have been a wrench for the Founders to move out of their ancient domain in Lothbury, but these developments marked a turning-point in the Company's history and did much to secure its future. It should be added that a decisive part in these events was played by William Meade Williams, whose many other services as historian and elder statesman have already been noted. It was also he who, in January 1854, during his second consecutive term as Master, informed the Court that he had found a freehold house in St. Swithin's Lane which was for sale and appeared to be suitable for the Company. After viewing this house, the Court resolved to buy it, subject to legal advice as to the power of the Company to acquire freehold property as well as hold it.

An application for a licence to hold the house in mortmain was made in May

IMPERIAL CROWN   153

1854, but Williams reported that it had not proved possible to obtain this licence before the day appointed for completing the purchase. He had therefore secured promises from 12 members of the Company to make advances totalling £3,500 to enable three of them to buy the house in their own names for the Company. Williams himself headed the list, the others being William S. Burton, Upper Warden, James Moul, Mark E. Marsden, William Christie, William E. Franks, William Devey and William Hems, all members of the Court; and Charles Warner, John Christie, Thomas Moxon junior and William Hems junior, all Liverymen. As had happened in 1531, when the first Hall was built, and again when it was rebuilt after the Great Fire, the Company relied on its own members for support and they gave it. The advances were repaid by instalments, the last one being cleared off in 1867.

In 1866, the freehold value of the Founders' new home at 13 St. Swithin's Lane was estimated at £7,000, a very small figure compared with the value it has since attained. The Electric Telegraph Company retained its lease of the Company's property in Founders' Court until 1863, when the tenancy was taken over by Messrs. Brown, Shipley, merchant bankers. In 1866, however, the Founders offered to lease part of 'the Lothbury house' to the Electric Telegraph Company at £200 a year, which suggests that Brown, Shipley did not occupy all of it, but the offer was refused. In 1876, the Court decided to pull down and rebuild the Hall in St. Swithin's Lane, but the work was not completed until 1878 owing to a strike by the masons. The cost was met by a loan of £8,000 from the London Life Assurance Company at four per cent interest which was repaid by instalments of £300 a year commencing in 1887. The Founders maintained their Court Room in this new Hall, with offices for the Clerk and Beadle and a 'weights office', but most of the house was let to tenants for offices and shops.

The Company's removal from Lothbury might be described as a logical result of historical evolution, since in common with other Livery Companies it had long lost its former position as a community of craftsmen serving their mutual interests and welfare. The last recorded mention of the craft connection is in 1811, when freemen of the Company working as 'journeymen brass founders' complained to the Court that Masters in the trade employed many men who never served any apprenticeship in it, and that the journeymen-freemen of the Company had applied to shops where they were refused employment. The Court made enquiries from which it appeared that there were often not enough 'free journeymen' to supply the trade, but there the matter seems to have ended.

It would be wrong to conclude that all links between the Company and the foundry industry were lost in Victorian times. The report of the City of London Livery Companies' Commission in 1884 stated that, although it could not be said that the Founders' Company exercised any general supervision over the trade, except on matters of weights, there were more members connected with it than was usual with City Companies. A Livery list made in 1867 shows a total membership of 125 and 80 of them gave addresses within the old City, probably referring to their place of work in most cases. In 1879, the President of the Royal Academy,

154 CITIZENS AND FOUNDERS

Sir Frederick Leighton, accepted the Freedom and Livery of the Company and was admitted by the Court at the *Star and Garter* hotel in Richmond.

Under new bye-laws adopted in 1853, quarterage payments were still required from members at nominal rates of 4s. yearly for a Liveryman and 2s. for a Freeman, but they are now commuted to a single payment on entry.

The 19th century witnessed a growing challenge to the rights of the Founders in supervising weights, though not without stubborn resistance. In 1811, the Master informed the Court that 'several persons were in the habit of stamping their own weights and neglected to bring them to the Hall for that purpose'. The Court resolved: 'That the Charter and Bye-Laws be delivered to Mr. Gatty, Attorney-at-Law, to consider the best method to proceed thereon', but his advice is not recorded. In 1825, the Company obtained a warrant from the Court of Exchequer authorising it to use as standards 'the weights under the Act IV, George IV', and these were deposited 'in the iron chest'. At the same time, the Court ordered a new set of 'punches' bearing the Founders' mark and coupled, in the case of all weights over one ounce, with figures denoting the date.

A serious threat to the Company's rights arose in 1834, when a Bill on weights and measures came before Parliament. The Court set up a committee to watch the Bill and it succeeded in getting a clause inserted which reserved the Company's position. In 1845, however, the Beadle reported that the Sadler's Wells Inspector required that brass weights bearing the marks of the Company and the City should have the County mark as well. He was also stamping weights himself which did not bear the Company and City marks, and a large number of them were being sent to the County Inspectors without passing through Founders' Hall or Guildhall. The Clerk was instructed to re-issue a statement of the Company's rights with a warning that any infringement of the Charter would incur legal proceedings, but this seems to have had little effect.

In 1853, when the Company was looking for new premises, a Court committee reported that the gross annual income from stamping weights had averaged £85 over the previous 11 years, out of which a commission averaging £17 a year was paid to the Beadle. The committee expressed doubts as to whether the Company's stamping of weights should be continued, but the Court decided to maintain a 'weight office' in the new Hall in St. Swithin's Lane.

However, the income from this source dropped very rapidly, amounting to only 12s. 1d. in 1866 and a little over £2 in 1869. The last entry for receipts from weights was made in June 1908, when nine weights were stamped at a halfpenny each. Parliamentary Acts on weights and measures passed in 1878 and later years contained a formal acknowledgment of the Company's title, and in 1888 the accuracy of the Company's weight standards was officially certified, but for all practical purposes its old jurisdiction was now a thing of the past. The only trace which still remains is the annual election by the Court of a 'Sizer' and a 'Searcher' from its members.

The rights of self-government which the old City had so long enjoyed were also

IMPERIAL CROWN

coming under pressure. In 1832, the Commissioners for Municipal Corporations requested the attendance of the Master and Wardens of the Founders, but were told that this would not be convenient as they were 'gentlemen engaged in business'. The Commissioners were asked to put their questions in writing for the Court to consider at its next meeting.

In 1852, a Bill came before Parliament for regulating City elections which proposed to confer the voting rights and privileges of Liverymen on all persons occupying premises in the City and paying rates on them. This would have abolished the ancient right of the Livery Companies to elect the Lord Mayor, Sheriffs, and Common Council, and the Companies joined together to resist it. A committee was formed for this purpose and the Founders were represented on it by two of their Court Assistants, William Devey and James Moul, who were chosen by a Livery meeting. This opposition was successful and, in January 1854, the Clerk of the Mercers' Company wrote to the Founders asking for a contribution to the costs incurred.

In 1863, the Master of the Founders, Richard Dale, and his Upper Warden took part in a meeting at Guildhall to consider a private bill tabled in Parliament for amalgamating the City and Metropolitan police forces. The Court authorised the Master to affix the Company's seal to a petition to Parliament, should the Bill be pursued, but in fact it failed.

The ever-increasing role of the State in education was marked by the Endowment Schools Bill, which came before the Commons in 1869. The Master of the Founders, Mark Eagles Marsden, and the Clerk, Algernon Wells, attended a joint meeting of Masters and Clerks to consider the clauses of the Bill and reported that it was 'very wide in its application to the funds at the disposal of the Livery Companies'. In 1872, the Master for that year, Francis Pritchett, represented the Founders on a Committee for the Promotion of Technical Education set up by the Lord Mayor.

The Company itself invoked technical aid in 1874, when it asked the City Commissioners of Sewers to lay down a 'noiseless pavement' in St. Swithin's Lane. The Commissioners replied that the request would be favourably considered, but gave warning of delays due to financial problems and pointed out that it had taken three years to complete a 'noiseless pavement' in Aldersgate Street.

The normal course of Company business was interrupted by news from overseas in 1857, when the laurels of Empire rested briefly on the Founders. In August 1857, the Clerk reported that he had received a copy of the *Graham's Town Journal* from South Africa which stated that the Arms of the Company had been assumed by the District of Aliwal North in the Cape Colony. There was no covering letter, but the Clerk thought that the article must have been forwarded by 'Mr. Chase of Uitenhage, the Civil Commissioner of Albert and resident Magistrate, a Freeman and Liveryman of this Company'. A gratified Court instructed the Clerk to write to Mr. Chase expressing its pleasure at this news and enclosing 'a careful copy of the Coat of Arms, authenticated from the original Grant made by the

156 CITIZENS AND FOUNDERS

Heralds College in the 32nd year of the reign of Queen Elizabeth, A.D. 1590'.

This produced a reply despatched from Uitenhage, Eastern Province, Cape of Good Hope on 16 November 1858, and reading as follows :

To the Master of the Founders' Company :
Sir,

I have the honour to acknowledge the receipt of a very gratifying communication, conveying a Minute of the Worshipful Company of Founders and the very handsome copy of the Coat of Arms of that Company, of which ancient guild I wish I were a worthier member and nearer neighbour.

You will oblige me by stating to the Court that I gratefully acknowledge this kind mark of their consideration and, while wishing you and the Members individually all happiness and prosperity, I beg to state that the town of Aliwal, North, is steadily progressing and is highly thought of by our present excellent Governor, Sir George Grey, who has just again visited it on his journey to mediate between the Basuto Chieftain and the Dutch Republic of the Orange Free State.

Believe me, dear Sir, Yours very truly,
John Centlivre Chase, Civil Commissioner and Resident Magistrate, Division (or County) of Uitenhage.

The Livery list for 1867 shows that by that time J. C. Chase was fifth in order of seniority and must have been of a ripe age, as he was admitted to the Livery in 1818. His address in 1867 still appears as Uitenhage, though he had probably retired by that time. The Company has had many proofs in its long history of the devotion it inspired in members, but the choice of its Arms for Aliwal North is certainly a unique example.

On 28 July 1865, and in accordance with historical advice given by W. M. Williams, the Company celebrated the great event of its 500th anniversary by a banquet at the Crystal Palace which started at five in the evening and went on till ten. It was attended by 150 ladies and other guests, among them being a reporter from the City Press who signed himself 'Alpha'. He wrote an account of the evening in a fruity Victorian style doubtless reinforced by a good dinner, but there are touches of shrewd observation and gentle irony which make him well worth quoting. He began thus :

There is nothing particularly dignified in assembling for the mere purpose of eating and drinking, proposing toasts and making indifferent speeches, yet such meetings go far to preserve and extend a kindly feeling among the myriad units of this vast community. The Companies must dine, and do well to make the necessity a pleasure.

Nearly sixteen generations have passed away since the Founders became a

IMPERIAL CROWN

157

brotherhood . . . Yet it may be doubted whether any of the great trading cities of Europe ever held such a festival. A few strokes of the pen suffice to typify 500 years, but how many empires have waxed and waned during the time? The Doges of Venice, the magnates of Genoa, the Dukes of Florence, and their High Mightinesses of Dutchland, where are they? None of them ever chronicled a 500th anniversary of commercial prosperity, while our glorious London boasts a whole band of princely Companies whose annals extend from four to nearly six hundred years.

Warming to his task and remembering the basic rule of relating events in their proper sequence, 'Alpha' then proceeded to set the scene :

The hall commands a broad platform with an outlook over the beautiful grounds of the Palace, and it was but a step for any guest who needed cooling after an extra glass of champagne. The tables had a really grand and tasteful appearance. They were covered with a profusion of flowers, with an adequate supply of glass and plate, and melons, pines, peaches, and other choice products of the hot-house or garden were awaiting the guests in tempting variety.

The delicacies and ornaments were elegantly walled in by the company; here a portly Founder and his stately wife, quite queenly in her moiré antique and rich jewellery; there a bright, blushing miss in her teens, keeping timorously close to papa, decorously solid and silent; then a young bride symbolising a blown rose, in contrast with the younger undeveloped blossom, and the fond young husband neglecting both his plate and glass to gaze at the charmer by his side. The Masters and Wardens, past and *de facto*, looked 'grave and reverend' on the cross seats, while on either side, and at the far end of the apartment, graceful folds of tamboured muslin mellowed the flood of sunny light and, while seeming to obscure portions of the richly coloured scene, really rendered it more beautiful.

The scribe then turned his attention to the more serious matters of food and drink, remarking :

The dinner was choice, well-cooked, well-served, no guest waited for a moment with an empty plate, some careful waiter was constantly soliciting attention to a fresh dish, and when a wish was expressed for something not offered, it was instantly gratified. Then the wines, 'Sherry or Hock, Sir?', both excellent in quality. 'Champagne or Moselle, Madam?', and these last were so liberally supplied that sealed lips began to grow vocal, and 'low, soft murmurs dropped from ladies' tongues'.

The actual dining occupied from half past five to eight o' clock, then the substantials 'melted into thin air'; custards and ice-puddings – how nice they are

158   CITIZENS AND FOUNDERS

– began to circulate, and while we were contemplating a bright lump of Wenham Lake in our hock glass, Stilton cheese and port, of unexceptionable quality, arrived and the comforted guests subsided into a resigned expectation of toasts to come.

The City Press man did not think much of either the speeches or the relays of singers who entertained between them. Commenting on a song entitled 'Her Pathway Strew With Flowers', he remarked that 'the singer has a powerful voice, but not much skill in using it'. Perhaps 'Alpha' was still trying to fish that bit of cheese out of his glass, but one must agree that bad singing has ruined many a good dinner. He also allowed that nobody making a speech could feel at his ease when scarcely one word in three could be heard and the rest were almost sure to be misinterpreted.

The breed of 'portly Founders' does not flourish today as it did when 'Alpha' so described them, and as for his 'timorous misses', they appear to be almost extinct, for better or for worse. If the guests at that Crystal Palace banquet could have foreseen what the next hundred years held in store for their country, as they drove home in their carriages that Victorian summer's night, they might have found it hard to sleep. They might now be turning in their graves.

CHAPTER XIII

A Sea of Troubles

NO EARLIER GENERATION of Founders was ever subjected to a tidal wave of change, both at home and abroad, so rapid, chaotic and destructive as the period since the death of Edward VII in 1910. Within living memory, we have experienced two world wars of unprecedented slaughter which have wiped out the old landmarks of Western civilisation. The British, French, and Austrian Empires no longer exist, while the rule of Tsars and Hapsburgs has given way to a Russian Communist domination, far more despotic and brutal, over formerly independent states and peoples in Central and Eastern Europe and in the Baltic. Britain herself has been reduced to the position of a second or third-rate power, partly by external forces beyond our control, but also by what sometimes looks like an irresistible urge for self-destruction.

In Ulster and many other parts of the world, the use of cold-blooded murder by terrorists as a political weapon has become a feature of daily life, and so have the hi-jacking of airliners, kidnapping of innocent hostages, and violent crime in general. Nuclear weapons now confront mankind with the threat of physical extermination, while old moral and spiritual values are challenged by a 'permissive' code exalting personal self-interest and self-indulgence. Modern industry and science have unleashed gigantic and unpredictable forces which governments no longer seem able to control.

We must hope and believe that these dangers will be overcome, and there is some comfort in recalling that the Founders, like the whole country, have weathered many past storms of religious conflict, civil war, threats of invasion, plague, fire and inflation. The task of adapting to change in modern times has been less difficult for the Founders, whose ancient craft has grown into a great foundry industry, than for some other Livery Companies whose original art or mistery has withered and died. In recent years, the Court has followed a policy of enlisting more new members from the industrial source. At the same time, the total numbers have been gradually reduced from a post-war peak of 150 to 129 in October 1975. By that time, the number of members associated with the foundry industry had risen to 55, or nearly 43 per cent of the total strength, and 72 Liverymen of all kinds were living or working near London. There is now a waiting list for new admissions, but the Court takes the view that the Company benefits from having a wide range

160   CITIZENS AND FOUNDERS

of interests and occupations represented in it, and that the present balance between foundrymen and others is about right.

For many years, the Company has given practical support to the industry so far as its means allowed. In 1910, the 'Founders' Medal' was instituted from a design by a Liveryman, Mr. A. S. Young, and struck by the Mint at Birmingham, some in silver and others in bronze. The Medal is awarded for outstanding services to the foundry industry and the Founders' Company. In more recent times, it has been presented, in 1958, to the late Dr. J. G. Pearce, a Past Master and Director of the British Cast Iron Research Association, and Dr. J. E. Hurst, Mr. C. C. Booth, and Mr. J. J. Sheehan; and in 1968 to Mr. Michael Hallett, all of whom played a leading part in the organisation of the Company's 'spring tours' of foundries at home and abroad. These tours, which began in 1951, have become a regular annual fixture and have taken Liverymen to France, Denmark, Germany, Ireland, Luxembourg, the Netherlands, Sweden and Switzerland, as well as visits to various parts of the United Kingdom.

In 1901 and again in 1910, the Company sponsored an exhibition of foundry designs, models, and castings at Ironmongers' Hall in the City, and gave prizes and medals for the best exhibits. The Company gave similar awards for technical processes at the Building Exhibition in 1935, and for a competition in 1957 for pattern-making and foundry practice arranged by the City and Guilds Institute. In 1924, the Court agreed to provide 'Founders' Company Scholarships' in the Engineering Faculty at King's College, London, and these were continued until 1941.

An important policy decision was taken in 1938, when the Court resolved that Company funds previously earmarked for charitable gifts to hospitals and other public causes, but excluding provision for relief of distress within the Company, should be used to create 'Founders' Company Fellowships' renewable for a second or possibly third year. Their purpose was to enable young men who had completed a normal course of technical training in foundry work to undertake a further full-time period of advanced training; and also to provide similar facilities for older men of proved ability who were preparing themselves for positions of leadership in the industry. The first fellowship was awarded to Mr. E. J. Ludlow in 1939, but further nominations were suspended during the war and thereafter the number of applications declined. This was largely due to the increased support for industrial training given by the Government, local authorities, and the industry itself.

Some Company Fellowships were still awarded, mostly to National Foundry College students, but in 1967 the Court decided, in view of changed conditions and the limitations of the Company's own finances, that the basis for the Fellowship grants must be revised. In the light of recommendations by Dr. Pearce and other specialists, it was agreed that the Company might make grants for research work in United Kingdom universities, technical colleges or polytechnics, concerned with any branch of foundry work. This particular aid would be financed from the Trust Fund given in his will in 1949 by Robert Warner, Master in 1933 and grandson of

A SEA OF TROUBLES

an earlier Robert Warner, Master in 1865 and 1882. Such grants for research served the purposes for which his trust was given. In addition, the Company's Fellowship fund could be drawn on to enable a young man of promise in the foundry industry to gain experience abroad befitting his record and prospects; or to provide support for an academic term or year in the case of a matured young man with foundry experience who had shown a capacity for rising to technical or managerial leadership.

In 1967 and 1968, the Company gave a diploma and cash grant for the best apprentice at the National Foundry Craft Training Centre, while in 1966 and 1969 it contributed cash prizes for the Inter-European Apprentices Competition. In 1970, the Company paid for three 'travelling scholarships' as part of a scheme initiated by the Foundry Industry Training Committee.

The Company has taken a special interest in bell-founding, an ancient and highly-skilled craft which has been dying out, like many others, in these modern times. It contributed to the cost of repairs made to the famous 'Bow Bells' in 1928 by the Whitechapel Bell Foundry, the oldest of its kind still surviving in Britain. This Foundry celebrated its 400th anniversary in 1970, in the belief that it started work in 1570, but a leading bell historian, George Elphick, has since suggested that the foundry began operating in 1420 in Aldgate, and moved to Whitechapel in 1583. Some of the names in the list of 'master-founders' of the Whitechapel Bell Foundry also appear as members of the Founders' Company, although in the earlier centuries they cannot always be positively identified as being one and the same. Thus, for example, James Bartlett took over the foundry in 1675 and a man of that name was admitted to the Founders' Livery in 1677. An earlier case was that of Thomas Lawrence, master of the Whitechapel Bell Foundry from 1523 to 1538, whose name figures among those admitted to the Founders' Livery in 1524, and who was Third Warden in 1529 and Second Warden in 1536.

In more recent times, the Mears family provided several links between the Foundry and the Company. Thomas Mears was Master of the Company in 1828, when he was also head of the Whitechapel Foundry, and he was followed by Charles and George Mears, who took over the Foundry in 1844. Charles Mears was Master of the Founders in 1849, and George Mears in 1854. Thomas Mears instituted the Company's Charitable Fund, described in the previous chapter. In 1970, to mark the 400th anniversary of the Foundry, two of its partners, Mr. William Hughes and Mr. Douglas Hughes, were made Freemen of the Founders' Company. Happily, bell-founding is an art still much in demand for repairing old bells and supplying new ones, both at home and abroad. In 1966, when the British Welding Association sponsored research work on cracked bells, the Founders gave it financial support.

In the hideous carnage of the First World War when the best of British manhood was slaughtered in Flanders, the relatively small Livery of the Founders lost eight of its members, three of whom belonged to the Warner family. In the war against Nazi Germany which followed in 1939, during which London and many other cities came under heavy air attack, the Company was more fortunate. Nine-

162 CITIZENS AND FOUNDERS

teen City Company Halls were destroyed, including that of the Salters in St. Swithin's Lane, but Founders' Hall was only slightly damaged by fire bombs on 11 May 1941.

This escape was in large measure due to the brave work of fire-watching done by the Beadle at that time, Charles Fountain, and his son John, who followed him as Beadle. Charles Fountain was appointed in 1929, on the retirement of William Westcott, who served the Company for 40 years. Charles himself was Beadle for over 30 years until he retired in 1961, and was held in high regard by Liverymen old and young. It is not easy to follow in such a father's footsteps, but John Fountain has proved a worthy successor. The Founders' records show no comparable period of continuous service as Beadle by father and son, both of whom were made Freemen of the Company.

In October 1938, when Britain reluctantly awoke to the threat of a new war, the Founders 'adopted' the London Irish Rifles, a Territorial Army unit, and helped its men with their family problems when they were on active service. On some occasions in post-war years, their Commanding Officer has been one of the principal guests at the Livery dinners, and the London Irish pipers have made a colourful appearance.

In 1940, when London was in imminent danger of air attack, the safe preservation of the Company's most treasured possessions became an urgent problem. A small pit was dug in the basement floor at Founders' Hall to hold the Weoley Cup, the Venetian goblet of painted glass given by Richard Weoley, Master in 1631 and again in 1640. The silver and other valuables were removed by the Clerk, Wilson Wiley, to banks at Oxford and Pershore, where they remained in safe custody throughout the war.

Wilson Wiley was appointed Clerk in 1936 and for 40 years he has been guide, philosopher, and friend to a host of Founders, admirably supported by his wife Connie. His devotion to the Company has been spiced with a lively sense of gaiety and fun, and his standing in the seasoned fraternity of City Company Clerks is shown by their choice of him in 1952 as Secretary of the Association of Clerks of those Livery Companies, other than the first Twelve, who own Halls. Of his many services to the Founders, one of the most notable was his leading part in the organisation of the 'Spring Tours', which have become a regular annual event.

In 1972, a portrait of the Clerk by Edward Halliday, President of the British Association of Artists, was presented to the Company by the painter and his wife in memory of her father, Robert Hatswell, who was Master in 1935. The Clerk is shown wearing the robes in colours of azure blue and gold which were re-designed in 1971 for the Master, Wardens and Clerk. He is seen holding the silver replica of the Weoley Cup which he gave to the Company in 1962 to mark his 34th year as a Liveryman of the Company. Not only is the Clerk's name, Wiley, very similar to that of Richard Weoley, who gave the original Cup, but by an even happier coincidence of history the silver replica was made by Richard Hart at his workshop in Chipping Campden, the birthplace of Richard Weoley, where he was also buried in 1644. The Clerk's gift thus forms a link in the Company's history extending for over 300 years.

A SEA OF TROUBLES   163

A striking example of family ties with the Founders is the Warner connection. It began with the admission of Edward Warner as a 'Love Brother' in 1767, and has continued to this day. John Warner was Master in 1784, and was followed in that office by Tomson Warner, 1786; John Warner, 1811; Joseph Warner, 1819; Robert Warner, 1826; John Warner, 1827; Charles Warner, 1847 and 1865; Robert Warner, 1866 and 1882; Robert Warner, 1933; and Stephen Warner, 1946.

In memory of Tomson Warner, a pair of candlesticks was given to the Company by Edmund Lucas, Master in 1916, who was related to the Warner family. In 1939, Robert Warner presented a fine Bible in memory of Edmund Lucas, and it has since been used to swear-in new members. This was the same Robert Warner who left the Company a trust fund for metallurgical research, as already noted in this chapter.

Another example of family links is that of the Young family. Henry Young, Master in 1918, was followed in that office, between 1931 and 1960, by his sons Percy, Stanley, Gordon, and Douglas. Henry Young's grandson, Harvey Young, was Master in 1966. Gordon and Douglas Young endowed the 'Young Trust or God's Gift', which presents a Bible to each new Freeman.

In 1972, the Court revived the ancient practice of electing 'Sisters' of the Company, originally widows who might have carried on their late husband's workshop or been married to a Master, Warden, Clerk or Beadle. The earliest case on record occurred in 1497, when the list of members making payments for quarterage and Mass included 'Mistress Hawke', widow of Richard Hawke, who gave the Company a standing cup and money for an annual 'dirge' in his memory. Later examples include Ann Story, admitted to the freedom by servitude or apprenticeship in 1729; Mary Winstanly, a widow admitted by redemption or purchase in 1759; and Elizabeth Ordway who received the freedom by patrimony, with her brother, in 1759. Under the custom of the City, the daughters of a Liveryman born to him after he joined the Company are eligible as of right, like his sons, for admission as Freemen. Three ladies were so admitted in 1972, and three more in 1973.

In recent years, the Court has sought ways and means of accelerating the promotion of Liverymen to the rank of Assistant and giving them an opportunity of election to the Court at an earlier age. The case for such action is strengthened by the longer span of life which now prevails, but the problem is one which admits no easy or instant solutions. The Court of a Livery Company relies very largely on the advice and views of men with mature and varied experience in many walks of life who, in the case of the Founders, are elected from Liverymen in order of seniority. It is a system which effectively combines traditional methods with the modern idea of a democratic process. It is true that in some Livery Companies, especially those with larger resources and a wider range of activities, a case can be made for selecting new members of the Court from Liverymen of outstanding ability, regardless of age or seniority. The risk here is that it may encourage nepotism and the rule of a small inner circle which may do more harm than good. The Founders have so far preferred to retain election to the Court by seniority as being the fairest method.

164   CITIZENS AND FOUNDERS

In considering how this system might be improved, the Court had to take into consideration a clause in the Company's Charter of 1614 which states: 'There shall be one Master, two Wardens, and fifteen Assistants'. As noted in earlier pages, this rule did not prevent some Founders' Courts in the 18th century from having as many as 35 Assistants, at a time when many of them failed to attend meetings. In 1777, the Court took the view that the Charter provision was intended to allow 15 Assistants as a minimum number, but not to confine them to that limit and no more. In 1962, however, largely on advice from the City Chamberlain's office, the Court decided that it must adhere to the Charter definition as meaning that no more than 15 Assistants could be appointed, in addition to Master and Wardens. Some other way of breaking the deadlock had to be found.

This was done by inviting members of the Court who had served as Master to become 'Honorary Assistants' of their own free will. They would still be entitled to attend and speak at Court meetings, but not to propose or second resolutions or to take part in voting. By accepting this invitation, they created new vacancies for electing Liverymen as Assistants without exceeding the Charter limitation of fifteen.

Mr. James Arthur Taylor, a senior and much respected member of the Court, gave the lead by becoming the first Honorary Assistant in 1962, closely followed by Mr. William Guy Fossick. In 1974, the Court widened the scheme by authorising the Master to write to five members of the Court who were 80 or more, and had passed the chair, to ask if they would be willing to serve as Honorary Assistants. They were Mr. H. C. Bradbrook, Mr. E. W. Moss, Mr. S. R. Walker, Captain William Gregson, and Mr. J. D. K. Beardmore. They all accepted this proposal, but for the time being only two of them, Mr. Bradbrook and Mr. Moss, were chosen. To mark its appreciation, the Court ordered that the names of Honorary Assistants should in future take precedence in the Court list.

The Company has revived its ancient link with St. Margaret Church, Lothbury. Services were held there in 1943, when Captain Alfred Hodsoll Heath was Master, and in 1957, when Major L. E. Cotterell held that office. Since 1958, an annual service for the Company has taken place there prior to the Court meeting for electing the new Master and Wardens. The Company has also taken part in the United Guilds Service held annually in St. Paul's since its inception in 1943. It has contributed to the cost of repairs, both in St. Margaret and St. Paul's, and also to Guildford Cathedral, where there is a window bearing the Company's name and arms.

The Company's financial position after the First World War was precarious, so much so that in 1919 the Court commended Mr. Harry Hughes, founder of the City Livery Club and a Liveryman of the Founders who was Master in 1929, for introducing no less than 15 new members and thus bringing in the useful sum of £500. Also in 1919, the Court appointed 15 Stewards at one fell swoop, whose office fines must have been welcome. Rents from offices and shops let out in Founders' Hall continued to be the mainstay of the Company's income, but in 1964, when Lt. Col. James C. Thomson was Master, events took a new turn which gave the Company a much stronger financial base. An offer was received for the

A SEA OF TROUBLES 165

freehold of the Company's property in Lothbury from the tenants, Messrs. Brown, Shipley, and the sale was made at a substantial figure. Still more fortunately, the business was concluded on the day before capital gains tax was introduced.

The severance of this last link with the old Founders' Halls in Lothbury had its sadder aspect, but the Company was thus enabled to rebuild and modernise the Hall in St. Swithin's Lane. The office rentals inside the Hall were terminated and the whole building converted for the Company's sole use. The alterations provided a new Court Room, a large reception room available for hospitality by the Company or its Liverymen, or for City and foundry industry purposes, offices for the Master, Clerk and Beadle, and a modern kitchen for serving lunches or dinners in the Court Room. There is not sufficient space for full Livery Dinners, which are still held either in the Mansion House, by kind permission of the Lord Mayor, or in other Company Halls. The reconstructed premises were opened on 25 September 1967.

On 29 July 1974, the Lord Mayor for that year, Sir Hugh Wontner, visited Founders' Hall and was entertained to lunch by the Court. He gave the Company a shield bearing his Arms to mark this occasion. Strange as it may seem, no reigning Lord Mayor had made such a visit before in the Company's long history. Conversely, the Founders have only provided the Mansion House with two Lord Mayors, Sir David Burnett in 1912 and Sir Frederick Wells in 1947. The office of Sheriff was held in 1958 by Mr. S. R. Walker, Master of the Company in 1962, and in 1960 by the late Mr. A. K. Kirk, who was elected to the Court in 1972.

The Founders celebrated their 600th Anniversary in 1965, in the same year that their old freehold in Lothbury was sold. Thus, while one chapter was closed, another opened in the Company's long story from medieval to modern times. The Company gave a banquet in Guildhall attended by over 500 Liverymen, wives and distinguished guests. The Master in this memorable year was Lt. Col. Thomson, whose name has already been mentioned and who joined the Company in the same year, 1934, as the present writer. At his suggestion, the Court initiated a 'Sexcentenary Fund' to mark the Anniversary. Its purpose was to contribute to national schemes for helping old people, and the young, and to buy for the Company some permanent memento.

In addition, each Liveryman was presented with a replica of the 'Bowen' Spoon. As earlier related, this was one of many silver spoons given to the Company by newly-admitted Freemen in Stuart times. All these spoons were later sold at intervals when the Company was in dire financial need, but the Humphrey Bowen spoon was saved, probably because of its delightful inscription : 'If You Love Me, Keep Me Ever, That's My Desire And Your Endeavour'. With the same thought in mind, the Court made a request that the replicas given to Liverymen should be returned to the Company after their death. As an outright gift, each wife of a Liveryman received a one-pound brass weight, stamped with the Company's Arms and recalling the rights formerly exercised by the Founders in this field. These weights were made in the foundry of Beardmore and Company, represented in the Livery by J. D. K. Beardmore and C. C. Rogers.

166   CITIZENS AND FOUNDERS

Another notable event was the installation in 1974 of a stained glass window bearing the arms and devices of the Company in the restored West Crypt of the Guildhall. The Master that year was Mr. Peter Blaxter, a distinguished surgeon, whose father and grandfather both served as Master. Nineteen Livery Companies were chosen by ballot for this distinction, and the Founders were among those successful. Their interest in the windows was first aroused by Mr. S. R. Walker, Past Master and a former Chief Commoner of the City, whose services both to the Company and the City Corporation deserve special mention.

There is good reason to believe that the West Crypt is the oldest part of the Guildhall and preceded the work of enlarging it which began in 1411. The West Crypt survived the Great Fire of 1666, but was severely damaged in the London 'Blitz' of the last war. It has now been restored to its ancient state, with vaulted roof and massive supporting pillars, and is lit by lancet windows deeply set into the walls and designed by Mr. Brian Thomas, O.B.E. In their warmth of colour and purity of style, these windows recall the medieval art of stained glass and make a vivil foil to the stark, monastic lines of the interior.

The Founders' window, placed next to that of the Blacksmiths, is a pictorial album of historical associations in stained glass. The central feature is the Company's heraldic device of a laver-pot in brass with a candlestick on each side, surmounted by a charcoal furnace and a pair of hands holding tongs over a crucible containing molten metal. This is flanked by various emblems signifying the Company's evolution, among them being an anchor and fountain representing the connection with the patron Saint Clement and the Company's origin as a religious brotherhood of laymen; the 'Founders' Medal' which has already been mentioned; and a globe denoting the annual visits made by the Company to foundries at home and abroad. The upper part of the window shows traditional products of the craft, such as bells, cannon, a cast-iron bridge and the brass weights over which the Company long exercised control. In the lower part, modern foundry products are shown, such as cylinder-blocks, crankshafts, marine propellers, pistons, pipes and valves.

The window is so placed that it catches the sunlight and is thus seen to the best advantage. Here in Guildhall, in the old heart of the City and within sight of St. Lawrence, Jewry, where the earliest Founders worshipped, is a memorial of which the Company may be justly proud.

This brings to a fitting conclusion the history of the Company which has been retraced in these pages through the long journey from 1365. There are still many aspects which remain obscure and offer a wide field for further exploration. If this book serves to stimulate such an interest in members of the Company, young and old, one of its main objects will have been achieved. It is possible that old Company records and papers which have disappeared are not lost beyond recall, but may still be lying forgotten in public archives or private attics and basements. In 1914, for example, the Founders' Order Book for 1763 to 1780 was offered for sale privately to the Guildhall Library and bought by the Company for £7. In 1948, Dr. Stannus, Past Master, made vain attempts to trace some old minute-books lost when

A SEA OF TROUBLES

in the hands of J. C. L. Stahlschmidt, Master in 1880. Old plans and sketches of the Hall in Lothbury may yet be discovered.

In January 1976, the Vicar of St. Margaret's Parish Church, Uxbridge, the Rev. Neil Pollock, wrote to the Master of the Founders, Mr. Frank Rowe, to say that the church had regained possession of a brass chandelier presented in 1735 by Robert Burton, a whitesmith in London. The chandelier was in need of repairs and the church was raising a fund for its restoration. We know that Robert Burton was apprenticed to Edmund Cooke in 1692, became a freeman of the Founders' Company in 1701, and was Master in 1715-16. The chandelier may well have been made in his own workshop. He was the son of Robert Burton senior, a cordwainer who lived in Richmond, Yorkshire.

Then again, while preparing this book for publication, I happened to see an offer in a magazine of a church or stable turret bell bearing the name of 'G. Mears, Founder, London 1860'. This must refer to George Mears, Master of the Founders in 1854-5, whose family connection with the Whitechapel Bell Foundry has already been mentioned earlier in this chapter.

The Founders' Company has undergone many a crisis in the past, but always emerged with its unity restored and its future committed to new hands. It began as a parish brotherhood of neighbours in an age of simple medieval faith and in an England tasting the first heady wine of national awakening. It then became a craft gild of working masters and men protecting their economic interests, but strictly upholding high standards of workmanship and fair dealing. That was followed by the transition to a Livery Company with a Royal Charter in which the old craft interest gradually died out. In our own time, the Company has gained a new vitality by forming its links with the modern foundry industry, while never forgetting that the Livery Companies are rooted in the old City of London which has a prior claim on their loyalty and service.

These Companies have played a decisive and creative part in English history. They won civic self-government for London from kings and over-mighty subjects. In their prime, they made the biggest contribution to our national wealth and commerce. Their example has shown what men can accomplish by free association in a common cause.

The Founders' Company has made its small mark on this scroll of history. It still has an active and continuing part to play as a bridge between past and present and a living proof of the strength which men draw from the ties of mutual trust and friendship. In the words of the Company's own toast, 'root and branch, may it flourish and prosper for ever'.

POSTSCRIPT

The Technical Evolution

BY MICHAEL HALLETT C.B.E., M.SC., F.I.B.F., F.I.M., F.S.A.

THE PAST six centuries have been a period of steady development in the foundry industry, as in other basic industries that have had to adapt themselves to meet the constantly changing and more severe demands of contemporary life. Several different themes may be distinguished in the evolution of foundries – appearance of new metals and alloys, growing ability to produce in larger and larger unit quantities, increasing efficiency and, in the present century, saving of labour by mechanisation and automation. The rate of change was slow at first but gradually accelerated through the 18th and 19th centuries to reach the breathless speed characteristic of today.

Often the details of the changes have not been documented but fortunately an outstandingly good account of the early period is available in the Pirotechnia of Vannoccio Biringuccio, a distinguished Italian, who eventually became head of the Papal foundry in Rome, a position he held until his death about a year before the publication of his book in 1540. Although written nearly 200 years after the establishment of the Founders Company, the practice described may be taken as typical of all the early period.

Biringuccio understood his foundry intimately and his general appraisal would hold in some quarters even now : '. . . he who wishes to practice this art must not be of a weak nature, either from age or from constitution, but must be strong, young and vigorous, so as to be able to handle things, as you almost always have to, that are heavy and inconvenient because of their weight – things such as bronze, iron tools, wood, water, clay, rocks, bricks and the like. Nor do I doubt that whoever considers this art well will fail to recognise a certain brutishness in it, for the founder is always like a chimney sweep, covered with charcoal and distasteful sooty smoke, his clothing dusty and half burned by the fire, his hands and face all plastered with soft muddy earth. To this is added the fact that for this work a violent and continuous straining of all a man's strength is required, which brings great harm to his body and holds many definite dangers to his life. In addition, this art holds the mind of the artificer in suspense and fear regarding its outcome and keeps his spirit disturbed and almost continually anxious. For this reason they are called fanatics and are despised as fools. But with all this it is a profitable and skillful art and in large part delightful'. To echo a complaint of many wives through the succeeding ages, 'As a result, as if ensnared, he is often unable to leave the place of work'.

In Biringuccio's time, the principal foundry products to which he devotes his detailed descriptions were guns, bells and cannon-balls. In each his knowledge was profound and he gives an account of bell-founding that does not differ fundamentally from present practice and which includes instructions on the design of bells and on the calculation of weights and thicknesses needed to arrive at particular results. Gun-founding had also been brought to a surprising state of perfection.

In general, the moulds were constructed of a plastic clay mixture which was smeared on to the pattern and subsequently baked. The clay was invariably strengthened by animal fibres such as wool cloth clippings, the whole being well beaten together and mixed so that it became absolutely uniform in the same way as in pottery. The problem of removing the pattern from the dried mould was generally solved by making the pattern in parts with separate loose pieces for undercuts. It was also possible to make the mould itself in sections and to re-assemble them after the removal of the pattern, though Biringuccio was well aware of the dangers of this procedure.

The cores were also made in a similar loam mixture but in this case with more fibrous matter such as the hair taken from skins during tanning. Core mixtures customarily contained manure to keep the structure open for passage of gas. The core for a gun-barrel was made in a manner still in use. A layer of rope was wrapped around an iron bar which served as the core spindle. On the rope layer was smeared the core mixture which was probably dried in successive layers. The central spindle was removed from the core before casting which, in the case of gun-barrels, seems to have been performed vertically. Suitable chaplets and ring supports to fix the core in position were introduced. In some cases wax patterns were employed and it was also possible for the core to be held in position by rods which passed through the mould and the wax pattern and into the core. It should be remembered that the lost wax process is of far greater antiquity than the medieval period. The whole assembly of mould and cores was reinforced by wrapping wire around before casting.

Biringuccio also mentioned the making of small castings in boxes. These were described as being in green sand but the sand was actually washed and calcined, mixed with bone ash and flour as a bond, moistened with such various liquids as water, vinegar, urine and wine. Interestingly, the cannon-balls made in iron were cast not only in such clay mixtures as those described but also in permanent moulds, themselves made of cast iron.

In the main, Biringuccio was dealing with bronze. This, according to the quantity required, could be melted in reverberatory furnaces or in small crucibles. The iron used for casting cannon-balls was melted in hearths of about the size of a smith's hearth, provided with a hole in the bottom through which the molten iron could be tapped.

THE TECHNICAL EVOLUTION

Cast iron

During the 15th century, cast-iron was appearing throughout Europe, though it had been used in China 2,000 years earlier. The discovery of cast iron had its origin in attempts to improve the simple types of hearth or low shaft furnaces in which a pure iron was made by direct reduction of iron ore with charcoal. These never achieved a sufficiently high temperature to melt the soft iron but as units became larger and the furnace shafts higher, a temperature was reached at which the iron dissolved carbon to produce a material of lower melting point which could be tapped liquid from the furnace and cast into useful shapes. In fact, most of the iron so produced was used for conversion into wrought iron, but appreciation of the properties of the new material, which was both harder and cheaper than bronze, gradually came to be recognised.

There is evidence that the first blast furnace to produce iron in England was in operation at Buxted in Sussex as early as 1496 and was unquestionably working at the time when Biringuccio wrote. The early products were mainly cannon balls, soon leading to quite large cannon, of which the first was cast by Peter Balde, already identified (p. 24) as a member of the Founders' Company. As early as 1549 a double furnace was in operation which comprised two furnaces mounted together in one structure like a Siamese twin, so making available double the quantity of metal for production of large castings. Another well-known early product was the cast-iron fire-back mentioned in the literature in 1547. Fire-dogs were produced at the same time and grave slabs became popular in some areas in the 1550s. In the following century, large rollers for sugar crushing were made and not unnaturally many of the parts of waterwheels and equipment used in ironworks were cast in iron and eventually domestic products such as pots and pans. Iron cannon cast in England enjoyed a very high reputation but it is not clear on exactly what grounds. In general, they appeared to be made with longer barrels for a given calibre which would, of course, increase the velocity and hence the range of the shot. Probably, the actual cannon were more reliable than those of some other European producers, perhaps because of better feeding and running techniques to ensure soundness of castings, perhaps even because of a fortuitous availability of more suitable grades of pig iron.

The next clear documentary evidence on the iron foundry industry came from a Frenchman, Réaumur, who lived from 1683 to 1757 and who published, in 1722, a work on the art of making cast iron malleable. A little later appeared another famous French work, the *Encyclopaedia* of Diderot and D'Alembert. The drawings in these two works are similar, and Réaumur accused Diderot (probably correctly) of stealing his plates and using them in the *Encyclopaedia*. In the foundries represented, making relatively small castings, moulding boxes were used which could be clamped together in a frame. Little detail was given on moulding practice, but it was clear that the moulds were still made in a baked clay.

Melting was carried out in small movable, stack furnaces not more than two or three feet high. The upper stack portion was preferably made of iron sheet lined with clay. This sat on top of a crucible or hearth made of a cast-iron kettle lined with about an inch and a half thickness of refractory clay. The blast came through a single tuyere blown by a pair of hand-operated bellows. This furnace was charged with charcoal, followed by successive layers of iron and charcoal. When all the iron had collected in the crucible, the top stack was knocked off and the crucible in its surrounding cradle was lifted either by a lever or by two men and the iron poured into the moulds. One variety of this type of furnace could be tilted complete.

While Réaumur was writing his account in France, great steps forward were taking place in England. In Coalbrookdale in Shropshire in 1709, Abraham Darby I solved, on a commercial production basis, the problem of smelting iron ore with coke. This freed the iron industry from the restrictions caused by exhaustion of forests for making charcoal and opened the way for larger scale operations. The Darby dynasty was composed of men of extraordinary character and ability who developed many iron products and processes on a larger and larger scale. Their introduction of the technique of true green sand-moulding in boxes enabled them to make articles such as the different sizes of the well-known Kaffir pots, which were relatively thinner than previous iron castings. Other firsts included the production of cast-iron rails. Coalbrookdale may justifiably be described as the cradle of the Industrial Revolution.

A spectacular advance took place in 1779 when Abraham Darby III cast and erected the first great iron bridge in the world, spanning the River Severn near Coalbrookdale. The span was 100 feet and the total weight of the bridge amounted to 378 tons. The individual members weighed up to five and three-quarter tons each. Only a coke-fired furnace could provide iron on this scale.

So far the cast-iron was tapped straight from the blast furnace, thus being directly smelted from the iron ore. For many foundry purposes this was an inconvenient method of melting and the advantages of using a separate melting furnace simply for the purpose of re-melting the primary pig iron came to be recognised and thus the cupola furnace was born. It may be regarded as a descendant of the small furnace described by Réaumur but the development was fundamentally due to the famous ironmaster and foundryman, John Wilkinson, who patented the first cupola in 1794 in the Black Country. His brother William may well have been responsible for the first in operation. Such families as the Wilkinsons and the Darbys worked in close co-operation with the various engineers developing new and improved steam engines. The success of Boulton and Watt in developing their engine could not have been achieved without the help of the foundrymen who were able to cast sound the large cylinders needed and also to develop equipment to machine the cast cylinders accurately. Wilkinson promptly applied such cylinders to make improved blowing engines for his furnaces, which in turn stimulated the production of larger and better castings.

These developments in England were rapidly followed in Europe and the United States. In a survey of the recent history of ironworks carried out by E. Vollhan in 1825, the existence of iron foundries provided with cupola furnaces, able to cast and machine large cylinders prepared both by sand-moulding and by loam-mould-

THE TECHNICAL EVOLUTION 173

ing, was reported at several locations in Poland and Czechoslovakia. Unfortunately, this report deals more with furnaces and smelting than with foundry practice.

During the first half of the 19th century, cast iron was in a predominant position as the main engineering constructional material and was used for many architectural purposes such as columns, beams, balconies and railings. Wrought iron, and, from the 1860s onwards, mild steel in particular, took over as the bulk material of construction but, although dropping behind as a proportion of the total output of ferrous materials, cast iron has continued to increase in absolute tonnage throughout the world.

Normal grey cast iron cannot be made to bend but a parallel material known as malleable cast iron, originating with Réaumur (though 50 years earlier Prince Rupert had taken out a patent), satisfies the need for an iron that can be cast and bent. Réaumur's type of product, whiteheart malleable iron, is still made but a stronger and tougher type, blackheart malleable iron, was invented by Seth Boyden in the U.S.A. in 1826 and still satisfies the bulk of the demand for malleable iron in the automobile industry. These two types of iron are so named because of the appearance of the fracture. In the 20th century, as a result of work both in the U.S.A. and in Great Britain, alternative methods of producing similar material with much less complicated or even no heat treatment were developed, the product being known as nodular iron or spheroidal graphite iron. It may also be noted that 20th century developments include the alloying of cast iron to produce materials resistant to wear, heat and corrosion.

Cast Steel

The process of melting steel in crucibles was invented by Huntsman in Sheffield in 1750 but he was interested in casting ingots for subsequent working into tools rather than in making finished castings. About 1825, in Europe, J. C. Fischer was able to make a low-carbon steel in crucibles and in the next 20 years gradually developed suitable refractory melting materials. In the 1840s, J. Mayer cast steel bells at Bochum. The first steel castings in the United Kingdom for railway crossings and cog wheels were cast in Sheffield, by Vickers in 1855. Production was limited by melting facilities and, to make large castings, batteries of crucible furnaces manned by innumerable workpeople had to be employed.

The development of the production of mild steel in open-hearth furnaces and in Bessemer converters provided bulk metal for steel castings but the first furnace specifically designed for use in steel foundries was the Tropenas side-blown converter which started work in 1893. Only two years earlier, steel was first poured into green-sand moulds. Later progress of steel foundries was intimately associated with electric melting furnaces. The industry also participated in the development and use of improved foundry methods in common with the other metals, and in the application of alloy and stainless steels.

Non-ferrous alloys

In the non-ferrous foundry field the casting of copper-base alloys had reached such an advanced state in the Middle Ages that there were no dramatic later advances. Certainly new alloys, such as aluminium bronze, of much greater strength and corrosion resistance, were developed and the melting of alloys in oil-fired crucible furnaces or in electric furnaces provided larger quantities of higher quality metal. The changes in the 20th century followed those in other types of foundries.

A newcomer to the non-ferrous field was aluminium. In 1890, aluminium was a rare metal worth about as much as silver but the processes for the mass production of pure aluminium by electrolytic smelting greatly extended the availability of the metal. The statue of Eros in Piccadilly was cast in aluminium before 1900 and many aluminium foundries were established early in the present century. These at first made their castings in sand but soon the problems of casting in permanent metallic moulds, usually of iron, were overcome and many die-castings of aluminium were used in the First World War. The early examples were simply cast by normal gravity into metallic moulds, a process still extensively used for high-quality castings, but during the two following decades pressure die-casting was developed, in which an exact quantity of metal at a low temperature was forced under high pressure into a metallic mould. These castings could be complex in shape and were of exceptionally good surface finish and high dimensional accuracy.

For certain special purposes, usually connected with aircraft, the even lighter metal magnesium is cast, often in sand-moulds of special composition, but for the cheapest die-castings, zinc alloys have definite advantages. Not only can the castings be made at a lower temperature but they can be made faster, cheaper and more accurately than aluminium castings. Zinc is better able than aluminium to accept surface finishes such as chromium plating but aluminium has the advantages of being lighter, with a better corrosion resistance, higher electric conductivity and greater stability than zinc alloys. The possibility of using zinc alloys was only achieved after some exceptionally painstaking research work which demonstrated that some serious types of internal corrosion in the early zinc alloys were due to small quantities of particular impurities. The production of high purity zinc has solved this problem.

Reference should be made to one other family of foundry alloys which has a very ancient history. These are the alloys based on tin and lead. Pewter, a tin alloy, has been known since Roman times and has long been cast in metallic moulds. Lead alloys used for toy soldiers were made throughout the 19th century in iron moulds. The process known as slush-casting was usually adopted for the soldiers, the mould being inverted soon after pouring so that the majority of the liquid metal ran out leaving only a shell of solid lead against the mould surface. Lead alloyed with antimony is the basis of type metal and the first attempts to produce machines for casting type metal, represented by patents in 1849, 1852, 1856 and 1877, eventually led to the linotype machines in which liquid metal was forced into moulds for newspaper work. Such machines were the forerunners of the die-casting machines used for aluminium and zinc.

The 20th century

As would be expected, development in the 20th century has taken place at a rate far surpassing that of earlier times. All sections of the foundry industry have

THE TECHNICAL EVOLUTION

been concerned in reducing the labour content of castings by mechanisation. Even at the end of the 19th century, continuous casting conveyors were in use but the moulds were made and placed on the conveyor by large numbers of operatives. Mechanised moulding machines of increasing complexity have been designed. They operate at ever greater speeds, producing harder moulds and therefore more accurate castings with much less production of dust and dirt. A present-day mass production plant may be completely automated, controlled from a central console, with mould-making, pouring of measured quantities of metal into each mould and the final knocking-out of the castings all being performed automatically.

As has been noted for non-ferrous metals, there has been a major swing in the direction of permanent moulds. The problems become more severe as the melting point of the material increases, but both copper alloys and cast-iron are poured into permanent metal moulds in substantial, though not predominant, quantities. One special form of the permanent mould is represented by centrifugal castings of tubular objects, particularly cast-iron pipe for water, sewage and gas services and cylinder liners for internal combustion engines, which represent an appreciable proportion of the total tonnage cast. The metal is poured into a rotating mould and the centrifugal force distributes it uniformly over the mould surface and holds the internal surface cylindrical until solidification takes place.

The production of cores which form the interior shape of castings has been revolutionised during the past 60 years. Originally they were made from loam mixtures, as described by Biringuccio, which were then baked hard and dry. In the 1920s, sands bonded with linseed oil came into general use, baking more rapidly and combining high hardness with high permeability. The last 25 years have witnessed the introduction of a series of core-making methods, all of which are based on the very rapid hardening of the cores in their core boxes. This has brought about much greater accuracy of the final core because its dimensions are determined while it is held rigid in the core box, whereas the earlier methods entailed removal of a relatively soft core, with the danger of sagging while being transferred to the core-baking oven. Some hardening methods have involved passing gases through the core mixture in its box; others have depended on heat to accelerate the hardening reactions, the heat being applied via a hot core box, while others entail the rapid mixing of a core-hardening binder with a catalyst to initiate a quick hardening action.

The use of heat in the containing core box has also been applied to the making of moulds by a process known as shell-moulding, where a hot pattern is covered with a thermally hardening sand mixture which sets rigidly before it is moved from the pattern. A combination of shell-moulds with shell-cores leads to castings of exceptionally good surface finish and dimensional accuracy. All these methods lend themselves to mechanisation and therefore to a satisfactory combination with the mechanised or automated moulding lines.

For a limited but very important production of castings of the highest accuracy and reliability, the old lost wax process has been resuscitated. In this process a wax pattern is made in a very accurate steel die. Around the wax pattern is coated, by

176   CITIZENS AND FOUNDERS

a succession of dippings into a slurry mixture followed by drying, a thick mould able to withstand the pressure of the liquid metal. At this stage the whole mould, still containing the pattern, is heated and the wax melts, leaving an exact impression ready to receive the molten metal. As with the modern methods of core-making the advantage here is that the dimensions are determined and the mould hardened while still in contact with the pattern. This process is also extremely flexible in terms of design as the usual problems involved in removing a complicated pattern from the mould do not arise.

Furnished with a bewildering array of machines designed to produce accurate castings of all sizes from fractions of an ounce up to hundreds of tons and in all numbers, coupled with the use of accurate cores and complicated equipment for cleaning and critically inspecting the castings made from metal melted under carefully controlled conditions, the foundry industry of today is serving all the needs of the world's engineering industries, which would not be able to exist without adequate supplies of appropriate castings.

APPENDIX A

Petition for Ordinances, 29 July 1365

To the honourable and right worthy Masters the Mayor and Aldermen of the City of London:

The good Men of the Mistery of Founders complain that, whereas some of the said Mistery do work and make their works of false metal and false solder, so that their said work, to wit, Candlesticks, Buckles, Straps, and other suchlike articles, when exposed to fire or great strain, crack, break, and dissolve, to the peril and damage of those who purchase them, and to the great slander of the City and the whole Mistery: Wherefore the good Men aforesaid pray that it may please your right worthy Masterships to grant that the points under-written may be conceded, allowed, and by you accepted and enrolled in the Chamber of Guildhall.

In the first place, That no Man of the said Mistery shall work in the said Mistery, or do any work, unless it be of good Metal.

That no one shall make any Stirrups, Buckles, or Spurs, unless of the best and finest Metal that can be found or obtained, and of Metal that will not break, and no other.

That no one of the said Mistery shall solder any Candlesticks with white Solder, or make Candlesticks, Lavers, Pots, or other things with any pieces soldered thereto but such things as in reason ought to be soldered, such as the pipes of Lavers and other like articles.

Also, that all the Work in the said Mistery called Closwork shall be made of good, fine, and pure Metal and no other.

Also, that no one of the said Mistery shall make any manner of moulding, or work in the said Mistery, by Night or on Saturday, or on the Vigil of a double Feast, when the Vigil shall begin after the hour of None [three o'clock] tolled at the Church where he resides.

Also, that no man that is not of the Mistery aforesaid shall receive or put any Servant, Apprentice, or hired person of the same Mistery to work with him in the said Mistery, on pain of paying to the Chamber each time he shall be attainted or convicted thereof, Forty Shillings.

Also, that no one of the said Mistery coming to the said City shall be suffered to keep a House or Shop unless he be first examined by the Masters of the said Mistery, who are elected and sworn to govern such Mistery, whether he be able and sufficient and knowing in the said Mistery, to have such state or not. And if he be able, sufficient, and knowing, that they may cause him to come before you to enfranchise him by the Masters aforesaid and not by others, so that they may know him to be good, sufficient, and profitable to the common people and to the City, under the same pain.

Also, that no man of the said Mistery, under the said pain, shall receive anyone to work in the said Mistery as a hired person before he be tried and proved by the Masters aforesaid whether he be able to work in the said Mistery as a hired person or not, and it be adjudged by the said Masters what he shall receive by the day; and that if he shall be found not able or knowing in the said Mistery, that he be ousted thereof if he will not be Apprentice.

178 CITIZENS AND FOUNDERS

Also, if any Master of the said Mistery and his Varlet or Servant shall disagree by reason of any contention between them, that no other Master of the said Mistery shall be so daring as to place or procure such Varlet or Servant to be put to any work until the Master and Varlet be reasonably reconciled.

Also, if any Varlet or Servant of the said Mistery has served his Master in the said Mistery for any certain term or covenant made between them, and no default shall be found in the Varlet or Servant, and the Master through malice will not pay to such Varlet or Servant his salary for his service according to the covenant made between them, or that the Master will compel him to serve contrary to his will beyond his covenant, well and lawfully fulfilled, that then the said Master shall suffer the penalty above written.

Also, if any Varlet or Servant of the said Mistery shall be found in any default towards his Master, whether by the deceit or enticement of another or by his own malice, he may be punished at the discretion of the Mayor and Aldermen according to the degree of the trespass.

Also, that no one of the said Mistery shall be so daring as to procure any Servant, Hired Person, or Apprentice out of the service of his Master before the covenant made between them shall be fully performed; and if anyone do so, and shall be convicted thereof, he shall pay to the Chamber each time he shall be attainted thereof, Forty Shillings.

Also, that two or three of the best Men of the said Mistery may be selected and sworn to watch and oversee the whole Mistery, and present to you all the default they may reasonably find in the said Mistery.

Also, that if anyone of the said Mistery, be he Master or Servant, shall be found rebellious or opposing to the said Masters elected and sworn, so that they cannot duly make their search in the said Mistery, he shall suffer the pain heretofore ordained in such case.

Also, that all the work of the said Mistery that may be found falsely wrought, or of false and brittle Metal, may be forfeited to the Chamber, in whose hands soever it may be found.

Also, that the Masters elected and sworn, together with a Sergeant of the Chamber, may have power to make their search as well over those who are not of the said Mistery and have articles touching the same Mistery to sell, as those who are of such Mistery.

APPENDIX B

Ordinances of 1489

Memorandum: The Wardens and other Good Men of the Craft or Mistery of the Founders within the Citie of London came into the Inner Chamber of the Guildhall of London before William White, Mayor of the same Citie and his Brethren the Aldermen, and exhibited and put unto them a Bill or Supplication, the tenor whereof followeth in these words:

To the Rt. Hon. the Lord Mayor, etc.,
Mekely beseechen your good Lordshippes and Masterships, the gode folks of the Crafte of Founders of the Citie of London, That it wold please your sayd Lordshippes and Master-shippes for the wele and gode rule to be had and kepte in the same Crafte, to graunt and establishe these Articles underwritten, from hensforth to be observed and kepte.

1st. That every Brother of the Crafte shall attend and wayte upon the Wardens upon due warninge by the Bedell. Also to wayte upon the Mayor, Aldermen, and Sheriffs at such tymes and seasons as has been accustomed upon payne of vi/d as often as any of them is found doing contrary without reasonable excuse, the fine of vi/d so paid, the one half to the use of the Chamber, the other half to the use of the Crafte.

2nd. Keeping of Masses, Burying of poor Brethren and other dede of Almes, and charge every Brother pay yearly his Quarterage to the Wardens. Every brother of the Clothing iii/d a Quarter. Every Householder not of the Clothing ii/d a Quarter. Every Journeyman i/d a Quarter. Upon payne to pay xii/d, one halfe to the Chamber, the other halfe to the use of the Crafte.

3rd. Every Brother of the Clothing, as those not of the Clothing, to attend upon the Wardens at St. Lawrence Church, Old Jewry, on the feste of the Assumption of our Ladye, there to have a Solemn Masse unless upon reasonable excuse, upon payne to forfeit vi/d to be divided as aforesaid.

4th. That if any Brother be misruled or of evil will and malice, to revile, call, or rebuke the Wardens or any other of the Crafte being in the Livery, to lye to him, or use unfitting language etc. in the presence of the Wardens etc., and being duly convicted, shall pay at every time iii/s iiii/d to the use aforesaid.

5th. That it shall be lawful to every Brother of the Crafte, being out of the Clothing, that is able with his own stuff and goodes to teche and find an Apprentice, to have one and no more, at once, except he show his Complaynt to the Chamberlain, and if he find him perfect and able, to have *two* Apprentices and no more, if the Chamberlain will admit him. Those of the Clothing to have two Apprentices and no more at once. And to him that has been Warden, iii and no more. The Upper Warden to have iv and no more at once. Every Brother of the same having no more Apprentices above rehearsed, at any time that any Apprentice goeth out of his tyme, to take another ii years before out of his tyme; if one die, to take another, so that he has not above the number aforesaid after

180   CITIZENS AND FOUNDERS

his degree. Who doth to the contrary shall, at every time he doth so, forfeit xx/s to the use aforesaid.

6th. Every Brother taking any Apprentice shall present the same unto the Wardens ere he be bounde, so that he may see he be right bounde for the Worshippe of the Citie, upon payne of iii/s iiii/d as often as any p'sone doth to the contrary, to the use aforesaid; any Act or Ordinance concerning the matter of this Article afore this made of any greater penalty than is in the same Article expressed notwithstanding.

7th. That every Brother going to any Feyre to the which he shall be by the said Wardens assigned unto him, shall shew his Wares unto the Wardens ere he pack them; the said Wares to be allowed by the Wardens to be able and sufficient for the King's liege people, upon payne of iiis/ivd to the use aforesaid; any other Acte afore this made concerning the matter of this Article notwithstanding.

8th. No Brother no tyme from hensforth shall vexe, sue, or trouble any Brother within the Citie, not without the Citie, without special license of the said Wardens, upon payment of iii/s iv/d to the use aforesaid.

9th. If any Brother of the sayd Crafte pay not their Quarterage as is aforesaid, or disobey, or do the contrarie to any of these Articles before specified, That no Brother from hensforth put himself to work until such tyme he come to the Wardens, and there submit himself to obey and fulfill all such Awarde and Judgment the Wardens shall shew him, upon payne to pay iii/s iv/d to be employed in manner aforesaid

The Bill above agreed to unanimously, and ordered to be entered in record by the Court of Aldermen.

(Guildhall ref. Whyte, Mayor, Lib.L.fo.278)

APPENDIX C

The Royal Charter

Signed by James I, 18 September 1614

James, by the Grace of God, etc., etc.

Whereas it is parte of our regall office to see our people justlie dealt withall, and amongst other things to take care that in Waights and Measures our Subjects doe deale one with another after a true proportion, wherein as we are informed there is a great abuse, as also the Workers in Brass and Copper Wares are not reduced into any certeine Company, nor the Men of that Misterie are not governed, nor their Workes searched and viewed as in other Misteries where there is a settled Corporation – We therefore for the prevention of such abuses have granted that from henceforth all and everie of our loving subjects the Founders of the City of London and the Suburbs thereof shall be one body corporate by the name of Master, Wardens, and Cominaltie of the Misterie of Founders of the City of London.

To be for ever capable in Law to hold Lands not exceeding £40 per annum.

To be able and capable to plead and be impleaded.

To have for ever a Comon Seale.

There shall be One Master, Two Wardens, and Fifteen Assistants.

The Master and Wardens to be elected yearly on the Monday next before the Feast of St. Michaell the Archangell.

The Assistants to be elected for life unless removed or dismissed.

To have Hall or House of Counsell.

Two persons to be nominated for Master who have served the Upper Wardenship, and reputed the Senior Assistants. One to be chosen.

Six persons out of the Assistants, or from the Livery, to be nominated for Wardens. Two to be chosen. The Master and one Warden to be present.

New Election for Master or Wardens, within fifteen days after death, dismission, or removal.

On death or removal of Assistants, new Election within convenyent tyme.

Master, Wardens, and Assistants to have full power to elect Officers, to hold Courts, and make Statutes, Laws, etc.

Touching the searching and finding out deceipts in Brass and Copper Works, Weights, and Wares; also as to Sizing and marking all Brass Weightes within the City and three Miles compas thereof, which shall be first brought to Founders Hall to be sized and marked with

182 CITIZENS AND FOUNDERS

their Comon Mark, taking payment as heretofore. All offenders against the Ordinances to be fined at the discretion of Master, Wardens, and Assistants, by distress or otherwise.

Discrete persons to be appointed under the Comon Seale and sworne to search all Shoppes, Warehouses, and other places, for deceiptful Works and Weights, and if need be by the Aid of the Mayor and Sheriffs of our City aforesaid, and the Justices of the Peace in whatsoever place within the compas of three Miles without the said City.

Given at Westminster, 18th September, 1614, in the twelfth year of our raigne of England, France and Ireland, and of Scotland, the Eight and Fortieth.

APPENDIX D

Charter Ordinances, dated 27 January 1615

To all Christian People to whom this present writing shall come, Thomas, Lord Ellesmere, Lord Chancellor of England, Sir Edward Coke, Knight, Chief Justice etc., and Sir Henry Hobart, Knight, Chief Justice of the Court of Comon Pleas, send greeting in our Lord God everlasting.

Imprimis: There hath of long time been a Company or fellowship of founders as a bodie collective, though not incorporate until now, and they have desired us that we would examine their said Statutes, Ordinances, and other hereafter sett down, and correct and amende in due and convenient manner and forme. We well considering their supplication, have all and everie of them seen, examined, corrected, reformed, and approved, the tenure whereof herafter ensue and bee these.

Imprimis: That Courts of Master and Wardens be held on Monday everie Week, Weeklie for ever, if occasion serve.

Courts of Assistants to be held by appointment of Master and Wardens as often as business shall require.

General Courts for the appearance of Livery and general bodie or fellowship, there shall be four of them called Quarter-day Courts; 29th October, Monday next Candlemas Day, Monday next May Day, Monday next Lammas Day.

Every person under the government of this Company shall then and there pay for quarterage 12 pence in money for the use of the Company, or in default thereof, or not performing such other rights and duties as may be required of him, shall forfeit Five Shillings. Any person not appearing at Courts by the time appointed shall forfeit 2 shillings, and not coming at all or departing before the Court ended without license, to pay 3s/4d.

That if the Master, Wardens, Assistants, or Liveries, shall repair to such Court without his Gowne, or being otherwise undecently attired, to forfeit 12 pence.

That if any person elected into the Livery do not within Fourteen days after notice given, prepare himself with Habit and Livery fitting thereunto, shall for the first offence forfeit Twenty Shillings, and the further sum of Ten Shillings Monthlie until he conform thereto.

If failing to attend the King's Majestie when repairing to or towards the Citty of London, or if appointed by the Master to any reasonable Service, either in Livery or otherwise by Horse or Foot, to forfeit Twenty Shillings.

In default of the Master or any of the Wardens not appearing for Service of the Lord Mayor at the hower appointed, to pay Five Shillings, or not coming at all, Ten Shillings, and every person of the Livery not attending at the Hower appointed to pay 3s/4d, and coming not at all, 6s/8d.

184 CITIZENS AND FOUNDERS

That if request be made to the Master and Wardens to accompany the dead Corpse of the brethren of the Livery deceased, or his or their Wife or Wives, if they the said M and W shall think fit, the whole of the brethren of the Liverie shall attend at the place and tyme appointed upon paine and forfeiture of Ten Shillings.

That as well the Master and Wardens as also all such persons as shall meddle or have anything to do with receipts or payments, or with the money or goods of the Company, shall within Ten days after being required present a true and plain Account to the Auditors, or in default thereof shall bind himself with sufficient Sureties to bring in whatsoever money, plate or other things, or the verie true value thereof, or shall undergo and suffer such lawful punishment as to the Master and Wardens and Assistants shall seem meete.

Every person refusing to take upon him the Office of Master to be fined Ten Pounds, and every person refusing to take upon him the office of Assistant to forfeit Twenty Shillings.

That if for the service of the King's Majestie or of the Citty of London, or of the affairs of this Company, any just or reasonable Assessments shall by the Master, Wardens, and Assistants be rated upon the Members of this Company, the same shall be obeyed and paid accordingly, and every person refusing to pay such sum as may be assessed upon him to forfeit the sum of Ten Shillings.

That if any Member shall revile, or give any blows, or speak opprobrious or unseemly words to any person of the said Misterie, whereby the King's peace or brotherly love may be broken or impaired amongst them, such person shall undergo and perform such just order or sentence as the Court may determine. Penalty for refusal, Twenty Shillings.

That the Master and Wardens, or such discrete persons as they shall depute, shall make view, and search once everie quarter, or oftener, through the Citie and Three Miles Compas thereof, for all kinds of deceiptful Worke in anie kind of Brass or Copper Wares, as also for all manner of deceiptful Weights made of Brasse.

That upon the day of Election of the Master and Wardens, Two of the Livery shall be nominated to take the place of Steward at the Assistants Dinner to be always kept on the Lord Mayor's Day, or such other Day as the Master, Wardens, and Assistants shall appoint, at the Cost and Charges of the said Stewards. At which Dinner, for the maintenance of brotherly love and familiaritee, the Master, Wardens, and Assistants and all or any of their Wives maie be present, as also all the full Liverie of the said Society. And if any one shall refuse or omitt to performe the same, he shall forfeit the sum of Five Pounds. None shall be taken to be Assistants unless he have first been one of the Stewards or paid his fine. No man to be twice called to the charge of Stewardshippe.

That every person working Brass or Copper Wares to mark the same with their own Mark, which shall have been allowed them by the Master, Wardens, and Assistants.

All penalties to be for the use of the Company.

Every person and persons which shall from time to time be appointed Master or Warden, or be of the Assistants, Liverie or freedom, or that shall be Auditors, Clerk, Bedell, Sizer, Searcher or Searchers, shall take the severall Oathes, as also the Oathes of Allegiance and Supremacy.

Ratified and approved this 27th day of January, in the year of the raigne of our Soveraigne Lord James, etc. etc. of England, France, and Ireland the Twelfth, and of Scotland the Eight and Fortieth.

APPENDIX E

List of Masters
Showing Year of Election

1365 John de Lincoln
1366-90 Not known
1391 Thomas Grace and
  Robert Newman, Masters
1392-1423 Not known
1424 Walter Adam, Nicholas West
1425-7 Not known
1428 Walter Adam, William Byrd
1429-30 Not known
1431 William Turner, Simon Sterne
1432 John West, John Russell
1433-7 Not known
1438 John Russell, Robert Reynolds
1439-96 Not known
1497 Robert Setcole
1498 Robert Setcole
1499 John Pinchbeck
1500 John Pinchbeck
1501 Robert Setcole
1502 Robert Setcole
1503 Randolf Austin
1504 Randolf Austin
1505 Randolf Austin
1506 Randolf Austin
1507 John Parker (or Sena)
1508 Robert Stacy
1509 Robert Wells
1510 Robert Wells
1511 David Mills
1512 Thomas Halifax
1513 Thomas Halifax
1514 Thomas Halifax
1515 Robert Wells
1516 Robert Wells
1517 Robert Wells
1518 David Mills
1519 William Grigby

1520 William Grigby
1521 Thomas Sweeting
1522 Thomas Sweeting
1523 William Grigby
1524 William Grigby
1525 Thomas Sutton
1526 Thomas Sutton
1527 Robert Bridgewater
1528 Thomas Sutton
1529 William Knight
1530 William Knight
1531 Thomas Green
1532 Thomas Green
1533 John Wise
1534 John Wise
1535 Thomas Paxton
1536 Thomas Paxton
1537 Thomas Railton
1538 Thomas Railton
1539 Thomas Paxton
1540 John Wise
1541 James Sewen
1542 John Goter
1543 John Beer (or Bere)
1544 Humphrey White
1545 John Goter
1546 William Abbott
1547 William Abbott
1548 Humphrey White
1549 David Southern
1550 David Southern
1551 Roger Taylor
1552 Roger Taylor
1553 David Southern
1554 Roger Taylor
1555 Christopher Stubbs
1556 Christopher Stubbs

1557	John Green	1610	Richard Rowdinge
1558	John Jackson	1611	Ezekiel Major
1559	John Jackson	1612	Ezekiel Major
1560	Roger Taylor	1613	John Hull
1561	Christopher Stubbs	1614	Richard Rowdinge
1562	Thomas Barley	1615	Ezekiel Major
1563	Robert Falconer (or Faulkner)	1616	John Hull
1564	Robert Falconer	1617	Edward Parnell
1565	John Jackson	1618	John Rawlings
1566	Thomas Barley	1619	John Hull
1567	Robert Shurlock	1620	Hugh Rogers
1568	Robert Shurlock	1621	Edward Parnell
1569	Uryan Daniell (formerly Evans)	1622	John Rawlings
1570	Robert Falconer	1623	Ezekiel Major
1571	John Chambers	1624	John Bowen
1572	John Jackson	1625	Francis Curwen
1573	Thomas Barley	1626	Abraham Woodall
1574	Robert Shurlock	1627	John Hull
1575	John Chambers	1628	Francis Curwen
1576	John Chambers	1629	Abraham Woodall
1577	John Jackson	1630	John Rawlings
1578	Edward Falconer (or Faulkner)	1631	Richard Weoley (or Willey)
1579	Edward Falconer	1632	Sisley Edwardes
1580	Edward Hearne	1633	Francis Curwen
1581	Edward Hearne	1634	Abraham Woodall
1582	John Jackson	1635	William Randall
1583	John Chambers	1636	Henry Carless (or Carles)
1584	Edward Falconer	1637	John Wright
1585	Edward Hearne	1638	Joseph Parratt
1586	Uryan Daniell	1639	Anthony Whaley
1587	Thomas Horton	1640	Richard Weoley
1588	Robert Waldo	1641	Sisley Edwardes
1589	Robert Waldo	1642	Henry Carless
1590	Nicholas Roberts	1643	Joseph Parratt
1591	Nicholas Roberts	1644	Thomas Bosworth
1592	John Chambers	1645	Richard Smith
1593	Edward Falconer	1646	Thomas Stead
1594	Edward Hearne	1647	Thomas Stead
1595	Robert Waldo	1648	Richard Smith
1596	Thomas Jackson (died in office)	1649	William Yardsley
1597	Nicholas Roberts	1650	Joseph Parratt
1598	Richard Rowdinge	1651	Henry Carless
1599	Richard Rowdinge	1652	Simon Cage
1600	Robert Waldo	1653	John Wright
1601	Nicholas Roberts	1654	William Yardsley
1602	Edward Hearne	1655	Stephen Pilchard
1603	Richard Rowdinge	1656	Simon Cage
1604	Humphrey Liddell	1657	William Burroughes
1605	Humphrey Liddell	1658	Stephen Pilchard
1606	Richard Rowdinge	1659	William Burroughes
1607	Edward Gaseley	1660	Marmaduke Almond
1608	Edward Gaseley	1661	William Ragdale
1609	Humphrey Liddell	1662	William Yeames

APPENDIX E: LIST OF MASTERS

187

1663 Marmaduke Almond
1664 William Ragdale
1665 Clement Dawes
1666 John Beauchamp
1667 Moses Brown
1668 George Dixon
1669 George Dixon
1670 John Stead
1671 Timothy Lane
1672 Moses Brown
1673 Andrew Grace
1674 Roger Fisher
1675 Clement Dawes (died in office)
     Andrew Grace
1676 Timothy Lee
1677 John White
1678 Abel Hodges
1679 Daniel Houghton
1680 Peter Causton
1681 Thomas Aylward
1682 John Armiger
1683 John Underwood
1684 Col. Theophilus Oglethorpe
1685 John White, Deputy Master
1686 William Rutter, ditto
1687 Richard Meakins, ditto
1688 William Crossfield
1689 George Chew
1690 Thomas Webb
1691 Henry Hemings
1692 Thomas Hawgood
1693 John Wingrave, John Attwick
1694 Thomas Watson
1695 Edmund Read
1696 Samuel Pilchard
1697 Matthew Beaver
1698 Noah Delaunay
1699 William Crossfield
1700 Thomas Aylward
1701 Noah Delaunay
1702 Noah Delaunay
1703 William Rogers
1704 Thomas Newman
1705 Richard Nevill
1706 Stephen Reynolds
1707 John Smith
1708 Noah Delaunay
1709 Joseph Dampney
1710 Samuel Newton
1711 John Brooks
1712 William Hayward
1713 John Meakins
1714 Daniel Hancock

1715 Robert Burton
1716 John Wade
1717 Anthony Giles
1718 William Warren
1719 Robert Turner
1720 Arthur Gardner, senior
1721 John Peel
1722 John Scott
1723 William Parsons
1724 Philip Davies
1725 John Richardson
1726 David Higby
1727 Daniel Hudson
1728 Robert North, dismissed
     Robert Burton
1729 John Halfhide
1730 Anthony Webster
1731 Capt. Richard Nevill
1732 Henry Hines
1733 Daniel Lawrence
1734 William Gardner
1735 John Sunderland
1736 Thomas Pearce
1737 Isaac Dobbins
1738 John Bridge
1739 George Meal
1740 John Giles
1741 Samuel Goadby
1742 William Ford
1743 John Beard
1744 John Bladwell
1745 Samuel Collisham
1746 John Walker
1747 John Bundy
1748 John Allen
1749 Nathaniel Clarke
1750 John Tillier
1751 William Gibbs
1752 John White
1753 Patrick Hawes
1754 Thurston Ford
1755 William Jones
1756 Richard Chapman
1757 John Marsh
1758 Thomas Tuck
1759 Richard Chapman
1760 Walter West
1761 Thomas Clark
1762 John Newton
1763 Daniel Bucknell
1764 Edward Lloyd
1765 Ambrose Denman
1766 John Cuttridge

188 CITIZENS AND FOUNDERS

1767 William Lister	1819 Joseph Warner
1768 William White	1820 William King
1769 Samuel Rogers	1821 William Barnes
1770 William Hone	1822 William Gillman
1771 Samuel Jacombe	1823 Robert Davies
1772 Tuffin Shepherd	1824 William Borradaile
1773 Edward Holmes	1825 William Roper
1774 Thomas Walker	1826 Robert Warner
1775 Sacheverell Hollyer	1827 John Warner
1776 William Lane	1828 Thomas Mears
1777 John Cole	1829 John Stott
1778 John Jenkin	1830 James Burrows
1779 Thomas Cartwright (died in office)	1831 James Chooling
Edward Watson	1832 William Devey
1780 William Kinsman	1833 John Moxon
1781 Joseph Keys	1834 Jeremiah Barratt
1782 John Trent	1835 W. I. Hurrell
1783 William Rogers	1836 I. H. Chapman
1784 John Warner	1837 John Burnell
1785 William Farm	1838 William Franks
1786 Tomson Warner	1839 Thomas Moxon, junior
1787 William Newman	1840 J. C. Stahlschmidt
1788 James Haygarth	1841 William Christie
1789 Samuel Taylor	1842 Francis Bacon
1790 John Hooper	1843 Charles Botten
1791 John Reynolds	1844 John Sexton
1792 John Cave	1845 William Huggins
1793 John Chamberlain	1846 William Hems
1794 James White	1847 Charles Warner
1795 William Borradaile	1848 Stephen Lowdell
1796 John Rea	1849 Charles Mears
1797 William Timmins	1850 James Moul
1798 Joseph Bramley	1851 Mark Marsden
1799 William Savill	1852 William M. Williams
1800 John Seale	1853 William M. Williams
1801 James Burrows	1854 George Mears
1802 Archdale Wilkins	1855 John Christie
1803 Thomas Hornsby	1856 Thomas Oliver
1804 William Dunbar	1857 William Hems, junior
1805 John Rea	1858 William Franks
1806 Joseph Thornhill	1859 William Burton
1807 Michael Barnett	1860 Thomas Moxon, junior
1808 John Batger	1861 William Christie
1809 Joseph Meyer	1862 Richard Dale
1810 Alexander Lean	1863 William Hems, junior
1811 John Warner	1864 Gervase Parnell
1812 William Timmins	1865 Charles Warner
1813 Robert Westley	1866 Robert Warner
1814 James Burrows	1867 James Franks
1815 James Burrows	1868 Mark Marsden
1816 William Gillman	1869 Edward Metcalf
1817 Edward Winter	1870 William Franks
1818 John Gray	1871 Francis Pritchett

APPENDIX E: LIST OF MASTERS

1872 Edward Baldock
1873 Edward Franks
1874 Joseph Holland
1875 William Fowler
1876 George Forrest
1877 Henry Hodsoll Heath
1878 George Aitchison
1879 M. H. Walker
1880 John Stahlschmidt
1881 Gervase Parnell
1882 Robert Warner
1883 Francis Pritchett
1884 George Berry
1885 Capt. Edward Baldock
1886 William Fowler
1887 William Evan Franks
1888 George Cockerell
1889 George Forrest
1890 Walter Franks
1891 Samuel Linder
1892 William White
1893 Henry Hodsoll Heath
1894 Frederick Harris
1895 Edward Bridgewater
1896 Charles Devey
1897 William Chambers
1898 Octavius Jepson
1899 James Dixon
1900 Richard Williams
1901 William Bruty
1902 Robert Wales
1903 Frederick Todd
1904 Walter Franks
1905 M. B. Herbert
1906 Henry Franks
1907 Charles Devey
1908 William Tetley
1909 Sydney Pollard
1910 George Hilditch Walker
1911 Wynne Baxter
1912 Ernest Hepburn
1913 Richard Williams
1914 William Cooper
1915 Alfred Brookman
1916 Edmund Lucas
1917 William Aitchison
1918 Henry Young
1919 James Taylor
1920 Henry Tait Moore
1921 William Devey
1922 Charles Miller
1923 William Hibbert
1924 Percy Horley

1925 Capt. Alfred Hodsoll Heath
1926 Soanes Gardner
1927 Augustus Blaxter
1928 Lt.-Col. Dudley Cookes, D.S.O.
1929 Harry Hughes
1930 Dr. Hugh Stannus
1931 Percy Young
1932 Stanley Young
1933 Robert Warner
1934 James Taylor
1935 Robert Hatswell
1936 William Christopher
1937 Francis Miles
1938 Robert Ababrelton
1939 Gordon Young
1940 Douglas Young
1941 Percy Horley
1942 Capt. Alfred H. Heath
1943 Augustus Blaxter
1944 Lt.-Col. Dudley Cookes, D.S.O.
1945 Charles Woodfield
1946 Stephen Warner
1947 William Fossick
1948 Leslie Corbould-Ellis
1949 A. P. L. Blaxter
1950 Jack Wheeler
1951 George Cotton
1952 Kenneth Adams
1953 Dr. Hugh Stannus
1954 Frank Greene
1955 Herbert Bradbrook
1956 Leonard Cotterell
1957 Rev. Richard Walker
1958 George Ilsley
1959 Arthur Jennings
1960 Douglas Young
1961 Ernest Moss
1962 Samuel Walker
1963 Charles Littler Smith
1964 Lt. Col. James Thomson
1965 Guy Hadley
1966 Harvey Young
1967 Dr. James Pearce
1968 Reginald Longcroft
1969 Paul Gunn
1970 Patrick, Lord Rathcreedan
1971 Capt. William Gregson
1972 John Beardmore
1973 Peter Blaxter
1974 John Cully
1975 Francis Rowe

Principal Sources

Founders' Company records in Guildhall Library

These are indexed and include the original Charter, Court Minute Books 1704-1902, Livery List Books 1681-1780, Weight Books 1741-9 and 1841-52, and many other documents.

Printed Books and articles

W. M. Williams, *Annals of the Founders' Company* (1867)
Guy Parsloe, M.A., F.R.Hist.S., *Wardens' Accounts 1497-1681* (1964)
W. N. Hibbert, *History of the Founders' Company*, compiled and transcribed from the *Annals*
H. S. Stannus, *Richard Weoley, Master 1631 and 1640* (privately printed)
George Unwin, *The Gilds and Companies of London* (2nd ed., 1925)
E. Lipson, *The Growth of English Society: a Short Economic History* (1964)
Professor G. M. Trevelyan, o.m., *History of England* (1937)
D. V. Glass, 'Status and Occupations in London' in A. E. J. Hollaender and William Kellaway ed., *Studies in London History* (1969)

Also at Guildhall

Journals of the Court of Common Council
Repertories of the Court of Aldermen

Index

NOTE: *The Index is divided into three sections, namely:* 1. SUBJECTS;
2. NAMES & PLACES, *showing Founders' Company names in italic;*
3. OTHER CITY COMPANIES, *References*

1. SUBJECTS

Aid to Industry:
Fellowships, 160
Founders' Medal, 160, 166
Prizes, 151, 160, 161
Research grants, 160, 161
Scholarships, 160, 161
Alms, 10, 12, 13, 14, 21, 22, 32, 33, 45, 46, 47, 77, 81, 89, 90, 91, 96, 127, 133, 135, 137, 143, 145, 149, 150
Annuities, 137, 150
Apprentices, 2, 10, 12, 17, 18, 19, 22, 25, 26, 27, 28, 32, 76, 97, 108, 121, 123, 126, 131, 137, 145, 146, 149, 151
Arms, grant, 22, 62, 155, 156
Assistants, see Court
Auditors, 33, 44, 74, 82, 85, 99, 120, 123, 127, 133

Banners, 13, 81, 112
Barges, 13, 33, 41
Beadle, 13, 33, 37, 64, 65, 74, 108, 110, 119, 120, 122, 123, 134, 139, 140, 147, 149, 151, 162
Bell-founding, 161, 167, 170
Bond's Legacy, 145, 151
Bowen's Spoon, 73, 165
Breakfasts, 33, 38, 119, 125, 137
Butler, 32, 79
Bye-laws, 136, 138, 154

Centenaries, 156, 165
Charitable Fund, 149, 150, 161

Charter, 10, 19, 33, 58, 65, 73, 74, 75, 87, 88, 89, 90, 91, 92, 93, 97, 113, 117, 135, 136, 144, 164, *Appendix* C
Chest, 13, 14, 15, 16, 108, 134, 145, 154
City Chamber, 16, 18, 27, 32, 39, 41, 46, 62, 75, 84, 144
City government, 4, 5, 8, 9, 24, 28, 130,155
City Police, 155
Clerk, 13, 37, 41, 64, 65, 74, 108, 110, 119, 120, 122, 123, 125, 126, 134, 140, 143, 144, 145, 147, 148, 162
Common Council, 5, 26, 28, 38, 43, 45, 56, 71, 97, 119, 130, 132, 133, 144
Cook, 79
Corn, 44, 70, 71, 84
Court of Assistants, 56, 57, 58, 74, 78, 88, 98, 126, 134, 135, 136, 138, 140, 143, 145, 146, 163, 164

Daysmen, 33
Dinners, cancelled, 14, 33, 38, 72, 77, 99, 118, 137, 143, 147
costs, 32, 40, 78, 81, 119
Dinners, food, drink, 32, 39, 40, 53, 146, 147, 157
occasions, 68, 72, 73, 77, 78, 132, 146, 156
payments, 13, 32, 33, 34, 57, 68, 72, 77, 98, 99
places, 132, 146, 147, 165

Discipline, 2, 10, 12, 19, 74, 79, 134, 136, 147
Disputes, lawsuits, 13, 14, 15, 17, 18, 19, 28, 32, 37, 46, 60, 61, 76, 78, 79, 80, 84, 86, 87, 88, 89, 90, 92, 93, 107, 122, 123, 131, 138, 144, 152
Dissenters, 110, 111, 134, 151

Election Day Service, 164
Exchequer, Court of, 17

Fairs, 10, 37, 58, 96
Finances, 12, 13, 14, 19, 22, 32, 33, 36, 37, 65, 70, 72, 75, 81, 82, 85, 99, 108, 109, 118, 119, 126, 127, 133, 143, 148, 149, 150, 164, 165
Fines, offences, 2, 10, 12, 16, 18, 19, 22, 26, 28, 46, 68, 72, 74, 77, 87, 89, 91, 95, 96, 97, 134, 141
offices, 74, 77, 78, 98, 107, 108, 109, 117, 118, 135, 136, 138, 145, 146
Foundry Tours, 160, 162, 166
Freemen, 22, 27, 28, 46, 59, 76, 95, 108, 126, 132, 133, 143, 144, 145, 146, 153, 163
Frost Fair, 112
Funerals, 1, 10, 22, 40, 72, 74, 79, 110, 134
Furnaces, 97, 172, 173, 174

194 CITIZENS AND FOUNDERS

General Courts, 74, 92, 131, 136, 143
Gifts, 11, 21, 22, 34, 36, 65, 70, 91, 95, 97, 99, 100, 108, 140, 141, 145, 148, 149, 150, 162, 163
Gilds, Misteries, evolution, 2, 3, 4, 5, 6, 7, 9, 11, 20, 27, 59, 60
Gowns, 23, 33, 54, 74, 79, 98, 133, 134, 147
Gowrie Conspiracy, 68, 72, 77
Great Fire, 99, 105, 106, 107, 109
Gun-founding, 24, 170, 171
Gunpowder Plot, 67, 72, 77
store, 54, 80, 81

Hall, Lothbury, building, 34, 35, 36, 107, 108, 112, 152
rents, 51, 52, 110, 111, 134, 152
repairs, 70, 81, 98, 149, 151
tenants, 12, 13, 36, 51, 52, 99, 109, 110, 111, 118, 151, 152
uses, 36, 51, 52, 110, 111, 146
Hall, St. Swithin's Lane, 148, 152, 153, 154, 155, 165
Hawke's Dirge, 22, 79, 163
Hawkers, 27, 95, 96
Hearse Cloth, 102, 103
Honorary Assistants, 164
Housekeeper, 120

Inflation, 12, 40, 45, 81, 112
Ireland, see also Ulster, 56, 69, 70, 84, 85

Jordan's Dole, 22, 45, 47, 91
Journeymen, 9, 10, 11, 16, 17, 19, 25, 27, 49, 59, 131, 153

Livery, admission, 9, 10, 17, 19, 22, 23, 97, 98, 115, 122, 131, 132, 145
dismissals, 78, 98, 134, 138
fines, 10, 12, 22, 23, 46, 72, 74, 77, 78, 79, 107, 108, 118, 132, 134, 135, 145, *Appendix* D
Lottery, 58
'Love Brothers', 132

Marks, 60, 62, 73, 74, 76, 96, 104, 112, 154
Mass, 1, 10, 11, 12, 13, 15, 19, 21, 22, 24, 25, 32, 45, 137
Master, Wardens, duties, 2, 3, 37, 46, 58, 77, 119, 120
election, 2, 3, 57, 72, 74, 78, 115, 135, 136
fines, 72, 74, 77, 98, 125, 134, 135, 145, 146, *Appendix* D
Master's Bond, 82, 125, 136
Membership, 9, 11, 12, 19, 24, 25, 49, 59, 88, 112, 131, 132, 134, 137, 145, 153, 159
Misteries, see Gilds
Monopolies, 60

Night Watches, 41, 42, 53

Origins, Founders' Co., 1
Ordinances, 1365, 1, 2, 90, *Appendix* A
1489, 9, 10, 12, 18, *Appendix* B
1508, 15
1516, 19, 21, 32, 57, 91
1592, 77, 97
1615, 74, 79, 81, 92, 97, 138, 144 *Appendix* D
general, 9, 10, 14, 15, 16, 18, 28, 73, 91, 109, 138
Orphan Fund, 149
Oyster Feast, 146

Parish relief, 51, 99
Parliament, 5, 14, 17, 24, 37, 38, 44, 84, 135, 138, 152, 155
Pensioners, 91, 137, 149, 150
Pie-Powder Court, 37
Plague, 16, 31, 99, 105
Poor Box, see Alms
Precedence, 40
Privy Council, 24, 50, 51, 58, 62, 63, 71, 72, 80
Processions, pageants, 32, 40, 41, 48, 49, 58, 71, 84, 103, 104, 141, 147

Quarterage, 10, 11, 12, 15, 19, 22, 24, 25, 32, 37, 45, 59, 70, 72, 74, 77, 80, 81, 87, 88, 91, 92, 109, 125, 131, 137, 144, 149, 150, 154
'Quo Warranto', 113, 115

Rates, 52, 81, 99
Rents, 12, 13, 34, 36, 51, 52, 59, 69, 70, 73, 109, 110, 111, 134, 148, 151, 152, 164
Robert Warner Trust, 133, 160, 163

St. Clement's Brotherhood, 1, 15, 21, 33, 45, 46, 166
Scots Church, 110, 111, 134
Search, 2, 27, 28, 63, 64, 74, 76, 87, 96, 104, 112, 121, 138
Sexcentenary Fund, 165
Ships, 56, 84, 104
Silver, plate, etc., 14, 15, 19, 22, 33, 73, 76, 81, 82, 107, 108, 143, 145, 148
Sisters, see Widows
Slaves, 112, 129, 130
Soldiers, arms, 43, 48, 49, 53, 54, 112, 119
Spanish Armada, 51, 54
Spiritual Court, 12, 13
Spoons, 26, 72, 73, 85, 165
Star Chamber, 14, 37
Stewards, 77, 78, 79, 95, 108, 125, 137, 138, 146, 164
'Strangers', 12, 23, 24, 25, 33, 37, 49, 58
Swan-upping, 59

Taxes, State, 44, 68, 71, 72, 83, 84, 85, 86, 112
City, 45, 56, 69, 70, 71, 81, 99, 104
Tobacco, 52, 112
Transfers, 97, 133

Ulster Plantation, 69, 70
United Guilds Service, 164

Virginia, colony, 52

Wages, 2, 16, 58, 59, 81
Water supply, 44, 99, 108, 112
Weddings, 36, 49
Weights, 60, 61, 62, 63, 64, 65, 70, 73, 74, 76, 89, 96, 107, 108, 121, 122, 123, 138, 139, 140, 149, 153, 154, 165, 166
Weoley Cup, 43, 93, 94, 108, 162
Widows, Sisters, 11, 12, 13, 36, 65, 70, 91, 136, 137, 141, 149, 150, 163

INDEX   195

Window, Guildhall, 166

Yeomanry, 9, 10, 11, 12, 15,

16, 18, 19, 22, 23, 28,
33, 36, 46, 47, 48, 49,
53, 55, 57, 58, 60, 63,

86, 88, 91, 92, 93, 131,
132

Young Trust, 163

2. NAMES & PLACES. *Founders' Company names in italic*

Abbot, William. Master, 57
Adderley, Capt. Charles,
    113, 118
Albion Tavern, 146, 147
Almond, Marmaduke.
    Master, 98
Apthorpe, John. Steward, 78
Ashe, John, 12
Attwick, John, 113
Augustine Friars, 34, 35
Austin, Maurice, 80
Austin, Randolf. Master, 14,
    17
Aylmer, Sir Laurence. Lord
    Mayor, 15, 19, 21, 33,
    47, 57
Aylward, Thomas. Master,
    116, 123, 124, 125, 126

Bacon, Sir Francis, 75
Baker, Daniel, 88
Baker, William, 57, 64
Banys, John, 13
Barbary Merchants, 52
Barnard, Anthony, 98
Barratt, Jeremiah. Master,
    143
Bartlett, James, 116, 161
Bassett, Thomas, 14, 17, 18
Basspoole, William. Clerk,
    65, 87, 89, 90, 92, 93,
    95, 96, 97, 120
Baude or *Balde, Peter,* 24,
    171
Baxter, Mrs. Thomas, 150
Beardmore, John. Master, ix,
    164, 165
Beauchamp, John. Master, 98
Beauchamp, Thomas, 107
Beaver, Matthew. Master,
    116
Beverley, Geoffrey de, 6
Bird, Edmond, 11, 14, 15, 17
Biringuccio, V, 169, 170,
    171, 175
Bishop, Benet, 53
Blaxter, Peter. Master, x, 166
Blowbell, John, 21
Bond, John, 53
Bond, William. Clerk, 145
Booth, C. C., 160

Borradaile, William. Master,
    136
Borradaile, William?, son,
    145
Boston, Thomas, 132
Botland, John, 14, 15
Bouchet, F. J., 143
Bowen, Humphrey, 73
Bower, John. Steward, 78
Bowyer, Mr., 46
Boyden, Seth, 173
Boyes, Francis, 48
Bradbrook, Herbert. Master,
    164
Bradley, John. Beadle, 120
Brewer, John, 36
Brewer, Thomas, 53
Bridewell workhouse, 26, 71
Bridges, Downton, 126
Broke, Sir Richard, 18
Broke, Sir Robert, 38
Brooks, John. Master, 135
Brown, Shipley & Co, 153
Brown, Thomas, 87, 88, 93
Bruce, Mr, 150
Bruce, Sarah, 149
Buckingham, Owen, 121
Bugden, John, 116
Burnett, Sir David. Lord
    Mayor, 165
Burroughs, William. Master,
    108
Burton, Robert. Master, 167
Burton, William. Master,
    152, 153
Bury, Adam de, Mayor, 1

Caesar, Sir Julius, 75
Calais, Wool Staple, 4, 6, 8,
    21, 48, 49
Campion, Charles. Beadle,
    120
Campion, Mother, 13
Cannon, Mrs Ann, 137
Carless, Henry. Master, 84,
    97
Carmichael, Alexander, 110
Causton, Peter. Master, 116
Charleston, R. J., 94
Chase, John C., 155, 156
Cholmley, Sir Roger, 38

Christie, John. Master, 153
Christie, William. Master,
    150, 152, 153
Clapham, Edmund, 80, 91,
    92
Clarke, George, 116
Clarke, John, 71
Clifford, Mother, 36
Clifford, Richard, 36
Coke, Sir Edward, 74
Cole, John. Master, 133
Collingwood, Edward, 26, 27
Collins, William, 80
Collyer, Dr, 111
Cook, John, and son, 97, 98
Cooke, Edmund, 167
Cooke, George, 135
Cooke, Leonard, 102
Cooke, Robert, 62
Cotterell, Major Leonard.
    Master, 164
Couche, Robert. Steward, 77
Croft, Father, 61
Croft, Robert, 48
Crole, Anthony, 111, 151
Crystal Palace, 156
Cully, John. Master, x
Curwen, Francis. Master, 73,
    99

Dale, Richard. Master, 155
Daniell, Uryan. Master, 49,
    61
Darby, Abraham I & III, 172
Darwin, F. Steward, 78
Dawes, Clement. Master, 82,
    92
Delaunay, Noah. Master,
    116, 124, 125, 126, 127,
    132, 133
Delwave, Charles, 139
Devey, William. Master, 153,
    155
Dickinson, James. Clerk, 65,
    112, 119, 120, 121,
    122, 123
Dixie, Mr, 46
Dixon, Anthony. Cook, 79
Dixon, George. Master, 107
Dixon, Richard, 59
Dovey, Humphrey, 71

196

CITIZENS AND FOUNDERS

Draper, Alderman, 59
Draper, Michael, 97
Drury, Mr, 134
Dumarosq, Stephen, 131
Dyer, Robert, 77
Dyos or Diss, William, 75

East India Company, 52, 114
Eastland Company, 52, 109, 111
Electric Telegraph Company, 152, 153
Ellesmere, Lord, 74
Elphick, George, 161
Embrey, Thomas. Steward, 95
Essex, Earl of, 85
Evans, Evan, 87
Evelyn, John, 105, 106, 107, 112

Fabott, Richard. Yeomanry Master, 59
Fairfax, Sir Thomas, 85
Falconer, Edward. Master, 60, 61
Falconer, Robert, 49
Falkener, John. Clerk, 65, 79, 80, 95, 120
Fendrey,* Henry. Clerk, 64, 65
Fischer, J. C., 173
Fisher, Harry, 48
Fisher, Roger. Master, 25
Fisher, Thomas, 141
Fleet prison, 17, 18, 126
Fleming, Mr, 111
Fleming, Roger, 123
Ford, Mistress, 12
Ford, William, 36
Fossick, William. Master, 164
Fountain, Charles. Beadle, 162
Fountain, John. Beadle, 162
Franks, William. Master, 153

Gauntlett, Mr, 76
Gibbs, Ezekiel, 116
Giles, Anthony. Master, 113
Glass, D. V., 131
Glover, William, 53, 59, 61
Goadby, Robert, 133
Goter, John. Master, 22, 23
Grace, Thomas. Joint Master, 1

Gray, John. Clerk, 147, 148
Gray, Richard, 57
Greathead, Dorcas, 70
Greathead, Elizabeth, 70
Greathead, Oswald, 70, 79
Green, Anthony, 95
Gregson, Capt. William. Master, 164

Hadfield, Joshua. Clerk, 126
Halifax, Thomas. Master, 14, 15, 16, 17, 18, 33
Hallett, Michael, C.B.E, X, 160, 169
Halliday, Edward, 162
Hamburg Merchants, 111
Harman, James, 64
Hart, Richard, 162
Haselton, Robert, 95
Hatfield, Thomas, 82
Hatswell, Robert. Master, 162
Hawgood, Thomas. Master, 116
Hawke, Mistress, 11, 163
Hawke, Richard, 11, 21, 22, 79, 163
Heath, Capt. A. H. Master, 164
Hedges, William, 121
Hemings, Henry. Master, 116, 121
Hems, William. Master, 153
Hems, William, Junior. Master, 153
Hibbert, William. Master, ix, 57, 93
Hicks Hall, 25
Higginson, Harry, 53
Hill, Richard. Yeomanry Master, 48, 49
Hobart, Sir Henry, 74
Hobbs, Gregory, 71
Hodges, Abel. Master, 87, 88, 95, 96
Hody, Sir William, 14
Hogg, Ralph, 24
Hollaender, Dr. A. E. J., ix, 131
Hollier, Charles. Clerk, 145
Holme, Robert, 13
Horn, Robert, 13
Horns Tavern, 132
Houghton, Daniel. Master, 116

Houlton, Thomas, 80
Howard, Catherine, 41
Hudson, Mr, 152
Hughes, Douglas, 161
Hughes, Harry. Master, 164
Hughes, William, 161
Hull, John. Master, 80, 82, 84
Humphries, John. Clerk, 123, 124, 125
Humphries, Owen, 116, 121, 122
Hunt, Robert, 48
Hunt, Walter, 53
Hurst, Dr. J. E., 160

Jackson, John. Master, 40, 49
Jackson, Thomas, 62
Jacombe, Mrs, 139
Jeffrey, Richard, 77
Jenkin, John. Master, 136
Jeny, James. Yeomanry Master, 58
Jewdrey,* Henry. Beadle, 64
Jones, Capt. John, 85
Jordan, Edward, 13, 22
Jordan, Henry, 22
Jordan, Thomas, 103

Keely, John, 99
Kemp, Ann, 137
Kemp, Richard. Cook, 79
Kerrison, Samuel. Steward, 78
King, Gregory, 114
King, John. Butler, 79
King, Thomas. Clerk, 140, 141
King's Head Tavern, 124
Kinsman, William. Master, 136
Kirk, Andrew, 165
Knight, William. Master, 17

Ladbroke & Co, 145
Lambart, Leonard, 73
Lambert, Francis. Clerk, 65, 107, 108, 120
Lambert, James, 62
Lambert, William. Steward, 78, 95
Lane, Thomas, 121
Lawrence, Thomas, 161
Lee, Timothy. Master, 123, 125, 126

* Jewdrey and Fendrey may well have been one and the same man acting as Clerk and Beadle, but confused by bad writing of the name.

INDEX

197

Leighton, Sir Frederick, 154
Lester, George, 53, 64
Lester, William. Yeomanry
    Master, 60, 61, 64
Levett, Richard, 121
Levett, Rev. William, 24
Liddell, William. Clerk, 37,
    65, 75
Lincoln, John de. Master, 1
Lipson, Prof. E., 6, 20
London Irish Rifles, 162
Lotall, Mr, 133
Loughborough, Lord, 136
Lucas, Edmund. Master, 163
Lucas, John, 87, 88, 104, 105
Ludlow, E. J., 160

Magson, Richard, 13
Major, Ezekiel. Master, 84
Major, John, 98
Maltby, James, 96
Mansfield, Lord, 136
Marsden, Jeremiah, 110
Marsden, Mark. Master, 150,
    153, 155
Martin, John. Beadle, 119,
    120, 139
Martyr, Messrs., 151, 152
Mayer, J., 173
Mayne, Col. Edmund, 113,
    118
Mayor, Joseph, 143
Meakins, Richard. Master,
    108, 116
Mears, Charles. Master, 150,
    161
Mears, George. Master, 148,
    150, 161, 167
Mears, Thomas. Master, 149,
    150, 161
Merchant Adventurers, 51,
    52, 99, 109
Meriell, William. Clerk, 13,
    37
Metcalfe, Alexander.
    Yeomanry Master, 58
Middleton, Sir Thomas.
    Lord Mayor, 73
Mills, David. Master, 17, 18,
    32
Monk, Davy, 53
Montague, Sir Henry, 75
Moon, Sir F. G., 147
Morison, Fynes, 52
Moss, Ernest. Master, 164
Moul, James. Master, 153,
    155
Moxon, John. Master, 146
Moxon, Thomas, Junior, 153

Moyle, Sir Thomas, 38
Mullins, John, 132
Muscovy Merchants, 52

Nell, Nicholas, 53
Nevill, Richard. Master,
    132, 133
New London Tavern, 132
Newgate prison, 13, 84
Newman, Robert. Joint
    Master, 1
Nicholls, William, 88
Nicolls, 'Goodman', 49
North, Robert. Master, 136

Oglethorpe, Col. Theophilus.
    Master, 113, 116, 117,
    118
Oliver, Mr. City Surveyor,
    107
Ordway, Elizabeth, 163

Palmer, Thomas, 64
Parker, John. Master, 11
Parnell, Edward. Master, 64,
    79, 80
Parratt, Joseph. Master, 84,
    92, 95
Parsloe, Guy, ix, 11, 33, 45,
    66, 81, 110
Paul's Cross, 102
Payne, John, 32
Pearce, Dr. J. G. Master, 160
Pearce, Richard, 79
Pecsall –, 14
Pendred, William, 22
Pey, John, 113, 118
Phillips, William. Beadle,
    140
Pilchard, Stephen. Master,
    89, 99, 100
Pincock, Thomas, 36
Pinder, Lawrence, 116
Plaister, Richard, 116
Platt, Thomas. Beadle, 37,
    64, 65
Pontifex, Mr., 144
Pope, Thomas. Steward, 78
Popham, Sir John, 65
Predyox, Mr., 36
Preston, John. Beadle, 37
Prince, John, 116
Prince, William, 150
Pritchett, Francis. Master,
    155

Rawlett, John, 36
Rawlings, John. Master, 73,
    75, 91, 99

Read, Edmund. Master, 116
Réaumur, R-A de, 171, 173
Reynolds, John, 87
Rivers, Sir John, 46
Roberts, Nicholas. Master,
    61, 82
Rogers, C. C., 165
Rogers, George, 26
Rogers, William. Master,
    116
Rowdinge, Richard. Master,
    70, 75, 76, 81, 99
Rowe, Frank. Master, x, 167
Rutter, William. Master, 116

St. Lawrence Church, Jewry,
    1, 10, 13, 15, 21, 166
St. Margaret Church,
    Lothbury, 13, 15, 21,
    99, 102, 118, 164
Sandford, John, 14, 15, 17
Sankey, John, 22
Setcole, Robert. Master, 11,
    14
Sewen, James. Master, 12
Sewen, Leonard, 53
Sewen, Mistress, 12
Sexton, John. Master, 152
Seymour, Jane, 40
Sheehan, J. J., 160
Sherwin, Henry. Steward,
    138
Shurley, Sarah. Housekeeper,
    120
Shurlock, Robert. Master,
    36, 77
Simpson, William, 53
Sims, James, 79, 138
Singleton, Dr. John, 110
Slaney, Alderman Stephen,
    28, 61, 62
Smith, Benjamin, 135
Smith, Richard, 93
Smith, Samuel, 133
Soame, Alderman Sir
    Stephen, 63
Sonlowe, John, 17, 18, 33
Soward, Mr., 146
Spencer, Peter, 48
Springham, John, 80
Stacy, Robert. Master, 16
Stannus, Dr. Hugh. Master,
    ix, 21, 93, 94, 166
Star & Garter Hotel, 154
Stead, Thomas. Master, 92
Stepney, Thomas. Yeomanry
    Master, 48, 49
Storer or Storey, John, 64
Story, Ann, 137, 163

198   CITIZENS AND FOUNDERS

Stringer, Nathaniel, 116
Sturmer, Daniel, 116
Sweeting, Goodwife, 13
Sweeting, Thomas. Master, 15
Symons, Richard, 116

Tabor, Rev. Humprhey, 102
Taylor, James. Master, 164
Taylor, Roger. Master, 65
Thomas, Brian, O.B.E., 166
Thomas, John, 151
Thomas, Philip, 88, 93
Thompson, Robert (3), 26, 64, 65, 73, 75, 80
Thompson, William. Under-Butler, 79
Thomson, Lt. Col. J. C. Master, 165
Thornhill, Frederick, 143, 144
Tiffin, John. Cook, 79
Tovey, Michael. Clerk, 144, 145
Trevelyan, Prof. G. M., 30, 31, 51, 53
Tristram, Lawrence, 71
Trott, John. Butler, 79

Uffington, Thomas, 111
Underwood, John. Master, 108, 116
Unwin, George, 3, 17, 24, 58, 103

Vaughan, Edward. Beadle, 147
Veron, Rev. John, 45
Virginia Company, 52

Vollhan, E., 172

Waldo, Lawrence, 82
Waldo, Robert. Master, 23, 62, 64, 82
Walker, Richard, 65
Walker, Samuel. Master, 164, 165, 166
Walmsley, William, 116
Warner, Charles. Master, 153, 163
Warner, Edward, 132, 163
Warner, John (3). Masters, 163
Warner, Joseph. Master, 163
Warner, Robert (3). Masters, 133, 160, 163
Warner, Stephen. Master, 163
Warner, Tomson. Master, 163
Warren, Henry, 116
Watkins, John, 138
Watson, Thomas, 116
Weller, Robert, 54
Wells, Algernon. Clerk, 148, 155
Wells, Sir Frederick. Lord Mayor, 165
Wells, Robert. Master, 32, 33
Weoley, Richard. Master, 43, 84, 93, 94, 95, 120
Westcott, William. Beadle, 162
Wheatley, Martin, 53
White, John. Deputy Master, 78, 113, 116, 121
White, William. Mayor, 9

Whitechapel Bell Foundry, 161, 167
Whittington, Sir Richard. Mayor, 26, 31
Wiley, H. Wilson. Clerk, x, 162
Wilkinson, John & William, 172
Williams, Rev. Philip, 110
Williams, Robert, 144
Williams, William M. Master, ix, 47, 57, 93, 94, 110, 111, 148, 149, 152, 153, 156
Wilson, John, 48
Wilson, Richard, 48
Winkles, James, 26, 27
Winstanly, Mary, 163
Wise, John. Master, 34
Withan, Mr., 134
Wolsey, Cardinal, 19, 31, 33
Wontner, Alderman Sir Hugh. Lord Mayor, 165
Wood, Adam. Clerk, 37
Wood, John, 134
Wood, Mrs., 137
Woodall, Abraham. Master, 84, 91
Woodcock, Sophia & Charlotte, 145
Wright, Roger, 22
Wyatt, Sir Thomas, 48

Young, Douglas. Master, 163
Young, Gordon. Master, 163
Young, Harvey. Master, 163
Young, Henry. Master, 163
Young, Percy. Master, 163
Young, Stanley. Master, 163

---

3. OTHER CITY COMPANIES. *References*

Ale Brewers, 5
Armourers, 5, 9, 11, 34, 41, 57, 76

Bakers, 5
Barbers, 5, 11
Blacksmiths, 5, 11, 166
Bladesmiths, 11
Bowyers, 56
Brass Potters, 1, 2
Braziers, 5, 11, 76, 97
Brewers, 5, 34, 57, 71, 97
Broderers, 82
Brown Bakers, 36
Butchers, 4, 5

Cappers, 5, 11
Carmen, 98
Carpenters, 28, 56, 97
Chandlers, 5
Clockmakers, 28, 92, 97, 109, 133
Cloth Measurers, 5
Clothworkers, 4, 6, 11, 92, 114
Cordwainers, 5, 6, 37
Curriers, 5
Cutlers, 5, 10, 75, 82

Drapers, 5, 9, 11, 35, 132, 134

Dyers, 59, 150
Fishmongers, 5, 6, 22, 69, 91, 133
Fletchers, 5, 56
Freemasons, 5, 28, 97
Fullers, 5, 11

Girdlers, 5, 11
Glaziers, 84
Glovers, 11
Goldsmiths, 4, 5, 6, 35, 89, 92
Grocers (Grossers), 5, 9, 34, 35, 56, 71, 82, 83, 84, 85, 103

INDEX

Gunmakers, 28, 97, 109

Haberdashers, 5, 11, 69, 70, 104
Hatters, 5, 11
Horners, 5

Innholders, 40
Ironmongers, 5, 75, 86, 103, 160

Joiners, 5, 84

Leather Dressers (Tawyers), 5, 11
Leathersellers, 5, 11, 34, 35
Loriners, 70, 109

Masons, 5
Mercers, 5, 6, 9, 35, 56, 57, 155
Merchant Taylors, 5, 6, 35, 56, 69, 84, 86, 92, 103

Minstrels, 56

Painter Stainers, 11
Painters, 5
Parish Clerks, 94
Patternmakers, 41
Paviors, 112
Pepperers, 4
Pewterers, 5, 35, 73, 75, 112, 131
Pinners, 5, 11
Plumbers, 5, 63, 64, 84
Pouchmakers, 5, 11
Poulters, 40, 41
Pursers, 11

Saddlers, 5, 84, 92, 99
Salters, 5, 151, 162
Scriveners, 28, 97
Shearmen, 11, 56
Skinners, 5, 28, 35, 104
Spurriers, 5, 11

Stainers, 5
Stationers, 92, 133

Tackle & Ticket Porters, 109
Tallow Chandlers, 9, 41, 60
Tanners, 5
Tapestry Weavers, 5
Tobacco Pipe Makers, 148
Turners, 69

Upholders, 28, 97

Vintners, 5, 6, 59, 60, 69

Waterbearers, 36
Wax Chandlers, 5, 12, 69
Weavers, 5, 6, 92
Whittawyers (Saddlers), 11
Wiresellers, 11
Woodmongers, 5, 97, 98
Woolmen, 56
Woolmongers, 5, 6
Woolwinders, 109